ANNO DRACULA 1959

DRACULA CHA CHA CHA

ALSO BY KIM NEWMAN AND AVAILABLE FROM TITAN BOOKS

ANNO DRACULA
ANNO DRACULA: THE BLOODY RED BARON
ANNO DRACULA: DRACULA CHA CHA CHA
ANNO DRACULA: JOHNNY ALUCARD
ANNO DRACULA 1899 AND OTHER STORIES
ANNO DRACULA 1999 (OCTOBER 2019)

ANGELS OF MUSIC
THE SECRETS OF DREARCLIFF GRANGE SCHOOL
THE HAUNTING OF DREARCLIFF GRANGE SCHOOL (OCTOBER 2018)
AN ENGLISH GHOST STORY
PROFESSOR MORIARTY: THE HOUND OF THE D'URBERVILLES

JAGO
THE QUORUM
LIFE'S LOTTERY
BAD DREAMS
THE NIGHT MAYOR
THE MAN FROM THE DIOGENES CLUB

VIDEO DUNGEON

ANNO DRACULA 1959

DRACULA CHA CHA CHA

KIM NEWMAN

TITAN BOOKS

ANNO DRACULA: DRACULA CHA CHA CHA

Mass-market edition ISBN: 9781781167571
Electronic edition ISBN: 9780857685353

Published by Titan Books
A division of Titan Publishing Group Ltd
144 Southwark Street, London SE1 0UP

First mass-market edition: April 2018
2 4 6 8 10 9 7 5 3 1

A CIP catalogue record for this title is available from the British Library.

Printed and bound in the USA.

For Silja

"I would like to have done a vampire sequence in one of my films, even though, personally, I cannot even look at blood, let alone drink it… But the vampire is a concept too strong for fantasy."
I, Fellini, Federico Fellini

"It is time for our culture to abandon Dracula and pass beyond him." *Burying the Undead: the Use and Obsolescence of Count Dracula*, Robin Wood

PART ONE

THREE CORPSES IN THE FOUNTAIN

NOTICE OF ENGAGEMENT, FROM *THE TIMES* OF LONDON. JULY 15TH, 1959

Asa Vajda, Princess of Moldavia, is to be married to Vlad, Count Dracula, formerly Prince of Wallachia, Voivode of Transylvania and Prince Consort of Great Britain. The groom has been married previously to Elisabeta of Transylvania (1448–62), Princess Ilona Szilagy of Hungary (1466–76), Marguerite Chopin of Courtempierre (1709–11), Queen Victoria of Great Britain (1886–8) and Sari Gabòr of Hungary and California (1948–9). The bride, a distant connection of the groom's mother, Princess Cneajna Musatina of Moldavia, is of the bloodline of Javutich. Since enforced exile from her homeland in 1938, she has resided in Monaco and Finland. The marriage will take place at the Palazzo Otranto, in Fregene, Italy, on the 31st of October this year.

1

DRACULA *CHA CHA CHA*

Alitalia offered a special class for vampires, at the front of the aeroplane. The windows were shrouded against the sun with black curtains. It added to the cost. The warm could pay a supplement and share the space – none did on this flight – but Kate couldn't be seated in the main cabin at the lower fare. The airline assumed the undead were all too wealthy to care, which was not in her case true.

The flight departed an overcast Heathrow Airport in mid-afternoon and was scheduled to arrive in Rome at sunset. In the air, she read well into *Saturday Night and Sunday Morning*. She didn't take personally the motto, 'don't let the bloodsuckers grind you down,' and identified more with Arthur Seaton than with the vampires who ran the bicycle factory where he worked. Alan Sillitoe was using a metaphor, not stirring up hatred against her kind. That said, England had pockets of real intolerance: she'd been caught in the Notting Hill blood riots last year, and was fed up with the crucifix-waving teddy boys who hounded her in the launderette.

She'd visited Venice in the 1920s and served in Sicily and the South during the Allied invasions, but never before been to Rome. Geneviève had offered to meet her at Fiumicino Airport, but Kate preferred to make her own way into the city. Geneviève was best off staying close to Charles. These were their last days. They deserved time together alone before Kate arrived to shoulder part of the burden and, incidentally and unavoidably, play gooseberry.

What was between Charles and Geneviève had always shut her out, even in 1888 when she was a warm girl and Geneviève was his first vampire. Kate loved him, of course, which made her silly and sad and would soon make her lost and alone. She was always last in line with Charles Beauregard: after Pamela, his wife; Penelope, his fiancée; Victoria, his queen; and, hardest to take because she'd be around forever, the sainted Geneviève Dieudonné.

Kate had to remind herself often that she liked Geneviève. It probably made things worse.

Toward the end of the flight, a snack was offered – a live white mouse. Not liking to feed in public, she declined. Looking up at the smartly uniformed hostess, she noticed a sky-blue scarf wound between her collar and her throat. Kate sensed the warm girl's bites and wondered if she were required to offer her neck to Alitalia's important vampire customers. More likely she had an undead boyfriend without much in the way of self-control.

'May I have yours as well?' asked another passenger, a thin-faced elder. 'I am peckish.'

He already had one wriggling mouse in his left hand.

Kate shrugged, politely. He reached over the aisle into the hostess's little cage.

'Thank you, Signora,' he said, claiming his prize.

The vampire opened his mouth like a python. Red membranes unfurled as his jaws unlocked, revealing double rows of fang-needles. He popped both treats into his maw and crunched out the tiny lives. He chewed the mice like gum, working the furry pulp into his cheek, sucking down juices in minute dribbles.

The elder wore full soup and fish: ruffled white shirt, black dickie bow, velvet morning coat, brocade waistcoat, Playboy Club signet ring, buckled boots, Patek Lioncourt wristwatch, black opera cape lined with red silk. He looked like a middle-European hawk: black patent-leather hair brushed back from a widow's peak; white face, red eyes, scarlet lips.

'Or is it Signorina?' he asked around his mouthful.

'Miss,' she admitted. 'Katharine Reed.'

The elder discreetly spat fur and bones into a paper napkin, which he folded into a small parcel and gave to the hostess for disposal.

Nodding a formal greeting, he introduced himself.

'Count Gabor Kernassy, of the bloodline of Vlad Dracula, late of *il principe*'s Carpathian Guard.'

In his Italian exile, they called Dracula '*il principe*', the Prince. He was born to the title, which distinguished him from the numberless counts – like this one – who floated around in his wake. Sly reference to Machiavelli's handbook for genial tyrants was also intended.

'This is my "niece",' Count Kernassy gestured at the vampire woman in the window seat next to him, 'Malenka.'

A glance suggested what species of niece Malenka was to the Count. She was dressed for an entrance, in a floor-length scarlet evening gown, cut to display an enormous outcrop of bosom. The neckline was more like a nipple-line, with a deep valley that almost reached her navel. Diamonds sparkled on the upper slopes of her breasts. Her growth of bright blonde hair was equally enormous, and her razor smile was a credit to either bloodline or Swedish dentistry. Her maroon eyes sparkled and dazzled with boredom, contempt and amusement.

Kate chided herself for unfairly detesting Malenka on sight. She had her down as a *nouveau*, one of those new-born vampiresses who attach themselves to convenient elders and try to pass among gentlefolk three hundred years their senior.

She waved tiny fingers at the woman. Malenka arched plucked eyebrows.

They were the only three vampires on the flight. Kate had an idea she might like the old rogue of a Count, who was on some level aware of the impression Malenka made. Kernassy paused sufficiently in a recitation of his part in several centuries' of court intrigue to ask her what she did and why she was going to Rome. She avoided the latter question by answering the former.

'I'm a journalist. For *The Manchester Guardian* and the *New Statesman*.'

'*Journalisti*,' Malenka spat, the first word Kate had heard from her. 'Ani-*malss*!'

Malenka smiled as if she were fond of animals, and enjoyed killing and eating them.

'My niece has been pursued by your press. She is highly visible.'

Kate didn't pay much attention to the society pages but had an idea she'd seen photographs in the *Tatler* of Malenka looking gorgeously bored at a coffee bar in Soho, or supporting a mushroom-cloud hat at Ascot. It was part of her job to keep up with all manner of publications. Also, she liked to know what people were wearing these days.

'Motion pictures are interested in her,' continued the Count. 'She photographs.'

Many vampires didn't. Only a few, like Garbo, were film actors or models. Monsieur Erik, angel-voiced spectre of the Paris Opéra, not only would not photograph but could not be recorded for gramophone records.

'So I imagine,' Kate snipped.

'Your accent? It is not English,' observed Kernassy. 'You are perhaps Canadian?'

'I am perhaps Irish.'

'They *loave* me in Ire-*land*,' Malenka declared.

'Malenka has performed a season at the Gate Theatre in Dublin. She was a very great success.'

Kate stopped herself from laughing at the image of Malenka as Molly Bloom.

'Many Ire-*land* men *loave* me,' Malenka announced.

'I'm sure,' Kate agreed. 'I can see that.'

Kernassy shared a secret smile. He liked being seen as a rakish 'uncle' to this spectacular but brainless creature. Kate wondered if he'd found her warm and turned her, or inherited her from another exhausted father-in-darkness.

'I do believe you will be much *loaved* in Rome,' Kate ventured.

'You hear that, Malenka?' said the Count. 'Our Miss Reed predicts formidable success for you.'

Malenka thrust out her breasts in a kind of seated bow,

nodding sharply at unheard applause.

'She is to be in a motion picture, in a leading role.'

'I am... *Medusa*,' she said, touching long fingernails to her snakeless tresses.

Kate could just about see the casting.

'No, *mia cara*,' Kernassy chided. 'You are *Medea*.'

'There is difference?' Malenka looked to Kate for support.

'One had adders in her hairdo and froze men to stone with a glance,' Kate said. 'The other helped Jason steal the Golden Fleece but got chucked and bashed their children to death.'

'I think they change ending in script,' Kernassy said. 'The original is – how was it put to me? – "not box office". And who would, as you say, "chuck" Malenka?'

'Who care for box orifice?' Malenka smiled. 'They will just care for *me*.'

Count Kernassy shrugged. The pilot announced they were near their destination and asked that all seat-belts be refastened, *per favore*. Malenka had to be helped with the buckle. The belt lay loose in her lap. Trapped in the corseted gown, her waist was tiny.

'You are in Rome for the wedding?' the Count asked.

Kate was startled. She didn't imagine anyone would think that, though the royal engagement had been thoroughly covered, even by the papers she worked for.

'I might write something,' she said, noncommittally.

Until now, she'd blocked the wedding from her mind. While she and Geneviève tended Charles's deathbed, the creature they thought of as blighting their lives for the last seventy years would, amid unparalleled pomp, be taking another wife. There were political and emotional ramifications. In the end, if she could control her hatred, she might indeed write something about it.

'We shall be at wedding,' Malenka said. 'Personal guests of *il principe*.'

Kernassy's eyebrows made Satanic V signs. Like many cloaked Carpathians, he seemed a cut-down imitation of his *principe*. Did Malenka intend to abandon him for a more distinguished uncle? If so, she'd have to best the Royal

Fiancée. Kate gathered that Asa Vajda of Moldavia – *la principesa*? – was not the sort to be seen off by a gold-digger.

'Perhaps you have other affairs?' the Count remarked, with an elder's insight. '*Mamma Roma* has many eternal attractions, some dolorous, some joyful.'

Dolorous? Curious word.

The plane touched down smoothly and taxied to the terminal.

Kernassy courteously let Malenka and Kate leave the plane before him. Naturally, Malenka went first and posed at the top of the movable steps.

There were explosions and flares. Kate thought she was being greeted by a fusillade. It would not have been the first time. Cold bright light battered her. Dazzled, she covered her eyes. Flashes danced in her skull.

A small orchestra struck up a tune. Incongruously for a welcome, it was 'Arrivederci Roma'.

Shouts came out of the darkness beyond the popping lights. '*La bella Malenka*... Signorina... swinging, baby... *bene, bene*... va-va-voom!'

Kernassy helped Kate back into the cabin. She took off her glasses and rubbed her burning eyes. Kodak were marketing a new film for photographing vampires. The flashbulbs that went with it produced nuclear sunbursts.

'Everywhere Malenka goes, there are paparazzi,' explained the Count.

Questions were shouted in several languages: 'Are you searching for love in Roma?' – 'What do you sleep in?' – 'Has your figure been surgically enhanced?' – 'What of the wedding?' – 'Do you favour the blood of Italian men?'

Malenka gave no answers, but outdazzled the flashguns with her smiles. She swivelled her torso to make a distinct silhouette, and bent forward to blow kisses, raising an animal roar of approval. Another battery of cameras went off.

Kate had attended press calls at London Airport. They weren't much like this: 'Will you attend any cricket matches,

Mr Sinatra?' – 'How do you like our English weather, Miss Desmond?' – 'Would you mind awfully posing for a few snaps for our readers, Mrs Roosevelt?'

The aisles filled with baggage-laden passengers wanting to get out of the plane. The hostess explained they would have to wait. *La bella* celebrity took precedence.

Malenka descended the steps as if entering an embassy ball, generous hips swaying. Photographers lay on the tarmac to shoot her from below, wriggling on their backs like up-ended beetles. Kate let Malenka get out of the way and off to one side, surrounded by her press, before leaving the plane again.

The orchestra finished their welcoming goodbye to Rome and began to pack their instruments.

'We are to be met by a woman from the House of Dracula,' the Count told her. 'She is to arrange transport into the city. You will come with us?'

'That's very kind, Count…'

'I insist. You have hotel?'

'A *pensione*, Count. In Trastevere. Piazza Maria, 24.'

'You will be delivered safely, Miss Reed. I give you the word of a Kernassy.'

The elder probably thought nothing of slaughtering peasant babies to slake his red thirst, but wouldn't leave an unaccompanied woman adrift in a foreign city. It was easier to go along with him than make an argument.

Malenka continued her performance. Behind still-popping bulbs, a troupe of photographers and reporters tumbled like acrobats. Kate had learned to look away from the flashes. There were newsreel cameramen and roving wireless reporters. Had she skipped a few too many pages in *Picturegoer*? Either Malenka was the new Marilyn Monroe or anybody who decorated an orgy scene rated this treatment in Rome.

'*Tangenti* have been paid so passports will be processed swiftly at customs,' said Count Kernassy, steering Kate past Malenka's act and toward a thinner crowd. 'Stay close, and you will go through under my cloak.'

For a moment, she thought he meant it literally.

Among the waiting people was a tall, slim vampire woman in a smart violet jacket and skirt, raising a hand in a matching glove. She wore black, horn-rim sunglasses and a Chinese-pattern headscarf, like someone in disguise. A double rope of pearls wound around her slender neck.

'This will be our *galoppina*,' Kernassy said. 'As you say, our fixer.'

The woman took off her dark glasses. Her tiny mouth opened in astonishment, showing piranha teeth.

'*Katie Reed*,' she exclaimed. 'Good grief!'

Kate supposed she knew Penelope was part of *il principe*'s household and was therefore in Rome. But, trying to give Penny as little thought as possible, she'd never considered she might be the first person she ran into in the city.

'Penny,' she said, lamely. 'Hello.'

'You are old friends, I see,' Kernassy deduced, not entirely accurately.

'Count Kernassy, this is Penelope Churchward. We knew each other, a long time ago.'

'A long time ago means nought to such as we,' he said, gallantly taking Penelope's hand.

The Englishwoman put on a smile that was significantly more convincing than Malenka's efforts. One had to know her well to distinguish its flaws.

'How you do turn up, Katie,' she said. 'You're here to see Charles, of course.'

At the time of her death, Penelope had been engaged to Charles. Her turning vampire ended the arrangement. Geneviève had something to do with it too, though not poor four-eyed Katie Reed. She wondered if Penny wasn't in Rome at least partly because of Charles. He certainly had a knack of keeping vampire ladies about him. Much like *il principe*.

'Have you seen him?' Kate asked, hating to.

'Not recently. He is an invalid. He must turn soon or be lost to us.'

Kate was hoping to persuade him of something similar. That Penelope should mention such a treatment wasn't encouraging. If it was Penny's idea, he'd probably be dead set against it. Surely he'd see sense as the last clouds gathered and the reaper sharpened his scythe?

Malenka swanned over, all teeth and teats. Paparazzi kept up with her. Discarded flashbulbs shattered like glass confetti. Penelope put her sunglasses back on and was introduced.

As the Count had promised, an official escorted them past the scrum for passport control. Half of the passengers on the flight were British and formed the beginnings of an orderly queue. Italians wedged themselves at the front, genially tutting at the eccentricity of a race that believed in waiting for turns rather than scrambling for position.

Kate was still too surprised by Penelope's presence to feel guilty about the slight corruption gaining her preference. She knew *tangenti* – bribes – from the War, when the black market and the open palm were the only way to get anything done. Peace hadn't changed Italy much.

The Count escorted Malenka. A large warm man in chauffeur's livery – Penelope addressed him as Klove – carried their many bags. Malenka's matching luggage was by Vuitton, Kate noticed. She and Penny walked together, wondering what to say to each other.

It had been *decades*.

'Thank you for the condolence card, Katie. It was a kindly gesture. You were always thoughtful.'

'I was fond of your mother.'

Mrs Churchward had died in *1937*.

'Mama always liked you,' Penelope admitted. 'You were the sensible one.'

'I'm not sure of that.'

'Do you have get?' Penelope asked, smiling sharply.

Kate shook her head. She had chosen not to pass on the Dark Kiss, to extend her bloodline. Only someone special, she had vowed. And someone special had never come along.

'I made a brood of sons and granddaughters in darkness. It's a fearful responsibility, my dear. I'm obliged to further the Godalming bloodline. In poor Art's memory.'

Arthur Holmwood, Lord Godalming, was Penelope's

father-in-darkness, the vampire who had turned her. Like Kate and Penny, he was one of the new-borns of the '80s. Like many of their peers, he hadn't outlasted his natural lifespan. Kate should be closer to Penelope. They were almost sole survivors of their world.

'I would found my own house,' Penelope continued, 'but I have duties. Whatever you think of him, we owe *il principe* a great debt, Katie. I know you were one of the firebrands who got him kicked out of England. But, like it or not, he's our leader.'

Neither Kate nor Penny were directly of the Dracula bloodline. They were free from some of the taints that had poisoned most of their generation.

'You must call at the Palazzo Otranto,' said Penelope, making Kate shiver. 'Things are hectic just now, what with wedding arrangements and ambassadorial conspirators. *He* would receive you, I'm sure. Charles is even invited, and that woman. If Dracula can forgive *them*, he'll overlook *your* little revolutionist enthusiasms.'

During the struggle to oust Dracula from the throne of Great Britain, Kate had spent seven years as an outlaw. Hiding from Carpathians who wanted to impale her, she'd edited an underground newssheet. Later, in the First World War, she'd been buried under one of *il principe*'s marvellous toys, the first breed of tank. She wasn't sure she could be as forgiving of him as the monster could afford to be of her. She also resented Penny's implied suggestion that political agitation was a passing hobby, something to fill out boring years of an eternity not spent furthering her bloodline.

She caught herself. Penelope was working her strings, as ever. Kate was not going to be that goggle-eyed wallflower again, scandalised by her prettier friend but hanging on every barbed word. When they were alive and Kate was often her chaperone, Penny was already a manipulative child. Now she had a great many more years of practice in the art of getting to people.

'Here are the cars,' Penelope announced.

They had hustled through the airport and out onto the

road. Parked at the verge were a red two-seater Ferrari and a hearse-like black Fiat. The Ferrari was a setting for Malenka.

More bulbs popped as Malenka was assisted into the tiny sports car. She stood tall and blew more kisses at the gathered crowd.

Penelope laughed quietly and shook her head, which made Kate think better of her.

'I'm reminded of twin torpedoes, Katie, *thrusting*.'

They *had* been friends, once.

'The rest of us shall ride out of the wind,' Penelope said. 'The bus is a lot roomier than the milk-float.'

A warm man loitered by the cars.

'Katie, this is Tom,' introduced Penelope, trailing fingers across his lapel to display ownership. 'He is a lost American in Europe.'

The young man was attached to the party in a subservient, unofficial fashion. His handshake didn't give anything away. Kate guessed he was a satellite, and noticed red scratches on his neck. She saw him thinking as he looked her over, and intuited he was totting up the cost of her clothes. His current job was to drive the Ferrari and duck low to stay out of the pictures.

Klove held open the rear door of the Fiat and Kate got in, daintily followed by Penelope. They sank together into a deep leather seat. Someone already sat opposite, smoking a cigarette. Count Kernassy gathered his cape and slipped in to join them. The chauffeur silently shut the door and went up front.

The Count embraced the smoker, kissing him on both cheeks without disturbing his cigarette.

'This is Signorina Reed, a discovery of our flight,' the Count explained. 'She is in your profession, Marcello. A reporter. From Ireland.'

The reporter leaned forward into the light. He was strikingly handsome in a bored, tired sort of way. His dark, wavy hair had a trace of unearned grey at the temples. Like Penny, he wore big black sunglasses. He was a living man, so Kate assumed the shades were an affectation.

Marcello extended a hand and took hers.

Electricity leaped between them.

She must watch herself with this Roman reporter. His casual, fag-dripping smile was insinuating. He was trim and smooth, but with an incipient plumpness that might be quite delicious. Under cologne and the tobacco was a scent of sweet blood. His neck was clean of bites.

He held her hand a few seconds longer than necessary, then turned to the Count and gabbled with him in Italian, ignoring her a trifle too deliberately.

Her heart beat faster. She knew Penelope quietly noticed her new interest. That would come back to haunt her. Penny was always good at storing ammunition for a rainy day.

Still, Kate was in Rome. And opposite was a beautiful man.

The sun was down by the time they were in the city proper. Kate realised the Count would be staying in the centre of Rome. Her *pensione* was in Trastevere, through which they were driving. She tried to persuade the elder to let her out, but he waved the request aside.

'Absolutely not, *mia cara* Signorina Reed. We have not done with you yet. I insist you join our party this evening. You and Signorina Churchward have much to talk of. And you must experience Via Veneto by night. It is the most exciting street in the world.'

Kate's rented flat was in the Holloway Road. Not even the most exciting street in North London. She allowed Count Kernassy to overwhelm her.

'You will escort Signorina Reed, Marcello,' Kernassy said, suavely commanding.

'But of course,' Marcello said, his first words of English.

'I'm rather afraid Marcello despises us,' Penelope said, politely. 'He's gathering material for a novel which will put us all in our places. His subject is the empty night-lives of the eternal rich.'

From the set of his mouth, Kate knew Marcello understood what Penelope had said. He had some fluency in English, which was a hopeful sign.

'Do you still write for the papers, Katie?'

'Yes.'

'I thought so.'

Penelope sat back. Kate feared she was reddening.

'Will you write about Malenka?' she asked Marcello.

Kate wondered why her stomach was tight. And whether she could have come up with a more inane question.

Marcello shrugged and expressively tilted his head.

'She is like a big doll,' he said, trying to sneer.

Kate knew at once the reporter was smitten with the starlet and felt unaccountably betrayed. The city was doing something to her. It was a hypnotic spell in 'Arrivederci, Roma'. She was turning into an idiot.

Her throat prickled with red thirst.

'But of course he will write of *mia cara*,' the Count said, arm snaking around the Italian. 'There must be tiny little words to put under the great big photographs. It is a legal requirement.'

Kate wondered if Marcello disliked the Count's patronising purr. There was steel in Kernassy's velvet, as if he had a hold over the reporter. Perhaps it was as easy to buy an Italian newspaperman as a passport official.

The Fiat crossed the Tiber at the Ponte Sisto and followed the Ferrari through the crowded streets of Campo de' Fiori and Piazza della Rotunda. Traffic horns honked a Spike Jones symphony, punctuated by rude shouts and appreciative cries. Couples on motor scooters zipped in between crawling cars, scarf-wearing girls grinned sweetly at stalled motorists. Pedestrians ambled along in the road rather than the pavement, squeezing between vehicles, talking blithely among themselves. There were even herds of sheep, blinking under the streetlights, driven by sharp-eyed children.

'Italian cars are for speed,' said Marcello, 'but Italian cities are not for cars. One can only drive through them at the pace of a walk.'

In the Largo di Torre Argentina, a football game was in process. Three-dozen youths booted a ball about among strolling crowds. When the Ferrari drove into the square, the match was abandoned and the players clamoured around.

Kate wondered which chassis they worshipped most, that of the car or that of *la Malenka*.

There was a great deal of whistling and stamping. Malenka stood up in the car and waved.

Everyone wanted red kisses. Malenka bestowed a few on favoured lads, nipping slightly. She licked blood off her lips, and made a gesture which parted the sea of people. They were able to drive on.

Hoots followed them.

Kate's teeth were sharp and her mouth watery. Inconvenient need nagged. Being a vampire meant living with something like an addiction. To blood, and all that came with its letting. The warm were addicted to food and drink, of course, and to air? But the vampire's need was stronger, crueller, more insistent.

'For whom do you write?' she asked Marcello.

He rattled off names of publications she vaguely knew. *Lo specchio*, *Oggi*, *Europeo*.

'Marcello once sold the exact same story to *Paese sera* and *Osservatore Romano*,' Kernassy said, laughing.

'She won't understand why that's amusing, Count,' Penelope said, sweetly. 'Katie, *Paese sera* is the newspaper of the Italian Communist Party, and *Osservatore Romano* is the Vatican paper.'

Marcello shrugged, showing no shame.

'They are deadly enemies, you see, the priests and the reds,' Penelope explained further.

Kate wondered if anyone would mind if she killed Penny.

The Count had a suite at the Hotel Hassler, a baroque remainder of old world magnificence at the top of the Spanish Steps. The elder tipped the doorman to the amount Kate expected to pay for a month's lodging in her *pensione*.

Kate, Penelope, Tom and Marcello sat in the crowded bar while Kernassy and Malenka settled in upstairs. Klove ferried many trunks from the Fiat up to the suite. Kate was self-conscious about her own tiny suitcase. Penny made an observation about her travelling light, implying – correctly – a poverty of wardrobe.

Marcello and Tom drank espresso, and Penelope insisted Kate sample the vampire fare. She summoned over a handsome, blank-faced young waiter. He wore a finely striped waistcoat and very tight black trousers. Penny ordered a measure for herself – to be sociable, she said – and one for Kate.

The waiter deftly popped a snap-fastener on his cuff and rolled up his sleeve. A tourniquet was tied around his elbow, and a steel needle was stuck into a fat vein in his lower arm, attached by a short clear plastic tube to a spigot.

He twisted open the tap and allowed a brief squirt of his blood into a thin cocktail glass. Penelope made great show of sniffing and tasting, then signalled him to go on. The waiter twice measured two inches of the red stuff over ice and a slice of lemon. Penny gave him a handful of *lire* and waved him away. He couldn't serve many vampire customers before having to be relieved. Kate wondered how many nights a week he worked. Did poverty-stricken Southerners dribble away their lives to send money home to their families? Or was everyone carefully vetted by a snobbish management?

Penelope raised her drink and smiled, delicate fang-points extended.

'Good health,' she said, clinking Kate's glass and sipping.

Kate looked at Marcello, wondering if he were disgusted by this display. She couldn't tell. He held up his tiny coffee cup in a parody toast.

All three of her companions looked at her as she touched her tongue to the cocktail.

It was a rush. She had not had human blood for weeks. She forced herself not to gulp. It was rich and would make her giddy if she tossed it down. She savoured a peppery mouthful, let it wash against the back of her throat, then swallowed demurely.

'Signorina Reed, is it true what they say of Italian men?' asked Marcello. 'Is our blood hot?'

'This isn't,' she said. 'It has ice in it.'

Marcello smiled with genuine sweetness.

'It would have to,' Tom said. 'Or you'd flame away.'

Kate sensed a fastidiousness in Penelope's American friend. If he disliked public displays of vampirism, why was he hanging around Penny? Was he jealous that she was drinking the decanted blood of an anonymous waiter, rather than taking his straight from the barrel?

It would take a while to sort all these people out in her mind. If, after tonight, she saw them at all. She could cheerfully avoid Penny for the rest of her visit and knew Tom would prefer her out of the way, but Count Kernassy appeared uncommonly decent for one of the old ones. And Marcello…

Malenka swept into the bar in a new dress and caused a sensation.

Kate assumed the Via Veneto was less likely to be bowled over by Malenka. The most beautiful, famous, notorious, and interesting people in the world gathered here nightly. She was sure she spotted Jean-Paul Sartre outside the Café de Paris, shrinking under the awning as Simone de Beauvoir arm-wrestled Ernest Hemingway into submission. Audrey Hepburn and Mel Ferrer strolled past arm in arm, a pack of worshipful urchins at their heels.

But Malenka conquered all.

Her gown, from the House of Massimo Morlacchi, was a masterpiece of architectural engineering. Midnight black velvet, it was cut low, slashed high and had round windows at the waist. Malenka was one of those vampires who didn't breathe. Any expansion of her rib-cage would explode the whole assembly. A white Wendigo fur wrap writhed on her wide, white shoulders – she had huge, lady-wrestler shoulders, Penny eagerly pointed out – as if it still had some remnant of life.

The Count displayed his niece. She rested a hand on his arm, her white flesh glowing, shoving the elder into permanent shadow.

Kate and Penelope, vaguely escorted by Marcello and Tom,

followed paces behind the main attraction. The faithful Klove was somewhere near in case anyone was too overenthusiastic in their attentions.

The paparazzi ran in a pack, snapping at Malenka, insatiable and insistent. Kate was sure she would show up as a smudge in the corner of a lot of pictures. She didn't photograph well.

They went from the Rosati to the Strega to the Zeppa to the Doney, stopping for drinks at each. Marcello stayed with espresso but Tom was on to *amaretti*. Penelope sweetly goaded Kate into more vampire cocktails.

She became quite drunk. There might be something in these stories of the virile blood of Italian men. She allowed Marcello to support her, but went rigid whenever she thought she was turning clingy or clumsy.

She stopped drinking. No one noticed. She could gut a nun with a breadknife tonight and no one would notice. She was carried along in Malenka's tide.

At each stop, youths offered their necks to Malenka. Some she petted, some she bit, some she almost drained. She must be glutted, and yet she was still white as bone and ice. Kate gathered that one warm lad turned cold in her arms and nearly died, happy, refusing to complain.

At each café, and in the streets, there was music. More orchestras, portable gramophones, tiny wirelesses. Humming, singing, stam-ping, cheering people. One irritating song was everywhere. When Kate realised what it was called, she had the presence of mind to be aghast.

Malenka sailed on in rhythm. Every few seconds she paused, and gave three sudden thrusts with her hips and elbows.

Cha cha cha…

'It's for the wedding,' Penelope told Kate. 'Embarrassing, really. Princess Asa hates it.'

Drac-u-la, Drac-u-la…

Dra… Cha cha cha…

Malenka danced as she walked. Supposedly phlegmatic sophisticates stopped to stare. Famous people allowed themselves for the moment to take supporting roles in the great Technicolor pageant of her procession. The television playwright Clare Quilty made an ostentatious point of ignoring the passing sensation, and said something waspish about overdevelopment to his wraithlike vampire companion, Vivian Darkbloom. The actor Edmond Purdom registered more emotion and interest on his face than he managed in any of his films. The Polish werewolf Waldemar Daninski howled and barked, like the big bad wolf in the Tex Avery cartoons.

Appalled and astonished, Kate looked at Marcello. Without taking his eyes off of Malenka's rotating *derriére*, he shrugged and lit another cigarette. She waved her fingers to catch his attention. He offered her his cigarette case and she took one, to smoke the taste of blood out of her mouth. He flipped open a Zippo lighter and she bent to suck flame. They bumped heads and apologised.

There was something here.

She looked around and saw Penelope and Tom lagging back. Penny talked intently at the American, gripping his arm. That must be another story.

Stray paparazzi, blocked from getting through to Malenka and the Count, pestered Marcello and Kate. He told them to go away and that he was a nobody like them, but they snapped and popped anyway. Kate knew enough to shield her eyes.

'I'll have to get some dark glasses,' she said.

Marcello laughed. 'Everybody wears them, I admit. We are all in hiding. It is a Roman tradition.'

Penelope and Tom were gone. The Count was taken up with Malenka. His promise to see Kate to Trastevere was gone with the setting sun. So much for the word of Kernassy.

She thought Marcello might look after her, though his attention, like everybody else's, was fixed on Malenka. No, his attention was different. She recognised an ironic distance. He wasn't involved. He took it all in, to write about later.

She was a bit like that too.

But Malenka had bewitched him, as she had all other men. It must be those ridiculous breasts. And all that hair.

A satyr-bearded man in a polo-neck jersey jumped out of a palm tree and threw himself down on the road, begging Malenka to '*cha cha cha*' over him. Klove picked him up and shoved him back into the crowd.

Cha cha cha…

Suddenly, it all seemed desperately funny. Kate began laughing, and Marcello politely joined in.

'Drac-u-la… Dra… *cha cha cha*,' she gasped, making fumbling arm movements. '*Cha cha cha*!'

It was all too silly.

Marcello stopped her falling down.

Time passed in a rapid blur. More cafés, more famous faces, more crowds. A constellation of flashbulb supernovae. Malenka wanted to visit this bar, to be snapped with that picturesque orphan, to sample a specific waiter's blood in a certain out-of-the-way trattoria, to be seen in front of every famous frontage in Rome, to hug a surprised country priest and show him her teeth.

Kate wondered how many of the crowd were staying the distance in the hope that Malenka's miracle dress would collapse completely. Already, her *cha cha cha* had torn new splits over her hips, causing great excitement. Kate half thought it the fashion equivalent of an ice sculpture, crafted to last for only so long. Before dawn, it would fall away in pieces and the photographers would finally get the shots they needed to complete their portfolios.

Marcello got Kate through it. Without him, she'd have been left behind in some café, like her suitcase (which was at the Hassler, she remembered). She considered a dozen different ways to ask if he would care to have her nip his neck, trying to frame it in a way that would suggest she was offering herself politely but not insistently to him rather than planning something close to rape.

He was a bit irritated with her. Every time it looked as if he might get closer to Malenka, she was in the way. Sensing how he felt, she tried to be sober and didn't do a good job of it.

Her expression must be comically solemn, for despite himself Marcello was forced to laugh at her.

The cocktails hadn't helped. The red thirst was gone, but the need was there. Blood was not enough. It was very civilised and mid-century to decant it into glass and take it like a tonic, but she needed human contact, her mouth on sensitive skin, her fangs piercing, the sighs in her ears, the unresisting body in her arms, the rush of *feelings*.

She was being silly, quite as stupidly blatant as Malenka. Penelope didn't have to go through all this face-pulling to attract attention. Or Geneviève, who was French and only had to ignore a person for a few minutes to make him her slave forever.

Kate noticed suddenly how hot it was. Midnight had come and gone, but the night was still balmy and tropical. Her face burned, as if she were warm. Blood-tides pounded in her temples, and she was unsteady on her feet.

How did it happen? The crowds melted away. Their footsteps echoed in empty streets. Malenka still hummed the 'Dracula *Cha Cha Cha*'.

Kate focused on something famous.

The Trevi Fountain. A statuary group depicted King Poseidon and his Tritons, pouring forth water from seashell spouts. One Triton struggled with a rearing sea-horse, the other led a docile creature. The sea-horses symbolised the unpredictable moods of the sea, her *Baedeker* said. She'd planned to visit the Piazza di Trevi on her 'Roman holiday', thinking even of tossing away fifty lire and making a wish.

A cat meowed. It padded elegantly along the rim of the fountain pool and nuzzled up to Malenka's plump, pale arm. She picked the cat up and rubbed its face against hers. Its white fur exactly matched her wrap.

'Poor little lost dear,' she said. 'He must have milk.'

It was a command. She looked at Count Kernassy, and he looked at Marcello.

'Everywhere is shut,' he said. 'Even in Roma…'

'There will be somewhere,' Malenka declared. 'It would not do to let such a tiny beauty die of thirst.'

She made kissing sounds. The cat climbed onto her head. It curled up, like a slit-eyed busby.

'Marcello, see to it,' the Count said, coldly. He handed over banknotes, which Marcello made disappear.

Kate was embarrassed. Marcello politely withdrew, in search of milk, fuming behind his sunglasses. She understood he was as much a pet as this suddenly adopted cat, and felt bad for him, bad about herself.

She was more like him than she was like these people.

Malenka leaped up onto the fountain. The cat slid off her head and landed unsurprisingly in her cleavage, slipping comfortably into the flesh valley. Malenka tightrope-tiptoed along the edge, then stepped into the water. It rose to her thighs. Her dress spread like a water lily.

The cat was spooked. It yowled and scratched. Malenka bit into its neck and threw it away. She wiped blood from her mouth with the back of her hand.

They wouldn't need milk any more.

Kate sat down on a stone bench. Her head span.

Whatever the cat had sensed made her tingle. She felt her claws starting.

Malenka's mood changed again. She waded among the waters, beseeching the Count to join her, letting the cascade fall on her hair, her face, her chest.

'There are coins. You can dive for treasure.'

'You are *mio tesoro, cara*.'

Malenka draped herself over a sea-horse, pointing her breasts at the stars.

One of the cocktail waiters must have been suffering from a fever. Kate was not feeling at all well. Impressions filtered into her mind in flashbulb bursts. Hot, dusty, empty landscape. Laughing famous faces. A dangerous crimson shadow.

She lay on the bench, head throbbing.

Something fast and red bounded into the piazza. Kernassy turned, cloak swirling, and was struck. The elder was lifted up and tossed into the fountain. His head was gone completely.

Blood fountained from his neck-stump. His torso tumbled backwards, tangled in the cloak. The head soared and crashed into a pool, face powdering off it.

Kate tried to sit up, but couldn't.

Malenka screamed in fury, talons and fangs starting. She leaped like a lioness. Something that flashed silver struck under her bosom.

Kate got up and tried to step forward. A hand took her by the back of the neck and made her watch. She had seen true death come to many vampires. Most elders went like Kernassy, turned instantly to dust and bones, centuries of age and decay catching up in seconds.

Something she'd never seen before happened to Malenka.

If she had grown old as a warm woman, Malenka would have become fat. It was in her body type, a ripeness ready to swell. Now, pockets of blubber bulged under Malenka's skin, inflating her face, her belly, her thighs, her torso, her arms. She ballooned, splitting like overcooked sausage. White stuff, veined with red, bubbled out of her rent skin. Her dress exploded.

Malenka boiled over. Her cheeks expanded, and her forehead, her jowls, her throat, even her lips. Her eyes stared in panic from the bottoms of their wells of flesh, imploring. Kate was stabbed with guilt for having taken a petty dislike to this woman. Blood poured from Malenka, along with masses of fatty tissue. Her hands were huge, meat hanging off their backs and the fingers.

Kate was held fast like a kitten. An outsize hand gripped the back of her neck, clamping her shorn hackles. She looked down. The Count's cloak floated like a wingspread of black duckweed. Coins lay like a scatter of eyes on the pool-bed.

She braced comparatively tiny hands against the low stone rim.

Operatic laughter roared out of the Piazza di Trevi and up the Quirinal Hill. The killer was bellowing gusts of triumphant hilarity. The fountain's rush was muted for a moment.

She was pushed slowly forward. Her elbows began to bend the wrong way. Her thick specs, blobbed with droplets, slid down her nose, blurring everything further. Fang-teeth sharpened in her mouth, an instinctive defence mechanism rather than a response to spilled blood. She felt no flicker of red thirst, only disgust and puzzlement.

The killer steadily forced her face to the water, as if he wanted to make this kitten drink. Maybe he thought her of a bloodline susceptible to running water or, considering the nearness of the church of Santa Maria in Trivio, holy water. If so, he was wrong. She wasn't even Catholic: water thrice-blessed by the Pope would only get her wet.

Kernassy's fleshless skull grinned from one of the upper pools. His empty boots lay among coins. Ribbons of old blood, the foul blood of the Dracula line, threaded through the water, not mixing. It was sucked up from the pool and sprayed from the jets, falling all around like dead rain.

Face near the surface of the water, dizzy from the stink of spoiled blood, Kate focused on the killer's rippling reflection: crimson skull-cowl, black domino mask, tunnel-mouth nostrils, Burt Lancaster grin. Bare-chested, he displayed an expansively muscled and oiled torso.

Her hands slipped from the rim and plunged into cold water. She was shoved forward and her chest slammed against stone. Her glasses fell off and splashed into the fountain. Without specs and with the agitation of the water, she glimpsed a dark image between the wavelets – her own reflection, rarely seen. It hadn't vanished altogether like those of some vampires, or been stolen away like Peter Pan's shadow. But, since her turning, it was hard to find. Only in extraordinary circumstances, like the imminence of true death, did her reflection come back.

For a mad moment, she was distracted. So this was how she looked with short hair. Not bad – very mid-century, a sort of existentialist Joan of Arc. She'd been tempted to hack off her waist-length red rope since the 1920s. Only now, with the European fashion for cropped bobs, had she dared ask her hairdresser to wield the silver scissors.

The killer, laughing like a demon of mockery, had a knee on her spine, pinning her to the edge of the fountain. He let go of her neck. She reached behind, and her fingers scrabbled on his muscular leg. He wore thick tights.

She was going to be murdered by a Mexican wrestler. It was too silly for words.

If he kept pressing, her ribs would shatter. If a broken bone stuck through her heart, she would die. Again. This time, it would take.

The killer wasn't a vampire. His strength of wrist equalled most elders, but his hand was hot, sweaty. She felt a strong pumping of blood in his thigh. He was a warm man, alive.

The noises of her body were more distinct than the crash of the water. Blood pulsed in her ears. Bones creaked inside her chest. Her reflected face, clear now even to her fogged eyes, looked up in rabbit-eyed panic. She seemed a young woman, the 25-year-old twit she'd been in 1888. She was hurting, not a common thing with her.

The pressure on her back let up slightly. The laughter stopped.

Kate's first thought, a universal journalist's instinct, was not to save herself but to understand. She scooped up her wet specs, sliding them on.

She still couldn't get up. Even if she bent her neck back as far as it would go, she couldn't see above the broad pool. At the other side of the water was another reflected face.

A little girl peered over the rim. In her upside-down face, a frowning crescent mouth floated above a sad eye. She had long hair, blonde like Geneviève's. Ripples made her shimmer, as if she were shaking her head solemnly. A tear crawled up her hollow cheek.

Kate tried to think of the Italian for 'run away'.

'*Va*,' she tried to shout, coming out only with a gasp.

The girl didn't move. She was a ghost in the water, stuck in time.

The killer removed his knee from her back. Kate tried to gather her vampire qualities. Talons slipped easily from her fingers. Her teeth became fangs. Strength uncoiled in her limbs.

She sprang up and balanced on the rim of the fountain, clawing at empty air, ready to kill… nothing.

The killer was gone, spirited away. Kate looked across the

piazza for the little girl. She heard the rapid pit-pat of the child running off down the Via delle Muratte and saw the last of her shadow, enormous on a far wall. The roaring hiss of the fountain returned, filling her ears.

Her flash of anger passed, her teeth and claws receded. In place of fighting rage, she had only puzzlement. She knew she had missed something. She stood alone in Piazza di Trevi with the truly dead.

Then Marcello came back with milk. He gently set the bottle on the brick pavement and came over to her. There was dawnlight in the sky. Hating herself for living the cliché, she swooned in his arms.

2

ON HER MAJESTY'S SECRET SERVICE

She wheeled his bath chair onto the broad balcony and positioned it in deep shadow. Beauregard welcomed the enfolding darkness as if it were a comfortable blanket. At his age, direct sunlight would kill him faster than it would Geneviève, and she was a vampire. She left his tea within his reach. Green gunpowder. He practically lived on the stuff.

From shade, he looked out at the grey light, down into the Via Eudosiana. This early in the morning, the misty haze – almost scented fog – was not yet burned away. It was already hot, promising a day in which flat loaves could be baked on sun-warmed flagstones.

A sleek, silver Aston Martin parked outside the apartment building. It attracted the awed interest of two small children. Beauregard deduced the guest expected at dawn was on his way up.

He heard Geneviève answer the door and admit his caller. She did not approve of his consenting to this interview.

She showed the guest onto the balcony and withdrew into the flat to make a racket, needlessly tidying. He understood her point, but had agreed to talk with the visitor as much out of curiosity as duty. If he was to be pumped for information, he would be paid in kind. Taking an interest was a way of proving to himself that he was still part of the world.

The vampire spy stood on the balcony and lit a cigarette with a Ronson lighter, flame reddening his forceful face. He exhaled smoke and looked down on Beauregard. His quizzical smile exposed a prominent fang.

'The name's Bond,' he said, with a slight Scots roll. 'Hamish Bond.'

'Good morning, Commander Bond,' Beauregard said. 'Welcome to the Eternal City.'

The new-born took a cursory look across Parco di Traiano, taking in the ruin of Nero's Golden House (one of Rome's many monuments to megalomania) and the jagged edge of the Flavian Amphitheatre, the Colosseum. Beauregard noticed with sadness that Bond was not taken with the scenery. Duty ought not blind one to the view. Indeed, it was the duty of those in their shared profession to pay attention.

Though travelling under his naval rank, Bond was out of uniform, dressed as if for baccarat at Monte. His white Savile Row dinner jacket was perfectly cut, loose enough to suggest to the observant the possibility of a shoulder holster. Beauregard knew exactly what this man was, even what was in the holster. A Walther PPK 7.65mm, worn in a Berns-Martin Triple-Draw, clip of eight lead-jacketed silver bullets. Nasty thing.

The breeze played with a stray comma of Bond's black hair. Smoke tore from his cigarette, a handmade Balkan-Turkish blend with three gold bands. Too distinctive for a fellow in his line, too memorable. Those custom gaspers suggested an attitude. Here was a vampire who knew how to shrug in a dinner jacket without rucking the collar, wore shirts of sea-island cotton and could draw a pistol as easily as he pulled his Ronson from an inside pocket. One would think he *wanted* to make an impression, to strike a pose for the gun-sight.

Charles Beauregard hoped he had never been like this.

If any Crown servant deserved a retreat to private life, Beauregard was that man. Yet the Diogenes Club – British Intelligence, if that isn't a contradiction in terms – was not an institution from which retirement was uncomplicated. For one thing, the notion that members might have a private life was discouraged. He had served the Club, rising on occasion to its highest office, for the best part of a century.

He looked out into brightening daylight, studying the

view Bond had already dismissed, finding it a source of endless fascination. This city was older than them all. That was a comfort.

'You're something of a legend, Beauregard. I trained under Sergeant Dravot. He donated the blood for my turning. It's a good line. He speaks often of you.'

'Ah yes, Danny Dravot. My old guardian angel.'

Beauregard discerned an echo of Dravot in Bond's rich voice, even in his relaxed but ready stance. The sergeant turned out sons-in-darkness with some of his calibre. Under the polish, Bond would be a good man, a reliable operative.

Dravot, turned vampire in the 1880s, would be a sergeant until the end of time. And would remain at the disposal of the Diogenes Club.

So much of Beauregard's life, of the considerable weight of memory anchoring him to his bed and chair, was bound up with that unassuming building in Pall Mall. If, as was increasingly the case, his mind drifted, a past of photographic vividness would blot out the fuzzy present. Often, he found himself back there: India in 1879, London in 1888, France in 1918, Berlin in 1938.

Faces and voices were clear in his mind. Mycroft Holmes, Edwin Winthrop, Lord Ruthven. Geneviève, Kate, Penelope. Lord Godalming, Dr Seward, the Prince Consort. The Kaiser, the Red Baron, Adolf Hitler. Sergeant Dravot dogging his steps. Dracula fleeing time and again, always finding a nest, never letting go.

He remembered his silver-plated swordstick. Had that been as ostentatious as Bond's Walther? Probably.

Now, it was not a question of drifting. It was a matter of casting, of trying to recall. That, infuriatingly, was more difficult. The game pie served at Simpson's in the Strand in 1888 came instantly to mind, the memory hot in his dry mouth. But he couldn't remember what was for supper last night.

'Head Office assume you've kept an eye on Dracula,' ventured Bond. 'It'd be out of character for you to let go. Especially with him so nearby.'

'Head Office?'

The jargon amused Beauregard. In his day, the slang was different. Before he was one of them, they were just the Ruling Cabal of the Diogenes Club. Then a faction of cricketers took to calling them the Pavilion. For a while, it was the Circus. The Cabal consisted of between one and five people, usually three. In the 1920s and throughout the last war, called back from his first stab at retirement, he had sat at the head of the table. Now, young Winthrop – 'young'? He was sixty-three! – occupied that chair.

'I beg your pardon, Sir.'

He had been worrying at his memories too hard and floated away from the present. He must concentrate. He should get through this quickly, if not for himself then for Geneviève. If he overstrained, she became upset.

She should know he was dying. He had been about it long enough.

'Yes, Commander Bond,' he replied, at last. 'I'm still interested. It's a hard bone to let go.'

'You're considered the authority.'

'Flatter the old duffer, eh?'

'Not at all.'

'You want to hear about him? Dracula?'

If he were to publish his memoirs – an enterprise from which he was forbidden by law – they would have to be called *Anni Draculae* – 'the Dracula Years'. The exile of Palazzo Otranto was the defining influence of his overlong life. The thing he most regretted about death was leaving the stage before the Count, not being there at the King Vampire's finish.

'*Dragulya*,' he repeated, drawing out the name, as Churchill always did. 'What would this century have been like without him? You've read Stoker's book? About how he could have been stopped at the beginning?'

'I don't have much time to read.'

Too busy running after warm wenches and getting into scrapes, Beauregard would be bound.

'A mistake, I think, Commander Bond. But then, I've had a great deal of time. I've read everything about Dracula, fact and fiction. I know more about him than anyone else alive.'

'With respect, Sir, we have people close to Dracula, who've been there for centuries.'

One of Winthrop's *idées fixées* was recruiting vampire elders to spy on their *principe*. So, Diogenes had finally pulled it off. There were moles in the Carpathian Guard.

'I said *alive*.'

He chuckled. That made his chest hurt. His laugh turned to a cough.

Geneviève, supernaturally attuned to every wheeze and creak, parted the curtains and stepped through the french windows. In a sleeveless cream polo-neck sweater and violet toreador pants, she was a beauty. Spots of colour on chalk-white cheeks showed her anger. She shot a chill look at Bond and knelt by Beauregard, clucking like a French governess. She made him lift his mug to his mouth, forcing him to take a swallow of the tea he had forgotten.

Unembarrassed, Bond leaned against the balcony, smoke pluming from his nostrils. Thin sunlight glinted in his hard eyes. He would have had to learn cruelty to serve Diogenes. Maybe he'd always had the knot inside him, waiting to be undone. He had been recruited warm and turned scientifically through tubes and transfusions, then trained and shaped to be the weapon required for the job. That was another of Winthrop's ideas.

'Charles-*Chèri*, you mustn't go on like this.'

Geneviève didn't scold or whine. She made a charade of fussing but understood exactly how much she could do for him and how much she could not. She laid her head briefly in his lap so he would not see the beginnings of pink tears in her eyes. Her honey-blonde hair spilled over his thin, heavily veined hands. His fingers stirred with an impulse to stroke her.

Bond looked at them.

With a flash of the insight Beauregard had developed in his career, augmented by the traces of herself Geneviève had left in him, he knew what Bond was thinking. A dutiful grand-daughter. No, *great*-grand-daughter.

She was by far the older, but he wore all the years she had cast aside. Geneviève was turned in 1432, at the age of sixteen. After five centuries, she seemed no older than twenty. Provided you didn't look too closely at her eyes.

It took him frustrating seconds to remember exactly how old he was. He was born in 1853, had received a telegram from the new Queen in 1953. The year was now…? He got it, finally, as always: 1959. He was 105 years old; 106 next month, August. He might not exactly look his age – another effect of her kisses, he knew – but he was undeniably old, inside and out, a living ghost of his younger selves.

He had almost outgrown pain. Ten or twenty years ago, he was stricken with all the aches and pangs of age, but they had faded. His body was losing the habit of feeling. Sometimes, he felt exactly like a spirit, communicating with the world through a half-witted medium, unable to get his message across. Only Geneviève understood, through a species of natural telepathy.

He controlled his coughing.

'You had better leave,' Geneviève told Bond, firmly.

'It's all right, Gené. I'm all right.'

She looked up at him, blue eyes penetrating. The trick with Geneviève was to not lie. She could always tell. Pamela, his wife, had been the same. It was not just a vampire trait.

The trick was to tell his truth.

'You can't let it go either, my dearest,' he said.

She looked away and he stroked her soft, fine hair. The electric touch took him back, to their first time together: her teeth and nails tracing trickling patterns on his skin, her cat-tongue tingling the love-wounds.

'Our Geneviève was the first woman to set foot inside the Diogenes Club, Commander Bond, the first to face the Ruling Cabal. Does that seem archaic to you? Mediaeval?'

'Not really.'

'You should be quizzing her. She hasn't let the bone go, either, the Dracula bone. And she's better able to do something about him than a living fossil like me.'

'He should be dead,' Geneviève said. 'He should *have been* dead a long time. Truly dead.'

'Plenty would agree with you,' said the new-born.

Geneviève stood up and looked at the young vampire's blockily handsome face. He had healed scars.

'Plenty have had opportunity to end it. To end *him*. Once, we... you know that story, of course – an old tale, tedious to you. Ancient history.'

Beauregard understood Geneviève's bitterness.

In 1943, it had been expedient for the Allies to come to a dark accommodation. It had taken Edwin Winthrop to negotiate the Croglin Grange Treaty, which brought the King Vampire into the war. The younger man, unfettered by what he sometimes called 'Victorian notions', was willing to take the responsibility and the opprobrium on himself. Despite everything, Beauregard had approved the policy. Even Churchill, detesting Dracula as he did Hitler, went along with the alliance, though he never shook the Count's hand. Beauregard had, turning away from the King Vampire's dagger smile. His personal defeat, willingly given, was in the name of a greater victory.

It was as well that Geneviève was in Java then, remote from the tides of history. She would have tried to rip out Dracula's throat.

'In this century, you've never understood Vlad Tepes,' said Geneviève. 'You've always thought he could be appeased and accommodated. He's never been a politician, like Lord Ruthven. He's a mediaeval man, a barbarian. His throne is raised upon a mountain of skulls.'

The wars of this modern age were different from those of earlier centuries. Partly because of new armaments which made conflict on a worldwide scale not only possible but inevitable, and partly because of the Changes – the spread of vampirism begun by Dracula's emergence into the Western world. Without vampires, Beauregard was sure there could never have been Nazis; if anyone was Dracula's heir, it had been Hitler. Though the Final Solution applied as much to vampires of the Dracula line as to Jews, Hitler had intended to turn once his Reich was absolute, to last the full thousand years. The creation of an undying master race by science and sorcery was a German project dating back to the First

World War, ironically as much Dracula's vision as Hitler's. If the Nazis hadn't excluded his bloodline from the register of purity, Dracula would have sided with them.

'You made him your ally,' Geneviève said, coldly.

Bond shrugged. 'Stalin was our ally too, and the Devil Incarnate after Yalta. Politics aren't my department, *mademoiselle*. Cleverer brains than mine struggle with that. Mine is but to do or die, preferably the former.'

'You've died once, obviously.'

'Of course. You know what they say…'

'No. What?'

'You only live *twice*.'

Geneviève stood, hand resting on Beauregard's shoulder. He was her last tie, he knew. When he was gone, what would she feel free to do?

'Pardon me for being blunt, Commander,' she said, 'but some of us have less time. What exactly are you here to find out?'

The spy couldn't give a straight answer. Winthrop was still thinking in zigzags, and his agent might not even know the point of his mission.

'I'm writing a report on the Royal Engagement.'

'You are perhaps a gossip columnist?'

Bond smiled, showing sharp teeth. With the beginnings of amusement, Beauregard saw the new-born was taken with Geneviève. If she worked him properly, she would have a conquest.

'Thanks to Beauregard and people like him, we know a lot about Dracula,' said Bond. 'You're wrong to think we've never tried to understand him. He's been a public figure since the 1880s. We know how he thinks. We know what he wants. It's always been about power. Since his warm days, he's seen himself as a conqueror. He's spread his bloodline to an army of get. Each time he's married, it has been to advance his cause, to build a power base.'

He heard Edwin Winthrop speaking through Bond. This was Winthrop's worldview. Beauregard could not argue with it exactly, but had come to understand – during the eras of Hitler and Mussolini and Stalin – that the Count was not a unique, or even uncommon, type. The coldest thought that ever settled in him was that Dracula had succeeded after all. Every nation on Earth – Great Britain not excluded – acted as if it were ruled by the King Vampire.

'The person we don't know about is the Princess,' Bond continued, exhaling more smoke. 'She flits in and out of the records, leaving no significant trace. What Head Office want to know is, why Asa Vajda? She's of the bloodline of Javutich, a near-extinct breed. Dracula has enough history. What he needs, as always, is geography – estates, a throne, a fastness. Like most elders' – Bond dipped his eyes at Geneviève – '*il principe* is dispossessed, a monied vagabond. Ceauşescu certainly isn't going to take him back.'

Hundreds of Transylvanian vampires, having survived Nazi death camps, were returned to their homeland after the War and promptly killed, with the shameful collusion of the Allies, by their warm countrymen. Nicolae Ceauşescu still conducted a campaign of extermination against vampires who persisted in an attachment to native soil that happened to lie within modern Romania. As terrified as any of his peasant ancestors, the premier took Castle Dracula for his Summer Palace, to show his mastery.

'Princess Asa is Moldavian,' Beauregard said. 'Dracula is a Wallach. Something like two-thirds of the world's vampire elders come from the horseshoe of the Carpathians. If Dracula is to have temporal power again, that's where he must begin, in what is now Romania. When one gets to be very old, homeland comes to mean a lot.'

Geneviève squeezed his shoulder.

'Head Office think along the same lines, Beauregard. But as a dynastic marriage, this doesn't ring true. By rights, Dracula should connect himself with a strong bloodline. Countess Elisabeth of the House of Bathory is an obvious candidate.'

'She's lesbian,' Geneviève put in.

'This isn't a love match, *Mademoiselle* Dieudonné. You have to admit it's a comedown. Going from the Queen of England to a backwoods hellcat with twigs in her hair and earth in the folds of her shroud?'

'The Count has his odd fancies. Ask Mrs Harker.'

'If it's bloodline he wants, Gené, I'm surprised he hasn't come a-courting.'

Geneviève shuddered. '*Très amusant*, Charles-*Chèri*.'

Bond shook his head. 'He's up to something. Dracula has never made a move that wasn't for his own ends first and last. But what are his ends?'

'Complete and utter subjugation of everyone and everything,' Geneviève said. 'Forever. There, I've told you his secret. Can I claim my five hundred francs?'

The spy cracked another one-sided smile. Sizing Geneviève up, he thought himself man enough to tame her. Beauregard chuckled again and found himself coughing. It was worse this time, jagged glass rolling around inside his chest. Breathing became a chore.

'This interview is over,' Geneviève insisted.

She knelt by him again, helping him drink, pressing a hand against his chest, willing him to survive. She forgot to hide her eyes. He saw the gathering red at her tearducts.

'Very well,' Bond consented. 'May I call back? If other lines of inquiry dry.'

Beauregard tried to stop coughing. He could not manage it.

'I'd prefer you didn't,' Geneviève said.

He tried to overrule her, but the words wouldn't come. It was best to let her decide.

'Let yourself out,' she said.

'Of course.' He extinguished his cigarette. 'Good day to you both. You can reach me at the Inghilterra.'

He slipped silently through the french windows and left the apartment.

Beauregard allowed his spasm to subside of its own accord. He spluttered, leaking foam from his mouth. Geneviève wiped his face, like his nanny.

As he had come to expect, the pain faded fast. His eyes and ears were still sharp, but he had almost no senses of taste or smell. Only memories.

'*Pauvre chèri*,' said Geneviève.

She wheeled him inside.

* * *

Though he had only lived on the Via Eudosiana for ten years, the apartment was crowded with a century of acquisitions. Bookshelves lined the walls up to the high ceiling. A great many odd objects picked up in all quarters of the globe were collected unsorted in corners. Geneviève often found an African mask or Chinese jade figure in a box or drawer and remarked on its quality or value. He had covertly made an inventory – such list-making upset her, he knew – and considered who would get the most out of each item. The library would go to Edwin Winthrop.

Geneviève helped him out of his bath chair onto the day bed in his study. He was so light now that even a warm girl could have lifted him up and set him down like a baby. Geneviève let him do as much as he could under his own steam. Using the last strength in his wasted muscles, he rose from his chair, steadying himself on her arm, then more or less collapsed onto the couch, allowing her to arrange his legs under a tartan blanket.

She smiled sweetly. It was like a pin through his heart. That feeling had not faded.

Sometimes he called her Pamela, and she let it pass. His wife had died after two years of marriage, nearly eighty years ago. The heat made Rome much like the hill country of India, where he and Pam had lived while he pursued what Kipling called the Great Game, the chess match of intelligence and counter-intelligence between the Russias and the British Empire over the disposition of the sub-continent – the first Cold War. Pam had said all along that no good would come of it, and had constantly been a thorn about duty, forcing him to question where it actually lay. Geneviève might be the last and longest-lasting of his loves, but he had a clearer sense of his brief time with Pam, of the joy and pain.

Guilt made him love Geneviève the more.

He took her hand and gripped it, squeezing with all the strength he had left.

She kissed his forehead.

It must be a grotesque sight, a young girl with an old

man. A song of his youth was 'A Bird in a Gilded Cage'. But Geneviève only *seemed* young, just as he was beyond old. Anything past a hundred was unnatural. An age for trees and turtles, not men.

'I need you, Charles,' she breathed.

It was not a lie. It was her truth, told in such a way that he could not refuse it.

She climbed onto the couch alongside him. When they lay together, he was still the taller. If her head was beside his, her feet barely reached past his knees.

She kissed his cheek and chin, smooth where she had shaved him an hour ago. Quite a bit of hair remained on his head, thick and white, but he no longer wore a moustache. He owed his hair to her, and probably his eyesight and the majority of his teeth.

She loosened his dressing gown from his neck and undid the top button of his pyjama jacket. She nuzzled the hollow of his throat and moved her mouth, feeling for the old wounds.

He was calm, spasms gone. In his heart, he was aroused. His blood flowed faster. In a way that would have astonished him as a young man, that was enough.

'This is absurd, Gené,' he murmured. 'You're…'

'Old enough to be your great-grandmother ten times over. You're the young lover with the elderly mistress, remember.'

Her fangs slipped into well-worn grooves in his shoulder, well away from the vein. He could never decide whether the tingling darts were hot needles or sharp icicles.

He shook with delight. Her tongue undulated against his skin. He felt her body tense against his and knew his taste was flooding into her.

Once, she would have drunk. Now, she sipped.

No, *tasted*.

He knew what she was doing. For years, she hadn't been drinking his blood. She opened his wounds and put her mouth to them, taking not substance but sustenance, drawing from his heart not his body.

And she gave him of herself.

He was as much a vampire as she. Geneviève kept him alive

with her blood. With the rough, sharp point of her tongue, she scratched away at the inside of her mouth, and dribbled smidgens into his wounds. It was in her power to force him to drink her blood, to turn him into her son-in-darkness, to make him her vampire get. But not in her character.

There were three vampire women in his life, all of different bloodlines. Geneviève, like Kate Reed, could not just take from her lovers. She had to leave something of herself behind, in the mind and body. Everyone she touched was changed by her, affected.

The other one had torn his neck and taken from him with contempt as much as desire. When he thought of her, it was with pity.

How many years did he owe Geneviève?

Her blood had kept him young, without him realising it. Because he hadn't wanted to realise. Now, he knew she was keeping him alive. The men of his family were not on the whole long-lived. An uncle had made it to ninety, and a nephew was still alive at eighty-one. But his father had died, of a Bombay fever, at forty-eight, and both his grandfathers were dead when he was born. For him, 105 was not a natural age.

In their communion, Geneviève sobbed silently, her sorrow coursing through his heart.

'Don't, my darling,' he said, comforting her.

He wanted to raise his hands, to touch her face, to blot her tears, but he was in a daze. His mind still darted, but his limbs were heavy, unresponsive.

'It doesn't matter,' she said.

Now would be a good time, he thought. Her warmth was inside him, would be carried along with him. He imagined himself shrinking inside his worn-out body, spirals of light and dark winding around him. His face arranged a smile.

Geneviève pulled suddenly away from his neck. He felt air on his wet skin.

'No,' she said, suddenly firm, selfish almost.

Through her blood, he had tugged at her. She knew what he was thinking, what he was feeling.

'No,' she repeated, tenderly, imploring. 'Not yet, please.'

His arms worked. They folded around her. He consented to live.

'That man was lying, Charles,' she said.

He knew.

'He doesn't make reports. He's not the type. He acts on reports.'

'Good girl,' he said.

As he fell asleep, lulled by the beat of his heart, he heard the telephone ring.

'Better… answer that,' he breathed.

3

GIALLO POLIZIA

Inspector Silvestri talked in high, musical Italian to uniformed subordinates, directing their activities in the Piazza di Trevi. Speaking English to Kate, his voice was entirely different, deeper. Flat-toned, like a bad actor.

'You saw the assassin?' Silvestri asked. '*Il Boia Scarlatto*?'

Il Boia Scarlatto – the Crimson Executioner.

In her mind, she still could. A face rippling in the pool.

'Only his reflection,' she admitted.

Silvestri noted that down. Despite the Roman summer, he wore the European detective's unofficial uniform, an off-white Maigret raincoat. He was a solid, middle-aged man.

'He had a reflection?'

'The man was not a vampire, Inspector.'

Two policemen lifted Kernassy's cloak out of the water like a hammock, holding his fragile remains in it. Minions from the coroner's office sifted with butterfly nets, scooping up stuff she supposed must be Malenka.

The Morlacchi gown had been spirited away, which irritated Silvestri. Some cop's fiancée or mistress had best not ask questions about the provenance of their birthday gift. Kate hoped it was cleaned and mended before presentation.

Merciless sun poured into the piazza. She had not expected the heat to be this bad. She didn't perspire – a trick of her altered body chemistry – but was thus all the more uncomfortable when the temperature rose much above the English norm. She was evolved to be a night creature.

Crowds of curiosity-seekers were roped back. The paparazzi who'd haunted Malenka were replaced by less frenetic, hungrier-looking crime reporters. On the Via San Vincenzo, angry carhorns honked. Despite the barriers, a lad on a Lambretta took a shortcut through the piazza, shooed on by gun-toting carabinieri.

The shadow Kate had found at one side of the fountain was shrinking. Her eyes hurt from the glare. She felt the tingle of sunlight on her face and hands, and knew she was going beet-red. Sun-scars sometimes took decades to heal. She'd planned to spend the day indoors like a proper vampire, and emerge after nightfall.

She looked around for Marcello. He was chatting easily with a couple of uniformed cops and some fellows she took to be reporters. They shared cigarettes and laughed. She recognised the professional callousness of those who trawl around where ghastly things have happened, pressmen as much as policemen. She was herself used to exchanging small talk over smokes while leaning against bullet-riddled, blood-patterned massacre walls.

What had Marcello told Silvestri? They clearly knew each other. The first thing the Inspector had done upon arriving was take the Italian reporter aside and listen intently to a lengthy explanation with illustrative gestures.

One of the coroner's men uttered a cry of disgust and fished out the dead, waterlogged cat. Everyone expressed sympathy for the poor thing. That suggested how vampires might stand in Rome. Dotted through the crowds like black scarecrows, nuns and priests glared disapproval at her. The Catholic Church was never going to be comfortable with her kind.

Kate guessed she was the favourite suspect. Marcello had come back to the piazza and found her alone with the remains of Count Kernassy and Malenka. He hadn't seen the killer, hadn't even heard his ridiculous laughter.

She'd retold her story three times and given a description to a police artist. They had worked up a sketch which looked embarrassingly like a comic strip villain, complete with mad grin. Next time, she'd be sure to be nearly killed by someone who could be taken seriously.

'Have you found the little girl?' she asked Silvestri. 'She looked sad, frightened. She saw the murderer.'

'Ah yes,' he said, affecting the need to jog his memory, flipping back his notes. 'The little girl who was weeping.'

'There couldn't have been many children on the streets. It was near dawn.'

'There are always children on the streets, Signorina. This is Rome.'

'She didn't look…'

What did she mean? She'd only seen the girl's face. No, the reflection of her face. Upside-down. She couldn't say what she had been wearing. She had an impression that the girl was not a ragged urchin, even that she came from wealth, old money. Why did she think that?

'Her hair,' she said, thinking aloud. 'It was long, clean. Well-groomed, looked after. It hung over one eye, like Veronica Lake's.'

Silvestri's mouth was fixed, but he smiled with his eyes.

'You observe,' he said.

'I'm a reporter. It's my job.'

His voice changed again, as he rattled off orders to his assistant, Sergeant Ginko. Kate caught a few words: *ragazza* – girl, *lunghi capella* – long hair, *Veronica Lake* – hubba-hubba.

They were taking her seriously now. Good.

'What else did you observe that you can report?'

She almost said something.

That upside-down face. Blonde tresses, sad-clown mouth, tears. The killer, dressed as an executioner – mask, bare chest, tights. A flash of killing red, sharp silver. Kernassy's skull, Malenka's eyes.

What's wrong with this picture?

'Go on,' Silvestri encouraged. 'Anything, even if you're not sure of it…'

'It's a puzzle,' she said. 'I keep trying to fit it all together. One of the pieces is wrong, but I don't know which. I'm sorry. It's as frustrating for me as it is for you. I have a sense of wrongness – some tiny detail. Something I saw, but can't put my finger on. I keep going over it.'

The Inspector was disappointed. He wrote his telephone number on a page of his notebook, tore it out, and offered it to her.

'If the puzzle fits together, you will call me?'

She took the number.

'Yes. Of course.'

Silvestri shut his notebook again. It was his favourite prop.

'You may go, Signorina Katharine Reed.'

She was a little surprised.

'You don't want to arrest me? On suspicion?'

Silvestri laughed.

'No. You have misunderstood. You arrived in Rome only last night, on the same flight as *il conte* and his "niece". That is confirmed by Alitalia. These were not the first killings.'

Even in the Roman sun, Kate felt a chill.

'Rome is not safe for *vampiri*,' Silvestri continued. 'They think themselves hunters of men, but here we have a man who thinks himself a hunter of them. This *Boia Scarlatto* has killed others, in ones and twos. Since the War. All elders.'

'Surely Malenka was a new-born. She seemed so... modern.'

Silvestri shook his head. 'She had her centuries.'

All elders. Why kill Kernassy and Malenka, but not Kate Reed?

There was no hard and fast age at which one became an elder. She supposed you had to survive your natural life expectancy, then live on at least another lifetime. After two centuries, you were getting there. Dracula was an elder, and Lord Ruthven, and Geneviève. Kate was ninety-six. If she'd stayed warm, she might still be alive.

Charles, ten years older, was.

Had the little girl scared off the Crimson Executioner? That didn't sound likely.

Silvestri ordered his men to lay down Kernassy's cape and looked at the body. The press photographed the scene with the famous fountain picturesquely blurred in the background. The Inspector put on a serious expression. Like Malenka, he gave the photographers different angles. He experimented with looks: contemplative, decisive, determined.

Reporters paid attention as Silvestri announced, *'I corpi presentano tracce di violenza supernatural,'* and proceeded to rattle off a statement they all jotted down.

Century-old schoolgirl Italian knocked around the back of her head, tainted by profane Sicilian picked up in the war. She didn't have to understand every word to catch the policeman's drift. It was a scene-of-the-crime speech, the same the world over. Every effort was being made and every lead followed. An arrest was promised in the immediate but non-specific future. Kate had first heard the song at the site of one of the Jack the Ripper murders, performed by the artist who made it famous, Inspector Lestrade of Scotland Yard.

Of course, Jack was never arrested.

Kate wondered if she should tell Marcello the police thought her innocent. He'd been startled enough by the moment of discovery. Even through *cool-baby* shades, he registered shock and suspicion. She knew the impression would be hard to shift. To him, she might always be a bloodthirsty monster.

Damn. There was always something.

She chided herself. Two people were destroyed and she was worried about impressing a warm man who, she was sure, found her as attractive as a face-rub with a dead fish.

She hadn't disliked Gabor Kernassy. And Malenka was more ridiculous than anything else. They might have been shallow, but they were kinder to her than convention obliged them to be. Even Malenka was funny. Kate had planned to write about the circus around the starlet. She'd have made money from them. Considering murder as news, she still might.

They had been slaughtered in front of her.

A long-bladed silver knife had fetched off Kernassy's head and skewered Malenka's heart. The police found the thing in the fountain, washed clean. Silvestri made sure it didn't vanish along with Malenka's dress.

Kate knew she wouldn't let this go. She had a great deal to occupy her in this city, unfinished business of long standing. But this was now her business too.

Someone called her name.

For an instant, she thought it might be Marcello. But it was a woman.

Geneviève.

She was behind the rope barrier, wearing a white straw hat and sunglasses. She waved at Kate with another hat.

'They won't let me through,' Geneviève shrugged, smiling.

She looked so *young*.

Her sun-blonde hair shone. Her smile was almost a little girl's. Her old eyes were out of sight. She was genuinely pleased to see Kate.

She'd given the police the telephone number. Silvestri must have had someone make a call. That was considerate.

'I've been told I can go free,' Kate said. 'I'm innocent.'

'I doubt that, Kate.'

She spoke English with the ghost of a French accent.

They hugged over the rope, cheek-kissing. It wasn't quite comfortable, as if someone were between them.

Charles, of course.

They were only friends in that they triangulated on Charles, and perhaps *il principe*. So many complications ran between them all. Edwin Winthrop fit into the pattern, too. And Penelope.

'I've brought you a *chapeau*,' Geneviève said. 'I knew you wouldn't expect the sun. The English never do and in this one thing I assumed the Irish would not be different.'

The rope was lifted by a policeman. Kate ducked under and took the hat. It kept the worst of the light off her face. Kate looked at the backs of her hands. They were red.

'You must take care,' Geneviève said, 'or you'll go off like a firework. In this lovely climate, spontaneous combustion is a hazard.'

4

MYSTERIES OF OTRANTO

The Palazzo Otranto might have been grown rather than built. It was neat as a snail's shell or a human heart, an architectural spiral. The main corridor began as a ledge inside the topmost tower, like the rifling of a gun barrel, and wound down through the building, the rooms off it larger the nearer they were to ground level, turning at last into a circular passageway around the cavernous basements. No staircases, just a constant helter-skelter slope and the occasional sharp step. Hell on the knees.

The palazzo was in Fregene, on the coast a few miles outside Rome, among pine forests and the usual ruins. There was a Temple of Pan on the grounds. The Dracula household celebrated eternal Saturnalia, a nebulous and never-ending party that attracted guests like flies.

Tom had been here since Spring and wasn't sure if he should stay much longer. There was no particular reason to move on and he certainly didn't want to return to the bailiwick of the New York Police Department. He'd left the States in the first place to avoid questions about a silly stunt some folk might call mail fraud though it hadn't gone on long enough for him to make money out of it, worse luck. The exclusive company of the dead was deepening his customary ennui. Someone dangerous might pick up on the irritation he attempted to conceal behind fashionable disinterest. The dead were clowns, but also killers.

This was, however, the life of ease and refinement he

always imagined would suit him best. Goodish paintings were about, mostly from old and fussy schools he didn't cotton to. A VistaVision Schalcken hung in his tower room, an angry horse with nightmare eyes. Renaissance schlock adorned the ballrooms, Biblical scenes heavy with bloody thunderclouds and gross nudes.

The dead clung to the fashions of their lives. The exception was *il principe*, whose premature enthusiasm for Van Gogh – he was the only person to buy from the painter in his lifetime – had paid off in his several exiles. Canvases worthless when bought now stood security for loans that kept the household among the wealthiest in Europe. Those daubs, at which Tom would have liked to get a look, were shut up in Dracula's private apartments, in the lower cellar depths.

In this topsy-turvy world, the most luxurious and sought-after quarters were the deepest underground, the nearest to Hell, the most like tombs or vaults. Penthouses that'd do for American millionaires were palmed off on half-living servants and enslaved blood donors.

In his months here, Tom had only set eyes on *il principe* once, with Penelope. He stuck to his apartments and rarely visited the party of which he was the host. He seemed like any other ancient dead man, with long white military moustaches and dark glasses like the wings of a black beetle. Nevertheless, Tom admired Dracula, for his Van Gogh craze if nothing else. That taste, once daringly radical, suggested an openness to the new uncharacteristic of the dead. Also, that – whatever his current circumstances – he could still be a dangerous man, a predator. Tom respected him. He'd leave *il principe* alone, and hope Dracula did the same for him.

In the mornings, before the household stirred, Tom took precious time to himself. He liked to sit in the Crystal Room, a conservatory on the first floor, looking out at the grounds through forty-foot walls of glass. Before noon, the room was a kaleidoscope of sunlight; he was rarely bugged by the dead.

He claimed a favourite chair to read the *International Herald Tribune* and drink continuous thimble-cups of bitter, strong espresso. The warm servants of the day shift, who rarely lasted long, were eager to keep him happy. Not a cruel fellow, he liked a little bowing and scraping. He felt he'd earned his leisure. It had taken not a little ingenuity and hard graft to get him here.

Sunlight danced around, flashing off the dragon-scale panes of the conservatory roof, illuminating columns of swirling dust, making angular patterns on the old carpet. Tom felt warmth on his face and was tempted to close his eyes and doze. He might not have to spend the day in a casket lined with Boston soil, but he'd still been up all night. Even the heart-punching coffee couldn't keep him awake forever. His habit was to siesta in the afternoon and early evening, to be out of the way when the dead rose.

Was his distaste just an American prejudice? There weren't many living dead in the States. Prohibition hadn't driven them out completely in the '20s, but they remained an underground presence, not the mushroom growth they were in Europe. Legal restrictions on their practices were stringently enforced. Tom fancied himself free from most convention, but something about the creatures crawled behind his eyes.

He opened his dressing gown at the throat and undid the top buttons of his Ascot Chang shirt. Dickie's shirt, originally. He hoped he was tanning. A Mediterranean brown would make the bite-marks stand out less. And he didn't want to be mistaken for one of the dead. He was with them so much that a wall was rising around him, separating him from the living.

It wasn't until he came to Europe, head a-buzz with his aunt's tales of bloodsucking monsters on every street corner, that he really found out anything about the dead. They weren't so fearsome.

In his own small way, he was a predator on the dead.

In Greece for no very good reason, Tom had run into Richard Fountain, a youngish newlydead. They knew each other from a weekend party in the Hamptons to which Tom had not exactly been invited. Dickie, now on the run from a tiresome girlfriend and a God-awful Cambridge College, was glad of the company, and took him back to his beach-house on Cyprus. Somehow, the Englishman picked up the idea that Tom was from money but estranged from it, a remittance man. Tom could never work out why life in England had become intolerable for Dickie, but it had, driving him south-east in a restless search for something indefinable. His course had led him to a dead peasant named Chriseis, who had turned him on their first night and ditched him in the dark.

Together, Tom and Dickie knocked around a little, hopping from island to island, having the usual adventures. Dickie, hooked on new experience, was obsessed with the dead of Greece. He rooted around everywhere for traces of Chriseis's bloodline, which he supposed went back to the *vorvolukas* of recent times and the *lamiae* of antiquity. It was a bit of a yawn but nothing that couldn't be coped with. After all, being bored was better than being in prison. It was Tom's intention never to go to jail. He loathed the idea of enforced proximity, of being in a tiny space with another man or men not of his choosing.

Through Dickie, Tom realised something important about the dead. When their teeth were stuck in your neck and your blood was washing around their mouths, they were in no position to notice you going through their pockets.

In his ignorance, Tom had thought the dead needed blood to survive the way the living needed water. It wasn't true. Warm blood could be like dope, or alcohol, or sex, or espresso, or sugar. Anything from a desperate addiction to a mild weakness. When the red thirst was on them, their famed powers of insight and persuasion turned to fuzz and fudge.

At first, Dickie was apologetic about bleeding Tom, and profusely grateful afterward. He didn't know the ropes. He said 'excuse me', 'please' and 'thank you' every time he bit some poor warm fool. Then he began to display an arrogant streak, as if he'd made Tom into his slave or something. In long, rambling monologues near dawn in the beachhouse, Dickie talked about sin and evil and gratification, of the need to go beyond guilt and embrace the full human potential. Words like 'sin', 'evil', and 'guilt' were meaningless to Tom. He had heard them often at school and been fascinated by their meanings, but only in an academic way as if they were discredited scientific theories centuries had been wasted on. The miracle was that Dickie still saw something in all that rot.

It became obvious to Tom that the arrangement could not last indefinitely. He'd had to cast around for a way of coming out of it comfortably.

A few trickles of blood fogged Dickie completely, made him uncommonly suggestible. After a month or so of this communion, the dead man no longer noticed if Tom borrowed things on a permanent basis. He liked to wear Dickie's English clothes, which were of a quality he appreciated. It was providential that they were roughly the same size.

When he accepted death, Richard Fountain threw away his life. It was only fair, then, that Tom should pick it up. He was best placed to enjoy it, after all.

Eventually, the set-up grew highly tiresome. Dickie's mad fiancée tracked them down to Cyprus. She made accusations which Tom found hurtful and upsetting. To sort things out, Tom and Dickie went off one night in a boat to argue it through and Tom stuck a broken-off spar into Dickie's chest. Though not dead long enough to turn to dust, he'd gone off like spoiled meat. Tom had tipped him over the side and watched him sink.

He fixed it so Dickie appeared to have left for an untraceable Greek island on a fool's search for the source of Chriseis's bloodline, leaving behind a small income signed over into Tom's control, 'for the maintenance of the house'. More importantly, Dickie left written instructions that Tom should have the use of his travelling wardrobe. No one was happy, especially the fiancée and the family. The cops were involved, but investigations and insinuations fizzled out.

Dickie was already deceased, so no murder case could be brought. Greece was one of those countries that had never rewritten its laws to accommodate the walking dead. If anyone was sought for the murder, it was the elusive Chriseis. The authorities had no incentive to search for a corpse that was probably unidentifiable mould anyway.

The money carried Tom to Italy and, despite his reluctance

to get mixed up again with the dead, eventually washed him into the Palazzo Otranto.

And against Penelope.

She had been dead a long time. Dickie would have said she knew the ropes. If you got close, you could tell her age. Her skin was white, but with an undertint of corruption that was almost bluish. If she were scratched with silver, Tom thought her wounds would peel open, festering. Her face and limbs were perfect, but she had scars, angry red circles, on her breasts and stomach, like bullet holes.

On Malta, he was approached by an English subaltern who originally mistook him, because of his clothes, for Dickie, with whom he had been flogged at school. The young officer had a package, brought out from England to pay off a favour. It was to be taken to an exile in Rome. Tom was offered the use of an already-booked room at the Rinascimento in Campo de' Fiori if he would deliver the package. Tom had planned to go on to Rome anyway, and this was as painless a way of arriving as any.

He was tempted to peek, of course. The parcel was small enough to contain a fountain pen or a hypodermic syringe. He assumed from the roundabout method of delivery that it was an artifact on its way to a new owner, perhaps without the consent of the last one.

The addressee was Penelope Churchward. They met at his hotel and he handed over the package, which she said was a wedding present. Afterward, she extended an invitation which, a few days later, he was pleased to take up. He knew from the first that she was interested in bleeding him. This was a comparatively new experience for him, but he was picking up on it. Was he one of those fellows who was attractive to the dead?

Penny found Tom useful for more than his blood. Her position in *il principe*'s household was undefined. She ran things, as much a housekeeper as a mistress. There were always chores Tom could do, like driving that dead cow Malenka through adoring hordes, or fetching goods from the city in broad daylight. He didn't even mind. There were advantages to being part of *il principe*'s entourage and yet a living man.

When she was bleeding him, she was as helpless as Dickie, as much addled by the taste of his blood. But she was more demanding, thirstier. Her red kisses drained him. He wondered how long she could last. At times, she was quite fun. She'd known Whistler and Wilde in her warm days, though not much understood their work.

His bites itched. He rearranged his dressing gown over them. Tom wasn't yet sure what to do with Penny. Something would come to mind.

It must be past noon. The sun had passed overhead. Shadows gathered like curtains in the Crystal Room.

Dead hands slipped around his neck.

Tom didn't have to guess who.

Penelope was in a mood, he realised. Working too hard on devil-may-care brittleness, she draped herself over an armchair as if it were a patron's lap, dangling one leg like a flirty fourteen-year-old. Her foot swung like a metronome. He guessed she'd like to kick someone.

She wore slacks, cut halfway up the calves to show off her pretty ankles, and ballet pumps. Her Nehru jacket was a sombre blue shade with frivolous filaments of something shiny mixed into the weave. Her hair was pinned up under an oversize sailor's cap with a red pom-pom.

Sunglasses dangled from her mouth. She had a habit of chewing the arms, sometimes snapping them off. He saw a tiny fang biting down.

'You must amuse me, Tom,' she decreed. 'I need to be amused. Desperately.'

It was because the elder from last night and his bovine 'niece' had run into the local murderer. Penelope could have cheerfully killed them herself, but resented the fuss made about this colourful atrocity.

The Roman morning papers were full of pictures. Malenka was everywhere, her luminously smiling face and ridiculous pout contrasted with grainier, less glamorous shots of the cops at the scene of the crime.

'Malenka came to Rome to be a star,' Tom observed. 'And has got her wish.'

Penelope snorted rather than laughed.

'You don't think the little witch will turn up unhurt, do you?' she said. 'That it's a publicity stunt? There isn't much identifiable in the way of a body, according to the papers. Even that blessed dress has waltzed off.'

'Count Kernassy is definitely identified,' he pointed out.

'She'd have killed for headlines. That one would kill for lunch.'

Penelope sat cross-legged on the seat, winding her legs together in a yoga pose, and lifted herself up on her arms, swaying slightly like one of those nodding dog automobile ornaments prized by vulgar people.

'Your English pal was a witness,' Tom said.

'Irish. Katie's Irish.'

'She gave a full description of their deaths. And of their murderer, this Crimson Executioner. Of course, she might have her reasons for being a liar.'

Penelope smiled nastily at the thought of her friend being in on murder.

'She can't be mixed up with it. She met Kernassy on the plane.'

'So she says.'

Tom did not believe for a moment what he was suggesting. He was spinning out a story to distract Penelope, to amuse her. She liked to think the worst of people. Except of him, oddly enough.

'It's not Katie Reed, Tom,' she said, having thought it through. 'You don't know her.'

'How well do we ever really know anyone?'

'I'm a vampire, you American clod. I can see into men's minds and hearts, and suck them dry.'

She flipped out of the chair and was close to him, faster than his eye could register. A cheap dead trick. It was supposed to unnerve and overwhelm.

Her hands rested on his shoulders and she leaned forward, glasses still dangling from her mouth, for a quick, bloodless kiss.

Tom felt a thrill of revulsion at the nearness of the dead woman. He let her peck his lips.

She was gone again, at the other side of the Crystal Room, leaning against a fireplace. Then she was back in her chair, sitting properly, knees together.

'I don't know what we're going to tell Princess Asa,' she said. 'She'll probably go spare.'

However irritated Penelope might be with Count Kernassy and Malenka, her real goat was Princess Asa Vajda, the Royal Fiancée. It was too obvious to think her simply jealous, for Tom knew she didn't dare imagine herself as even a consort for *il principe*. Though she'd taken on the organising of the household, she was clearly not one of Dracula's sluts. Tom had seen them about, mindless dead women in shrouds, and a damn nuisance to any warm man within reach.

Sometimes Tom thought Penelope hated everyone but was too well brought-up to mention it.

She had a history, but it was too dull to delve into. It was as if he had walked into a movie theatre during the last reel of a complicated but not very interesting melodrama. His best policy was to ignore it, cluck the occasional agreeable or amusing comment and let the dead sort themselves out.

'Think of it this way, Penny,' he began. 'You've two free spaces in the chapel for the ceremony. You can bump up some of the poor relations.'

One of Penelope's chores was to assemble as many of Dracula's get as possible for the wedding. *Il principe* had been profligate for centuries, turning his mistresses and officers, disseminating his bloodline like a dog wetting trees.

'You've no idea how superstitious all those Middle European barbarians are,' she said. 'Reluctant to plonk their bottoms on a truly dead man's chair. Some still light black candles for the Devil on Walpurgis Night.'

By the time of the wedding, Tom wanted to be done with the dead. The ceremony was to be in the palace chapel, probably because the Pope wouldn't let Dracula use St Peter's. Otranto would be thronged with dead things.

The doors of the Crystal Room were flung open. Princess Asa made an entrance.

She wore six-inch high heels and a black bikini swimsuit, not an atypical ensemble for her. Transparent layers of floor-length shroud were draped over her head, fixed by a wide floppy black hat. Her waist-length hair was as dark as the proverbial raven's wing. Through all the grey lace, her huge round eyes glowed like red neons. Her cheekbones were sculptured ice, her lower lip was reckoned the lushest in Europe, and her tummy was tight as a drum skin.

On leashes, she had two mastiffs the size of ponies.

'Signorina Churchward,' she shouted. 'Can you not be entrusted with even the simplest task? Can you not fetch a valued friend from the airport without losing him to the mob?'

Penelope stood, affecting unconcern.

'Are we all to be found in our coffins and destroyed, as in the old times? You moderns remember nothing of the persecutions. Why were precautions not taken? Why was this atrocity allowed to happen?'

As she spoke, with a hollowly venomous voice, the Princess's shrouds fluttered around her like anemone fronds. She stalked the room, heels putting penny-sized holes in the old carpet, lace drifting behind in an angry froth, thin white thighs scything.

Penelope knew better than to shrug.

'*Il principe* will be distressed,' shouted Asa.

Tom wasn't sure the Princess had ever met her Prince. Theirs was more an alliance than a marriage, with everything negotiated beforehand. She seemed able to speak for him at all times, though. It would be interesting to see how much authority she might actually have.

One of the dogs snarled at Tom. Animals didn't like him much, which was a shame.

Princess Asa wheeled to look at him.

Her eyes burned through lace. Her eyelids curled like snarling lips. She flashed white teeth.

'I should take him from you, your toy,' she said, to Penelope. 'As punishment.'

Her dead face loomed close, eyes the size of saucers. Tom caught a whiff of grave-breath.

'But such treatment would be wasted on you,' the Princess said, wafting across the room, fluttering toward Penelope. 'You are a stupid, unfeeling woman. You care for nothing and no one.'

'As you say, Princess.'

Princess Asa picked up a Chinese plant pot older than she was, and smashed it on the floor, skewering earthy roots with a heel.

'Kneel, Englishwoman!'

Penelope's face tightened.

The Princess drew herself up, shrouds gathered, and towered over Penelope. A mediaeval tyrant in a snit, a Victorian lady with steel in her spine.

Princess Asa lifted a taloned hand in command. Her fingernails raised points in her shrouds.

Penelope went down on one knee but didn't lower her head.

'Kneel as if you meant it, woman.'

'As you say.'

Penelope looked briefly at the carpet, then got up, brushing dirt from her knees.

'Satisfied?' she asked Princess Asa.

'Eminently.'

'Good. If you'll excuse me, I have errands to run.' She looked at the shards of china and the trampled plant. 'I'll find a servant to clear up this mess. That was Tang Dynasty, by the way. Ninth century. A gift to Prince Dracula from Kah of Ping Kuei Temple. The High Priest probably didn't expect his tribute to be used as a flowerpot. Ugly object, I always thought. But apparently quite valuable.'

Penelope withdrew with strange dignity. Tom was proud of the old girl.

He was left alone with the Royal Fiancée.

She growled at him, like one of her dogs. He relaxed a little. She might make great display of her wrath, but Princess Asa was far less dangerous a creature than Penelope Churchward. For Tom, the Royal Fiancée was easy, almost disappointing.

He adjusted his collar, touching always-open bitemarks. He got his fingertips a little bloody and rolled them together.

Princess Asa, struck by red thirst, forgot his face, and looked at his sticky fingers. Pretending to have noticed her interest only now, Tom apologised and searched for a handkerchief. Then, shyly, as if it were an afterthought, he held out his hand, fingers dangling.

The Princess hesitated, looking around to see if they were observed. She gathered her shrouds and threw them up over her hat, tidying them behind her white shoulders. Her skin was like polished bone.

She moved as fast as Penelope, darting close to Tom, dipping her head, licking his fingers clean, then retreating, cleaning her mouth on gauze.

He saw how his taste affected her. Her skinny ribs rose and fell, like the legs of a contented centipede. She was shuddering with delight.

She would never give him a thought again.

5

GELATI

She looked Geneviève's Vespa over with some trepidation. The little motor-scooter was white with red trim, aerodynamically styled like an American wireless set. A great devotee of the bicycle in her younger days, Kate hadn't had much luck with motorised vehicles. In her experience, wonderful new contraptions had a habit of trying to kill her.

'It's the only way to get about,' Geneviève declared. 'I can nip in and out between stalled cars.'

'I'll bet you get honked at a lot.'

'Well, yes.'

Geneviève smiled as if Kate happened to be in town to sample the nightlife and look at the ruins.

They hadn't talked, really. About Charles.

Geneviève sat forward on the long seat, telling Kate to climb up behind and hang on. The ride was swift and thrilling, affording the welcome comfort of a breeze and a few routine brushes with death. Geneviève knew her way about the narrow streets and through hidden courtyards and piazzas. She handled her trusty steed with practised expertise. Whizzing past stalled motorists, she waved cheerfully at a chorus of rude horns.

Clinging to Geneviève's back, with blonde hair blowing at her face, Kate realised she was at the point of being seduced. When she returned to London, she'd consider buying a scooter. She might cut a tidy figure going around Highbury Corner on a little dream machine like this. She'd draw appreciative sighs outside the coffee bars along Old Compton Street. And she could cut through the knot of Teds who liked to block her way to the launderette.

They zigzagged away from the Piazza di Trevi toward the Piazza di Spagna, then up a steep side-road. Kate clung to her hat. Geneviève drove her back to the Hassler.

In the hotel lobby, she reclaimed her suitcase from an imperious uniformed functionary. She wondered if the management had cleared out Count Kernassy's suite.

Sergeant Ginko, Silvestri's pet, was questioning some maids. The investigation must be proceeding along the usual channels, trying to establish something in the Count's past that would lead to the killer. It wasn't likely to be a fruitful avenue: she thought Kernassy was murdered for what he was, not for anything he had done.

Had the news got to Penelope? Was it in the daily papers? Surely, Marcello must have sold the story. Kate would have done in London.

Geneviève lifted her sunglasses to examine marble and gilt. Rich people with expensive luggage streamed steadily into the lobby.

'You came straight here from Fiumicino? You must like the high life, Kate.'

Kate shook her head. She felt out of place here, a mouse at a banquet.

'I went along with things because it was easier. As usual, it's landed me in trouble.'

She remembered the cadre of bellhops swarming in Malenka's wake, trying to claim her luggage from Klove. Only half a day ago.

'They say the waiters here are *très* delicious,' Geneviève said, peering into the empty, shadowed bar.

'They are,' Kate agreed.

Geneviève looked, almost admiring, at her.

'You are a dark horse.'

Geneviève was fond of English idioms. She picked them up from Charles.

Kate had an idiom too. 'When in Rome…'

'I think you are a wicked girl,' Geneviève said, affectionately. 'Charles should've warned me.'

It was the first time Geneviève mentioned him. They would have to talk. Soon.

Geneviève realised it too, and suggested they slip off for *gelati*. Kate agreed. They left the lobby, Kate carrying her suitcase. Geneviève's Vespa looked impertinent parked outside the Hassler, so near the Spanish Steps. Geneviève gave her scooter an affectionate little pat, and tipped the doorman to watch over it.

They walked down the steps, against the human tide. Warm people in summer dresses strolled past. The few early-bird vampires among them wore enveloping robes like desert sheiks. Everyone had huge hats and dark glasses. Kate spotted fashions that would be in London by Christmas.

At the foot of the steps, a row of young artists – all berets and beards, as if they were dressing the part – sat on stools, doing sketches of the tourists. Kate could never walk past a group like this, in London or Paris, without being tempted. After seventy odd years without a reflection, she had a constant, nagging curiosity about how she looked. She remembered the shadow she'd seen in the waters of the Trevi Fountain, and shivered.

Geneviève knew a café opposite the house where John Keats had died. It was surprisingly neglected by the tourists who frequented the Museo Keats-Shelley.

'It's a vampire place,' she explained. 'Alive by night.'

They were given a table under a black awning. The cool shade was delightful. Kate touched her face and found it still hot from the sun. Geneviève ordered in Italian, and two tall glasses of soft crimson ice cream were presented. Kate touched hers with a long spoon, dislodging the cherry on top.

'The management claims they import Abyssinian virgins, but they use sheep's blood really.'

Kate had tried blood ice cream before. Crunchy rather than creamy, it was an unsatisfying blend of tastes and sensations. This was different.

'It's lovely,' she admitted, throat a-tingle.

'This is a city for the senses,' Geneviève said. 'A place for the heart, not the head. If you want to think, you go to Paris; if you want to feel, you come to Rome. After a while, it'll drive you mad. I'm not sure how much longer I'll be able to stand it, after…'

She left the sentence unfinished.

'How is he?' Kate asked, directly.

Geneviève angled her head in thought, frowning a little. She slipped her sunglasses up into her hair like an alice band. Kate saw hurt in her eyes.

'From day to day, he fades. There's no single illness, only old age. The things which hold him here are passing.'

'Is it too late? For him to turn?'

Geneviève pondered a moment. Kate knew she must have been fretting with the question. Why hadn't she done anything, made a decision?

'The Church says there's such a thing as deathbed conversion,' said Geneviève. 'I don't know why it wouldn't be possible. To turn, you only have to be near death.'

'You have no get?'

The other vampire shook her head.

'In all these centuries, there's been no one?' Kate asked.

Geneviève looked a little sad and shrugged, a very French gesture.

'For the first four hundred years, I had to hide. You weren't a vampire then, Kate. Before Dracula came to London and the undead population exploded, many vampires felt turning was a curse, not a blessing. They believed they'd sinned so dreadfully they were barred from Heaven. Even now, I'm not sure the Changes were all for the best.'

'You can't mean that, Geneviève.'

'You are still young, Kate.'

Kate felt pinpricks of anger. Geneviève was acting like the typical elder. Seen everything, done everything, know everything. Pretty much bored with it all.

'You have no get, either.'

'I'm not sure about my bloodline,' Kate said. 'Of the many my father-in-darkness turned, I'm the sole survivor.'

The majority of those who turned vampire failed to live out their normal lifespan, let alone become elders. New-borns of tainted bloodline did not grow true. When a warm person turned, they went through a moment of liquid malleability. At that point, it took a strong mind to stay whole. Many condemned themselves to a brief, painful shamble through the dark.

'Charles is alive because of us, Kate. You and I, we have drunk from him. Touched his life. We have not turned him, but we have changed him. He is a part of us and we a part of him. Sometimes, he gets us mixed up in his mind. He looks at me and sees you.'

'And Pamela?'

Now Geneviève was pained. Skilled readers of emotion, they could hold a conversation via tiny expressions.

Kate regretted her angry spark. She shouldn't underestimate the depth of the woman's feeling for Charles. What distinguished Geneviève Dieudonné from most elders was that she could love, genuinely. Many elders couldn't even love themselves.

'Yes,' Geneviève admitted. 'More and more, there is Pamela.'

'You never knew her.'

Pamela Churchward, Penelope's cousin, had been a few years older than Kate. She'd known how Kate, then a near-blind warm adolescent carrot-top, felt about Charles, and always took the trouble to be kindly. Pam died young, in India, miscarrying Charles's child. The terrible, bloody business had affected Charles, turned him toward duty, away from himself.

Charles's engagement to Penelope was a futile attempt to get Pamela back. That hadn't been fair, especially to Penny. Kate thought not being Pam was what had driven Penny to Lord Godalming and the Dark Kiss.

'Pamela was more like you than Penelope,' Kate said.

'And more like you than me,' Geneviève replied.

'Only because I wanted to be like her. Penny did too, and even Mina Murray. Pam was the original and we the poor copies.'

'*Tchah*! You've had eighty years to become a real live girl,

Kate. Pamela had a few summers of seeming perfection. Even Charles knows that had she lived, she'd have been like the rest of us. Not a saint, but a struggler.'

Unexpectedly, Geneviève took Kate's hand.

'One of us must turn him,' she said, red tears in her eyes. 'We can't let him go.'

'Even if that's what he wants most? To be with Pamela, not…'

'Not me? Or you, Kate.'

When Charles died, it would be the end of the warm world for her. He was the last living survivor of her girlhood. But it was Charles the man she wanted to hold on to, not Charles the Victorian, the right-thinking, honourable, good-hearted servant of Queen and Country.

This century was such a *mess*.

'After true death, is there anything?' Kate asked.

Geneviève let Kate's hand go as if it were electrified.

'How should I know?'

'All your years. You were a supernatural being.'

'We are all supernatural beings, the warm no less than the undead. When I was a girl, I couldn't separate religion from the Church. That was a temporal institution, devoted to the perpetuation of its power. When I turned, we were persecuted. Those who tracked us down and destroyed us did so in the name of God. In this century, we are all creatures of science, our mysteries dissected. Those who have tried to destroy us have done so in the name of science, in a calculated attempt to eliminate an evolutionary competitor. It's all the same.'

The Nazis had tried to purge most vampire bloodlines. Even now, Kate occasionally heard warm people mutter that Hitler had been right about that.

Ever since she could think for herself, Kate had been an agnostic. Now, she wondered about the immortality of the soul.

'There are vampires, Geneviève. There are werewolves. Are there ghosts?'

'I think so, though I've never seen one.'

'As a girl, I fancied I saw dozens. I went through a spiritualist craze, along with half the world. Ectoplasm and table-rapping. It was all very "scientific", you know. We Victorians wished to map the afterlife as we had mapped Africa. We wanted to believe death was a change, not an ending. Of course, that's exactly what it turned out to be for some of us, for me. When I turned, I lost interest. Only recently have I realised the puzzle wasn't solved but abandoned. At first, being a vampire seemed like being immortal. Then I realised how few of us even live a long time. Last night, I saw two elders die in an instant, like anyone else. We'll both end, Geneviève. Then what?'

Their *gelati* had melted.

'This is perhaps an overly momentous conversation for such a time and place,' Geneviève said. 'This is a city of life and death. Those great matters will attend to themselves without us. We are just a pair of pretty old ladies…'

'Less of the "old", Grandmama.'

'We should take young lovers and have them buy us clothes.'

Kate thought of Marcello and blushed.

Damn. Geneviève would, of course, notice.

Kate looked away, letting the shadow of her hat fall over her face.

'Kate?'

Geneviève reached over and lifted up Kate's hatbrim.

Wiping away tears, she found herself giggling.

'Kate, you've been here less than a day…'

Geneviève was astonished but not displeased. She laughed out loud.

'Kate Reed, you're a dark horse. And no mistake.'

6

FROM MOLDAVIA WITH LOVE

As evening fell, his blood rose. His eyes clicked open in the dark. Through the afternoon, he'd slept the sleep of the dead in a shuttered room at the Hotel Inghilterra.

Hamish Bond regretted the loss of those periods of half-sleep he had enjoyed as a warm man. After a fine meal, a day of exertion or making love to a beautiful woman, he would relish the slow departure of consciousness. As a vampire, he simply willed himself to rest as if turning out a light. His mind stopped along with his heart. It was compensation that he only needed three or four hours' sleep – coffin-time, they called it – in a given month.

At once he knew he was not alone.

He had sealed the door and the windows, of course. He would have been alerted if the seals had fallen.

'It's no use lying still, Commander Bond,' purred a silky voice. 'I saw your eyes open.'

The room was pitch dark. His companion was like him, a vampire.

Casually, he sat up in bed, hand closing on the Walther PPK under the covers. He slept in a Japanese pyjama jacket, belted tightly at the waist.

He could see in the dark too.

She was on the other side of the room, breathing smoke through large, elegant nostrils. One of his cigarettes angled like a scalpel between her long, slender fingers.

She was sitting naked in an armchair, one knee demurely

propped on the other. Though she had the throat for jade and the earlobes for diamonds, she wore no jewellery. Midnight-black hair grew straight back from a pronounced widow's peak and cascaded over wide shoulders and onto proud breasts.

Her face was broad, Slavic with an almost Mongolian cast. Her fluorescent, violet eyes had suggestions of epicanthic folds. Her face was the beautiful mask of a pagan idol, luxuriant lips parted sweetly to afford a glimpse of savage fangs.

He knew at once she was an elder.

Her crossed legs were long. He appreciated the stretch of velvet-sheathed muscle from hip to knee. Halfway down her shins, flesh and bone thinned, trailing away into a wisp of white mist.

He'd heard of the trick, but never seen it done. She'd willed herself to become living fog, flowed under the locked and trip-wired door, then reassembled herself in his armchair.

The last of the mist coalesced into sculptured white feet.

'Bravo,' he complimented her.

'I don't know why I went to the trouble,' she said, vowels smoothing over an old accent. 'A very expensive Balmain is lying crumpled in the corridor, with a pair of emerald earrings that are sure to be stolen. Oh, and twenty tiny petals of dried nail polish.'

She flicked away the still-burning cigarette and stood, delightfully immodest. She crossed to the windows and opened the shutters. The last light of sunset gave her skin an inviting glow. An inrush of air disturbed her mane. Her hair was full-bodied, heavy. It curled up slightly at the ends, like a row of tiny fishhooks.

'I'm Anibas,' she said, turning to look at him, her right hand pressed to her heart. 'You know who I am.'

He did.

'My great-great-aunt is Princess Asa Vajda, the Royal Fiancée. I'm to be a bridesmaid. You should see the abominable dress they want me to wear.'

He relaxed by the moment, savouring the presence of this wild creature. But he would never be off his guard around someone like her.

Suddenly, she was on the bed, crawling on all fours like a vixen. His hand closed on nothing.

'Looking for this?'

She dangled the pistol from her forefinger.

'You're very fleet.'

She giggled, nastily. 'And you're very fortunate.'

Anibas tossed the pistol across the room and touched his face.

'Your Mr Winthrop said he was sending me a gift,' she said. 'Do you think I'm pleased?'

'You can always throw me back into the sea.'

'I think not,' she said. Nails like razors drew across his face, a fraction of an ounce of pressure away from breaking the skin. 'I think I keep.'

Even a warm woman of Anibas's physique could put up a spirited fight. She had the legs of a runner and the hands of a karate expert. She was a vampire elder, his senior by centuries. She was playing with him. If she meant instant harm, she could have ripped his heart out while he slept.

He'd told Beauregard that Winthrop had people close to Dracula. That was something of an exaggeration. The several vampires of *il principe*'s household who reported to the Diogenes Club were probably doubles, letting slip only what their master wished. But that might be about to change.

This was the woman he was in Rome to see.

Anibas traced jagged scars across his chest, sliding his jacket over his shoulder.

With the marriage, the House of Vajda would be absorbed into the House of Dracula. A pecking-order that had been secure for centuries would change. Genuine discontents were stirring and could be turned to England's advantage.

'My great-great-aunt is a horrifyingly dull woman,' Anibas whispered. 'You would not like her at all.'

'Does she know where you are?'

'Undoubtedly. She's been suspicious forever, always seeing conspiracies against her. She thinks every unfamiliar face is a Jesuit sworn to stick iron skewers through her eyes. She is an embarrassment.'

Of course, Anibas wished to take the Princess's place. The long lives of elders were an inconvenience for poor relations waiting to inherit estates, titles and positions.

'I've signed myself in to the hotel under another name. Sabina. Clever, *hein*? It's my name in a mirror. Sabina. Anibas.'

Why were vampires so enamoured of that trick? Had anybody ever been duped by an alias like 'Alucard'? If he were to sign hotel registers as 'D. Nob', no one would ever be fooled. Was it an elders' quirk he'd come to appreciate?

'You and I,' she said, face close to his, 'we are to plot, are we not? To scheme and plan like snake and swine. To the ruination of Princess Asa and the abandonment of this unwise match? What need we Vajda of the thin blood of Vlad Tepes? We were ancient and honoured when he was buggering Turks with large sticks. Rightfully, he should crawl to us.'

Winthrop had warned him to watch Anibas carefully. This second, she seemed to have common cause with them. But who knew how things might turn out? And there were always others in the ring.

She was crawling on top of him now, hair hanging in his face, breasts against his chest. She flicked an active tongue over her generous lips.

He understood very well the game being played.

He took Anibas by the shoulders and shoved her down against the mattress. He rolled over onto her, letting his weight lie on her body, his legs pinning hers.

She squealed, pretending to be trapped, and clicked her tongue at him, tossing hair out of the way. Her white throat arched.

He bit savagely into her neck, and drank her elder's blood.

When he came out of the bathroom, towelling his hair, he found her bathing in the moonlight. The doors onto the balcony were open and night breeze cooled the room. The wounds on her neck and breasts faded fast, disappearing as he watched. He would sport the scars she'd given him for weeks, maybe longer.

She had fetched in her evening gown. The backless, strapless dress was hardly more decent than nudity. Her earrings were chunky emerald clusters. In the East, size and intricacy counted for more than taste.

He was full of life. Literally.

Of course, he'd had vampire blood before. That was how he had been turned, in a private hospital near Marble Arch, with a measured amount of Sergeant Dravot's vampire blood exchanged for his warm red stuff. Since then, in the field, he'd killed vampire enemies and glutted himself on their gore, drinking from their gashed throats. They made him stronger, the Chinese doctor and the Jamaican voodoo master. Memories still occasionally bubbled up inside his brain, as if he were the continuance of their bloodlines.

But he'd never tasted the blood of an elder.

It was like a drug, shifting his senses to another plane entirely. Her mind almost blotted his out. He knew much about Anibas that she'd not told him. Impressions from her long life flooded his memory. The freezing palace where she was born, with its filthy floors and priceless tapestries. He felt the mouth of her father-in-darkness – an ancient retained by the Vajda to further the bloodline – at her throat and his hands under her skirts. He shared the panic of flight from homeland, the stern-faced mob waving torches at their carriage, spade-bearded orthodox priests with silver scythes, burning scaffolds bright in the Moldavian night.

He was tense, when he should have been relaxed.

Not all the impressions were ancient history. She'd had her fun. Now she was to kill him. Her arrangement with Diogenes was not exclusive. She had offered the same services to Moscow, and decided the Kremlin could best help her gain control of the House of Vajda. After all, her ancestral estates were behind the Iron Curtain.

There was a moment of regret. She'd genuinely enjoyed him. He knew that.

She turned from the open window, lovely face stretching. Her mouth widened in a gash, fangs crowding out from her jaws.

He lowered the towel and shot her with the gun he'd wrapped in it.

Anibas was almost faster than the bullet. He'd intended to put silver in her heart, but the red wound exploded in her shoulder.

Damn. He was probably dead.

A hundredweight of angry animal slammed him in the chest, knock-ing him onto his back and carrying him through the bathroom door.

She was unrecognisable.

A black snout dipped toward his throat. Wolf eyes blazed at him. Clawed forepaws dug into his chest. Her backlegs scrabbled on the tiled floor.

He had one hand on the underside of her jaw. Pine-needle bristles sprouted against his palm. His forearm was straining iron, holding murderous teeth away from his throat.

Blood still poured from her shoulder. Furred skin closed across the wound but melted at once, failing to scab over the silver-gouged divot.

He angled the pistol up, trying to shove the muzzle against her eye. She shook her head and bit the Walther, fangs scoring deep lines in the barrel. He lost the gun, lucky to keep his fingers.

She formed a human face.

'How could you? After what we've meant to each other?'

She exaggerated her plea, a snarl behind the simper.

She was an animal again, more bear than wolf. Her bulk was crushing him. The Balmain was a ragged sash. Earrings still hung from the high, pointed, foxbat-ears. He gripped one and tore it loose, ripping the flap.

Anibas howled.

It was the vanity of elders to wear jewellery with silver settings, to show off their supposed invulnerability to the deadly element. He tried to jam the bauble into the vampire woman's left eye.

He only managed to enrage her.

There was a flurry of movement and the weight was lifted. He almost breathed relief. Wide jaws clamped to his torso, just under his left armpit. Fangs sank in like butcher's hooks.

She was going to tear out his ribcage and eat his heart.

And that would be that.

The grip relaxed and there was a great gush of blood, soaking him completely. A foul stench made him choke. He thought for a moment that he was dead. No, he could sit up.

Anibas's mouth detached from his side and her head rolled into his lap. In an eyeblink, her head turned from cartoon wolf, neck cleanly severed, to a woman's, fan of bloody hair spread out across his knees. Then she was a spilled bowl of mist, flooding away. An inch of white fog settled on the bathroom floor, rippling slowly.

The bitch was dead.

He felt his ribs knitting again.

In the doorway, he saw legs. A well-built man in red tights. From his hands dangled a length of cheesewire, shining silver coated with thick red.

Maniacal laughter filled the room.

He tried to look up to his saviour's face.

Something tugged the man in red away, leading him back into the bedroom.

He was too drained to stand and follow.

The laughter grew louder.

He blacked out, dimly aware of a hammering at the door, of his name being called.

7

THE LIVING

They ascended in the cage lift, a contraption of polished brass and lattice wood. Geneviève hesitated outside the apartment, apprehensive for her friend. She held her keys and looked at Kate, wondering how to phrase her concerns.

'It's been several years, hasn't it?' she said.

'Charles was in his late nineties the last time I saw him,' said Kate. 'He was already old. I shan't be shocked or upset.'

Geneviève wasn't so sure.

The warm aged and died. She did not. Though she'd had centuries to get used to, it left her often bewildered, blinking back tears. Surely, a whole life couldn't run past so swiftly. It wasn't fair.

Carmilla Karnstein, a vampire girl Geneviève had known in the eighteenth century, grieved for lost friends as if the warm were her pets, grown suddenly ancient in dog years during the eternity of a human childhood. Carmilla was gone too now. Twice. It had never apparently occurred to her that her favourites wouldn't have died if she hadn't been so fond of them that she had to have so much of their blood. That had been the death of her.

Treating the warm as pets or cattle was one way elders coped with estrangement from human time. In this century, with so many nosferatu about, things should have changed. But Geneviève worried that she couldn't change. Evolution was something one's successors dealt with. Vampires like Kate Reed should tackle those issues.

'He's past a hundred, Kate,' she said.

'I'm not so very far off it.'

'You know it's different for us.'

'Yes. I'm sorry. That was a silly thing to say.'

Geneviève opened the dark-wood double doors. They were nine feet tall, more appropriate for a castle than a flat. Romans liked impressive entrances.

'Come in, come in,' she bustled.

Kate stepped over the welcome mat and put her suitcase down. She looked around the foyer, admiring bookcases and brass lamp-fittings.

'Very Victorian,' she said, 'very Charles.'

Geneviève kept bowls of dried rose petals, for the scent.

'Come through,' she said, leading Kate around the corner of the passageway, toward the study. The apartment was spacious, but the corridors – and the kitchen and bathroom – were cramped, squeezed into the plan between two large bedrooms, the study, and a dining room.

The french windows were open, and evening breeze stirred the curtains. The last of the sunset threw an orange veil over the city.

'Charles likes to sit on the balcony,' Geneviève explained.

There was some fussing outside.

'Charles-*Chèri*,' Geneviève said, quite loudly. 'Kate is here.'

She left Kate and stepped out onto the balcony. Charles had managed to turn the bath chair around with slippered feet, but his fingers couldn't get a grip on the rims of the wheels to move it forward. He was frustrated with the failure of his hands, but more amused than irritated. He accepted frailty as he had always accepted strength, as a comparative thing.

Without needing to be asked, she wheeled Charles into the room. Kate waited, eyes watery behind thick glasses, fidgeting with the seam of her tartan skirt. He smiled, and his age-lines stretched. He looked oddly childlike, almost a baby.

Kate flew at him and went down on her knees. She took his hands in hers – making him wince with her uncontrolled vampire grip – and laid her head on his lap.

'Charles,' Kate sighed, 'Charles.'

Charles managed a coughing laugh.

'Stand up and let me look at you,' he ordered.

Geneviève turned on the electric lights. Even after decades, she felt she ought to be reaching for a taper to light the candles. Sometimes, she'd try to twist a light switch as if it were the key of a gas lamp.

'I'm not sure that hairstyle is becoming,' Charles clucked. Kate's hands went to her exposed neck. 'It's more like a hair*cut*.'

Kate blushed, freckles darkening. She held herself rather awkwardly, refusing to believe she might in a certain light be appealing. Victorians were prejudiced against red hair, so she'd been taught to be ashamed of her looks. Now tastes had changed and she might pass for fashionable. She was petite enough for the New Look. Even spectacles weren't the disfigurement they'd once been considered.

'I had short hair when I was warm,' Geneviève said. 'It was the fashion. Jeanne d'Arc set it.'

Charles thought about that. 'You were one of those girls who passed as a boy to go to sea and become a pirate. Kate is in a more respectable profession.'

'Many would disagree with you, m'darling.'

Kate got off her knees and kissed Charles.

Geneviève had a pang. Her nails became fractionally more like claws.

Thinking about it, she knew Kate had earned her kiss. She'd been there when Geneviève hadn't. While Geneviève had avoided the twentieth century, Kate had been a part of it and stuck by Charles through the nightmare years.

Kate dabbed her eyes dry with a hankie.

'Look,' she said. 'I'm crying. You'll think me a fool.'

'Not at all,' Charles said, kindly.

'Kate has already got mixed up in murder,' Geneviève said.

'So I've been reading.'

Charles indicated the afternoon editions of *Il quotidiano* and *Paese sera*. They lay on a kidney-shaped coffee table, the newest piece of furniture in the room.

'I had to rescue her from the police.'

'Who's in charge of the investigation?'

Geneviève looked at Kate.

'An Inspector Silvestri,' Kate said. 'Do you know him?'

'I know of him. He's reckoned a good man. He caught that couple last year, the ones who left bloodied butterfly brooches on the corpses of their victims. Of course, he hasn't stopped these murders. According to the papers, you saw the Crimson Executioner?'

'Actually, I saw his reflection,' said Kate.

'A fine distinction, but worth making.'

Charles was livelier than Geneviève had seen him for weeks, livelier even than when the British spy was consulting him. She hadn't known that he took an interest in the murders of vampire elders but it didn't surprise her. Was he concerned for her safety? He was occasionally solicitous of her, but she had put that down to the fussiness of advanced age. She'd underestimated him. Again.

'Counting last night's, there have been seventeen murders since the liberation,' Charles told Kate. 'All vampire elders. All in Rome, and mostly in public places. Tourist spots, even. Professor Adelsberg was staked in Castel Sant'Angelo. That lieutenant of Dracula's they used to call Radu the Repulsive was beheaded on the steps of the Museo Borghese. And the Duchess Marguerite De Grand, who was reckoned such a beauty, was destroyed in the shadow of the statues of Castor and Pollux in the Piazza di Quirinale.'

'I've heard of Adelsberg,' Kate said. 'Wasn't he a war criminal? One of Hitler's vampire doctors?'

'It's possible he wasn't a Crimson Executioner victim. The others were real elders, four and five hundred years old, mostly of the Dracula line and with titles and decorations to prove it. The Professor barely had his century. The Israelis may have sent their fellows after him. Or he might have been killed on general principle, by someone with good cause. As you know, that happens when these murderers get a run. Other crimes are laid at their doorsteps. It becomes easy to slip in an unrelated killing. Like hiding a pebble on a beach.'

'As elders go, Count Kernassy didn't seem such a monster.'

Geneviève wasn't sure about that. Kate had only known the Count for a few hours at the end of four centuries of life. Kernassy was one of *il principe*'s Carpathians, and they tended to be a brutal lot. It might be that this one's manners were a bit above the average.

'Still, it's a rum go,' said Charles. 'You wandering into all this.'

'She met someone at the airport and was dragged off on an adventure,' Geneviève said. 'Penelope.'

A cloud of fatigue passed over Charles's face.

'Poor Penny,' he said, quietly. He blamed himself too much for what had happened to Penelope Churchward, for what she had made of herself.

'She does turn up rather like the proverbial bad one,' said Kate. 'Penny, I mean. What's she after doing with Dracula?'

Charles tried to shrug but couldn't lift his shoulders.

It was still a moot point whether Geneviève had stolen Charles away from Penelope, or whether Penny had abandoned him for her father-in-darkness, the ill-remembered Lord Godalming. Geneviève thought neither was entirely true. Charles had left Penelope to her own devices because he felt a greater duty, and Geneviève happened to coincide with that duty. If it had been otherwise, she knew he'd have kept his promise to Penelope, no matter how unhappy it would have made them both.

He was, in many ways, an impossible man.

'Do you see her?' Kate asked them both.

'She has called,' Geneviève admitted. 'Infrequently.'

'I'm not surprised.'

'It was a long time ago,' Charles said, remembering.

Not for Geneviève, it wasn't. And not, she suspected, for Penelope, or for Kate.

At the end of his life, Charles was forgiving.

Kate and Charles had known Penelope well as a warm girl, of course. Geneviève knew her first as one of those new-borns who didn't understand anything. Just after turning, Penelope had drunk bad blood and made an invalid of herself for a decade. A quack who treated her with leeches hadn't helped matters much. If anything, Geneviève – working then as a doctor – had saved Penelope's life. That had been her duty, so she supposed she wasn't that different from Charles.

'She was the first to tell me I should turn,' Charles said. 'She wanted us to become vampires together. It seemed the done thing, if one wanted to be advanced.'

Kate shot Geneviève an alarmed glance. He was forestalling their carefully composed argument.

'Gené, Kate,' Charles said, looking at them as if they were his ashamed grandchildren, 'I know you don't mean it as she did, but you ask the same thing. The thing I cannot do.'

Kate covered her face, to hide the tears.

'I'm sorry, Kate,' Charles said, touching Kate's elbow. 'It's nothing wrong with you. Or you either, Gené. It's me.'

Despite the strength of his feelings, he was fading before their eyes. Every day, perhaps every hour, he became fainter, a vaguer presence, losing substance.

'You're not too old, Charles,' Geneviève said. 'You can turn. I'm sure of it.'

He shook his head.

'You could be young again,' Kate sighed.

'*He* grew young,' Charles said. 'Count Dracula. I doubt if he'd much pleasure of renewed youth. He has always struck me as a profoundly sad individual. When he turned, he lost something. Most vampires do. Even you, my undying darlings.'

He looked serene, but Geneviève heard his excitement. His heart beat faster. His brow was dampened. His voice was near cracking.

'Am I so selfish?' he asked. 'To want to leave?'

Later, after nightfall, they sat together, and talked about the past, forcing themselves not to talk of the present and future. Kate prompted Charles to tell Geneviève of many things she had missed during her time away from him this century.

She had realised, of course, how close Charles and Kate had grown in the First World War. Now she saw how they had fixed so much of their hope in Edwin Winthrop of the

Diogenes Club, whom she'd spent an interesting weekend with in 1923. She almost regretted not being there in the bloody mud of France, in the thick of intrigue at once absurd and terrifying.

She was a creature of a slower age, where time was measured by seasons, not wristwatch ticks. She had never adjusted to this century of jet planes and Sputniks, of CinemaScope and rock 'n' roll. Charles had lived through more than she ever would and been affected more by it. She recognised her own untouchability as weakness.

Kate would have to do instead. She talked about the Second World War, which she'd seen from the ground as Charles had from maps and despatches. Her commitments were so selfless, to make the world a more just place. Her passion burned with a fierceness Geneviève regretted she could never match. If there was a God, Kate must be closer to Him.

Charles grew tired but insisted on staying with 'the girls', nodding at their conversation, dozing even.

'It looks like Lord Ruthven won't be Prime Minister after the next election,' Kate said. 'He's never really recovered from Suez. But we've thought him gone before. When Winston took over in the war, I swore that was the last of him. But he came back. That's one thing I could do without, politicians whose careers go on forever. Then again, Ruthven is such a chameleon. He keeps fading into the scenery and popping out again as a different person.'

Geneviève asked Kate about new films, plays, books, music. How had London changed? Who had she seen recently? Who was famous?

'The *Daily Mirror* ran a poll about vampires recently, asking who was the most admired, the most disliked. It was to do with an exhibition at Madame Tussauds. Who do you imagine is the most admired vampire in Great Britain today?'

Geneviève couldn't think. 'Edmund Hillary?'

'Good try. No, *Cliff Richard*.'

'Who?'

'A pop singer. "Living Doll"?'

Geneviève had heard the song.

'Think of it, Geneviève. He's never going to get old, never going to lose his voice. Would there ever have been a Caruso if Farinelli had still been around? Could Wagner have competed with a hundred-year-old Mozart? In forty years' time, when singers who haven't yet been born should be coming into their own, Cliff Richard will still be there, mooning over his crying, talking, sleeping, walking living doll.'

'They say few vampires achieve distinction in the arts,' Geneviève said.

'There've been exceptions. Trust me, Mr Richard is not one of them.'

Kate tried to hum the song she'd been talking about. Geneviève laughed.

'History is dwindling into a hit parade,' Kate said. 'And we have all been doing the Dracula *Cha Cha Cha* for too long.'

A bell sounded.

Swiftly, Geneviève answered the door. It was a liveried footman, with a message. Geneviève took it and bade him goodbye, slitting the envelope open with an extruded thumb-claw. Three gilt-edged cards shuffled out. She returned to the main room, where Charles was alert and Kate intrigued.

'We've been invited to a party,' Geneviève announced. 'By Prince Dracula and his intended, Princess Asa Vajda. Now fancy that.'

PART TWO

LA DOLCE MORTE

FROM THE PARLIAMENTARY REPORT, *THE TIMES* OF LONDON, JULY 30TH, 1959

…the Honourable Hamer Radshaw (Lab.) asked: 'Have you received an invitation to the wedding of Vlad Dracula, former Prince Consort, and if such is the case, will you attend the nuptials of this disreputable character and his blood-spattered bride?'

The Prime Minister, Lord Ruthven (Con.) replied: 'If such an invitation were received, representatives of Her Majesty's Government and, indeed, Her Majesty's Loyal Opposition, would of course give every consideration to an appropriate response.' Mr Radshaw further asked: 'Is Her Majesty also expected to traipse off to Italy to watch a former relation by marriage make yet another dynastic match?'

The Prime Minister replied: 'I have not had the opportunity to discuss this matter with Her Majesty, but I am certain she would wish to extend hearty congratulations to her valued ally and sometime countryman, Count Dracula.' A commotion on the floor of the House prevented further debate.

8

JOURNALISM

Kate's room at the *pensione* was a tiny cupboard at the top and back of the building. A tall, thin window looked out into a narrow alley bridged by clothes lines. Shirts and sheets flapped lazily in the warm wind. This was the room set aside for vampires. Instead of a bed, a rough wooden coffin lined with a folded blanket stood on trestles. Less faded patches on the wallpaper showed where a crucifix and a mirror had been taken down. If the Gideons had left any reading matter, it was tidied away.

She imagined accommodations at the Hotel Hassler were of a different order.

Having arrived in Trastevere just after dawn, the night talked away with Charles and Geneviève, she crawled into the coffin intent on blacking out for most of the day. For once, her tininess was an advantage. She fit snugly into the box. At the point of sleep, she thought back to the Piazza di Trevi. She didn't want to relive what she'd seen there, but something still nagged her.

Count Kernassy, Malenka, the Crimson Executioner… the little girl.

Had she seen anything different? Kate would like to find and talk with her.

Marcello, with a milk bottle.

She smiled, and death-sleep crept over her.

* * *

At first, she was told the telephone in the hallway was for the exclusive use of the landlady's family. After she passed over five hundred lire to the landlady's son, the situation was explained in more detail. It appeared that in emergencies she would be allowed to make calls. A further five hundred lire was convincing proof that this was indeed an emergency. She specified that the emergency under discussion was likely to last the length of her stay, and parted with a final banknote to convince him.

'As you say, Signorina,' the landlady's son replied. A fifty-year-old stay-at-home, he wore a white string vest pricked through by chest hair. Braces cut like cheesewire into his doughy middle. A victim of maternal cuisine.

He left her alone, pocketing the cash.

Using the telephone would be a challenge, given her rudimentary Italian. In London she did most of her work on the phone. She should be able to convert her skills to this new system.

First, she tried Inspector Silvestri. He was out, but she got through to Sergeant Ginko, who remembered her. She gathered there were no official developments on the Piazza di Trevi murders and, judging from his careless talk, no unofficial ones either. Silvestri was over at the Hotel Inghilterra, where there was some fuss. The sergeant cut himself off in mid-sentence and changed the subject. Hotel Inghilterra. She made a mental note of that. Maybe there was an unofficial development after all.

With her best helpless little foreign-girl wheedle, she told Ginko she'd arranged to meet Marcello but got mixed up and lost the details. Did he have the number of the newspaper he worked for? Ginko knew whom she meant, said he was a freelance without an office, and suggested she try the Café Strega. It was in Via Veneto, of course. She thanked him and hung up.

Next, she called Geneviève. Charles was still sleeping. From Geneviève's tone, Kate could tell he'd had a bad day. A tiny barb of guilt hooked her. Had her visit been too much of a strain? She was here to help, not pester. Geneviève, intuiting

Kate's qualms, tried to reassure her. Serious things were unsaid between them. The phone was no good for things like this. As vampires, they were both too used to skimming minds, picking up on nuances of expression, breathing in feelings. Falling back on muffled words was like being forced to use semaphore.

She thought about telephoning Penelope, but didn't.

Café Strega. The Witch's Coffee. That conjured up an image: cream and newts with that, Signora? She tried to remember which of the pavement places it had been.

Unusually, she gave some thought to what to wear. A dress was called for, and she'd only packed three: one white and elegant (Christian Dior, once removed), one black and simple (Coco Chanel, according to the stall-holder in Portebello Market), and one dun and practical (Marks & Sparks). She should save the elegant for the Engagement Ball at Palazzo Otranto, which prompted her to favour the simple over the practical. The trouble was that the simple made her look like a lost schoolgirl. She was nearly a hundred; she didn't want elderly men offering her lollipops. Hang it, she would go with the elegant. It was good enough for Audrey Hepburn.

For the ball, she'd buy something new. Geneviève would know where to shop. She was an old hand at this *haute-couture* lark. Kate liked the idea of something spectacular by Piero Gherardi.

By the time she was ready to leave the *pensione*, it was nightfall. She found a taxi on the Viale Glorioso, outside the *Ministero della Pubblica Istruzione*, but had to abandon it not long after they crossed the river. As she'd already discovered, Rome was not best organised for swift journeys by anything with more than two wheels. The best way to learn a city was on foot anyway. She paid off the unconcerned cabbie, and set off on her own. It was a short stroll to Via Veneto, but not uncomplicated.

She wished momentarily that she had opted for the simple or the practical. In her elegant frock, she felt overdressed.

Some warm loungers in the Piazza Barberini wolf-whistled at her. She knew she was blushing. Invitations which fortunately – or unfortunately – she did not understand were called out after the gentle Signorina, which she assumed meant her. Actually, she decided, she didn't mind overly much. She wasn't often whistled at. They probably gave the treatment to every woman who passed. It wasn't an especial compliment or insult. No Italian had pinched her bottom yet. Of course, they might be afraid of her.

A few new-borns were about early in the night. Across the piazza from the loungers was an equivalent group of beautiful vampire youths, sharp-faced and sharply dressed, pale-faced sheiks with dear little fangs. They had the post-war look: white Nino Cerutti suits, those omnipresent sunglasses, tight-fit Casa Lemi shirts open at the throats to show gold tat pendants. The *vitelloni* let Kate pass without comment, but lowered their shades in unison to stare at a warm girl who was happening by, flexing their combined powers of mesmeric fascination.

Kate giggled. But the approach probably worked. The girl, a waifish Pier Angeli lookalike, stopped in her tracks. One of the new-borns made gestures of imperious enchantment, beckoning with long fingers, projecting 'you are under my power' at her mind. As if a puppet on invisible strings, she turned slowly to the vampire crowd, pretty face blank of expression. The new-borns sprouted fanged smiles. The great hypnotist was quietly triumphant.

The girl laughed at them and walked away. She hopped into a blinding-white Maserati and cuddled up to a warm man in his sixties. He had a definite bald spot and a foot-long cigar. The sports car cruised off.

The hypnotist was crestfallen. His fellows chided him for insufficient skill, thumping him with the heels of their hands. Another girl breezed into view, this one along the more generous lines of Elsa Martinelli. The hypnotist recovered his momentarily jarred confidence and began again to cast the 'fluence.

Kate walked on.

* * *

Two nights on, the murder of Malenka didn't seem to have affected the mood of the Via Veneto. The cafés were still thriving and the paparazzi still out after famous faces. Kate had to step over Hemingway, who growled something up at her. She didn't feel like reminding Papa that they'd met during the First World War, before he got old and drunk and famous, back when he was pretty nearly a good writer.

Marcello wasn't at the Café Strega, but she found a table where three newsmen were arguing over a bill. They pretended not to understand her in Italian or English, so she paid the bill and bought their attention. After exhaustive apologies, a button-nosed French reporter whose stiff forelock stood up like a wood shaving admitted he knew who she was asking after and sent her off to yet another café, the Zeppa.

A muscular figure ambled down the middle of the road. Kate had a start. The broad shoulders and swelling chest reminded her of the Crimson Executioner. This fellow had a curly beard. He wore a peplum, the classical belted tunic of the ancient world, and sandals. He might be an actor, still costumed after a hard day of wrestling papier-mâché serpents and bosomy starlets at Cinecittà.

'That's Maciste,' a crone explained, in English. 'The great hero of Rome. Whenever the city has need of him, he appears. He is the messenger of the Gods.'

Kate thought that was Hermes.

Maciste strolled on, heroically. The muscles in his back and thighs bunched and relaxed as he moved.

She remembered the grip at her neck. The Crimson Executioner could have squeezed her head off.

At the Zeppa, she did find Marcello. He was at a table on the pavement, with a gaunt-faced, austerely robed priest, whom he introduced as Father Lankester Merrin.

'And, Father, this is… I am sorry, I misremember…'

'Kate Reed,' she said, cut to the heart.

'Of course. Signorina Reed.'

Though an invitation was not forthcoming, she joined them, pulling across a chair from another table.

'I've read your book on African religion,' she lied to the priest. 'Very provocative.'

The priest smiled thinly. He had piercing eyes. She wouldn't risk another lie with him.

A waiter brought her a glass of chilled lizard blood.

'You're the other reporter who was there at the destruction of the elders, Count Kernassy and Malenka?' asked Merrin.

She admitted it.

'Marcello has been consulting me on a related matter, and now you chance along. Providence has a way of arranging these things, Miss Reed.'

'Call me Kate,' she said.

'Thank you, Kate. You may call me Father Merrin.'

She wasn't sure whether that was a joke.

From the reviews of his book, she couldn't remember which side of the vampire debate Father Merrin took. It would be rude to come out plain and ask him if he considered her a being with a soul or not.

'Marcello was on the point of politely accusing me of taking part in a secret crusade against your kind, Miss Reed.'

Marcello shrugged and tried to wave away the suggestion.

'Everyone in Rome believes in secret crusades,' Merrin continued. 'If the Vatican isn't behind it, then it must be the mafia, or the Communists, or the Si-Fan, or the CIA, or the Diogenes Club, or the Illuminati.'

'Do you believe that, Father?'

'Belief is relative. Rome is eternally complex.'

Marcello stuck a cigarette in his mouth and lit up, eloquently. He had a way with small gestures.

The late Pope Pius XII – the second coming of Savonarola or Torquemada, depending on whom you talked with – had issued a bull reaffirming the Vatican's traditional position on vampirism. Upon death, the soul fled to its reward and the remains should be decently buried. Vampires were untenanted corpses, demonic imitations of those who were formerly in residence. If bell, book and candle failed, the suggested treatment was fire, silver and the stake. Though strictly there shouldn't be a need for the measure, to turn was to invoke automatic excommunication. Then again, so was voting Communist, and Palmiro Togliatti's party regularly took a quarter of the popular vote in Italian elections.

Many vampires were extremely devout Catholics. Ironically, they tended to be the breed who blistered when splashed with holy water, choked bloodily on communion wafers, and shrank in terror from the sign of the cross. In the last hundred years or so, theologians had struggled with the vampire question. A growing body of Catholic thought considered that the undead were indeed possessed of their original souls and thus should be reclaimed for the Church. It was rumoured that the newly elevated John XXIII wished to moderate the nosferatu doctrine, stopping short of recognising vampire priests, but had been until now dissuaded from that path by his conservative Secretary of State, Monsignor Tardini.

'What's this I hear about the Crimson Executioner and the Hotel Inghilterra?' she ventured.

Marcello raised an impressed eyebrow. Her random shot convinced him she had well-informed sources.

'Someone dressed like the murderer was seen climbing the front of the hotel. Like a big red spider.'

'And has any crime been committed?'

Marcello shrugged. 'Hard to tell. There was trouble in the room of a British naval officer. He denies anything more than a drunken liaison. A maid has sold information that the liaison might have been spectacular, and not so pretty. There was blood, a gunshot. This Britisher is a vampire. Oh, and everyone knows he is one of your spies. His automobile is far too ostentatious for a sailor.'

'Not one of mine. I'm not British.'

Marcello shrugged again, which made her want to break his dark glasses.

'Was an elder involved?'

'That is a question. One of the hotel's guests has vanished as if into smoke. She signed a false name, but was clearly

Lady Anibas Vajda. A relation of Princess Asa, the Royal Fiancée. A vampire elder.'

Kate had vaguely heard of the woman. Nothing good.

'She hasn't turned up murdered?'

'Not yet. But there are whispers. The very old ones sometimes do not leave remains to speak of. Coroners resent that.'

'I understand Inspector Silvestri was called in.'

Marcello nodded. 'He is the latest in charge of the Crimson Executioner case. Three other detectives have been reassigned or reduced in rank for their failures. Silvestri must be wary. Last year, an inspector of the *Sureté* who has some reputation as a sleuth was imported in a great explosion of publicity. He vowed in a bizarre accent that the felon would be apprehended within the month, then fell flat on his face several times and was, I understand, demoted to traffic duty in an undesirable quarter of Paris.'

'This is fascinating,' Father Merrin said, standing, 'but I must leave you young people now. I am sure you'll see the matter to a satisfying and thrilling conclusion. After all, the answers to such mysteries are very often found under the soles of our shoes.'

Marcello and Kate stood, out of respect, and the priest left, vestments billowing. She watched him stride through the crowds, a lone ascetic among voluptuaries. Beneath his knife-logic mind was a not unkindly soul, she thought. But he'd cleverly dodged the question about secret crusades.

She sat down and, after a moment's hesitation, so did Marcello. He was still uncomfortable with her. Was it because he'd seen her crouched by the corpses of Kernassy and Malenka? Or had he been reserved before that? He was with vampires at the airport, so he could hardly have a phobia about her kind.

No, she realised, it was her usual curse. Whenever she met a man she liked, she gave everything away at once. She broadcast some signal that made the object of her interest privy to her hopes and desires and, at the same time, rendered her faintly repulsive to him. She'd tried being cool, being friendly, being clever, and being blatant.

No approach modified the first impression.

She scared them off. That was all there was to it.

With those damned sunglasses, she couldn't tell what Marcello was thinking. Geneviève would've seen through the black lenses and read his shrinking soul. Kate worried that he was trying to think of an excuse to escape from her.

'Have you written up the murders?' she asked.

With an apologetic turn of the head, he admitted he'd passed on the bare details to several editors. She couldn't believe he was as bored as he affected to be. No newspaperman could walk into the scene of a double murder and fail to smell a by-line and a paycheque. And he'd taken the trouble to consult Father Merrin. He was posing, pretending a profound disinterest he couldn't possibly feel.

'I've been thinking of doing an article on the Crimson Executioner,' she said. 'He's unknown in Britain. By chance, I'm in the middle of the news. But I need more than just the one close shave. I need background, and I need to stay on the story. We should work together.'

That was too blunt. He'd run screaming now.

'Perhaps we might even get to him ahead of Silvestri,' she ventured.

Marcello's mouth pressed into a thoughtful line. Brows knit above the rims of his dark glasses. He let out a plume of smoke.

'Perhaps,' he said.

Perhaps. That was almost as good as a *yes*. Better than a *maybe*, and not a *no*.

'Partners?' she suggested, offering her hand.

He stubbed out his cigarette, lit another one, sucked in smoke, let out smoke, considered a moment, and took her hand, not squeezing, not shaking.

'Partners,' she confirmed.

9

LIVE AND LET DIE

He knew he was being followed. Three of them, two large, one small. Bond, on foot today, took the opportunity to dawdle in the Parco di Traiano, to smoke them out.

Strewn about were all manner of ancient things worth a touristy look-see. Whenever he peered at a plaque, or pondered a chunk of broken statue, he enjoyed the thought of his tails getting uncomfortable under their collars. Each stop made them more conspicuous. Actually, they were about as unobtrusive as a Korean wrestler at an English golf clubhouse. He wondered why they'd got into this business in the first place. The point, as he'd been told many times, was to blend in, not stand out. Then again, Bond liked a dash of the ostentatious. It wasn't exactly easy to overlook an Aston Martin, for instance. And his other car was a Bentley.

He guessed they were from the Other Side, the people Anibas had thrown in with. They wouldn't be happy to lose a valuable vixen like her, and might even be inclined – somewhat unfairly, but what could you expect from that shower? – to blame him for their loss. Another possibility was that the larger of the two large fellows was this Crimson Executioner, to whom he owed his life but whom he wouldn't be especially keen on tangling with again. After all, the vampire killer might not always confine his garrotting activities to elders. The situation in Rome was complicated, as Winthrop had warned him. He needed to consult the old man again.

From the park, he could see Beauregard in his bath chair on

his balcony, nodding perhaps in sleep, sometimes looking out at the view. In the Diogenes Club, the old man was a legend. Youngsters who'd come up in the war tended to get a touch fed up when fossils of Edwin Winthrop's generation harped on about the daring exploits of Charles Beauregard, the man who faced Dracula in his lair and lived to tell of it. Having met the fellow, Bond began to understand what all the fuss was about.

He stopped dead and lit a cigarette, fixing his tails' positions in his mind.

The larger of the two large ones was very tall, well over seven feet, anchored by clumping asphalt-spreader's boots. His complexion was a greenish-grey, not very healthy. The oversize bowler perched on his flattish head, shaded heavily lidded, watery eyes. His teeth, glimpsed when thin black lips stretched in an approximate smile, flashed steel. The collar of his black duffel coat bunched up around his neck, covering protuberances. He moved slowly, lumbering, and his long, scarred hands seemed spindly. But there was great strength there. He would not be easy to kill.

The other large one – Bond assumed it was human – was broader, bundled up in a clay-stained overcoat, legs like stiff tree trunks, doughy face the brown of freshly scooped mud. On a head the shape of a plum pudding was a strange wig-hat, somewhere between a page-boy bob and an upturned flowerpot. A Star of David hung around its throat, perhaps to ward off vampires.

These were not undead in any sense he understood, but he was convinced they weren't exactly alive either.

At least, they clod-hopped enough to be obvious. They'd picked him up a few streets away from the Inghilterra and trudged purposefully after him all afternoon and into the evening, making a bad job of loitering aimlessly whenever he slowed down.

The third was the most interesting, a long-necked ballerina with a doll-like white face and porcelain arms. She drifted along on her points like a stray from a *commedia dell'arte* troupe, skirts slightly bedraggled. He hadn't been sure of her at first, but she definitely triangulated with the others.

A team of three meant something serious. If he was only to be tailed, less noticeable agents would have been deployed. And if he were to be assassinated, a sniper with a silver bullet could handle the job. Considering how often the Other Side had decreed he should be truly dead, it was a surprise they hadn't yet called in an East German Ladies' Rifle Champion to get him cleanly out of the way. It was always nonsense with venomous spiders under the eiderdown or bizarre strong-arm characters. Like these.

He left the park and looked up at Beauregard's balcony. The old man saw him at once and dropped something over the parapet. Bond's hand snaked out instinctively. He snatched the keys from the air. He was being invited up.

He assumed Beauregard's vampire companion wasn't at home. That might be a good thing. The Dieudonné woman didn't care for him much. Which was a shame, since she was interesting, with arresting eyes and an electric grace. A fiery spirit burned inside her supple body. It would be an interesting challenge to bend spirit and body both to his will, to unleash centuried passions and join them to his own relentless hunger.

On the stoop of the apartment building, he paused and looked around. His three tails converged, striding or tripping through the low mist of the park.

The weight of his Walther was comforting under his armpit. Whatever these characters were, a silver bullet or two in the head or heart ought to see them off. He hoped it wouldn't come to that. Having a licence to kill was all well and good, but he had to fill in forms in triplicate whenever it was exercised. And even friendly foreign governments, like whoever was running Italy this week, whinged when British Intelligence killed folk on their patches.

He yawned with calculation, exposing fangs to the night air, tasting the breeze. He was still quickened by Anibas's potent blood. Sometimes, he felt an enemy's fear on the tip of his tongue, could suck out of evaporated sweat an idea of purpose. Now, there was a riot of Roman senses, but nothing from the three comrades.

Nothing at all.

Not vampire, not warm.

He let himself in to the large, dark lobby and took the cage lift up to Beauregard's landing. It rose with a satisfying clunking and rattling of chains.

He unlocked the door of Beauregard's flat and stepped inside. The old man called to him to come through to the study. Bond found Beauregard wheeling in from the balcony, exerting himself a little.

'You must excuse me, Commander Bond. Gené is not at home. She's out picking a dress for a special occasion.'

'A wedding?' he ventured.

'Yes, but it'll have to do for a funeral too. So our Crimson Executioner has destroyed the Lady Anibas?'

He wasn't surprised Beauregard should know. The man still had his sources of information.

'You were in Rome to see her, I presume? To turn her, as it were. One of Edwin's little operations. As might be predicted, she wasn't quite prepared to sign up. What happened? Did the Russians get to her with a better offer?'

He only had to confirm Beauregard's suppositions.

The old man shook his head knowingly. Still obviously frail, he was a little flushed too. He might be a warm man, but he'd picked up – from his vampire mistress? – the trick of sapping energy from associates.

'Their section chief in Rome is very able,' said Beauregard. 'You've been briefed on him.'

'Gregor Brastov.'

'Count Gregor Brastov, he was once. A proper Carpathian. Not many of the breed in Smert Spionem. Over centuries, he's developed the skills one needs to survive successive purges. They call him the Cat Man. Always lands on his paws.'

Smert Spionem – Death to Spies! – was Lavrenti Beria's Soviet Intelligence department. The Other Side's equivalent of the Diogenes Club. Bond had tangled with their long-range employees before, and was fascinated by the colourless Beria's love of eccentric and flamboyant lieutenants.

'Winthrop says Brastov is one of the most dangerous creatures in Europe.'

'Typically acute,' concurred Beauregard. 'Brastov is more isolated in Rome than he might be. Mario Balato, a local Communist Party bigwig, is a vampire-hater of the first water. He is forever citing passages in Marx to justify the prejudice. Aristocrats draining the lifeblood of the noble peasantry, dead labour leeching off the living. Our American cousins think, in their slightly simple-minded manner, that Moscow runs all foreign Communist Parties with an iron hand. Certainly, Khrushchev wishes that were true, as much as Stalin did. But the Italian reds are too bolshy, as it were, to go along with Comintern more than half the time. Brastov imports his own people, and there's been friction with Balato's crowd – factional killings, safe houses blown up, that sort of thing. One theory has the Crimson Executioner as literally a Red Vampire Killer, acting on Balato's orders.'

'Liquidating Anibas was as much an attack on Brastov as on the House of Vajda, then. She was a prize. Three unique individuals have stumped around after me all afternoon, which suggests Smert Spionem are rather upset.'

The old man's thin hands darted like birds, waving away the theory.

'The Executioner's too theatrical to be one of Balato's knifemen. To be honest, his activities strike me as being more in *our* line.'

It had occurred to him, of course. The Crimson Executioner had saved his life, eliminating someone who was on the point of killing him. Winthrop could be running another agent in Rome without letting Bond in on it. That sort of 'need to know' trickery wouldn't be surprising from Diogenes.

Beauregard wheeled backwards, heels trailing on the carpet. He rolled over to a low table and offered brandy from a decanter.

Bond accepted.

'I have to watch my measures,' Beauregard admitted, 'but I can derive vicarious pleasure from your enjoyment.'

It was a good, not quite excellent, Courvoisier. He let it sing on his tongue for a moment. Since turning, his palate had become extraordinarily sensitive. He feared he was spoiled for anything less than truly first rate.

Beauregard took a Havana cigar from a box and accepted a light. He puffed, and looked a little sad.

'I've lost surprisingly little in extreme old age,' he said, with quiet pride. 'But taste is going.'

Bond knew he was unlikely to last, even as a vampire, to the age Charles Beauregard had attained. He was not the type to rise, as Winthrop had done and Beauregard before him, to the Ruling Cabal. Few field agents went on much beyond forty. It was a question of nerve, not willingness. As a vampire, he might have four or five more decades in the game than a warm man, though he risked, in the picturesque phrase of a colleague from the CIA, 'going blood simple'. One of the less comfortable factors of turning was that it was never certain what exactly one would turn into.

'Did you see the Crimson Executioner?' Beauregard asked.

'Just his hands. They were red.'

'Bloody?'

'No. Well, yes. There was blood. He had a silver wire, thick with the stuff. But his hands were red. Dye, or some sort of stain.'

'Witnesses describe a red face. Not just a mask, though he wears a domino and a cowl. That used to be a fashion among the more unusual criminals of Paris – Fantômas, Irma Vep, Flambeau. Now, it's a European tendency – Kriminal, Diabolik, Satanik, Killing. Absurd names, leotards, masks. A little like us, I suppose. These fellows never grew out of dressing up and playing pirates.'

'He wasn't playing. He was being.'

'Yes, yes. Quite, quite. This one is of a different order. He's not a thief. He takes no souvenirs. I don't think he's working through a private pattern, like most mad murderers. I believe him to be an assassin. He is the catspaw of a faction or individual. He kills because he is told to, and he spares some – like you or my old friend Kate Reed – because their deaths have not been included in a well worked-out plan.'

'Who do you think is behind him?'

Beauregard smiled. 'Now that's the question, Commander Bond. If it's not Smert Spionem and it's not us, who does that leave? It's a dreadful temptation to rope in Dracula, isn't it?'

'The victims are his friends.'

'Friends? I doubt if he can have friends. But that's a question for another night. Certainly, the dead elders are his contemporaries, even his supporters, connections, retainers. *Il principe* is capricious. He spread vampirism throughout the world, made it safe for the undead to live openly. Perhaps he has changed his mind and wishes to drive the undead back into the shadows.'

'Anibas would have betrayed him.'

'So would any of the dead elders. As a breed, they aren't long on loyalty. Dracula has always commanded through fear, not love. He expects treachery at every turn, even feels there's something wrong if it isn't constantly lurking. Elders have strength of will, not personality.'

'What about…?'

'Geneviève? She's unique. Haven't you noticed?'

He had.

'There are other players,' Beauregard continued, 'waiting in the wings, shuffling in the dark. Literally dozens of domestic political or religious factions. Leagues of Vampire Killers, underground or semi-public. Churches and banks and faiths and fancies. The Pope of Rome and the Mother of Tears. The victims are all elders. There are other ancients in the world, institutions which prize their histories. Perhaps some are jealous and wish to be unrivalled in their longevity. Now, there are only a handful of elders. Soon, there will be a great many more, as the new-borns of the '80s and '90s settle into permanence. Vampire elders will then be a very significant force. They might even be the ones to decide the shape of human history in the next millennium. We have always feared the rule of the dead.'

He swallowed brandy, and pondered.

There was a crash outside, in the hallway. The front door burst in.

The Walther PPK was out of its holster and in his hand. He crouched cat-like, alert. Beauregard rolled backwards, into shadow. Bond would have to look out for the old man. They might use him as a hostage.

Someone heavy lumbered down the corridor and stood at the door to the study. Clayface entirely filled the door-frame. It had no weapons but its own huge, thick-fingered hands. They were probably deadly enough. Bond fired twice into the fudgy mass of its head. Silver bullets hit with a sound like pebbles thrown into mud, and had about as much effect. The holes closed over. He tried firing at the heart area. No result, either.

'The Star of David,' shouted Beauregard.

He took aim on the amulet but something fast slammed his arm, bowling him over. His hand was stamped on and he lost the gun. A sharp toe-point jammed into the side of his head.

The ballerina had come over the balcony.

She kicked him, many times. It was a strange dance, frenzied but poised. He felt jabs of real pain as some sort of razor sliced through his clothes, stinging.

He rolled with the kicks and grabbed an ankle. Her leg felt like cold china. Her pump was tipped with a two-inch silver blade, smeared with garlic.

The knife neared his face. He needed all his strength to hold her off.

Looking up, he saw her pretty, blank face. Dots of red on bone-white cheeks, eyes blinking slowly like clockwork, sausage curls bobbing.

There was inhuman strength in this frail doll.

His elbows bent outwards. The knife almost touched his eye.

They must have a detailed dossier on him. He was of a bloodline susceptible to garlic.

'Excuse me, Miss,' Beauregard said.

The old man had scooped up the Walther and rolled his chair across the room, rucking up the carpet. He tapped the ballerina's outstretched leg with the pistol, and held the barrel to her knee.

The ballerina's painted expression didn't change.

Beauregard pulled the trigger. The explosion of the gunshot was enormous, ear-ringing. The gun kicked in the old man's hands and pushed him back in his wheelchair.

The ballerina's knee exploded. Shards of china blasted all around. Oiled wires worked up and down inside her wound. Gears and cogs spilled out of the rupture. Her lower leg came loose.

She hopped back, still perfectly balanced. Wires unrolled from her loose shin, stretched tight, and yanked the lower leg and foot out of his hands. Clear oil spilled on the carpet.

The ballerina was a mechanical toy. All three of the team were artificial to some extent.

Bond climbed swiftly to his feet. Instinct had taken over. His fangs were fully extended and his bloodlust was up. Having escaped death, he must feed soon. In turning and training, his circuits had been rewired. After danger, he must have blood.

The ballerina, damaged but incapable of feeling pain, was still dangerous. The third assassin clambered over the balcony, snarling anger.

Beauregard's chair was trapped by folds of carpet. The centenarian was out of the game, befuddled by the noise of the gun, and the suddenness of the whole thing.

Clayface had come into the room, and blocked the door.

Being big was no guarantee of toughness. Bond launched himself into the air and sank talons into the lumpy ruff that passed for a neck. He gripped the broad waist with his knees, opened wide his maw, and sank fangs into thick flesh, anticipating the rush of blood into his throat.

A muddy, dirty ichor trickled into his mouth. It was not blood.

Heavy arms clamped around him, holding him in an inescapable embrace. He felt strain in his lower back. He was about to be snapped in half.

The impression of a face was close to him. He saw the mouth was just a line scored in mud. The eyes were glittering pebbles in holes. There was life here, but nothing he could feed off or overwhelm. Knowing few men could best Bond, Brastov had sent inhuman assassins.

Beauregard shouted something.

Bond's ears rang with the blood squeezed into his head. The throbbing was the low bass-line of an electric guitar, rumbling ominous yet driving chords, a signature-tune for death and danger.

He couldn't understand. What was the old man yelling about?

The Star of David amulet was in front of his face. The assassin's shoulder was ripped open, indented with the marks of his teeth. Inside, the flesh was wet soil, swarming to fill the hole and smooth over.

A few of Bond's ribs snapped. Stabs of agony ran up his body.

'The Star of David,' Beauregard shouted again.

Bond had no feeling at all below the waist. His ribs knit together with the accelerated healing prowess of a vampire, but broke again and knitted out of true. Jagged pain scratched his heart and lungs.

He spat and spewed, voiding his mouth, and bit into the amulet. A mild sensitivity to religious objects stung his mouth. Clayface's grip froze. Bond worried at the amulet, pulling it this way and that. He got a better mouth-grip and tore it away completely.

The semblance of life fled. Clayface became a soft statue.

Bond was dropped. He spat out the amulet and took a deep breath, inflating his lungs, expanding his ribcage. He hoped the bones would settle into their proper places.

The ballerina still hopped around, and the third assassin, the flat-headed man, was in the room. He took off his bowler hat.

Bond stood up, stepping to one side.

The bowler flew across the room like a razored discus. The assassin's snarl showed steel. The hat smashed into the clay statue, embedding itself. The brim must have been reinforced.

Bond took the hat out of the mud wall of the statue's chest and spun it back. The assassin batted it aside with a growl and loped across the room, arms outstretched. His boot-falls shook the floor.

Beauregard must have imperturbable neighbours.

The assassin paused a moment by the old man, looking down at him, thinking. He was the one with flickers of independent animal intelligence, able to deviate from the plan to take into account unforeseen factors. If it hadn't been for Beauregard, either of the other killers would have finished Bond.

The assassin raised a hand, prepared to land a killing blow.

Calmly, Beauregard tossed the remainder of the brandy at the greenish face. The tall man shook his head like a dog, blinking and spitting. He was confused. Beauregard blew on his glowing cigar and flicked it up into the man's face.

A puff of flame engulfed the assassin's head, singeing his lank black hair to stubble. He clawed at the fire with black-nailed hands, roaring like an animal in pain, blundering around in a blazing panic.

Bond pushed over the statue, which shattered on the polished wood floor of the hallway, then waded through clay fragments towards the exploded front door.

He'd only just made it out of the flat when something landed on his back and clung. A leg wrapped around him, scissoring his ribs, abusing his recently broken bones.

Cold, stiff fingers took his head and shook it, as if trying to wrest it from his shoulders.

The ballerina sang as she tried to kill him, a high, perfect ululation. It blended with the thrumming of his blood, producing an exotic, threatening, promising song. A crimson wash rose over his vision. White porcelain arms, stained with trickling red, writhed to the blood-music.

He threw himself around the landing, slamming his back into the walls, trying to get rid of this strange toy.

The tall assassin, face blackened, stalked out of the flat. His steel teeth clicked together in a slow castanet rattle of death.

Bond floundered back and collided with the barred door of the lift cage.

Had the thug killed Beauregard before coming after him? That old man was the best in the business. He had understood what he was facing and known what to do. If Bond lived to be a hundred, he'd never match that.

He was unlikely to live to a hundred. Ten dagger-point nails were working their way through his gullet. He was on his knees, bent over backwards.

With his free hands, he scrabbled as far behind him as possible, reaching for the lift doors. His fingers brushed the loose bars. He stretched, extending his nails, and got a grip.

The doors parted and he heaved his shoulders, jamming the ballerina into the shaft. She freed one hand from his throat and grabbed a bar, bracing herself. He wriggled and pushed but couldn't shift her further.

The tall assassin watched with malign interest, cunning sparking in his pained eyes.

There was a rattle inside the liftshaft. Someone was coming up.

10

CAT O'NINE TAILS

Mildly distracted, Geneviève pressed the button for her landing and looked through her purse for her keys. Though not of a sun-shunning bloodline, she'd run late throughout the day and missed the bank. However the world might change, bankers were not about to alter their opening hours for the benefit of the nocturnal.

She was living off investments which yielded enough to cover her expenses. She was supposed to be getting familiar with Charles's estate on the assumption that she'd soon be its trustee. She'd made him swear not to leave it all to her. A particularly distasteful species of vampire gold-digging involved ensnaring hapless mortals to the point where they bequeathed you all their worldly goods, waiting for the inevitable, then cashing in and looking around for the next prospect. She didn't want the world to remember Charles Beauregard as her dupe.

The lift ascended with its usual clanks and rattles. She found her keys. Something in the air caught her attention.

Spilled blood. Spent energy. A hint of cordite.

Damn. It was starting all over again. Couldn't she leave Charles alone for an afternoon?

Just before her floor, the lift shrieked to a stop. Then, chains hauling, it rose again, by inches. Metal and something else screamed.

Through the cage door, she saw a dangling dress. A broken white mannequin leg kicked.

People were on the landing. Hamish Bond, and a flat-headed goon she didn't recognise.

A panic hand took her heart.

Was Charles hurt? Worse?

She wasn't ready. Despite his gentle drifting away, she wasn't ready to lose him. Just a few more weeks. Days, even. Things had to be settled first. If this was love, it was horrible.

A crushed body writhed in front of the cage doors, jammed between the slightly parted outer doors and the pull-across screen of the lift itself. It was pinned at the neck between the edge of the doorway and the top of the lift, head stuck out into the shaft.

The scream was musical.

The neck came apart and the thing in the dress fell, spewing clockwork.

Bond coughed up blood. His once-immaculate dinner jacket was sliced to ribbons across his sides.

Flattop stood over the British spy, harrowing hands reaching down.

She'd put a stop to this.

Tearing the cage door open, she stepped onto the landing and fixed Flattop with her eyes. The creature was brutish, but had a brain. He could be willed to stand down. The automaton would have been different. Geneviève made tiny fists and reached out with her mind.

Flattop staggered. He snarled, mouth showing metal.

The apartment door was smashed. She saw ruins in the passage. This was going to be expensive.

She was coldly furious. 'Commander Bond, explain this.'

Bond couldn't stop coughing. Holes in his throat healed.

'I'd best take that initiative,' said an unfamiliar voice.

She hadn't sensed any presence, so it must be someone old, with powers.

'I am Brastov.'

She'd heard of him. A tall, wide man stood in shadows, forked beard giving his head a distinctive shape. In his hands was a large white cat which shone in a shaft of moonlight from a high window. The cat's slit eyes were scarlet. The man wore a

Chinese-style mauve cotton jacket and *muzhik* pantaloons.

'I wish only an interview, for the moment,' said Brastov.

Geneviève realised she had made a too-easy assumption about this creature. She wondered if Bond had been misled too. She remembered Charles mentioning this Brastov, the Cat Man. He was supposed to be a Soviet spymaster.

'You are Geneviève Dieudonné, an elder,' said the Cat Man. 'An innocent party, perhaps, but involved. I shall have to ask you to accompany Mr Bond.'

She extruded claws.

'If you put up no fight, we shall leave Charles Beauregard as he is and not put him to the trouble of coming along with you.'

She drew in her nails.

'He is overexcited, but unhurt. You have the word of Brastov that no harm was intended to him. He has a reputation in our profession. One would not wish to show disrespect.'

Brastov's voice was snake-like, hypnotic. Thick fingers kneaded the fur of the cat's throat.

'That old man saw off three of your best,' Bond spat.

'Indeed he did,' Brastov purred, suavely unruffled. 'Lessons have been learned. A car waits downstairs. You will come with us.'

Geneviève stiffened.

'You may look in on Mr Beauregard, Mademoiselle. I am not without feeling. But only for a moment.'

She nodded gratefully.

Flattop blocked the smashed doorway.

'If you would recover Olympia's head,' Brastov ordered his underling. 'It would be a shame to lose such an ingenious and pleasing device. She can be rebuilt.'

Flattop grunted and got out of the way. He reached into the lift shaft and wrestled free the object he found there. The automaton's eyes blinked.

Geneviève stepped into the flat. The hallway was littered with wet clay.

Charles was in his study, propped in his chair, breathing heavily. He seemed stunned. There was a weal on his cheek, a rising bruise.

She smoothed the crumpled carpet – she knew it sometimes trapped his wheelchair – and checked Charles's pulse. His eyes opened fractionally, telling her he was awake.

'You are satisfied as to his health?' asked Brastov. He was in the flat now, eyes on them.

'To strike a man his age,' she protested.

'My associate will be punished. He doesn't like fire.'

Charles smiled, too tiny an expression to register across the room. Geneviève adjusted the blanket over his knees and felt under it for his hands. Her fingers closed on something cold. Bond's gun. Charles pressed it on her. She manipulated it out from under the blanket and into her armpit, hidden under her shawl.

Charles patted her hand. She kissed his forehead.

'Very touching,' Brastov commented. 'Now, if you will be so kind as to come along. Mr Bond has had a trying evening.'

By the time they were out of the apartment, the pistol was in her handbag.

Geneviève and Bond were blindfolded and hustled into a Daimler. They were driven a short way and assisted out of the vehicle and through an iron gate which scraped on gravel.

'You'll have been memorising tiny sounds and scents, to fix the journey,' said Brastov. 'I too have played that game. It is no matter. If your Diogenes Club isn't up on our addresses, I should be very surprised.'

The blindfolds were removed. They were in a large garden, with nondescript ruins. The man with the cat stood by an entrance to a tunnel sloping down into the earth. He led the way inside. Geneviève and Bond followed. Flattop brought up the rear.

The passage was narrow and low. They were taken through catacombs. Flattop kept banging his forehead against the rock roof. Alcoves in the walls contained hunched-over corpses, preserved bags of bones. Some faces were twisted in death, as if they had been walled up alive.

'"For the love of God, Montresor,"' Geneviève quoted.

'Yes indeed,' said Brastov, amused. 'Do you know Mr Poe? He is in Rome at the moment. One sees him at social gatherings, glooming about in the corner. De Laurentiis has him under contract. He has been working on the script for one of those Cinecittà epics, *Gli Argonauti*.'

The passage widened into a chamber. Its walls were made from jawless skulls, layered like macabre bricks. Flattop reached for a particular relic, sliding thick fingers into empty eye-sockets. He pulled the skull and the wall parted, sliding out of the way.

'Come through, into our lair,' said Brastov.

The man with the cat stepped into the dark beyond the wall of skulls. Lights automatically came on. Without needing to be prodded, Geneviève and Bond followed. They stood on a platform which descended like a miner's lift, into a huge underground space. The cavern was hewn out of naked rock, shored up with modernist steel struts.

Banks of equipment stood among broken classical columns and armless, headless statues. Large television screens hung from stalactites. Symbols crawled across animated maps of various continents. Devices the size and shape of refrigerators, huge whirring spools of tape on their fronts, stood in ranks between rock-pools – up-to-date computers.

Pretty girls in tailored white jumpsuits were busy with the equipment, receiving and sending messages, tabulating information. Swarthy men in orange boiler suits watched over them, sub-machine guns casually slung over their shoulders.

They walked through the operations centre and were shown into changing rooms. Bond was allowed a shower and given a fresh suit of clothes. Geneviève considered the evening gown she was offered, but decided to stick with her current practical outfit. She didn't want to put down her handbag for fear of losing the gun.

While Bond sang a calypso in the shower, Geneviève looked at the hard-faced matron assigned to watch over them. She was a new-born, with typically slavic features. Few of the people in Brastov's lair were obvious Russians or even Eastern Europeans, though his operation was strictly Soviet, often at odds with the Italian Communist Party and even the local criminal organisations.

Bond emerged from the changing room, perfectly groomed. He wore a lightweight suit, charcoal grey, with a double-knit blue tie. He expected her to compliment him on how he looked, but she disappointed him. She was too concerned with Charles, back at the flat alone, perhaps hurt.

The matron ushered them into a luxuriously appointed office. The famously stolen Basil Hallward portrait of Lord Ruthven hung behind a desk the size of an aircraft carrier. A clump of life-sized mannequins dangled from a wooden frame, posed in a strange array. Geneviève saw a gap and guessed that was where Olympia had been. The most impressive of the remaining dolls was an eight-armed dancing Kali.

The man with the cat was behind the desk, face again in deep shadows. A spotlight fell on the cat's white fur. The animal luxuriated, as if sunbathing.

'May I offer you something to drink?' said Brastov. 'We have a well-stocked cellar. There are always expendable warmfellows. You may kill one if you wish, Mr Bond. After your exertion, you must have a touch of the red thirst.'

Geneviève wouldn't trust Brastov not to palm off a hopeless drug addict or tertiary syphilitic. She declined his offer. So, after a moment's thought, did Bond.

'Very well. To business.'

The cat stretched on the desk, rolling over. He was the size of an Alsatian, and doubly fanged. Pampered, but obviously a terror to his prey.

'We were most saddened by the loss of Anibas Vajda.'

There was steel in the conventional sentiment.

'So were we,' said Bond.

'I doubt that. Her loyalties wavered. At the time of her decease, they were wavering in our direction. Frankly, we wondered if you mightn't have eliminated her yourself.'

'As it happens, I didn't. Not for want of trying.'

'That is as we thought, Mr Bond. This business between us, between East and West, may seem impenetrable to outsiders like Mademoiselle Dieudonné, but we understand the game, we know its rules. In this instance, we were playing for a very small prize, the possibility of exerting influence on the House of Vajda and, through that, getting close to Prince Dracula. He still has a certain following in our sphere of influence, and is capricious regarding the use to which he puts it. He could be useful or a nuisance to either of us. Since the war, he has sat in his palazzo, withdrawn from the world. He has had such moods before. They do not last.'

Despite herself, Geneviève was interested.

She gathered the Russians were as in the dark as anyone else about *il principe*'s intentions.

'This Crimson Executioner is the tool of a third force,' said the Cat Man. 'A major player, perhaps. But not one who has stepped into the field honestly. We speak of a hider in the shadows.'

Geneviève almost laughed.

'One might think some Chinese mastermind from an earlier era were reviving his enterprises in the present day.'

She knew whom he meant.

'Or one of the others – Herr Doktor Mabuse, Monsieur Anthony Zenith, even the astronomy professor. We thought them all retired or dead, but those conditions are seldom permanent with such men. In the second half of this century, the nature of shadow kings has changed. Secret societies abound, but they have become like corporations. You saw the wonderful boxes outside, adding machines and thinking machines and killing machines. Where are the robes and rites and curses of yesteryear? Do you know, Mr Bond, I miss all that. In my network, I have as many accountants as assassins.'

'One hopes they are of better quality,' Bond said, resting his hand on one of Kali's upper arms. 'Or I should fear even for the Kremlin's deep pockets.'

'We're not quite at that stage, old fellow.'

Kali's eyes sprung open. Bond wasn't startled.

'She is more than a machine,' Brastov commented. 'Kali is a work of art, plaything of an ancient despot. You have to admire the artificer who could bring such a beauty to life. Her embrace is final but her victims die in unspeakable ecstasy.

Really. Spirit mediums have sought them out in the afterlife to confirm it.'

'I've had too many final embraces these last few days.'

The cat's mouth opened in a mocking yawn.

'That you have, Mr Bond. You sought out Charles Beauregard to quiz him about the Crimson Executioner?'

Geneviève had guessed as much. She felt a knot of useless anger. Later, if they survived, she'd settle with the British spy. He had pointlessly endangered a dying man. Like Brastov, he was so intent on his game that he never gave a thought to the breakable human pieces.

'I imagine he thinks along the same lines as myself. He is a man of quality.'

'He mentioned the possibility that friends of yours might be involved,' ventured Bond. 'Mario Balato's shower.'

Brastov hissed a laugh. 'He might have mentioned the possibility, but he would not subscribe to it. Our unruly children are a bother, I admit. They believe in too much, don't know the rules of the game. Another unwelcome twentieth century trait. But this isn't their sort of business. No, we've to look a little deeper, under the stones. The answer to this question is old, as old perhaps as Rome.'

Bond shrugged.

'Mademoiselle,' Brastov addressed her, 'have you heard of *Mater Lachrymarum*?'

'She's supposed to be one of Three Mothers,' Geneviève said. 'Witches or Goddesses or Patron Demons – *Mater Suspiriorum*, the Mother of Sighs; *Mater Tenebrarum*, the Mother of Darkness; and *Mater Lachrymarum*, the Mother of Tears. Guardians of the Sick Soul of Europe, or some such. Thomas De Quincey wrote an essay about them.'

'You impress me. I had expected that. Officially, I have little time for such arcane nonsense. It smacks of alchemy and pointed hats. Moscow deplores such things as un-socialist. But I have many sources. *Mater Lachrymarum*, the Mother of Tears, is the oldest of the three, and her legend is inextricably bound up with the history of Rome. She was here before Romulus and Remus, they say. She has presided over her invisible court throughout the city's history. Caligula sacrificed to her and Rodrigo Borgia was her lover before he became Holy Father. Myths and rumours and fairy tales, but at their heart is a truth that affects us all. There's a whisper that the Mother of Tears is more than an ur-legend and that this Crimson Executioner is in her thrall.'

Geneviève realised they'd been brought here not to be questioned, but to be given an answer.

This was all about dropping a name.

Mater Lachrymarum.

The interview was ended. Brastov had concluded his business. One of them would be let free, to do with the information as they would. The other would be killed, to underline the seriousness of the matter.

'Perhaps you'd care to dance with Kali,' Brastov said.

The automaton's spider-arms closed, just missing Bond's chest.

The Cat Man laughed.

Geneviève took the Walther out of her bag and tossed it to Bond. He was the one who knew how to use the wretched thing.

He stepped forward, drew perfect aim, and shot the man behind the desk. In the chest, twice. The cat-minder snapped into his swivel chair, then pitched slowly onto his face.

She couldn't believe Bond had made such a mistake.

'That was hardly gracious,' said Brastov. 'Russians are so hard to train.'

Bond was astonished. Geneviève was exasperated.

'Not the man, you idiot,' Geneviève shouted. 'The cat!'

Brastov flowed across the desk like furred lightning, padding on swelling paws. He assumed a slightly more human shape, back legs longer, forepaws fingered.

Bond shot again, but barely brushed Brastov's shrinking tail.

A flap opened in the wall and Brastov slipped through it.

Bond was at a complete loss. Geneviève shook her head.

'I'll get you out of here alive,' Geneviève said to him, feeling her talons and teeth coming, gathering the fighting strength she was about to need. 'But that's it. You'll be on your own. My patience with this silly game is exhausted.'

11

THE DANCING DEAD

Penelope was all a-flutter, like a little bat. Tom wasn't the only one to notice. He overheard one of the waiters call her *Signorina Pipistrella*. Perhaps it was what they called all dead women behind their backs. If so, it was unwise. Like bats, the dead had big, sensitive ears. He knew Penelope could segue from desperate gaiety to homicidal rage on the spin of a coin.

They were under the Baths of Caracalla, searching out some new cabaret. Penelope had heard wondrous whispers of a coloured singing group from America, the Kool-Tones. She was one of those Europeans who valued American exports for their vitality and brashness. Tom suspected he fell into that category of American himself, though he didn't care to think of himself as either vital or brash. The last thing he wanted was to traipse through a city thousands of years older than New York in search of some doo-wop spades who couldn't get a paying gig in Harlem.

The Kit Kat Klub was mostly underground, its entrance among ruins. An orange neon sign fizzled among the remnants of a classical frieze. Everyone was aware of the vulgarity, and took pains to distance themselves by passing ironic comment.

'It's like transforming the Taj Mahal into a music hall,' snipped Penelope.

Though he'd never seen it, Tom thought the Taj Mahal vulgar enough without cocktail waitresses dressed as French maids or crooning contortionists. Popular taste had never been good. He'd heard from something disgustingly old that classical Rome had been a hideous riot of bad taste, marble covered with violent layers of ghastly paint. Busts which now seemed the essence of white serenity had originally looked like demonstration masks for circus makeup.

They sat at a good table near the stage, talking and laughing loudly enough to drown out the struggling Kool-Tones as they did their worst to 'Blue Moon'. Penelope jabbered to everybody but Tom, though under her wrap her clawed hand was hooked around his elbow. It was as if she were clinging to him for support, or to remind herself that one toy was still hers alone. He wondered if she were old enough to melt to nothing if her heart were punctured by silver. Probably not. She was one of those Victorians. She'd dwindle to a ragged skeleton with wisps of white hair. And maggots.

Since Princess Asa's dressing-down, Penelope had run on the edge of hysteria, under a compulsion to be terribly amusing and modern. She'd rounded up this group of second-stringers and parasites from the palazzo and various bolt-holes around the city, and was leading them on yet another expedition. 'Damned by dawn,' was her motto.

He was the only living man at the table except for another American, a yard-wide, corn-fed Kansas quarterback named Kent. He had won a body-beautiful contest back home and been brought to Rome to appear as Ercole in Dino de Laurentiis's motion picture of *The Argonauts*. It had just been announced that Sylvia Koscina was to replace Malenka in the role of Medea. Kent's hair was dyed a blue-black that would register as lustrous on film. His blocky, hero face was made thoughtful by sensible glasses, which didn't disguise eyes that missed little.

Penelope's dead friends were the minor poet Roger Penderel, still trading thinly on the desperate disillusion he'd picked up in the First World War; Irena Dubrovna, a catty little Serbian frail who kept making scratches in the tablecloth and apologising; the English *avant garde* painter Anthony Aloysius St John Hancock, sporting a beret and a foot-long cigarette holder; Nico Otzak, a strange, breathy German blonde thing who was either very lost or very drugged; an extremely boring 700-year-old Count; and an obscene little hunchback who communicated only in neanderthal grunts.

From somewhere, Penelope had dug up a bright-eyed newlydead American couple, the Addamses. They laid it on thick, with off-the-peg copies of fashions set by the writers Clare Quilty and Vivian Darkbloom, the husband in an offensive pinstripe suit and the wife a clinging silk shroud. Their faces were whited-up, their hair dyed black. Mr Addams had made his money in railways and munitions, and treated his wife and himself to death and resurrection as a retirement present. She wore sweet little bat earrings.

After the Kool-Tones had finished, with 'Flying Saucers 'Rock 'n' Roll', the Kit Kat Klub offered the once-in-a-lifetime-and-thank-heavens-for-it pairing of the stately Bianca Castafiore, the 'Milanese Nightingale', and the 'beat poet' Max Brock, a Yank in a false beard. The poet began free-associating run-together words, many inappropriate for mixed company, while the diva screeched wordlessly behind him.

'This is my Song for Europe,' Brock began:

A sad serenade of Sisyphean solicitude,
Strangling the strange seraphim of shameless slop
Gurgling in a gutter of galloping garbage
Gorging itself on gross guppies of Grecian goo,
Humiliatingly humping Henry Harry Herman Herbert Hoover
Haruspex of horribility, holocaust of human heartburn,
While in the icebox, it is the children's hour…

La Castafiore hit a high note that made the dead react like dogs to a silent whistle, gritting their fangs and jamming napkins in their ears. Tom realised he was enjoying the performance.

I spent my birthday in a telephone box,
Sorting out your present of igneous rocks…

Max Brock paused, aghast that he had accidentally

produced a rhyming couplet, and stamped around the stage in fury, tossing rhetorical questions into the audience like hand grenades.

'What's the taste of purple? When's the colour of February? What's on second? Why did the bat cross the moon? What's the thirty-nine steps? Who is the Mother of Tears?'

Someone hissed. Seriously. Not like a disgruntled patron, but like an angry serpent from hell.

Max Brock turned his back on the audience. La Castafiore shrieked a trill. Glasses exploded all around the club. Shards and blood spattered over the table.

'Cool, man,' someone shouted. 'Straight from the fridge!'

Irena laughed like a kitten and Nico looked at the girl as if she were dinner. Penderel made a drunken point about metre, and hailed Max Brock the greatest poet of an age that couldn't, by very definition, produce even a good poet.

'You say he's great, but not good?' asked Mr Addams, eyebrows doing a Groucho wiggle. 'That seems to be a contradiction.'

'I say he's great, and utterly dreadful. This is the age of dreadful. Don't you agree Mr Hancock?'

'Not half,' said the English painter, who was taking napkins out of his ears and might not have heard the question. 'I should cocoa. That bloke's got a flaming nerve.'

'I like that in a man,' cooed Mrs Addams, sucking in her cheeks to make a black bow of her mouth.

'Who is your favourite poet, Mr Kent?' Penelope asked, cruelly.

'Walt Whitman,' he replied.

'Very Herculean,' she commented, tartly.

Tom admired romantics and decadents, but recognised a puritan-American streak in himself that deplored moderns who might think themselves romantic or decadent. Like this mob.

'Eddy Poe, the writer on *Argonauts*, says he hasn't written poetry since he turned,' said Kent. 'He claims creativity dries up when you become a vampire.'

'In my case, that's not true,' said Penderel. 'I was a mediocre verse-man when alive.'

'My genius is immortal, mush,' said Hancock, aggressively.

'I'm AB negative, you know. It's all I can drink.'

'No offence,' said Kent, 'but I've met so few of you. Vampires.'

'Oscar Wilde wrote "The Ballad of Reading Gaol" after he turned,' said Mrs Addams. 'You have to admit that's good.'

Penelope's eyes narrowed. She didn't care for talk of Wilde. Even doubly dead, he was an embarrassment.

'Dalí is a vampire,' Nico said.

'Never liked him,' Hancock moaned. 'All those bowler hats.'

'But Picasso is a warm man,' put in Kent. 'And T. S. Eliot, Thomas Mann, Shostakovich, Joe DiMaggio, Ludwig Wittgenstein, William Faulkner. None of them turned. Yet they're the century's best.'

'Their careers have ended, or will end,' said Mrs Addams. 'To turn is to change, to embrace a darkness within. It must be a spur to creativity. Since I turned vampire, I have been far better able to express myself.'

She was what they used to call a 'murgatroyd'. Having risen from the grave, she was determined to dress the part. Almost invisible on her jet hair was a black lace veil, weighted by black pearls. Her low-cut, floor-length dress had trails like octopus tentacles. Her pallor was artificially heightened, with strategic dabs of violet shadow.

Kent, who had a mind inside his muscle, was working through a private problem.

'Maybe there are better ways to become immortal. Through work, perhaps? Or by having children?'

Penelope was on the point of ripping off Tom's arm.

'I'll take immortality any way I can get it, old fellow,' said Penderel, signalling the waitress to come open her vein into his beer *stein*. 'Sometimes it doesn't last long.'

Kent shrugged, Hercules shoulders straining his lightweight blue suit. He'd have looked conservative but for the red and yellow swirl of his hand-painted necktie.

'What about the existentialists?' asked Mrs Addams. 'Surely, their ideal modern man is a vampire? A being outside hypocrisy and convention? A creature alone in the night?

Appetites and urges unfettered by history?'

'History is all some of us have,' said the Carpathian, Oblensky.

Tom had read Camus and Sartre and didn't see what all the fuss was about. Thin books with thinner stories.

'History could end at any moment,' said Nico, making an explosion in the air with her fingers. 'Ka-pow!'

'Ah yes,' mused Penderel, 'the boom-boom Bomb.'

A dance band began playing. Penelope cut short the philosophy by forcing everyone onto the floor. She claimed Tom for herself, and partnered Kent with Mrs Addams, Penderel with Nico, Hancock with Irena, and Mr Addams with the surprisingly light-footed and enthusiastic hunchback. Count Oblensky scooped a warm film extra out of the crowd, and nibbled her throat sickeningly.

Penelope, brought up not to look into her dancing partner's eyes, held her spine ramrod straight, stretching her lovely neck to advantage.

The dead made dance halls tricky prospects. They clung to the fashions of their lifetimes, yet wished to be seen to embrace the modern. Penelope had learned to dance when the waltz was dominant, but elders were schooled in mediaeval gavottes or rowdy Russian kicking. Moderns carried over elements of the Charleston or the jitterbug.

The band played neutral dance music. A skinny crooner sang 'Volare' as if he meant it. The floor accommodated everyone's writhing. Mercifully, it was dark.

Penelope was thinking. Tom knew that made her dangerous.

Her hand crept up his back, fingers settling around his neck. She twisted his head and looked at him. Her fangs were out.

'Beautiful, blank-faced Tom,' she said. 'I wonder what goes on in there. But, also, I wonder what goes on in here.'

She touched the extended finger of her free hand to her head then her heart.

'Do I really feel anything?'

Tom was uncomfortable. Did she want him to reassure her of her humanity, or confirm her élite estrangement from the living?

'Or only imitations of feelings? Animal instincts tricked up for a complicated brain. I wasn't prepared for any of this, Tom. I was going to be a wife and mother. A hostess, a lady of some standing.'

Her tongue slipped across her fangs.

'Am I even a woman?'

Tom would rather have answered one of Max Brock's nonsense questions.

'I'm dead, Tom,' she said, piteously. 'Hold me.'

'I am holding you, Penny.'

'Yes.'

They danced on, not missing a step.

Tom knew he would have to tread carefully. He was close enough to see how unstable Penelope really was. She could pose as an ornament, displaying pleasure and amusement in such a way as not to stretch her face out of its beautiful true. But sometimes, there were cracks. And beyond cracks, the chasm.

Princess Asa was behind some of it. For a Victorian to be treated as a vassal by a mediaeval tyrant was humiliation enough. But the Princess was just the most recent irritant. Penelope's moods went deeper, and her troubles back to the age of Wilde and the Terror.

In the end, it was Dracula. And perhaps her onetime fiancé, this Charles. Tom knew both men were nearby, yet distant from Penelope. Had she come to Rome because of them?

'I'm sorry, Tom,' she said, hugging him. 'It's unfair of me to go on like this.'

He relaxed. She was thinking about him for a moment, not herself. Excellent.

'I'm also sorry about this, but…' She bit his neck, deeper than usual, opening the old bite-wounds. The pain was a shock. Her fingers dug into his ribs. She sucked ferociously.

They were still dancing. Others were bleeding. No one noticed.

For the first time, Tom felt panic.

The dead were dangerous. Really.

She set him down gently on a chair, letting him slip from

her hands. He couldn't move his limbs or even hold up his head. As he slipped into a daze, he saw Penelope dab her lips with a napkin.

She looked as if she had made a decision.

12

DEAD SOULS

More people were in Piazza di Trevi tonight. It wasn't yet midnight. Couples – other couples, Kate corrected herself – looked at the fountain, tossed in coins, made wishes. There was a policeman on guard.

'The little girl was standing there,' Kate said, pointing across the piazza. 'Where that woman is.'

Marcello tried to brush her hand down, but came up against her vampire strength of wrist.

'Be careful, Signorina Reed…'

'Kate,' she insisted.

'Kate. It does not do to attract attention. Especially with such creatures.'

The woman sat alone on the rim of the fountain, sucking at a cigarette, legs dangling like a kid's. Her tiny face reminded Kate of the little girl's, her blonde hair was cropped short. She wore a ratty fur cardigan, a sweater with horizontal stripes, and a tight, short skirt.

By gesture and ellipsis, Marcello tried to imply wordlessly that this woman was a prostitute.

'Marcello, don't be silly. Do you think I don't know a tart when I see one?'

On the whole, Kate got on well with prostitutes. She'd interviewed dozens, dating back to the Whitechapel of Jack the Ripper. Sometimes, when animals weren't enough, she had bought their blood. Just now, she didn't want to think about that.

She concentrated on Marcello. He was annoyed.

The little whore noticed them. She stubbed out her ciggy and dutifully sashayed over, calculatedly manufacturing a smile that didn't go with the puppyish openness of her big eyes. She was warm, with extensive scabbing around her neckline. Her pallor suggested she made herself available to too many vampires.

'*Ciao*,' she squeaked. 'I am Cabiria. It means "born from fire".'

She spoke accented English. Cabiria was the name of the heroine of an Italian film spectacle Kate had seen before the First World War. Obviously, its memory lingered. Since then, Italy had produced fire enough to birth many heroines.

Marcello tried to shoo off the whore, but Kate shushed him.

'Do you come here often?' she asked.

Cabiria was astonished by the question.

Kate laughed. 'I'm sorry. I really mean that. Are you often in Piazza di Trevi?'

'Sometimes,' Cabiria said. 'It is good place. Many tourists come here. Nice men, generous. How you say, big spenders?'

'I'm after a little girl. *Ragazza*. I saw her here.'

The whore looked shocked and drew away. Kate realised Cabiria thought her a bloodthirsty child molester. Sometimes being a vampire gave the wrong impression.

'I think I can help you not.'

'No,' said Kate, touching the woman's arm. 'I didn't mean it like that. She was lost, I think. I want to talk with her. She saw something. You've heard of the murders, of the Crimson Executioner?'

Cabiria crossed herself and spat.

Kate had thought the whore little more than a girl. She was tiny and frail. Her face was unlined and open, almost clownish. But she must have been in her thirties. She was frayed a bit, like her clothes. Kate guessed she'd often been bruised.

'Perhaps you should see fortune-teller,' Cabiria suggested.

Marcello snorted. He was trying to move off, to pull Kate away. Kate held still. She was interested.

'I can take you. It is not far. Near my home.'

'We have a car,' Kate said.

Marcello was coldly angry. He didn't want a whore in his car, the precious red Ferrari (which wasn't actually his – Penny let him have the use of it for reasons Kate couldn't understand and was worried about). That decided Kate. The Italian must learn his lesson.

'Signora Santona is the great fortune-teller of my district.'

'Where do you live?'

'I Cessati Spiriti,' Cabiria said.

Dead Souls. Kate sensed Marcello's rush of fear.

'It is impossible,' he said. 'Kate, you do not know what such a place is like.'

For most of her life, men had been telling Kate things were impossible, that places were terrible and off-limits. They usually meant that poor people lived there. Or there were shameful circumstances it would be distressing to read about in the papers. If Marcello had known her better, he'd have understood that telling her a place was impossible was the best way of making her want to go there.

'I've been in bad places, Marcello,' she said. 'Worse than you can imagine.'

'Perhaps. But you have never been in I Cessati Spiriti.'

'It sounds fabulous.'

'It is not so bad,' Cabiria said. 'The dead there are not swift like you, *vampiro*. They are *morti viventi*, slow. You have to watch over your shoulder.'

Kate led them to the sports car. Cabiria was struck with wonder at the machine, and treated it with the reverence due a religious object. 'Ferrari,' she repeated, over and over, eyes brimful, relishing the 'r'-sounds, stroking the mirror-finish of the body. It was a nice car, but Kate couldn't see what the fuss was about.

Getting three of them into the two-seater was a squeeze, but Kate and Cabiria were smaller than average. Cabiria put on a cloche hat. Kate feared a little for her Dior. Marcello let off the brakes and freed the beast under the bonnet. For the first time since Kate had met him, he smiled genuinely rather than to punctuate boredom with politeness. At the wheel, he was a little boy with a new toy, going 'broom broom' under his breath as he drove the Ferrari through the narrow streets at inadvisable speeds.

On the drive across the city, Cabiria told her a little about I Cessati Spiriti, with Marcello adding ominous footnotes. Then a site of fighting between the partisans and the Germans, the once-prosperous district was bombed heavily by the Allies. A famous priest had been executed by the Nazis when Rome was an open city, prompting a minor uprising. After the war, I Cessati Spiriti became a shanty-town, home to the dispossessed, a dozen varieties of refugee, many who wished to avoid the peacetime authorities, and the traditional poor. The unplanned community expanded and collapsed in on itself many times.

Ten years ago, the De Gaspero government initiated a massive public works programme to clear the slums and rebuild I Cessati Spiriti, but the funds allocated were diverted to the mafia. Much of the building work that got done was so shoddy it fell down at once. The population of the district still swelled, flooded by escapees from the drought-ridden South. With them came a new bloodline. An epidemic cluster of the risen dead, brains burned out by fever, prompted much of the warm population to evacuate. A hardy minority stayed behind in the ruins, learning to live alongside shambling *morti viventi*. Cabiria had lived here ever since the War. She seemed quite fond of the place. Marcello, it turned out, had never been here.

As it slid over trackless wasteland, cruising between huddles of patchwork shacks and piles of festering rubbish, the Ferrari must have looked like a spaceship. Kate was reminded of the trenches of France during the German onslaught of 1918. Open fires burned on the wastes like tribal beacons.

Nearby, a knot of *morti viventi* was encircled by warm feral children who tormented them with flaming torches. From a distance, the walking dead seemed like crippled tramps, easily bested by the fast, vicious kids. One creature got too close to fire and went up like a screeching roman candle. It fell in flames, and two youths battered its head with crowbars.

Cabiria directed them to a street lined by the hulks of bombed-out and patched-up buildings. There were no streetlamps but braziers burned, casting flamelight on bullet-pocked walls. It was hard to believe this was in the same city as Via Veneto, but it was hard to believe Whitechapel was in the same city as Kensington.

It annoyed her that so much of the world was still like I Cessati Spiriti when it didn't have to be.

'I live there,' ventured Cabiria, pointing to a shattered apartment block, obviously hoping one or other of them would suggest dropping by for a 'visit'. Kate intended to pay the whore for her troubles but didn't want to take advantage of her services. 'And Signora Santona lives here.'

Marcello parked by another ramshackle building. It had once been a church. The roof was gone, replaced with polythene sheets. Some windows had patches of stained glass between the beaten tin cans and taped-in cardboard.

'I shall stay with the car,' Marcello announced.

Kate couldn't argue that wasn't a sensible idea.

Perhaps he'd be attacked by monsters and she'd have to rescue him. That might impress him. Then again, he might blame her for getting him into an attackable situation in the first place. Men were always unreasonable.

Marcello sat in the car, angling the wing mirror so he could look in as many directions as possible.

Kate and Cabiria got out. Standing on the pavement for a moment, Cabiria listened to the wind. There were faint cries. She shook her head and ventured on.

The front door of the former church was boarded up, but a little door at the side led to a staircase that went down into the basements.

'It is all underground,' she said. 'Watch your shoes.'

At the bottom of the staircase was a long, wide corridor. The only light came from an oil lamp somewhere. An inch of stagnant water lay on top of a furry carpet. Rough planks propped on bricks made a walkway, with tributary planks leading into rooms. Nailed-up blankets hung from lintels, edges trailing in the water.

Business was being transacted in some of the rooms.

A scratchy gramophone record was slowing down. A waltz ground to a halt.

Cabiria balanced like a tightrope walker on the planks, arms out. Kate, wearing heels, tottered a little as she followed.

From one room came a growling and chewing. Behind the thin blanket burned a fire that made a fine crosshatch of the weave. Something spurted and splattered against the blanket, and dribbled down. There were swirls of red in the water.

Cabiria pulled Kate on, past that room.

'Here is the *signora*'s apartment,' she said.

This doorway had an actual door. It was bright blue, with gold crescents and silver stars. Cabiria knocked on the door and a hole opened in the centre of a painted eye.

'To see the fortune-teller,' Cabiria explained.

The door was opened and the women allowed in.

The fortune-teller's servant was *morti viventi*, the first Kate had seen up close. A cage-muzzle was nailed to his cheekbones, over the constantly grinding jaw. Facemeat was flaking away. Staring eyes betokened no intellect. Kate understood this was a breed of vampire, given to chewing blood out of flesh rather than drinking from the vein. Most people thought of them as zombies. Maybe classing someone as a reanimated automaton, entirely vacated by its former personality, was an excuse not to treat them as human. On this brief acquaintance, she wasn't ready to argue the assumption.

The servant was dressed in shabby genteel style, a good suit gone to the bad. He had no shoes or socks. His feet were black and ragged.

He didn't try to eat Kate or Cabiria, but led them into a labyrinth. The fortune-teller's apartment was large, and full of items perhaps accepted in payment. Stacks of furniture, bundles of books, a pile of broken bicycles, jars of specimens floating in brine, several bedsteads, a surprising amount of scientific equipment, empty gilt picture frames, a rack of rifles. Off in curtained rooms, *morti viventi* performed chores Kate didn't understand.

Santona sat cross-legged on a canopied palanquin, her barrel-body swaddled in many-coloured shawls, neck and wrists heavy with jewellery. She was an old woman, though her face was unlined and her oiled ringlets were youthfully dark.

Two more *morti viventi* attended the fortune-teller.

'They were '*ndrangheta*,' Santona explained. 'From Calabria. Criminals. They tried to move North, but brought this taint with them. Most don't last long, but I have trained these and make use of them.'

'I'm Katharine Reed. From Ireland.'

She extended her hand, but Santona didn't shake it.

'I know,' she said. 'You are in this city for the dying.'

Cabiria crossed herself.

'That's as may be,' Kate said. 'Just now, I'm looking for a little girl I saw in Piazza di Trevi. A witness to a crime.'

'The man in the red hood. He is like these '*ndrangheta*, only a servant. A tool. There was no little girl.'

'I didn't imagine her.'

'You didn't see *her*. You saw a reflection.'

The fortune-teller must have been skimming her mind. Some warm wise women had a little of that vampire sense.

'Reflections can mislead.'

Kate had thought that. Something still bothered her about the scene. Had she misunderstood what she saw?

'Was she a dwarf?' she asked.

The ripples in the water could have made a child's face of a withered mask of age.

Santona laughed and shook her head. She held out a hand.

Kate produced five hundred lire, which disappeared. The fortune-teller had snatched it.

'Not everything can be revealed.'

This was what she expected from a proper con woman. Pointless mystification and disappearing money.

'You shouldn't look for this girl. She will find you.'

'She's looking for me?'

'You have shared something.'

Kate shuddered.

'You have troubled the Mother. This is important.'

'The girl's mother?'

Santona shook her head, insistently. 'No, Rome's. *Mater Lachrymarum*. She has always been here, under and around us.'

'The Mother of Tears?' Kate remembered her Latin.

The *'ndrangheta* were disturbed. Red-orange trickles slipped through their muzzles onto much-stained lapels.

'There are tears everywhere,' the fortune-teller said. 'The stones of the city pour forth tears.'

'What does that mean?'

'Enough. This is all. You have been warned.'

More money was required to end the interview. Kate handed it over. She wondered if Cabiria would get a cut.

Santona shut her eyes and lay back on cushions. One of the *'ndrangheta* massaged her forehead, pickled fingers working away at her temples.

Cabiria tugged Kate's arm. They were required to leave.

A small crowd of the walking dead had gathered around the Ferrari. Marcello kept them back with pages of *Osservatore Romano*, rolled into torches and set alight. When one burned down, he'd shoo the ash away from the car and light another.

Morti viventi had stumbled out of their holes. These weren't under Santona's spell or muzzled. Some were red-mouthed, others hollow-chested and hungry. Many were feeble and fell apart with a kick, but some had prospered, perhaps through cunning, and retained strength in their limbs and jaws. They were dangerous.

Marcello was relieved to see her.

'They took a little boy last night,' Cabiria said. 'An orphan. He said his father was an American. He was fast but he got tired. They ate his stomach out.'

Kate wondered why Cabiria was telling her this.

'He has risen tonight. That is him. Dondi.'

Among the *morti viventi* was a child in baggy shorts, with an oversized American soldier's cap. As if he'd heard his name, he turned to look. Olive eyes glittered, but only with wetness.

His t-shirt was torn away from his scooped-out belly, and his mouth was chewing.

'They first try to eat themselves,' Cabiria said.

Kate felt sick.

As she walked through the loose crowd, *morti viventi* backed away from her. Whatever they craved didn't run in her veins.

A woman-creature sniffed at Cabiria, who squealed. Kate took the *morta viventa* by the chin, which detached with a snap. A long dog-tongue dangled. Embarrassed at what she had done, Kate gave her back her jawbone.

Nothing could be done for these revenants.

Were they indeed dead souls, all reason and person fled from reanimated carcasses? Or should she feel pity for the spark that might be left behind?

Perhaps, in the end, all undead became like this.

Was she the same person she'd been when alive? Or did she just mislead herself that she was? Had Katharine Reed flown off to Heaven or elsewhere, leaving behind a shell that could deceive itself into pretending to live out her life?

No.

She looked into the empty angel eyes of the newly risen Dondi and knew she was different from him. Kate still felt, still fought. If there was a kinship, it was more tragic. The *morti viventi* might have a distant awareness of their situation. Kate was weak-kneed with useless love, empathy with something that felt only hunger and pain.

'You can kill them easily,' Marcello said. 'Smash their heads. If their brains are broken, they stop moving.'

'That's not the same as being dead.'

He shrugged and lit up the sports pages.

'Please,' said Cabiria. 'He was my friend. When I was ill, he… he stole for me.'

'She wants you to kill it,' Marcello said.

'Like a sick dog. To be put out of his misery.'

Kate was crying. She hoped her tears were not bloody.

Cabiria hugged Dondi, who was only just shorter than her, and tried to cradle his head. He opened his mouth wide, to bite into her tiny breast.

Kate took him away from Cabiria and twisted his head around. The spine snapped, but it wasn't enough. Head on back-to-front, Dondi crawled toward them, jaws working like mandibles. He was drawn to living flesh, like a bee to pollen. His brain was purged of all that made him human, but there were still instincts.

Sobbing now, Kate found a stone and battered the dead boy's head to paste. The body twitched, but ran down. Whatever had remained seeped away.

It took her a moment to compose herself.

'We must go, Cabiria,' Kate said. 'Will you be safe?'

Cabiria smiled a one-sided smile and hitched up her shoulders, pulling her cardigan around her thin body.

'It's not far from here,' she said. 'My place.'

Kate gave her more money than was sensible. Cabiria looked at it sadly.

'Make me like you,' she asked. 'When I turn, I don't want to be a zombie. I want still to feel. To be Cabiria, not a woman-shaped dog. Not to be Dondi.'

Kate bit her lip.

'I can't,' she said.

What was she saving herself for? She'd found virginity a ridiculous inconvenience', and had lost hers twice (when she turned, her hymen had grown back again). She'd drunk the blood of children, had killed when she'd had to (and perhaps when she hadn't), had loved many.

Why had she not given the Dark Kiss? Why had she not turned any children-in-darkness?

She would have given Charles her blood, had offered to open her veins for him. Why not this warm orphan?

It wasn't a curse. It was an opportunity. She wasn't lost to God. She wasn't lost to herself. It wasn't death, it was life.

It would be simple.

But she couldn't.

And she couldn't explain.

Cabiria smiled sadly again and rubbed her fur collar against her bites.

'It doesn't matter.'

'*Ciao*, Cabiria.'

'Goodbye, Kate.'

Kate kissed Cabiria and got back into the Ferrari. Marcello drove away. Kate didn't want to look back at the bowed figure trudging away from the *morti viventi*, searching for the warmth of a fire. She didn't want to, but she did.

13

OLD LOVES

Geneviève could look after herself and Bond was trained for this sort of thing. Beauregard told himself he shouldn't worry about them. It was probably not worth Brastov's while to have them liquidated, as they said in these jargon-happy times. At the very least, Winthrop would insist on reprisals – murdering their top man in London, probably – and that was how cold wars heated up. Unless someone did something stupid, they'd be back before dawn.

Of course, there was always room for stupidity.

He remembered Geneviève hauling him out of Buckingham Palace in 1888, after they had delivered to the Queen the instrument she would use to free herself from Dracula, the silver scalpel of Jack the Ripper. He was badly wounded, and they were surrounded by the most dangerous creatures in Europe. They'd had help, of course, inside and outside the palace, but had only barely escaped.

He'd thought he was going to die. At thirty-five, he'd been better prepared for it than he was now.

'Charles, I can save you,' she'd whispered urgently, before biting into her wrist and bringing forth the bright blood. 'Charles, darling, drink… Turn, and live.'

That was the closest it had come. Her blood spilled on his lips. That alone had probably given him an extra twenty years of youth. It would've been so easy to drink. He didn't even know why he hadn't.

'You don't have to be like *him*,' she said, meaning Dracula.

'You don't have to be like *me*. You just have to live...'

He gurgled a farewell, 'I love you forever.'

And she repeated, 'Forever?'

Then, with dutiful anticlimax, he got better. He didn't die and return as a vampire. He just survived his wounds, got on with the work of booting Dracula out of Britain, rose in his profession, fought other battles, got old, got tired, tried to keep up, came to Rome...

Why?

Because of him. Dracula.

It was his duty to stay close to Dracula, to guard against his return to power. When he died, others – Winthrop, mostly, perhaps Geneviève – would take over the task, and perhaps keep *il principe* off the world stage forever.

Forever?

Was anything forever?

He had loved Geneviève in 1888, and he still loved her in 1959. That seemed like forever. Yet he'd never stopped loving Pamela. Loving the dead did not preclude loving the living.

This close to the end, he was still learning. Through reason and emotion, he'd settled an old quandary. Whatever might be true for most of vampirekind, Geneviève was alive in every sense that counted. And she was not alone. Kate too could grow to be that kind of elder.

He wasn't leaving the world to the walking dead.

Over the years, Geneviève had bled him, passionately at first, tactfully of late, never again pressing her blood upon him. Once, as Geneviève had offered herself to him, he had offered himself to Kate. During the First World War, when she was bled dry, he had given her his wrist and said, 'Go ahead, pretty creature, drink.'

Then, in 1918, Geneviève was on the other side of the world. At least part of the reason he let Kate bleed him was that he'd missed the sensation, the commingling and draining. He could admit that now. It did not feel like faithlessness.

The communion, renewed on occasion, had given him strength, and Kate too. To her he owed the most, for she'd always jostled for a place in his life, never quite coming to the front. If it hadn't been for… he and Kate might have…

As much as the Queen, Kate needed to be freed. To be free of *him*, of his distracting presence. Without him, she would grow. Perhaps, of their group, she was the only real hero, because everything was difficult for her.

The strong-arm creature had struck him across the face, probably no more than a swat. It didn't even hurt. But Beauregard's brains had taken a good shaking. The lights were going out.

All this thought of the past.

That was dying. This was what dying was like.

At last.

'I suppose I'm the last woman you expected to see, Charles.'

Pamela?

He opened his eyes and found he was still in his body, in his chair, in his flat.

'That French person is clearly an inadequate housekeeper.'

She stood at the doorway of the study, looking with distaste at the knocked-over bookcases, the scatter of *golem* detritus, and the disarrayed furniture.

Not Pamela.

'Penelope. Penny.'

Every time he saw her, it was a shock. Very slowly, she'd lost her girlishness, had sharpened and grown sleeker, into the image of her cousin, his wife. He understood why he had nearly married Penelope, and why that would have been a very great unkindness.

She had fed recently. He could tell from the colour in her cheeks and on her lips.

Had his neglect, as much as Godalming's blood, turned her into a predator?

She stepped into the room and right-sided some chairs.

'You are very old, Charles. I should have expected that.'

She picked up the bookcase and propped it in its place. Then, with undead swiftness, she put books back on the shelves, in any old order. She just wanted them off the floor, to look neat. He would have to rearrange them later.

No.

He wouldn't.

'I'm dying, Penny.'

She paused and looked at him. 'And whose fault is that, Charles? No one need die. Not really.'

'No, Penny. I'm dying *now*.'

A wash of expression disrupted Penelope's red-lipped primness. With her startled eyes, she looked like a little girl again, arranging her dolls because there was safety in tidiness, retreating from chaos that might hurt her.

'I am sorry, Charles.'

She was like a schoolmistress, conventionally sympathising with a charge whose tears are his own fault and who will have to learn to sleep in the bed he has made for himself.

'No, I'm sorry,' she continued, actually flustered. 'I didn't mean that. It's difficult for me to mean what I mean. That sounds absurd. It is. I'm not a monster. I've tried to be, but I'm not. I feel for you. As much as I can.'

He wanted to touch her, to lay a hand of comfort on her. But he could not lift a hand.

Penelope was in the middle of the room, away from all the walls, alone. Her hands rose to her face. Books fell from her grip, very slowly. He did not hear them thump on the carpet.

She uncovered her face. Her eyes were red, her fangs extended. She looked at once fiendish and sad, a little girl playing the devil.

'I don't know when I stopped wanting you to turn,' she said.

When they were engaged, she was a warm girl, desperate for them both to become vampires, to advance themselves in the world Dracula had shaped. She was dispassionate and matter-of-fact about it, unexcited by immortality or blood-drinking or all the senses of the night, but certain rising from the dead would secure invitations to the best houses, would excite the envy of friends and admirers.

Of all the vampires he had known living and undead, she had changed the most. She'd sought out Arthur Holmwood, Lord Godalming, and taken his blood, transforming herself.

Then, learning fast, she'd purged herself of her ambitions, her limitations. Beauregard remembered her discovering how much of a monster her father-in-darkness had been and vowing to be a monster herself.

For a while, she was mediaeval, glutted on stolen blood. She turned sons- and daughters-in-darkness, creating a coven for herself.

'They're all gone,' she said. 'My get. I turned my lovers, but the weakness of will that made them susceptible to me made them poor vampires. I was taught as a little Victorian girl to prize strength of character. But everything I have done, I've done through weakness.'

Beauregard wanted to contradict her, but couldn't.

'You want to speak and can't,' she said, sorry as much as triumphant. 'How I would have adored that in a husband, once upon a damned time. It was me, that time. You knew that.'

He did.

Penelope was his third vampire lover. Shortly before the turn of the century, with the Terror just over and the business of putting the country back together as yet undone, he'd been accosted one foggy night in Chelsea, dragged into a dark place between two buildings, and bitten. Raped, he supposed. He remembered sharp teeth savagely tearing open the wounds Geneviève had made gently, and thinking he was to be exsanguinated completely and left to die. There were still vampires like that in London in those days, stranded by the withdrawal of their King-Emperor, preying on the unwary.

'I had planned to take you to the point of death and make the offer of the Dark Kiss. I imagined you begging me for life-giving blood, then becoming my slave. By turning you, I could have had you, owned you. But you don't only take blood when you drink. You take all sorts of things. With the taste of you on my tongue, I knew you would have turned me down. As you turned down others. You would have died.'

He had recovered. He never even told Geneviève he suspected he knew who had assaulted him.

Vampire kisses were more than wounds. Some called those distinctive scabs the Seal of Dracula. Fangs weren't darts, but hooks. Invisible threads led back to the creature who bit you. And the line ran both ways.

Penelope took his hands and looked at him, close up. She was struggling to remain in control.

'Katie was never in the contest,' she said. 'And I could have bested the French person. You don't think so, but I could have. She's not a goddess. It was Pamela. If it hadn't been for her, we would have been together. You've never seen me as me. If you ever loved me, it's because I was her reborn, back from the grave. All your women die and come back.'

He tried to say he was sorry. He had known she was in pain, but had done nothing.

'Do you know why I went to Art? To seek the Dark Kiss?'

He shook his head. It was a supreme effort.

'Because he was the closest I could get to Dracula. I wanted to give myself to the vampire you hated most. I would have become one of the Prince Consort's mindless mistresses. If you wouldn't rule my life, then he would. He could have been like you. He is more like you than you know.'

All their lives had been a dance with Dracula. What had Kate called it, 'the Dracula *Cha Cha Cha*'?

'At last I have fulfilled my mother's expectations, Charles. I have made myself useful. I am part of a Royal Household. There are dreadful things about the position. This wedding is a nightmare. Princess Asa is a witch. Dracula will wake. It'll start all over again. The conquest. And I'll be part of it. You didn't stop him forever, you just set him back a century.'

That was what he was most afraid of. Was she being sincere or cruel?

'The world needs you, Charles,' she said.

For the last decade and a half, he had remained alert almost solely to keep close to the monster. When Dracula was found a seaside palace, in reward for his services in the war, Beauregard followed him to Italy. He had hoped they were both in permanent retirement, a slow slide to eternity.

'I need you too, but that's beside the point. I've fed tonight. A young man, an American. He thinks he's clever, but he's an amusement for all that.'

She unbuttoned her blouse. Underneath, she wore a black brassiere. Her white bosom still bore the circular scars left years ago by leeches.

'I'm going to finish what I started, Charles.'

She drew a fingernail across her breast. A line of blood welled. Bright scarlet, with a coppery tang.

Perhaps this was for the best – to have no choice. To be forced to life. He could not struggle. He could barely move. Penelope would suckle him into a new life.

'Penny?' someone said, from across the room.

Penelope closed her blouse, flushed with embarrassment.

He felt the moment slipping away. And was not sorry.

The newcomer was Kate. He could imagine how upset she must be, on several levels, to walk into such a scene.

'Penelope Churchward,' Kate said, sternly. 'What exactly do you think you're doing?'

Penelope stood straight, determined to see it out through *hauteur*. Blood seeped through the thin material of her blouse. She looked across the room at Kate, eyes burning, fangs sharp.

'You know exactly what I'm doing, Katie. It is what you, or the other person, should have done long ago. Very well: if your consciences bother you about saving a life, I shall step in. I have no such encumbrance. We can all debate about what a monstrous harpie I am after I've given Charles what he needs to live.'

Good God, she even sounded like Pamela now.

He remembered Pamela at the last, ordering the doctor to let her die and save the child. If Beauregard hadn't hesitated, hadn't urged the incompetent butcher to save both, perhaps his son would have lived. And perhaps the sight of him would have given Pam heart, forced her to rally, to strangle death. Perhaps.

'Penny, I know how you feel,' Kate said, eyes watering. 'But you *can't*...'

Kate stepped forward. Her fangs extended too.

'Katie, me darlin',' Penelope said, in the imitation brogue she had used to make fun of her friend when they were children, 'if I have to, I'll fight you. I admit you're not the drip we used to think you, but I was stronger than you in the nursery and I can *destroy* you now.'

He tried to protest.

They hissed in each other's faces.

'Yes,' Penelope said. 'I can take you.'

From the doorway, Geneviève said, 'And what about me, new-born? Can you take me?'

Penelope turned, snarling.

14

DITCHED – ITALIAN STYLE

Tom thought he might be dead. Or worse. Turned. He was very cold, and so depleted of blood that his fingers and toes tingled. He had blacked out propped in a chair, near the coat-rack. His knees had buckled, and when he woke, he was curled up behind the coats, shivering.

What had Penelope been thinking?

Actually, he knew all too well. She'd stopped seeing him as a person, and started seeing him as a convenience. Most people treated most other people like that most of the time. He certainly did.

He had been afraid she would suck his mind empty.

If she knew about Dickie Fountain, she might kill him on principle, assuming he planned to do to her what he had done to him. That wouldn't have been fair. Penny was different, and deserved different treatment. Tom was involved with her for what he could get, he admitted that. He did not necessarily plan to destroy her.

Though…

He stood up, unsteady. He must have looked as pale as a ghost.

Music still played. 'Papaverie Papare'. Some of the group he had come in with were still here. The Dubrovna chit wasn't getting far in putting the moves on Kent. Tom looked about for Penny, but couldn't find her.

A waiter was ready for him with a tonic, a thick English fruit drink dosed with vitamins and iron. Vimto. He drank it down, not minding the taste, and asked for more. It was provided.

It took a certain genius, he recognised, to spot a gap in the market and fill it. Though never advertised explicitly as such, Vimto was what the living lovers of vampires drank to get their strength back up again after a bleeding.

He had no idea if it did any good.

He was told that the signora had ordered the drink for him before leaving.

That showed some consideration.

His bites itched and it was all he could do to prevent himself scratching them raw. He seemed to have lost substance. His clothes hung loose on him. There was an insect buzz in his ears.

A third Vimto at least got liquid back into him.

What now?

On the street, among ruins, Tom let the brief chill of the dead of night clear his head. The cool wouldn't last. He smoked a cigarette and tried to ignore the feeding and fumbling taking place all around in the dark. Mr and Mrs Addams had forced Max Brock against a column, and were furiously sucking at several bites. Mrs Addams was soothing the poet with threats about leeching away all his talent. Max Brock was looking up at the stars, at a temporary and merciful loss for words. Tom hoped the Addamses had killed the opera singer first. It was important to get one's priorities right.

'Ciao, Tom. You have escaped from Penelope, then?'

It was Marcello, the Italian reporter who was always hanging around, who'd been at the airport when Count Kernassy and what-was-her-name had arrived, who'd been there when that strange Irish dead girl saw the Count being murdered.

'Other way round, old fellow.'

Marcello looked drained too, but had no obvious bites. His cheeks were sunken. The reflective lenses of his dark glasses suggested the empty eye sockets of a skull.

'You look as if you've had a bad night of it,' Tom said.

'You too.'

'I wouldn't argue with that. Damn all dead bitches.'

Marcello bummed a cigarette and lit up, exhaling with weary anger.

'I have been to Hell and back,' the Italian announced.

'I didn't make it back.'

Marcello laughed.

'I would gladly exchange you Signorina Churchward for Signorina Reed.'

'Little Irish corpse?'

It took Marcello a moment to catch on. '*Si*. Little Irish corpse. She has a grip, that one. Will not let go. We went to I Cessati Spiriti.'

Tom whistled.

'I don't suppose either of you chaps could lend a hand,' said a deep, bone-tired voice.

It was a dead man, in a suit that had suffered. He'd plainly been in a fight. Several fights. Wounds in his clothes looked like bullet holes, and one sleeve was skinned away completely.

'I think we've something in common. I'm back from Hell and abandoned by a vampire girl too.'

He took a few steps out of the dark and collapsed.

Marcello looked at Tom over the dead man's back. He shrugged.

15

SUNRISE

Now, she was prepared to rip off Penelope's head and stuff it into her chest cavity. After fighting her way out of Brastov's lair, dragging Bond behind her, and enduring an anxious trudge back to the Via Eudosiana, Geneviève was not in a mood to deal gently with an uppity nosferatu nuisance like Penelope Churchward.

Kate faltered, stepping back, allowing Penelope to hiss at Geneviève. The Englishwoman's blood was up, her fangs were out and her eyes were wide. She might have frightened an infant who has never seen Mummy pull a face, and was probably strong-willed enough to overwhelm her warm prey. But she didn't have the mettle to cow an elder.

Geneviève didn't pop her claws or teeth.

She'd fought enough during the night, and bled several of the Russians. She would not be frenzied, she would be purposeful.

Penelope stepped forward, but Kate put a hand on her shoulder, holding her back. Kate nodded toward Charles, who was in his bath chair, barely alive.

The first pink of dawn slipped into the room.

From Charles's face, Geneviève knew this was the last day. An icicle transfixed her heart.

She remembered her first sight of him, in a crowded room in 1888, at an inquest. He had seemed untouched by the squalor and violence all around, the only man in London prepared to do something, even at extreme cost, to make things better. Later, she learned he wasn't a *Boy's Own Paper* good-fellow, no muscular Christian hero, but a man who tried always to do the right thing even when there were no right things to do.

If men like him had stayed in fashion – if they'd ever really been in fashion – this century would have been happier. Charles had refused to accept Dracula as his Lord, and had never let himself become like Dracula in his attempts to best the King Vampire. Edwin Winthrop and Hamish Bond, his successors, had learned too much from their enemy, had too much of Dracula in them.

There was blood on Penelope's blouse. Her own.

'She was trying…' Kate explained.

'I know what she was trying to do.'

The anger in Penelope's eyes swirled and broke apart. She was frustrated and afraid, like everybody else. For a tiny moment, Geneviève wanted to hug her, not kill her.

Then the idiot ruined it.

'He must be turned,' Penelope said. 'He is too far gone to be sensible about it. One of us must become his mother-in-darkness.'

Geneviève went directly to Charles and knelt before him. His eyes were still open. She felt the ebb of him, dwindling, disappearing. But he was still thinking, still determined.

With great effort, he lifted a hand to her face and into her hair. She kissed his palm, her teeth against his flesh. She tasted him but did not break the skin.

Even now, it wasn't too late.

And even now, he wasn't afraid to go on.

He'd often said he had nothing against vampires, but just didn't want to be one. Though she'd long ago got over being ashamed of what she was, she understood.

Geneviève blamed the first dead woman in his life, the one who hadn't come back. Pamela.

She thought the offer into his mind.

'Do you want me to?'

A tiny, gracious, grateful shake of his head told her.

Tears started in her eyes.

Penelope and Kate came near, anger subsided, children

again. At least there would be no cat-fighting.

Geneviève swallowed her resentment of the intrusion. She had always had to share Charles, with duty, with memory, with others who had a better claim.

She'd lived four centuries before Charles. In that time, no one had come remotely as close to her heart, not her father-in-darkness, not those she had bled pale. She might live another four centuries, or more, after Charles.

Sunlight spilled over the carpet, creeping toward them. She should warn Penelope, who was sensitive to the sun.

Geneviève kissed Charles's lips.

She couldn't blame his death on anyone, not Penelope, or Bond, or Brastov's goon, or Edwin Winthrop, or Prince Dracula. If they had disturbed his last days, then it was her fault for letting them near him, and his for not being able to concentrate on his own life to the exclusion of the world.

She had failed to persuade him to accept the Dark Kiss. But he let her know that she had not failed with him.

His blood sang inside her.

'I love you forever,' he whispered, too soft for the others to hear.

'Forever?' she prompted.

'Forever,' he confirmed.

The sun rose up and bathed them all in stinging warmth. By the time it became unbearable, Charles was cold.

Geneviève knelt again, arranging his blanket around his legs, putting his hands into his lap, brushing back his hair, closing his eyes. It was like playing with a doll. Whatever Charles Beauregard had been was gone.

She stood, walked away from Charles, and snapped a slap across Penelope's face, fetching the Englishwoman off balance, leaving an angry red mark.

'That's for what you did in 1899.'

Penelope didn't protest, didn't make fists. Something was gone out of her.

The room was orange with dawnlight, and hazy.

One of them had to cry, so the others could comfort her, could cry themselves. Geneviève had thought it would be Kate, but it was her. From deep inside came sobs that racked her whole body. Penelope, the handprint fading fast, hesitated and stepped forward to embrace her, to whisper soothing nothings. They hugged and cried together, then broke apart and extended arms to Kate, who was more bewildered than bereft.

Kate joined them, letting flow her own tears. They huddled together on a divan, blood and water on their faces, sobbing not for what was lost but for what must stay behind. The room was filled with light that made each random dust mote a spark. The dust danced around them all.

PART THREE

L'ECLISSE

NOTICE OF DEATH FROM *THE TIMES* OF LONDON, AUGUST 1ST, 1959

Charles Pennington Beauregard, 105, died peacefully yesterday in Rome, *writes Miss Katharine Reed.* A distinguished diplomat whose services to his country were rarely recognised in his lifetime, Beauregard was, in a lengthy career, variously attached to the Indian Civil Service, the Foreign Office, the Royal Air Force, and Lord Ruthven's wartime Government of National Unity 'think tank'. He was a lifelong member and sometime official of the Diogenes Club of Pall Mall, a private institution that remains club of choice for many public servants.

Born in India in 1853, son of Major Marcus Aurelius Beauregard of the Fourth Bombay Native Infantry and the former Miss Sophie Pennington of Loxley Barrett, Charles Beauregard was educated at Dulwich College and Merton College, Oxford. Briefly married (1882–3) to the former Miss Pamela Churchward, of Chelsea, he had no issue. He twice refused a knighthood. His few publications include two books of verse, *The Matter of Britain* and *The Britain of Matter.* He will be buried privately in the Protestant Cemetery in Rome, final resting place of Keats and Shelley.

16

KATE IN LOVE

Since the funeral, Kate had been on a blood bender, drunk with red thirst. She'd been back to her *pensione* at least twice in the past week, but had not slept. Even after feeding and lovemaking, she couldn't drop off, tormented by restless thoughts and persistent memories. Marcello, however, went out the second he was spent, sunk into a torpor deeper than any vampire lassitude. When they were in bed together, he took off his dark glasses but left on his socks. Very romantic, she supposed. Perhaps that was how Italian men won their reputation as great lovers.

They were in his apartment, a modern box in a suburb that was a mess of concrete and glass bunkers set down in featureless grasslands. At its edges, Rome was as distinct from the countryside as a cliff is from the sea.

The flat was fashionably under-decorated, with little furniture and none of the reference books or piles of periodicals Kate expected. Her own rooms were in danger of filling up entirely with paper. Marcello didn't even own a typewriter. He dictated all his articles, mostly delivering notes rewrite people worked up into actual prose. One room contained nothing but a white dial telephone – the famous *telefono bianco*, once a touchstone of luxury in Italy – on the floor, long golden cord snaking across bare boards.

Though Kate knew Marcello body and soul, inside-out on the deepest level, she was still ignorant of a great many details about his life. She'd found out his surname at some point, but presently it escaped her. Where was he from? Were his parents still alive? None of that mattered. He was a for-the-moment person, a present-tense man, just right for that atomic-age sense of impermanence. He knew as little about her, but had opened himself entirely.

She lay naked next to him as he snored slightly, feeling the swell of fresh blood in her face. It was as if she were wearing a fleshy, pulsating mask. Bloated with his blood, she feared she was growing careless, taking far too much from this one lover.

The light fixture above the bed swung like a gibbet. Was it moving or was her head swimming? It didn't matter. She wasn't such a fool as to believe nothing mattered. It was just that nothing mattered for now. Not a fig. Charles was dead and buried. She had to stay behind.

The fact of his death, a sunburst in her mind, had blotted everything else out. She'd planned to help Geneviève with the funeral arrangements and any legal complications, but had instead fled, sought out Marcello, frankly overpowered him, and made him distract her.

By the time of the funeral, she was in a fog of blood.

Had Edwin Winthrop come over from England? She thought so, but hadn't been able to connect the kindly old man with the clipped white moustache with the cold young maniac she remembered from the First World War.

There were few other mourners. Marcello had propped her up, and she made love to him near Shelley's ashes. All of the poet but his heart was buried in Rome. That was how she felt, too.

At first, Marcello was shocked, perhaps even unwilling, but she set out to enslave him and, rather surprisingly, pulled off the trick. Without Charles's civilising influence, she might grow into a proper vampire, a monster of the old school.

Marcello was relieved that she was leaving the Crimson Executioner alone. There had been no more jaunts to I Cessati Spiriti, no more questions asked of suspect persons in threatening locales. The more she became wrapped up in him, the less the big mysteries meant. There had been no new murders, no new clues. The paparazzi had taken dozens of photographs of Sylvia Koscina as Medea, and the material on Malenka was filed away to be forgotten. Other sensations would come along.

She shivered with fullness. Her heart coursed. Colours and shapes floated on her eyes. Her skin felt stretched tight, on the point of bursting. She had drunk so much to glut her red thirst that it came alive again and wheedled inside her, spurring her to action. Her fangs prickled in her mouth, razor-edges cutting her gums as they slid out of their sheaths. There was a little dental sensation, on the edge of tingling, jabbing over the line into pain. Delicious pain.

She wanted to feed again.

With a snort, Marcello turned onto his back and settled between pillows. Crescent grazes on his neck and chest, and other places under the sheets, trickled a little. Her bite marks were all over him. He was growing pale under his tan.

It might even be love. They had shared so much.

And Charles was gone – she was free to love.

She thought she was in synchronisation with Marcello's beating heart, his gently dreaming mind, his worn-out-by-love body. She'd cut through his pose of indifference and tapped into the real person underneath. There was kindliness in his makeup, passion under his cynicism, secret hurts she could winkle out and ease, and a warm strength that would keep her going.

He wanted to write real books, she knew – novels, history, philosophy. He admired Lankester Merrin profoundly, not just for his wisdom but for his prose. She could encourage him, nag him into giving up worthless-tat journalism, gently force him to do real work. She'd buy him a typewriter, keep others away from him while he wrote, modestly accept the dedication of his first masterpiece 'To Kate, without whom…'

God, yes.

His eyes twitched under their lids, dream-movements.

He always wore his dark glasses until the last possible moment, kissing her with them on. Their frames would tangle with her spectacles. When there was nothing else between them, he'd slip off her glasses and then his own, propping them intertwined next to the statue of the Madonna on his bedside table.

When they made love, his naked face was a blur to her. It was a quirk of bloodline that becoming a vampire changed her in many ways but left her eyesight as useless as it had been when she was warm.

She didn't know what colour his eyes were. It didn't matter. She had a sense of what lay behind them.

Slipping under the thin sheet, pressing herself against his body, feeling his warm skin with her cool belly and breasts, she tried to fit herself against Marcello as if they were the complementary halves of a puzzle. It wasn't comfortable, so she slid up over his hip, stretching one leg between his, draping an arm across his chest, hand creeping into his armpit and up behind his shoulder.

Marcello stirred in his sleep.

His heartbeat was a steady thump in her head. Like an addict, like a pathetic thing, she needed to complete the circuit, to become one creature with her lover. She opened her mouth wide and found one of the recent bites, in the meaty part of his chest, beside a lightly haired nipple. Her sharp teeth sank easily into the grooves they had made. She worked the wound with her tongue, pressing until blood welled up into her throat.

She felt the *rush* in her heart and head.

The blood made her forget.

As she drank, Marcello rose from the depths of his swoon and ran hands down her back, massaging her waist and bottom. She humped her middle up a little, tenting the sheets, and he fitted his penis into her.

She guided their rhythm with her mouth and hips, suckling blood and coaxing semen in tidal cycles. After all these years, she couldn't remember what lovemaking had been like as a warm girl – she'd only managed it the once, with her father-in-darkness, Mr Harris – but turning certainly increased the range of pleasures she could give and receive.

Marcello screamed and his entire body stretched taut, as if all his sinews were piano wires. She thought momentarily that she'd killed him, but the blood pouring into her mouth was rich and alive.

He collapsed under her, dragged down into unconsciousness.

She wanted more of him, and gnawed his chest almost to the bone.

If she kept at it, she would truly forget.

17

GENEVIÈVE IN MOURNING

She didn't know how long she should stay on in Rome. There was the business of Charles's things, making sure they were dispersed according to his will. As executrix, she'd have to go to London soon, though she didn't think she would stay there either. Once her duties were discharged, her best bet would be to go to a country she didn't associate with him. There were still a few corners of the world where she had never lived – Samoa; Tierra del Fuego; the Pacific North-West; Swansea, Wales.

The apartment was empty. There was a silence in her head where there had been a constant whisper. For the first time in years, Geneviève was alone. The crying lasted only a few days. Then came the chill. This time, grief bit like a trap.

Kate was no help. The poor girl had gone completely to pieces, and ran off with a warm Italian body. Surprisingly, Penelope was considerate, making telephone calls that eased the practicalities of interment. She took it upon herself to send telegrams to Charles's surviving nephew, himself too old to travel to the funeral, and his onetime protegé Edwin Winthrop, who had made the journey across Europe with his companion, Miss Catriona Kaye.

Winthrop said he thought Charles should have been buried in Westminster Abbey with full state honours. Geneviève was unprepared to find Winthrop turned into a handsome, kindly old man who plainly hero-worshipped his just-dead friend, and was stricken by his not-unexpected passing.

The funeral was a tiny ceremony. Charles had outlived his warm generation. However, telegrams had come from all over the world, including apparently sincere tributes from the Queen's Household – which had a very long memory – and Sir Winston Churchill. There was even a hand-delivered, black-edged card of conventional condolence signed with a thick-nibbed 'D'.

She sorted the telegrams and cards. They would go into the last of the many packets of papers she was to turn over to Winthrop for the secret archive of the Diogenes Club. Among the documents was a transcript of the phonograph diaries of Dr John Seward, covering the period between 1885 and 1888. She shuddered, remembering the discovery of those wax cylinders, the rush through the fog to a tiny room thick with dead blood. The Seward papers would be sealed for centuries. The open presence of the very long-lived in the world meant that files which would once have been shut up for a scant hundred years were now *sub rosa* perhaps forever.

Charles had been meticulous. Everything was in order. She didn't really need to go through the papers, but this was the last of him. She wanted to keep something for herself. If only memories.

A few pages, evidently surviving fragments of a book-length manuscript, contained stirring paragraphs on duty and sacrifice, the need to shuck one's individual humanity in the service of humankind. Were it not in German, she'd have thought the manuscript was about Charles. Reading on, finding an account of an aerial battle, she deduced that the pages were from a ghosted autobiography of Manfred, Frieherr von Richthofen, vampire air ace of the First World War. She wondered who'd written them, and how they'd come to be of interest to Charles. Winthrop had been involved in the destruction of the so-called Bloody Red Baron, she knew. Doubtless, the archivists of the Diogenes Club would know in which puzzle to put these odd pieces.

There was much more, including highly sensitive material that revealed a good deal of the secret history of the twentieth century. She found scribbled notes, in Charles's handwriting, for Edward VIII's abdication speech. That had been a major constitutional crisis. Since the death of King Victor in 1922, no vampire had sat on the throne of Great Britain, but Edward's fiancée, Mrs Wallis Simpson, intended that they should both turn and rule the country in perpetuity. Evidently, it was Charles who'd informed the King that if he became a vampire, he would be legally dead, and the rule of succession would be invoked.

It was an important precedent in the United Kingdom. In questions of inherited position, turning vampire was equivalent to death. Lord Ruthven, Prime Minister then as now, was forced to renounce his title and buy it back at great cost from an impoverished collateral descendant. Elders who styled themselves 'Count' or 'Baron' were quietly levelled to 'Mr' at Dover or Heathrow. Edward and Wallis, nosferatu together, ruled over their estates in Bermuda, and a warm woman sat on the throne of Great Britain.

She would have read on, picking through secrets, but her appetite was glutted. Every note she found from Charles, every scrap he had saved, was like a mocking message. It was as if he had escaped from her.

A week ago, she was prepared to kill Penelope to prevent her forcing the Dark Kiss on Charles. Now she wanted to dig out her own heart for failing to turn him herself. She recognised that as a selfish impulse. But was it wrong to want someone you loved to live forever?

Charles hadn't *wanted* to die. But he had accepted death.

Had she had enough of life? When she was born, few women lived past their twenties. She had lived so far past. How much future could she bear?

Since Sputnik, many children wanted to be spacemen when they grew up. It was likely, if Earth survived the next hundred years without nuclear self-immolation, that humanity would spread to the stars. It might be an option for her, a wonder-journey to Jupiter and beyond. She had read an article by Arthur C. Clarke in *Time* magazine that suggested vampires like her, elderly enough to be stable, would be ideal for long-haul space flights, more resilient than the norm, long-lived enough to undertake voyages that might last human generations. There were even ways round the problem of feeding.

She was laughing. Her train of thought had started with the question of whether she should leave Rome to escape her memories. Now she was seriously thinking of leaving the Solar System. How would she look in one of those Dale Arden numbers from the funny papers, with a fishbowl helmet and a transparent leotard? Real spacesuits looked less like harem outfits.

Charles had been interested, even as a centenarian, in the possibilities of space travel. On his desk when he died was a report from the director of the British Rocket Group, annotated in Charles's hand. They were both struggling to keep the moon project on a scientific rather than military basis. How many other causes would suffer for the lack of Charles's acuity and influence? She made a mental note to send a contribution to CND.

Using Charles's wheelchair seemed indecent – she must find a hospital or an old people's home to donate it to – which meant she had to perch on a kitchen stool to work at his desk, the only suitable surface for the sorting-through she had to do. Her back and shoulders ached from the long hours.

She had promised Winthrop she'd have the material for the Diogenes Club boxed up by the end of the week, to be shipped to London in the diplomatic bag. The Beauregard Papers warranted a personal escort, though her malicious suggestion that Hamish Bond be given that position had been curtly declined. The spy had appeared at the funeral, but had not met her eyes.

She climbed off the stool and walked across the study, stepping around the carpet on which Charles had died, wandering up to the wall of bookshelves. Charles had been an inveterate annotator, which meant some volumes ought to be included with his papers. His library was a personal bequest to Winthrop, not the Club. She supposed she could trust Winthrop to turn over anything which should be part of the Papers.

A book stood out. She took it down. *Dracula*, by Bram

Stoker. This was the first official publication, of 1912. With a memoir by the author and an Introduction by no less than Miss Katharine Reed. Geneviève had first read the book, which was completed about 1897, in an underground edition, one of the many that circulated during the Terror. The manuscript was smuggled out of the concentration camp in Sussex where Prince Consort Dracula confined his enemies in England, and Kate – then a heroine of the underground – arranged for broadsheets of the text to be run off on the presses of the *Pall Mall Gazette*. The novel had been a rallying point of the resistance during the hard years after Queen Victoria's death, when Dracula was trying to cling to the throne of Great Britain with increasing brutality and popular rebellion was spreading.

It was a curious novel, Geneviève had thought then. Stoker had imagined a world in which Dracula did not rise to power in Great Britain but was defeated by the foes he had bested in reality, Professor Van Helsing and his followers. Knowing something of the real histories, she was moved by his portraits of Mina Harker, Dr Seward and Arthur Holmwood as they might have been had they found the strength to resist. Presented as a collection of documents and diaries – some authentic, like Jonathan Harker's journal of his trip to Transylvania and Mina Harker's remembrances of Lucy Westenra – the book was designed to feel like a work of history, an account of events that had happened rather than events which should have happened.

The conventions of 'imaginary history' in literature dated back at least to Louis Geoffroy's *Napoléon et la conquête du monde*, a novel she'd read in 1836 that concerned a Buonaparte who triumphed at Waterloo. But Stoker, civil servant turned theatrical fixer turned revolutionary, popularised the 'if things had been otherwise' narrative. Since *Dracula*, there had been any number of novels on the theme: George Orwell's *Big Brother*, an account of a grey and grisly Britain in a world where a Communist regime came to power in 1917; Sarban's *The Sound of His Horn*, about a Nazi victory in the Second World War; and Richard Matheson's *I Am Legend*, in which

Dracula chose to migrate across the Atlantic and invade America, creating a world in which the last warm man was surrounded by an entire population of the undead. Subtlest of these works was Anthony Powell's *A Dance to the Music of Time* novel-sequence. Geneviève had been halfway through the fourth novel, *At Lady Molly's*, before she realised the change Powell had wrought in his fictional world. He had imagined the history of the twentieth century as it might have been without vampires.

She opened *Dracula*. It was signed to Charles, by Kate. How was Kate? She had been in a bad way at the funeral, puffed up with too much blood, befuddled by grief.

Stoker was dead by the time his book could be openly published. There was a falling out between Kate and his widow, Florence. This edition, with Kate's never-reprinted Introduction, was a valuable curio, but it also had other significance.

She decided to keep it. She knew Charles wouldn't mind.

The book fell open. An oblong of card and a folded paper had been put between its pages. The card was the invitation to Dracula's Engagement Ball, two nights from now. The paper was a memo, written sometime in Charles's last two days, maybe on the day before his death.

An alliance, cemented by marriage, between the House of Dracula and the House of Vajda will establish, for the first time this century, a standard under which vampire elders can gather, probably in pursuit of temporal political power. Already, many of the great fortunes of Europe are in undead hands. If Dracula returns in triumph to Transylvania, an empire will rise again. Princess Asa Vajda is a tyrant manqué, evidently with ambitions to become the nosferatu Eva Perón. The unknown factor in this alliance is, as ever, Dracula himself. From close study, Edwin, I should say that our Count has...

* * *

The memo was unfinished. There was nothing in it Winthrop did not know. But since it was obviously intended for him, she would pass it on. He'd returned to London, but Bond was still in Rome and could probably be prevailed upon, out of gratitude for his life, to become a postman.

She wondered what observation Charles had formed but not set down.

She tapped her teeth with the invitation. Should she go? The last time she'd been invited – with Charles – by Dracula to a palace, an empire had fallen and there'd been a great deal of fire, bloodshed, and kerfuffle. Of course, this was likely to be less interesting.

She had the dress, though. Suitable for funerals and weddings. Only worn once.

18

FREGENE

Outside the city, Kate encouraged Marcello to let the Ferrari loose. It wasn't a long drive but the roads widened enough to allow the car to get up speed. She wanted to travel fast. Wind hammered her face, pressing her swollen skin with invisible fingers, jamming behind her spectacles into her open eyes.

Her head didn't clear. She told him to go faster. Ever the willing slave, he obliged. Sheep scattered. It was hilarious. A shepherd's curses were lost in their wake.

They rounded a corner. The Palazzo Otranto stood on its promontory peak, suitably ancient and sinister. A gentle slope led down to the beach. For the Engagement Ball, Dracula had declared a holiday. The town was like a carnival, full of pale people in elaborate costumes.

She ordered Marcello to cruise along the seafront. This was not like Brighton or Blackpool. Vampire women exposed dead-white bodies in swimming costumes that would never get wet. Servants scuttled along with parasols the size of the big dish at Jodrell Bank, keeping circles of safe shadow over their mistresses. There was music and dancing and feeding and drinking. Kate was one of them, a vampire bitch with a human lapdog, crab-crawling across the beach, teeth and claws clicking and clacking, leaving a snail-trail of blood. All faces were skulls, cheekbones and teeth gleaming, eye-sockets empty. All voices were shrill, shrieks of cruel laughter. The sun bleached everything to the colour of sand.

Marcello was afraid of her, could deny her nothing. That made a change. Usually, Kate was the person denying nothing, empty when abandoned. For once, she was free to think only of herself, her desires and dreams. To hang with the rest of the world.

She vaulted out of the Ferrari, limber with the quickness of the blood in her, and landed like a cat, even in heels. She had found a black and tiny Piero Gherardi gown and tossed away most of her *lire* on it. She wore it with scarlet scarves that matched her hair.

People on the beach took notice of her. Some boys who were hauling a sea creature out of the surf turned to whistle. She posed like Malenka, wind whipping her scarves like squid tentacles. She wanted to roar, like a lady panther. The boys throbbed with blood. If they came near her, she would rip them open with love.

Marcello parked the car, and came after her, one hand cupped around a cigarette. He was being impatient, practical, hustling her on, telling her not to pay attention to the sea-boys. He was acting like her father.

She slapped him, to teach him a lesson. Infuriatingly, he gave her a 'well, if that's how it is' shrug. The slap was a mistake, too obvious. She exerted her control over him, reaching out through his blood, turning his arteries into puppet strings, jerking him to her, inflicting a sharp kiss on his mouth. He surrendered, which irritated her more.

She was tiring of him. No, of this. Her head was spinning. She had been in this whirl for days now. Weeks?

She didn't want to think of loss. She nipped Marcello's neck and scraped some of his blood onto her tongue. The rush made things better again, for the moment.

The boys cheered Marcello. He managed a smile and a wave.

Kate had his complete attention. But he held back something. He surrendered his blood and his body, but a ring of ice surrounded his heart. She knew what he was thinking, but rarely what he was feeling. He must love her. By his actions, by his words, she could tell. His love was a cloak, a protection. She might not want or need it, but it was there.

The boys dragged their sea monster up the beach and dropped it in tribute to her. It was a living wing, with a long, barbed tail. A single eye, lashless and round, looked up at her, clouding over. What did this dying thing see?

She knelt in the fine sand – careful of her dress – and touched the cold, scaly skin. The creature was aflap with the last of life. Its wriggling, departing spirit disturbed Kate, brushing past her as it fled. Any movement now was mechanical.

'It's dead,' a boy said. 'You can tell by the eye.'

The eye was a white marble.

A spell of dread passed over Kate's mind. She had missed something important.

This was not what she wanted. She was at the seaside, on holiday. She wanted Punch and Judy, Brighton rock, cream teas. She wanted to find fossils, messages in bottles, driftwood carved into exotic shapes. She wanted to be a girl again, at Lyme Regis, wondering what it was her father wouldn't tell her about the gaunt, beautiful woman who stood at the end of the Cobb, gazing out to sea. All these years later, she knew exactly what that nameless woman had been feeling. Love and loss.

Cars passed through the town in a sombre procession. The passengers were the more distinguished guests of *il principe* and his fiancée, the fashionable and the fierce.

The palazzo cast its shadow on the sea. Kate looked up, shading her eyes from the setting sun. That was where the Devil lived these days.

It was important that she look on her host's face. In all these years, in this century of the 'Dracula *Cha Cha Cha*', she'd never met him, never seen him. Once, he'd put a price on her head, declaring her a dangerous enemy of the state. But then he had been overwhelmed by a rising tide of more powerful enemies and had (she supposed) forgotten her. She'd felt his touch, though: in the silver sword-scrape sustained in an escape from the Carpathian Guard during the Terror, and the iron treads of the German tank that rolled over her in the trenches. With Charles gone, she was alone in the world with

Dracula. They should meet. Perhaps, if things were settled between them, they could both be free. It would all be over.

The uncertain future frightened her. When the music stopped, when the *cha cha cha* was over, what then?

The blood wasn't burning in her so much now. Blocks of bright colour still overlaid everything, and penumbrae fuzzed around living or moving things. But her mind was coming in to land, plummeting almost.

'Take me to the palace,' she ordered.

Marcello gave a nasty little bow and offered her his arm.

19

THE PARTY

She wore black velvet. The gown left her shoulders bare but swept to the floor like a train. It was heavy, but Geneviève could carry the weight. An unappreciated advantage of vampirism was the ability to dress spectacularly but comfortably in outfits that would choke, constrict, strangle, or hobble a warm woman. She didn't wear the veiled hat that went with the dress, which she had needed at the funeral.

Since the funeral, she hadn't been out of the apartment for more than an hour. As she left, she picked up Charles's invitation as well as her own. It might be amusing to give it to a random stranger, and let them enjoy *il principe*'s hospitality. Then again, the welcome of Dracula had occasionally proved fatal. He was probably over his craze for nailing guests' hats to their skulls or impaling lieutenants who complained about the stench of the dying, but it was best not to take chances.

The invitation specified that transport would be provided to Fregene if she were to be at the Piazza del Quirinale between six and ten o'clock. It transpired that a fleet of cars was going back and forth to and from the Palazzo Otranto for guests who chose not to make their own way.

She was sharing a Daimler with people she didn't know. Jeremy Prokosch, a Hollywood producer with crimson glasses and a little red book for jotting down ideas; Dorian Gray, the Italian actress not the English libertine; Dr Hichcock, one of *il principe*'s personal physicians, and his silent wife, one of the many women of fashion who made herself up to look as much like Princess Asa as possible; and an unhappy-looking hollow-cheeks named Collins.

Geneviève would have been interested in talking with Collins, a rare American vampire, but Prokosch delivered a showbiz monologue. Apparently, he'd just missed being in the car before, with Orson Welles, who was playing Argo in the *Argonauts* film, and John Huston, whom Prokosch wanted to hire for a movie of *I Am Legend* with Charlton Heston. She hadn't seen any of the films the producer had made. They were mostly about orgies, but based on classical (out of copyright) sources.

'The best way to keep costs down on a costume picture is to cut out the costumes,' Prokosch said.

Collins tried hard to smile at her.

'Have you ever done any modelling?' the producer asked.

'Not recently,' she said.

By the time the car pulled up outside the Palazzo Otranto, night had fallen. Geneviève felt as if she'd been clubbed over the head with a rolled-up copy of *Variety*. There was a delay in escaping from the Daimler because the official door-openers were trying to prise Orson Welles out of the car in front. Welles, bearded and enormous, couldn't stop laughing as he wriggled like Winnie the Pooh stuck in Rabbit's hole. Finally, John Huston stabbed a lit cigar against Welles's enormous backside, and the spherical genius was ejected like a ball from a cannon.

Prokosch produced a script from under his cummerbund and scuttled off after Huston. Geneviève wished him 'boffo boxo' and stepped out of the Daimler. She looked up at the palazzo. Very nice. More baroque than gothic. Swirly columns and uncontrolled ivy.

'It looks like a big onion,' she remarked, to no one in particular.

She joined the human stream flowing toward the huge doors. A cadre of warriors, with fur-trimmed armour and teeth like cashew nuts, checked invitations and waved in the guests. Paparazzi crowded around the Tartars but were discouraged from getting in the way. Broken cameras, indeed broken photographers, littered the driveway. She saw a pest dashed against a solid-stone wall.

Her invitation passed muster and she was allowed in. She drifted along a corridor which opened into a ballroom the size of a cathedral. An all-girl orchestra played dance music by Nino Rota, under the direction of a skeleton-thin figure whose face was a blank mask. A buffet was set out on two hundred-yard tables, offering cold meats and salad for the warm and a selection of still-living animals for the undead. Waiters and waitresses, healthy warm folks, paraded with bare necks and wrists, spigots already inserted into their veins. She accepted a measure of human blood and sipped.

Scanning the room, she recognised many guests: Princess Margaret and Anthony Armstrong-Jones, representing the Queen; John and Valerie Profumo, representing Lord Ruthven; Senator John Kennedy and Ambassador Clare Boothe Luce, representing America and hating each other; Carlo Ponti and Sophia Loren; Alberto Moravia, the author; Gina Lollobrigida and General Mark Clark, liberator of Rome; Frank Sinatra and Dean Martin; Pier Paolo Pasolini, the poet; Jonas Cord, the aviation millionaire; Rita Hayworth and the Aga Khan; Totò, the Italian clown; Moira Shearer and Ludovic Kennedy; Enrico Mattei, head of the state petroleum concern; Palmiro Togliatti, the Communist Party chief; several screen Tarzans, and the genuine Lord Greystoke; Zé do Caixão, the Brazilian celebrity undertaker; Magda Lupescu, a vampire once famously the mistress of the King of Romania; Mrs Honoria Cornelius and Colonel Maxim Pyat; Salvador Dalí, sporting long curved fangs like the mirror of his famous moustaches; Edgar Poe, the screenwriter; Dr Orlof, the controversial plastic surgeon; Yves Montand and Simone Signoret; Lemmy Caution, the American adventurer; Gore Vidal, whose work she admired; Amintore Fanfani, the just-deposed government bigshot; Michael Corleone, the olive oil tycoon; Prince Junio Valerio Borghese, an ex-fascist with ambitions; and, representing the Vatican as unobtrusively as possible, Bishop Albino Luciani.

And the elders: Saint-Germain, the famous enigma; Karol

Lavud, back from Mexico; Armand of Paris, the theatrical manager; Gilles de Rais, called *barbe-bleu*; Baron Meinster, the golden-haired toady; Sebastian de Villanueva, disgraced alchemist of the Manhattan Project; Elisabeth Bathory; Drago Robles; Innocente Farnese; Faethor Ferenczy; Don Simon Ysidro. There was even a clutch of elders who held themselves apart from the rest, like a separate species entirely: Edward Weyland, Joshua York, Miriam Blaylock, Hugh Farnham. One octopoid shape-shifter went so far in dissociating itself from humanity that it claimed to be a native of the planet Mars. If any of the secret societies dedicated to the memory of Abraham Van Helsing were to stage a terrorist attack, they might practically exterminate the breed.

Her appalling contemporary de Rais, a hero of France in her warm days, reminded her she was of an age to style herself an elder if she so chose.

She excited little interest among so many famous faces.

'I'm the only person here I've never heard of,' she thought.

Of course, one famous face was unseen.

Princess Asa Vajda made an entrance, born on a palanquin shouldered by six gilded youths, bat-wing fans stuck into her mountainous beehive. But her fiancé had not yet put in an appearance.

Geneviève could wait.

She saw Penelope through the crowd. The Englishwoman looked tastefully pretty in a simple formal dress, hair done up. She wore an expression of exasperated harassment. They made eye contact. Princess Asa swept down on her like a parrot-plumed hawk with a series of demands. She had to concentrate on being reasonable, smoothing over some minor crisis. Geneviève remembered Penelope's tendency to domestic tyranny and wondered if she were repenting her sins here in Otranto, suffering the exact torments she had inflicted on so many servants.

Cagliostro and Orson Welles faced off inside a circle of onlookers and duelled with magic. The warm conjurer bested the nosferatu sorcerer with showmanship, smiling broadly as he used trickery to accomplish his stunts while the Count sweated blood as he worked genuine but affectless magic. Cagliostro had relied for so long on supernatural powers that he was at a loss in this century of everyday miracles. A pretty girl giggled as Welles found a mouse in her cleavage. Spectators tucked long-stemmed glasses into the crooks of their elbows so they could applaud with both hands.

Geneviève was well into her second drink – the waiter claimed to be a virgin of a good Catholic family, and his blood certainly had a tang to it – when she rounded a pillar and found Hamish Bond, immaculate in white dinner jacket, surrounded by disposable popsies, languidly smoking one of his special cigarettes, instructing a waitress that he wanted her blood with vermouth and an olive.

'Shaken, not stirred,' he purred.

'What a ridiculous way to go about things,' Geneviève said.

Bond cocked an eyebrow at her.

'Mademoiselle,' he acknowledged.

The popsies – beauty contest runners-up and orgy extras – faded. She liked the effect.

'I suppose I shouldn't be surprised that you're here,' said the spy. 'You're the type who might turn up anywhere.'

'Weddings and funerals,' she said. 'And hairs-breadth escapes.'

'I've yet to thank you properly.'

'Don't mention it. Have you seen our friend with the whiskers? Brastov is bound to be here. Penelope will have set out a saucer of bloody milk for him.'

Bond's face darkened. He didn't like to be reminded.

'Everybody is here,' the spy said.

'I spotted Villanueva,' she said. 'The defector. Shouldn't you kidnap him? When he skipped behind the curtain, he left those Rosenbergs to take the blame. This must be his first peep in the West in five years.'

'That's Johnny Yank's business. Besides, this seems to be a half-holiday. Otranto is a bit like Spandau prison. Neutral territory, with presences from all sides. When they renewed the Croglin Grange Treaty at Yalta, they agreed to leave Dracula alone but keep their eyes on him. The palazzo has been infested with spies since '44. I shouldn't be surprised if everybody here was a double agent. Except me. And you.'

'Thank you for the compliment.'

'Don't think of it. You're yourself.'

She felt a tiny pang. She knew what he meant. With Charles gone, she had no loyalties except to her own heart.

He sipped his bloody martini.

It had been a gory business hauling him out of Brastov's lair. She had reverted almost to a feral creature, scything through Smert Spionem minions, ignoring bullets, tearing down walls. It wasn't something she cared to do often. It disturbed her to be reminded how easy it was to shape-shift not in body but in mind, to streamline her intellect for mere survival, to set aside empathy.

That scene with Penelope and Kate, at Charles's side, had been a messy afterthought. She'd not settled back into herself, and had been forced to cope with a roomful of volatile emotions.

Bond was completely over it. She'd left him a ragged survivor, but he sprang back together like Wile E. Coyote, donning armour of suavity and brutal polish like his Savile Row tuxedo, ready again to do meaningless battle, to see off the faceless hordes she stubbornly insisted on seeing as inconvenient, bleeding individuals.

Penelope marched past them, intently lecturing a white-faced warm youth.

'I ran into that fellow after you left me,' said Bond, nodding at Penelope's companion. 'Our hostess's American friend. Tom Someone. Something not right about him, you know. Well, more than that. He's got something missing.'

'Like all of us,' she said.

'You're gloomy tonight.'

'The man I've loved since 1888 died this week. That tends to take the wind out of your sails.'

Bond was politely taken aback. He couldn't imagine anyone taking death seriously. It was so much a part of his daily life. Charles had never let himself become like that. The retreat behind callous irony wasn't even a vampire thing; it was a twentieth century thing.

Suddenly, she felt only sorry for this spy.

'You'll fall in love too,' she said. 'And she'll die.'

Bond tried to shrug, but froze. He knew she was right. It had happened to him before and would happen again.

'I'm sorry,' she said. 'That was needlessly cruel. You're right. It's a half-holiday. We're all dressed up and allowed out. It's a night for dissembling, not for inconvenient honesty.'

He looked at her.

'You're a remarkably beautiful woman, Geneviève.'

She laughed at him, but was flattered a bit.

'Earlier, a film producer asked me if I did any modelling.'

'You couldn't. Too much character in your face.'

'Too much overbite, more like.'

She clicked her sharp teeth.

20

OPERAZIONE PAURA

Passing through the doors of Palazzo Otranto was like stepping into the mouth of a dragon. Kate felt the laws of the universe bend out of true. This was how it was in the Royal Presence.

Marcello noticed her hesitation. They held up traffic. A press of guests built outside the doors, like the fizz behind a champagne cork.

They popped.

Guests flowed through the corridors of the palazzo, pulsing in organ-like chambers, throbbing toward the heart. The vaulted ballroom was immense, and crowded.

She was in the grip of red thirst. Everyone here, living and dead, was a sack of blood. She'd gone beyond being glutted by Marcello, and was on the fringe of mania. She'd seen other vampires in this state, but never been here herself.

It wasn't so bad from the inside.

Her eyes must have been glowing scarlet, enlarged by her specs. Her teeth were daggers, her fingernails talons. She was a bit of a dragon herself.

The orchestra played 'Dracula *Cha Cha Cha*'. His Majesty's subjects danced, trailing black and red velvet across a polished mosaic floor. Black ostrich plumes bobbed like insect antennae above elaborate headdresses. Red jewels sparkled with firelight. White faces glowed like stains in the dark.

She was entranced.

'Let's dance,' she said to Marcello, taking his arm and stepping onto the floor.

It was easy to surrender to the music. Marcello kept up with her, warily. He was blank behind his dark glasses, but she owned him entirely. She had made of him a slave, like that poor mad fellow Jack Seward had been treating in 1885. Renfield.

...he killed the flies to catch the spiders, he killed the spiders to catch the birds, he killed the birds to catch the cats...

Dancing was like feeding, drinking the music. All around, in the throng, were creatures like herself. Stiff-haired muzzles, bestial paws with lace cuffs, rotted fangs with gold dental work, leathery wings freed by backless gowns, red eyes lined with blue shadow.

These were Dracula's guests.

The Prince himself did not need to be in the room. He was not a creature of the heart. He would be below them somewhere, in the earth. At the climax of the evening, he would rise to be with his subjects.

They danced past people she knew. Geneviève was in a corner, warily flirting with a handsome vampire Brit who had been at Charles's funeral. Penelope was snatching a quick ciggy, looking as fraught as a nanny whose charges are running wild. Kate found that amusing: She had often had to look after little Penny, the pretty terror. The only way Penelope could grow up was if everyone else turned back into children.

Orson Welles was sawing a Czechoslovakian blonde in half with a sword, keeping up a constant light patter as he levered the silvered blade through her lovely stomach. Inspector Silvestri and Sergeant Ginko, dressed as waiters, kept an eye out for threats to vampire elders, warm plods laughably employed to protect the most dangerous group of people in the world.

She caught the rhythm at last.

Drac-u-*la*, *Drac*-u-*la*, Dra... *cha cha cha...*

Father Merrin, in simple robes with a prominent pectoral cross, observed the throng with more pity than disapproval. And, good God, there was that rogue Sebastian Villanueva. He was supposed to be in Star City, dreaming up rocket weapons. If Villanueva was even tentatively in the West, that was a story. She should find a telephone and call her editor.

No, she was dancing.

Drac-u-*la*, *Drac*-u-*la*...

Tonight, she didn't care about news.

...Dra... *cha cha cha*...

She writhed close to Marcello, elbows on his shoulders, long-fingered hands teasing his lightly-oiled hair.

Drac-u-*la*, *Drac*-u-*la*, Dra... *cha cha cha*...

She licked her mouth, feeling the rough of her tongue on her full lips. She stuck out her tongue and touched her nose with the pointed tip. The trick had sometimes delighted Penny enough to distract her from mischief. She had enjoyed laughing at poor, staid old Kate. Marcello didn't so much as flinch a smile. To him, dancing was a serious business.

Drac-u-*la*, *Drac*-u-*la*, Dra... *cha cha cha*...

She whirled around, hips punctuating the dance with precise *cha cha cha* thrusts, and stuck her tongue out at Penelope – who was bad-temperedly stubbing her cigarette on a waiter's hand – then exploded with the giggles. Marcello kept her upright, and she let the music take over.

She couldn't remember Charles ever dancing. She had seen him fence, though. He was light-footed and imaginative. He would have been a fine dancer. Perhaps it was just that he'd never danced with her.

She missed a step. Damn. Always, she was bothered by ghosts. It was absurd. A vampire should trump a ghost.

Among so many hypnotic elder stares, she spotted kindly blue eyes of warm wisdom. Merrin. He watched her, feeling for her. He had no right. She was a monster. She needed no sympathy.

With a thumb-talon, she slit open Marcello's neck. She craned to catch the spurt in her mouth, and sucked back the blood, feeling it bursting behind her eyes. Electric taste wiped away what she had been thinking of, worrying about.

Marcello wasn't dancing. He was spasming in her arms, too much blood pouring from his depleted veins.

Discreet footmen stepped onto the floor and took Marcello from her. One slapped a large sticking-plaster over the wound and said something in Italian about Vimto. They took him away from her as if taking a broken toy from an unruly child, careful not to express disapproval but nevertheless clearly miffed by her heedlessness.

One of the servants indicated his chin. It took her a moment to realise what he meant. She took her hankie and wiped away an obstinate trickle of blood.

Marcello was walked toward an alcove. As the curtain whisked aside, she glimpsed a row of beds and a stand of drip-feeds. Nurses were in attendance. She was not the only vampire to lose self-control under the influence of the *cha cha cha*.

As a lone woman, she was suddenly open season. General Iorga, a tubby elder who'd been head of the Carpathian Guard when they were sworn to cut off her head, tried to whirl her in a gavotte. The General lost her to a beatnik bleeder with a beret and a goatee who jerked her back into *cha cha cha*-mode. An amulet on a long chain danced between them, thumping against his black pullover and her *décolletage*.

She was torn from the Maynard G. Krebs-type by a woman elder who took advantage of a momentary slowing of the music to French-kiss her. As an alien tongue probed her mouth for licks of Marcello's blood, Kate realised this was the strangest of all elders, Casanova. Upon turning, he'd shape-shifted permanently into a woman, a miracle which had no effect whatsoever on his character.

Then she was detached from the great lover, a process that involved much unlocking of mouth-parts, by a ravaged, bloated warm fellow whom she recognised, under many layers of dissolution, as Errol Flynn. The former matinee idol had a spigot in his neck. Kate could not resist the blood of Robin Hood. It was more vodka than gore, but rich with Caribbean spices and gunpowder.

She left Flynn, and stumbled, drunk in several ways, through the crowds.

A huge chest blocked her way. She raised her head to look at the face, but it was a crimson blur. The man wore tights that showed thick columns of muscle in his thighs and calves.

A cold cloth dropped on her brain.

Where were Silvestri and Ginko? Where were the Carpathian Guard?

Fright seized her.

Her eyes focused. She had been mistaken. This was not the Crimson Executioner. A bespectacled, handsome, kindly face, built of solid blocks, looked down at her. It was an actor, Kent. She'd seen pictures of him as Hercules.

He wasn't even dressed in red. His tights were blue.

'Are you all right, Miss?' he asked.

She waved him away, trying to make a sober arrangement of her features. He wasn't sure about her, but took her reassurance as authentic.

Beyond the muscled American, she glimpsed a smaller figure. A tiny woman, or a child. A wing of blonde hair over one eye. She'd been wrong about the Crimson Executioner, but this was the little girl from Piazza di Trevi.

'Excuse me,' she said to Kent, brushing past him.

The girl was gone.

Now, Kate wanted to cry. She knew she was in a dulled, insensate state. She wanted to be sharp, wanted to be herself. She needed herself now.

A red ball bounced on the floor and rolled to her feet. She bent to pick up the plaything, but clumsily tapped it. The ball leaped like a balloon, and hopped away like a Chinese vampire. It bounced off Private Elvis Presley's head and against Edgar Poe's chest, making the writer spill his drink, then loped onwards, sliding between Gina Lollobrigida and an elder Kate didn't know. It was as if it were trying to escape. Kate kept her eye on the ball, and followed.

21

CEMETERY GIRLS

Someone small brushed by Geneviève.

'Past that child's bedtime, I should have thought,' said Bond.

She looked around but saw no child.

'Naughty little devil,' the spy mused.

'In this company, you shouldn't judge age by looks, Commander Bond. Melissa, my grandmother-in-darkness, is one of those forever children, turned as a six-year-old. She's been "fwightfully cwoss" for the best part of a thousand years.'

She wondered if Melissa d'Acques were here. Geneviève hadn't heard of the old girl in over a hundred years. Once, that would have meant that the elder had been destroyed. Now, it suggested she was one of that circle who disapproved of Dracula's showboating. Some were so used to living in shadow that they would never forgive *il principe* for taking the public stage, shattering forever the exclusivity of vampirism.

The word went round that Dracula was expected soon.

Penelope was receiving orders from Princess Asa, who had changed her outfit twice already during the party. Two hundred years hadn't altered her imperious looks. The odd creation she now wore was as apt for Mongo as Moldavia.

Asa had a savage, almost Mongol face. Currently, it was framed by a demon ruff of lizard-like material, which served as collar for a turquoise satin train supported by a pair of dwarves made up as turbaned blackamoors. Under the cape, she wore an abbreviated brass Valkyrie breastplate and a short skirt of chain mail and leather. The spike heels of her thigh-length jackboots added as much to her height as her topiary tower of hair. The Princess carried a coil of bullwhip, the like of which she must have used to *knout* her peasants back in the good old days.

Bond was taken with the Royal Fiancée. Geneviève thought the Princess looked ridiculous, but in this company it took a lot to stand out. And Asa Vajda certainly stood out.

Penelope nodded curtly as she accepted each royal decree. There would be trumpets, torches and a cannonade from the battlements. Penny argued that it might be more politic for the cannons to be pointed out to sea rather than over the town.

'A fall of chain-shot is a poor substitute for confetti, Princess,' she said.

'Pah!' declared Asa. 'What care we for mortals! They should be grateful to bleed and die in commemoration of my happiness. If we fire out to sea, what will happen? Only fish will die. I like not fish.'

Penelope looked at the end of her rope. Geneviève had an impulse to help the Englishwoman.

'It's traditional for Dracula's guns to fire at the sea,' she put in. 'To avenge the flood of 1469, which cut off the retreating Turks and prevented Vlad's armies from hacking the foemen to pieces.'

Foemen, that was good. Very fifteenth century. Asa swivelled her enormous eyes.

'The Dieudonné girl,' she said. 'Carmilla Karnstein's little friend.'

'So pleased to see you again, Asa.'

Three hundred years ago, Melissa d'Acques had called a gathering of female elders in the Black Forest. They were supposed to debate some point of nosferatu protocol none could understand, but Geneviève alone realised it was because her grandmother-in-darkness was lonely for new playmates. They'd spent the month dressing up and chasing huntsmen in the woods. Princess Asa hadn't liked Geneviève then, and wasn't about to change her opinion now.

'*Chut*,' Asa said, which might be either a Moldavian greeting or a deadly insult.

'*Chut* to you too, *chèrie*.'

'This flood of 1469…?'

She had made it up, of course.

'A rebuke to Poseidon. *Il principe* will be honoured.'

'Very well,' decided the Princess. 'Englishwoman, you may bombard the waves.'

Penelope was relieved. Like Caligula, she could now claim victory over the sea.

A red ball bounced off the dance floor. Asa looked at it as if it were an interloper.

'And have this ball burst,' she ordered.

The point of tyranny was to be arbitrary. Asa had probably read her Machiavelli and was trying to surpass his model. Sometimes, it did to issue meaningless commands to see how swiftly one's retainers snapped to.

Kate Reed stumbled out of the crowd, apparently following the ball. She was in a state. Her eyes were enlarged and red. There was blood on her mouth and down the front of her dress. She was so fixated on the ball that she tripped.

Geneviève caught the woman. Kate struggled a bit, then slowly recognised her.

'If it isn't Mademoiselle Perfect,' she said.

Geneviève knew better than to be hurt. Kate was well gone into the red madness.

'Do you know how you make the rest of us feel?' Kate continued. 'You, the lady elder, the vampire saint, the marble adventuress? Sixteen and milky-white on the outside, with all that genius and generosity of spirit caged up inside you?'

Geneviève looked at Penelope and Asa. Neither commented.

'I'm like you, Kate,' she said. 'I'm not special.'

Kate laughed bitterly, to the point of tears.

'It's no wonder you won him,' Kate said. 'None of us had a chance. You're like a statue. Beside you, we're all ratty little kids. We change and shrivel and die, and you go on and on and on, always perfect, always modestly triumphant. The rest of us are the wreckage left behind.'

'I think you've had enough to drink, Katie,' said Penelope.

'Yes, I know. I'm sorry, Geneviève. You're right. I'm not being me.'

Despite everything, a sliver of ice got through. Kate was drunk, but could still think. Perhaps drink only freed her to say what she'd always thought. Perhaps Geneviève was an impossible presence. In the end, everyone she knew suffered.

She tried to find the love in her heart, the thing that made her different from Asa Vajda or Prince Dracula, the constant throb she'd felt for Charles, and through him for his warm world. Momentarily, she thought it was there no longer.

'I've hurt you,' Kate said, reaching out for her cheek, fingertip touching a tear. 'I'm sorry. I'm wrong. You're still alive.'

Kate was crying too. Penelope held her tight.

Again, the three were joined by tears.

'No one must weep at my party,' Asa said. 'This I decree. All must smile, all must be happy. On pain of impalement.'

'I apologise, Princess,' began Penelope. 'My friend meant no…'

Asa flicked out the tip of her whip and slapped Penelope across the face as if with her open hand.

The whipcrack was like a gunshot.

Bond flinched, hand slipping into his jacket. Then he relaxed. This was women's business. He could enjoy the show.

Kate was suddenly calm. She set the shocked Penelope, whose face bore a broad red mark specked with blood, down in a chair, and faced up to Asa Vajda, who was at least eighteen inches the taller.

'You old cow,' she said, and punched the Princess in the throat.

Asa staggered under the blow, unsteady on her heels. Her imps tripped under the train and tugged it off her shoulders. A clasp at the neck snapped. The Princess emerged from her satin shroud and lashed again with the whip.

Kate caught the leather snake with her forearm and wrapped it several times around her wrist, tugging on it like a lasso, further unbalancing Asa. Both women wore heels, but

Kate could kick off her Perugia shoes and fight in her stocking feet. She did so, and lost another three inches.

Princess Asa's face swelled at the sides, as if teeth were sprouting around her eyes and along the insides of her jaws.

'It's not a good idea to bash the bride,' Bond said. 'Why don't you girls kiss and make up.'

Kate yanked hard on the whip, pulling Asa toward her, within range of her clawed hand. She got her fingers in the Princess's hair and dismantled the beehive, flopping black strands over her face. Red wheals were scratched across Asa's cheek, but healed at once.

With terrier-like ferocity, Kate lifted Asa off the floor and slammed her several times against a column. The Princess's head slapped back and forth and she screeched with fury. Kate dropped her and stood back, letting her recover a little.

Asa kicked out with a booted leg and caught Kate behind the knees, sweeping her off the floor. She fell badly, whip still around her wrist, and the Princess placed a boot-toe on her forehead.

'Yield,' she said, an Amazon addressing an ant.

Of course, everyone in the room gathered around, watching. Flashbulbs popped. Kate lay like a beached fish, the fight gone out of her.

Geneviève felt more tears on her cheek.

'That's enough, Asa,' she said.

'She must yield,' the Princess said. 'For that, I will reward her with a swift, merciful death.'

'You can't do that any more, Asa. You haven't been able to do that for years. You don't own serfs any more. You don't have a right to take their lives.'

Asa looked down at Kate, then at Geneviève. She was not a stupid barbarian. That was what frightened Geneviève. Nothing was worse than a clever barbarian.

'You are right, Geneviève of the line of d'Acques. In this century, we have let things slip. Peasants dare to strike their betters…'

'I'm not a peasant,' gurgled Kate. 'I'm a journalist. *Haut bourgeois*, I admit. Remember the bourgeoisie, Princess. We superseded feudal chieftains in the eighteenth century.'

Asa slipped her heel into Kate's mouth, shutting off her talk.

'This is where everything changes back,' decreed the Princess. 'This is where things become as they ought to be.'

Geneviève knew she would kill Asa before the Princess could further hurt Kate. And then she would be torn apart herself. Dracula would arrive at his party just in time to dip his fingers in her cooling blood.

It had been the same at Melissa's gathering. Put female vampire elders in a room and they take to fighting like cats.

Princess Asa reached out a hand.

'You there, fat man with a beard,' she said, to Orson Welles.

The genius was surprised to be singled out, but not displeased.

'I have need of your sword,' Asa said.

Welles held what looked like a silver-plated cavalry sabre, already stained red.

'Let it be known,' shouted the Princess as she took Welles's sword, 'that, as in Moldavia, I am prepared to act as my own headsman.'

She took her foot off Kate's face and raised the sword.

'So perish all who defy the Princess Asa Dracula!'

The sword flashed as it came down on Kate's neck.

22

THE MAGIC SWORD

She couldn't stop laughing. Her throat had taken a bruising, and blood was backed up in her mouth.

'You stupid, *stupid* bitch,' Kate spluttered.

She felt her neck. It wasn't even broken.

Princess Asa Vajda looked at the sword in her hand as if it were a snake. It seemed straight, sharp and silver. Red stuff dripped from its edge. Not blood, strawberry jam.

'It's a *magic* sword,' Kate said, sitting up.

Orson Welles looked sheepish. Asa stabbed at his enormous torso and the sword appeared to pass through his chest without harming him.

'Not your kind of magic, Princess,' Kate said. 'Not necromancy and sorcery. Just trickery, *prestidigitation*.'

The Princess looked an utter prawn. Kate wasn't the only one laughing. Penelope desperately tried to keep a straight, sympathetic face, but couldn't contain her delight at the humiliation of the Royal Fiancée.

'You try saying "prestidigitation" in my state,' said Kate.

'What manner of sword is this?' the Princess demanded of Welles.

'A conjurer never reveals his secrets,' he said.

Asa Vajda had made a big mistake, and while making it had taken the name to which she was not yet entitled. A subtle hint of terror crept across her beautiful, mask-like face. Dracula would hear of her presumption, probably already knew about it.

Tartars seized Kate and hauled her upright. Geneviève laid a hand on one of them, calmly powerful and impossibly lovely. Princess Asa nodded to the guards. Kate was released.

Penelope handed Kate her shoes. She was crying with suppressed laughter. The mark of Asa's whip had disappeared.

'I think you'd better leave, Katie,' said Penny, biting the insides of her cheeks to keep from exploding.

'I think you're right.'

Kate kissed Penelope.

'Lovely to see you, as always, Penny,' she said, really hugging her friend. 'And you too, Geneviève. I withdraw unequivocally my ill-judged rant of a few moments ago. You're the best friend a girl could have.'

Geneviève kissed her too.

Asa muttered about the barbarous lands and isles of the West. Ireland, England, and France were far from Moldavia. The customs of those places were absurd.

'Princess, good night,' said Kate. 'Do enjoy the rest of this democratic century.'

'Out,' Asa spat.

Kate left.

She was outside the palazzo before she remembered that Marcello was inside, probably choking on Vimto and cursing her appetites. Should she wait for him, or hitch a lift back to Rome by herself?

Music filtered through the barred windows and spread out over the town. Kate sat on the broad front step and slipped her shoes back on. She was still drunk, but now under control. The danger had passed, her red rage was spent. She would not attack anyone else tonight. Unless she ran into someone ghastly.

She could laugh about it, but her fight with Asa Vajda had been scary. If the Princess had found a more reliable sword, Kate would be a head shorter, and truly dead. Even if she'd avoided the blade and gouged out the vampire elder's slippery guts, she'd have wound up dying for it. Only a moment of comedy had saved her life.

Something red rolled on the driveway: the ball she'd been following. It was as if it were waiting for her. Even in her current state of not thinking straight, she knew toys were not supposed to have minds of their own.

A cannon sounded from the battlements. Something whizzed out to sea then exploded, scattering fiery chunks down onto the waves. She smelled the stink of gunpowder and conquered an impulse to throw herself flat on the ground. She'd been in too many wars.

In the flash of powder, she saw a small figure at the edge of the cliff. She looked at the dark and couldn't see the little girl any more.

She had been there.

A fog of boiling blood rolled across her brain, the beginnings of a truly spectacular headache. She wanted to curl up and go to sleep here beside the stone lions that guarded the doors of Dracula's palace.

The girl had left a silhouette burned into Kate's eyeballs. She momentarily took off her glasses and rubbed her eyes. In the red darkness, the child stood out.

She had a flash of the sad face she'd seen in the waters of the Trevi Fountain. The look she knew was wrong. She almost understood what was wrong with the picture.

The ball was at the edge of the cliff. She stood up and walked across the drive onto a stretch of long, wet grass that sloped down gently until the land broke sharply away. Below the battlements was a sheer drop. Waves crashed against the base of the cliff, hammering the foundations, slowly eroding them.

Eventually, the Palazzo Otranto would fall, like Mr Poe's House of Usher. And a good job, too.

The red ball was trapped by a shrub that clung to the very edge. Kate reached down to free it and was struck dizzy at the worst possible moment, attention caught by the froth of foam hundreds of feet below. The waves came up at her and went away again, a trick of vertigo.

She did not fall.

Where had the little girl gone?

She looked along the side of the palace. The wedge of green grew thin, where the cliff had crumbled away. After a few yards, the wall and the cliff became one, without even the thinnest of ledges. There was no way past the building.

A stab of guilt thrust into her heart. Had she frightened the child? Made her fall?

Kate sat down, feet dangling over the edge. There was spray, like waves of fine rain. Coolness seeped into her mind, wiping away the fog. She liked the saltwater specks on her face.

Another cannon went off.

This time, she was looking down as the flash lit everything up. The dark rock face momentarily bleached white, and a small figure was visible.

Was she moving, waving her arms? Or was she still, animated by the flash?

Kate called out.

'Little girl. *Ragazza*.'

Her voice was lost. Waves roared like the blood in her ears.

She waited, but the next cannon blast was a long time coming. She had time for fear. The girl must have fallen. Was it Kate's pursuit, or the shock of the cannon going off? Had she been chasing her ball and overbalanced, only to be caught on an outcrop?

Obviously, there was more to the child than random wandering through Kate's life. She'd been in Piazza di Trevi when the Crimson Executioner had struck, and now she was here at the Palazzo Otranto for her face-off with the Princess. Somehow, she had become Kate's angel of violence.

The ball sailed off the cliff and out to sea.

Kate knew what she'd have to do. She needed to remove her shoes again. This was going to ruin her stockings, and her expensive dress. But the party was over for her anyway.

She stood on top of the cliff, arms outspread like a diver, judging the wind and the spray. Not too strong, thank heavens. She knelt on the edge and leaned over, bending down below the lip of the cliff, reaching for a handhold a few feet down.

Pulling herself over the edge, she clung to the rock, feeling her weight in her shoulders and hips. She crawled down like a lizard, worried her glasses would slip off and be lost forever. Her elbows and knees grazed rock, but her fingers and toes found holds.

She clung like a heavy fly, looking down into the dark. If the girl was still there, Kate could not see her.

Slowly, she made her zigzag way down. Her soaked dress clung to her back and bottom. Some vampires could grow wings and fly. Kate Reed had to crawl.

Another cannon fired.

Kate saw the girl looking up at her. The tiny face was shockingly close, still half-masked by that unnaturally beautiful hair. A single tear stood out from her exposed eye. And she was smiling like the Cheshire Cat.

When the flash was gone, the darkness came back.

She knew what she had failed to see the first time. It was the mouth, the downturned crescent of sorrow. She had seen a reflection, upside-down, of a smile. At the sight of the Crimson Executioner murdering Kernassy and Malenka, the girl had not been shocked, but possessed with unholy delight.

In that innocent face was Evil.

Kate reached out for where the girl was, and her hand closed on nothing. There'd been no cry. The child hadn't fallen.

She lurched forward, hands free of the cliff, and scrabbled down a few yards. Her feet found holds and she dangled. There was a hole in the rock. Not a cave, but a man-made entrance. She got her hands around the hewn edges of the ingress and clung on tight.

Inside the cliff, the little girl ran.

23

BLOODY PIT OF HORROR

She thought she should look for Kate. There was nothing here for her at the party.

Geneviève was momentarily distracted by Orson Welles. He was so *enormous*. His cravat would have served most people as a cloth for an occasional table. He produced objects from every pocket of every jacket. Birds, mice, drinks, coins.

Didn't anyone here ever get tired of all this? She knew one person did. Him. Prince Dracula. He wasn't here yet. But he was on his way. That changed the feel of the party. Kate's scuffle with Princess Asa had helped the chill along. It showed how uncertain everything was.

What would Dracula do when he got here?

He was capable of having the doors locked and burning the palace down, holding out to the last so he could follow his guests to Hell. Or he could be a gracious host and send everyone away with a Renaissance masterpiece as a party favour.

She remembered the last time. In 1888, when she'd stood beside Charles at the foot of a throne in the sty Dracula had made of Buckingham Palace, surrounded by monsters and victims.

The Prince had taken a few knocks since then.

Geneviève looked around. Apart from Welles, she'd lost sight of them all: Kate, Penelope, Asa, Bond, Kate's journalist escort, Penelope's Tom. All she saw were the famous dress extras.

The music changed. A march played, something pompous and magnificent. Great curtains parted. Attendants held them aside like nurses keeping open a giant's chest cavity during heart surgery. A pair of empty thrones stood on a dais. Geneviève recognised one as having been stolen from Buckingham Palace. It was Victoria's, with the arms of Vajda tacked over the lion and the unicorn. The other, taller chair was something stark and mediaeval, a cathedral-shaped gothic throne from the reign of the Impaler.

Columns of blue fire rose, threatening the curtains. Trumpets lifted, and sounded a fanfare.

'He's coming up from his tomb,' Welles said. 'What an effect. It's like Ivan the Terrible meets the Wizard of Oz.'

'He's a whiz of a wiz all right,' she said.

The blue flames twisted like barber's poles, and puffed into the shape of dragon wings.

'That's the effect I wanted for my *Caesar*.'

Warm monarchs liked towers, the undead favoured lairs. A living king might descend to be among his subjects, but the King Vampire must come up from underground.

A funnel of cold grave air shivered the fire dragons and billowed the curtains. A section of floor slid open and a couple of minor guests fell into the abyss.

Princess Asa, veiled now, strode to the edge of the pit and knelt, touching the floor with her forehead. She was intent on cancelling out the presumption she had shown in taking the name of Dracula in vain.

'They say this will be their first meeting,' Welles commented. 'Tonight, Dracula will look on the face of his bride. Old-fashioned, isn't it?'

Geneviève wasn't surprised. This was a dynastic match.

There was a rumble in the depths of the palace, and a clanking of vast iron chains. A platform was being hauled up by the bodily effort of dozens of servants. A flutter of the curtain gave her a glimpse of sweating, shirtless bodies and huge black chain-links.

From out of the depths rose a head.

She recognised Dracula: thick scarlet lips, rope-like twists of moustache and eyebrow, jet black fall of oiled hair, aquiline nose, nostrils like flared tunnels, hatchet cheekbones, protruding fangs like sharp thumbs. And red eyes, swimming in blood. There was more blood around his mouth. The Prince's face was a stiff mask.

The platform clicked into place.

Dracula's head surmounted a black, all-enveloping cloak which rose from a circle on the floor and completely concealed his frame. He was much thinner than she remembered, a round-shouldered scarecrow.

The fanfare concluded. The blue flames settled into their jets and burned orange. Applause began and swelled to hysterical clapping. Women sighed and prostrated themselves, captivated by Dracula's musk. Men looked with hatred, envy, arousal and love. Vampire elders went down on their knees. Geneviève hotly refused to bow to this monster. He was not her king, her commander.

He was just an elder, one of many.

'My God,' breathed Welles, 'I never dreamed. Such presence, such *power*. He is a dark god, a prince of hell, an avatar of the apocalypse.'

She couldn't see it, but was alone in that.

Welles huffed as he sank to his knees, an elephant doing a trick. No one save her dared look into the monster's face. She saw something was wrong.

Had Dracula gone blind? His eyes were red marbles.

The last echoes of the fanfare died. Applause petered out. A sobbing woman got control of herself. Silence. Someone coughed. *Il principe* said nothing. His head hung there. A trickle of blood ran from one exposed fang, along a feeler of moustache, dripped onto the cloak, and slid down a fold.

Princess Asa looked up and cast back her veil, exposing her face. Dracula paid her no attention.

'My prince…' she said.

Geneviève stepped forward, dreading the pull that would come when she entered Dracula's zone of power, the clash she'd feel as his mind tried to enfold and dominate hers. But there was nothing.

She walked across the room, through the frozen crowd.

A whisper began. Was this a wax statue?

She stepped over the Princess, who was struggling with incomprehension. She looked up into Dracula's face. It might as well have been a Halloween pumpkin, with a carved grin. The candle inside guttered, and the eyes jerked to focus on her, in a spasm.

Geneviève reached out and took a fold of Dracula's cape. She whipped it away and cast it across the room. The voluminous garment fell in a heap, exposed swathes of scarlet lining like slashes in the hide of a brave bull at the end of the *corrida*.

Someone – the Princess? – screamed.

Dracula's head was stuck on a wooden pole. It had been raggedly sawn off.

…minutes later, she was running down a passageway. Plastered walls gave way to rough stone. Attendants ran with her, the flames of their torches trailing the low roof.

A steward – Klove – was guiding her to Dracula's lair.

After all, there was more to his body than his head.

The Princess was in shock, demanding that the murderers be put to the sword. The Carpathian Guard had sealed off the palazzo. Half the catering staff turned out to be policemen. Inspector Silvestri kept pace with her. He was the detective in charge of the Crimson Executioner case.

The name had been spoken first in a whisper. Now, it was being yelled from the battlements.

The Crimson Executioner! If this was his work, then it was the most daring coup of all time. Not even Abraham Van Helsing had been able to carry off the head of Vlad Tepes. Prince Dracula had died before, of course – even, she was sure, had been beheaded – but this was true death.

That roll of the eyes, a final focusing on her, was the last of his tenacious spirit, fleeing the flesh, disappearing into the wherever. Any other elder of his age would have turned to dust, but Dracula's great will staved off bodily dissolution.

There were offers already to buy the head. The Inspector had left it in the care of Edgar Poe. Famous quacks – Drs Hichcock, Schuler, and Genessier – were promoting their services for the autopsy. Zé do Caixão had already tried to get close to Princess Asa and put in a bid for the funeral.

Orson Welles was with them, keeping up astonishingly for someone of his bulk. He'd been caught by the Ariadne thread of story, and was following it to the end.

Cobweb curtains parted and the small party entered a tomb.

The body lay half-out of a magnificent catafalque, still leaking profusely at the neck-stump. Dracula had been wearing a suit of midnight black. A red flower was pinned to his chest with a silver sticker.

The painted ceiling and walls of the tomb, which might date back to Ancient Rome, were redecorated with modern-art splatters of rich blood. The Prince had drunk an ocean of blood in his undeath. It all poured forth now in a ghastly torrent. The place stank of the death of Dracula. It was indescribably foul.

Her attention was drawn by the silver knife in *il principe*'s heart. It was a familiar object, one she had supposed long lost. The silver scalpel of Jack the Ripper. Charles Beauregard had smuggled it into Buckingham Palace, to free Queen Victoria of her bondage. Now it had been used to end another royal vampire's life. The red flower was a frozen clot of Dracula's heartsblood.

'Someone is here still,' Silvestri said.

Geneviève heard whimpering, sensed movement. She looked at Welles's grey face floating in the gloom. Klove drew a curtain aside. Cold air flowed into the tomb.

An exhausted woman tumbled out, covered from head to foot in blood. Kate's round glasses were thickly painted red, her hair was matted with gore.

PART FOUR

FUNERAL RITES

NOTICE OF DEATH FROM *THE TIMES* OF LONDON, AUGUST 9TH, 1959

The true death is announced of Count Dracula, formerly Prince of Wallachia, Voivode of Transylvania and Prince Consort of Great Britain. Born in 1431, turned vampire in 1476, Dracula was in warm life a ruler of his homeland and defender of Christianity against the Turk. As an elder vampire, Dracula was a central figure of the modern age. By marrying Queen Victoria in 1886 and disseminating his bloodline in Britain, he established himself not only as a statesman and world leader but as father-in-darkness to fresh generations of vampire breeds. Before Dracula, vampires were covert creatures, considered by most sources to be legendary spirits. His presence in London made public the existence of the nosferatu.

Though he was driven from the throne of Britain in 1897 and fell from power in Germany with the defeat of the Kaiser in 1918, Dracula survived the eddying tides of this turbulent century for far longer than most of his critics would have believed possible. Having signed the Croglin Grange Treaty with the Allied powers in 1943, he rallied an underground of elder and new-born vampires in South Eastern Europe to assist the invasions of Greece and the Carpathian Nations. Without his influence, victory in the Second World War might have been a far costlier and more protracted affair. Since the War, Dracula has lived in modest retirement near Rome, though the recent announcement of his engagement to Princess Asa Vajda fuelled speculation that a return to the stage of international politics was imminent. Tributes have poured in from surviving wartime Allied leaders: Lord Ruthven, President Eisenhower, Marshal Zhukov, and General de Gaulle. Alone among his peers, Winston Churchill has refused to pay homage in death to the King Vampire.

It has become a commonplace in recent years for the new-born vampires of the 1880s and '90s, bewildered by the rapid changes of the atomic age, to express nostalgia for the certainties and values of Dracula's comparatively brief reign in England. The accepted image of Dracula as a tyrannic monster was enshrined by Bram Stoker's *Dracula* (1897) and the concluding chapter of Lytton Strachey's *Eminent Victorians* (1918). This traditional portrait is qualified in revisionary, sympathetic biographies like Montagu Summers's *Dracula: His Kith and Kin* (1928) and Colin Wilson's *The Impaler* (1957), though the old view is reinforced with conviction by Alan Clark's *The Monsters* (1958) and Asa Briggs's *The Age of Impalement: 1885–1918* (1959). Daniel Farson's controversial *Vlad the Imposter* (1959) advances the theory that the vampire Count Dracula was not the former Vlad Tepes, but an as-yet unidentified Transylvanian who assumed the name and title. Farson lists many discrepancies between Dracula's accounts of himself and what can be established of Vlad but, with his passing, it is unlikely this question will ever be resolved. In death as in life, the Prince took pains to maintain his air of mystery.

In Rome, a suspect is in custody in connection with the murder but no announcement has been made of an arrest or charges. Police Chief Francesco Polito has declared all effort will be made to bring the murderer to justice. It is speculated that the destruction of the most famous of all elders is the latest in a series of atrocities carried out by a vampire slayer who goes colourfully by the name of the Crimson Executioner. Garlands of traditional black flowers have been sent by well-wishers to

Buckingham Palace, where they pose an embarrassment for a Royal Household which would perhaps prefer not to be reminded that Dracula was once Prince Consort. The disposal of the estates and fortunes has yet to be decided; it appears that, after defying death for five hundred years, the Count died intestate. The corpse is in the custody of the Rome police, but pressure is growing in demand for release and burial. Nicolae Ceauşescu, President of Romania, has refused permission for reinterral of the remains in their original grave on the island monastery of Snagov, and Lord Ruthven, the Prime Minister, has ruled that a space in Westminster Abbey is 'Sadly, out of the question'.

See also (in our weekend-special edition):

*DRACULA, AS I REMEMBER HIM, by the Prime Minister, Lord Ruthven

*THE END OF AN ERA: THE PASSING OF THE FIRST AMONG VAMPIRES, by Dennis Wheatley

*UNSOLVED CRIMES: THE FIVE HUNDRED YEAR CAREER OF VLAD TEPES, by Catriona Kaye

*DRACULA: STATESMAN, GENERAL, HERO, by Enoch Powell

*IS DRACULA REALLY DEAD?, by R. Chetwynd-Hayes

*... AND GOOD RIDDANCE TO BAD RUBBISH!, by John Osborne.

24

CADAVERI ECCELLENTI

Her holding cell was underground, like Dracula's tomb. Kate supposed Silvestri intended she be reminded of the bloody pit. The strategy didn't work. She remembered the little devil girl's terrifying smile and being hauled out of a pool of blood by Geneviève, but everything between was a red mist. She tried and tried, but a murderous hangover blotted out her mind. If it hurt this much, she didn't want to remember.

She had been questioned several times. Someone was supposed to be getting in touch with the Irish Embassy. Mostly, she was left alone, with orders to think hard.

For the moment, she was a witness. Not a suspect.

When they had told her Dracula was dead, she'd let out an instinctive hallelujah of unlovely gloating. That hadn't made a good impression, especially since she was still plastered with the deceased's congealing blood. Even now, the last rinds clung stubbornly to her hair and under her nails.

She didn't even know whether she was guilty or not.

Objectively, she was the assassin type: idealistic, obsessive, frustrated, prone to fits of emotion, equipped for violence. On the night of the murder, hundreds of witnesses saw her pick a drunken fight with the dead man's fiancée. She had a long history of enmity with the House of Dracula. As a reporter, she'd have picked herself as the likely killer.

But surely she would remember?

No news was allowed through to her, but she could imagine how the world was reacting. Those who thought her guilty would be sharply divided: Dracula's supporters calling for her public impalement on television, his enemies hailing her as a heroine and a saint. It should have been Geneviève. She was better fit to handle all this.

What stopped Silvestri charging her? The pounding in her head didn't entirely blank her intuition. The Inspector didn't think she'd done it. Marcello had told her the policeman specialised in those very Italian murder cases where nothing was ever what it seemed and weird combinations of suspects with twisted motivations perpetrated unwieldy, unlikely and baffling atrocities. His usual quarry were black-gloved, hooded fiends who took straight razors or strangling cords to fashion models or nightclub hostesses to pose as sex killers but actually sought contested inheritances, double indemnity insurance claims or to preserve the reputations of even more unpleasant relatives. To Silvestri, the victim's worst enemy found at the scene of the crime covered with his blood and with the deceased's wallet in his back pocket was obviously an innocent red herring.

She tried to think back.

Dracula's tomb was elusive, but more and more she found herself going over the past. It was all there somewhere.

In 1943, she had walked across most of Sicily in the wake of General Patton's armoured forces. 'Operation Husky' met little resistance from Italian troops on the island – King Victor Emmanuel had just dismissed Mussolini, and Pietro Badoglio was negotiating Italy's change of sides – but 40,000 German soldiers put up a desperate fight.

The press tagged along with the second or third wave of liberators. Chain of command wouldn't let Kate up front in the fighting like Ernie Pyle. By the time she got anywhere, it was supposed to be pacified, suitable for writing-up as a morale-boosting victory. She was encouraged to file stories about Sicilian-American GIs visiting relatives in the old country, being welcomed as saviours with picturesque peasant feasts.

Actually, she saw the bureaucratic mess of a changeover

from failing fascist authorities to a provisional Allied military government and then to whoever could best exploit the situation. Most of the partisans who assisted the Allies turned out to be mafia *soldati*, clawing back territories Il Duce had wrested from them. In order to make the campaign swift and successful, the Allies were prepared to make use of the likes of the bandit Salvatore Giuliano and the gangster Charles 'Lucky' Luciano. She saw unsmiling Sicilian villagers waving flags at gunpoint to give a welcome to 'exile son' Luciano, and wept to see not liberation but an exchange of oppressors.

'You brought them *back*,' spat an old woman.

Kate always remembered that peasant, face worn, back bent, sons and grandsons dead on all sides. To her, the Germans (only recently hostile) were alien beings, unpredictable and implacable as the weather. The mafia, whom she was now expected to welcome, had been around all her life. They were people she could hate, arrogant and quixotic, suddenly violent, always demanding more tribute.

An American officer confided in Kate that he couldn't understand these people. 'They're free. What more do they want, blood?' Then he realised what he had said and tried to apologise. Two nights later, she bled him anyway, though she never slept with him.

The disbelief and disgust of the old woman stayed with her.

In the Balkans, it must have been worse. There, the Allies installed not mafia *capi* but elder vampires, grave-mould scum out to reclaim their castles and feed off the grandchildren of the villagers they'd slaughtered in years gone by.

'You brought them *back*.'

She still shuddered at that.

'Have you found the little girl?'

Inspector Silvestri had heard that before.

'It was the girl from Piazza di Trevi. She must be a part of this. I think she's mixed up with the Crimson Executioner.'

The policeman sighed.

'*Il principe* Dracula was not killed by *il Boia Scarlatto*.'

He stated it as a matter of fact. Kate was surprised.

'On the night of the party, the night Dracula died, *il Boia Scarlatto* was seen more than a dozen times in Rome. He was in a frenzy. Seven elder *vampiri*, all on their way to or just returned from Fregene, are dead by his hand. He has grown bold. Most were killed in public. The assassin and an elder named Anton Voytek fought like wrestlers in Piazza dei Qinquecento, outside the railway station, causing much damage. Voytek's heart was torn out and tossed to the dogs. The other dead are il conte Mitterhouse, Webb Fallon, Richmond Reed, il conte Oblensky, Lady Luna Mora, and a Madame Cassandra. There may be more. It's difficult to identify heaps of ashes. The thing is that all these died in Rome, not the Palazzo Otranto.'

'How convenient.'

'Indeed. It has occurred to us that there might be an army of identical assassins. In that case, who is their *generale*? This lost child of yours?'

'She wasn't a vampire.'

And yet, she wasn't warm either, not in the sense Kate understood.

'Sometimes the Devil looks like a little girl,' she said.

Silvestri threw up his hands. 'You can't expect me to arrest *il diavolo*. Besides, he was put on trial once before and sentenced. The American law of Double Jeopardy must apply.'

'Very well, I confess. I am the mastermind. I decreed the deaths of all elders in Rome. I personally destroyed the King Vampire. Now I am Queen of the Cats and shall reign throughout the eternal night.'

Silvestri chuckled.

'But you are innocent, Signorina Reed.'

'Prove it.'

'Show me your hands.'

Surprised, Kate laid her hands on the desk between them. The Inspector took her hands and turned them palm up.

'A silver scalpel was stuck into Dracula's heart. *Argento*. That killed him. The decapitation was only a flourish. He was killed by another *vampiro* – which also rules out *il Boia Scarlatto* – and your hands aren't scarred. Silver is like hot iron to the undead.'

'I could have worn gloves.'

'And still got your hands bloody? So bloody that you would have red stuff under your nails?'

Kate was self-conscious and made fists, trapping Silvestri's thumbs. She could have ripped them off if she'd been so inclined. She let him go.

'There was also skin on the scalpel. A residue.'

'I heal fast. Even after silver.'

'You didn't have any weal on your palm when we found you that night. I observe too.'

'I take it you've asked for a show of hands?'

'Many *vampiri* were at the engagement ball. Few have chosen to remain in Italy for the funeral. And who can blame them? *Il Boia Scarlatto* is the Grim Reaper with a silver scythe. Incidentally, are you an elder?'

'I should think not. I'm not even a hundred.'

'A thousand pardons, Signorina. But the question had to be asked. I should not care to release you into peril.'

'You're releasing me?'

'Discreetly. Your name has not been made public.'

Kate was grateful for that. She knew the pandemonium her life would become if her part in this were generally known. Her colleagues of the Fourth Estate would scent blood in the water and descend on her in a feeding frenzy of pestering questions.

'Thank you, Inspector. You are a wise and a good man.'

'Perhaps. I am also, unless these murders are cleared up, soon to be a traffic policeman on the island of Lampedusa.'

He shrugged, and let her out of the interview room.

Someone – Marcello? Geneviève? Geneviève – had retrieved some clothes from the *pensione* and sent them to the police station on Piazza Venezia, so she did not have to change into the remains of her party dress to be let out.

It was early evening, the sky purple. On the steps of the police station, she drew breath. She had looked forward to something other than the stale air of the cell.

A cry went up from across the piazza. A horde of pressmen, who had been lounging by the Victor Emmanuel Monument, rushed up at her, hastily grabbing cameras, microphones, and notebooks. Flashbulbs exploded, questions were gabbled in many languages. Light and noise assaulted her.

She covered her eyes.

25

THE ORDER OF THE BOOT

Princess Asa Vajda was on her knees at the foot of her bed, face pressed to the eiderdown, hair a thistly tangle. The coverlet was streaked with bloody tears.

Tom tried warily to get her attention. The last time he'd been sent to ask after the Princess, she'd tossed a Fabergé Devil Egg the size of a hand grenade at him. The door was dented and the bauble lay unnoticed on the thick carpet, its surmounting inverted cross bent out of shape. It was priceless but in hideous taste.

'Princess,' he said.

Asa's back was racked with sobbing. She was like a dark Ophelia, driven out of her mind with grief.

'Princess,' he insisted.

She looked up from the eiderdown. Ropes of hair hung like seaweed over her eyes. Smudges of blood were smeared on her cheeks. She'd chewed her lush lower lip. There was even a little water in her tears.

'Penelope… Miss Churchward… wondered if you would like to come down, and have tea. The police have left.'

Inspector Silvestri was tactfully refraining from pressing the Princess for an interview. But the cops came back to Fregene every day and had still not finished their investigation of the scene of the crime. Many areas of the Palazzo Otranto were roped off and guarded.

Asa's hands crawled over the bed like white spiders. Tom tensed, in case she was looking for another weapon. Instead, she stood up. She'd been wearing the same soiled white gown for days, the wedding dress she was cheated out of. The garment would do for a shroud.

The room was musky with an odour of the dead. A basin of shrivelled violets stood beside the bed.

The Princess ran fingers through her hair. Her knuckles caught on snaggles and knots. She was not fit for society.

The dead bitch fastened Tom with a mad stare. He was proof against her fascinations. Penelope had overwhelmed him totally. It was not that he had the strength to resist an elder like Asa, but that he had no will of his own to be dominated and broken.

Asa gave up.

'Tea will be served in an hour,' he said. 'Company is expected.'

What he felt for Penelope might be love. He'd once assumed he wasn't capable of love, frankly doubting the emotion everyone talked about actually existed. Now his whole person was wrapped up with another, a dead woman at that. His contentment and ease of mind were dependent on her moods. If he hadn't been in such a daze from the bleedings, he'd have been terrified to have stepped so far off the track. Now he understood why people spoke of 'falling in' love rather than 'ascending to' it. He was plummeting.

She was in the Crystal Room, working at a paper-strewn desk. In late afternoon, the sun didn't shine into the room, but she still wore a wide-brimmed hat and dark glasses. The murder of *il principe* had thrown the rest of the household into a panic, but Penelope showed an English cool head. She coped with everything from an avalanche of condolence cards to easing relations between the cops and the Carpathian Guard.

'I've told Princess Asa about tea,' he said.

'Will she come down?'

'I don't know.'

Penelope's mouth narrowed. 'Very well. Come here, would you, Tom?'

This time, he would not obey. He was determined. But he found himself standing by Penelope's desk, a schoolboy summoned to the headmaster.

She stood, bent back her hatbrim, and stuck her mouth to his neck. The electric shock of penetration came, and a little more of him flowed into her. She swallowed, dabbed her lips with a hankie, and sat down, looking again at the ledger open on the desk.

Tom swayed a little, unsteady on his feet. He was not sure if he was dismissed.

Though Penelope was bleeding him as regularly as ever, she was more businesslike about it. She nipped without passion, as if he were an animal or a servant. She was concerned with too much else to spare time for coaxing him along. He didn't even mind. Just so long as he could stay.

'I think we have discovered why the late Prince was so attractive to the House of Vajda,' Penelope said.

She stabbed a finger at a column of numbers.

'Not to put too fine a point on it, Asa is stony broke and has been for two hundred years. She inherited a fortune with her title, but spent it all on living from decade to decade. She has never had any income except plunder, never made any investments. Without Dracula's gold, the poor dear will have to throw herself on the mercy of her creditors. Or find herself another wealthy fiancé.'

Penelope spoke as if this discovery didn't please her. She seemed to express genuine sympathy for the Princess.

'That's the trouble with elders,' she said. 'They live forever and don't realise things run out. They were born in an age when stewards ran households, and never learned to balance the books.'

A little of his blood was smudged at the corner of her mouth. He didn't point it out.

She slammed the ledger shut.

'Asa's bankruptcy is a minor inconvenience. Since no connection was actually made with the House of Dracula, she can safely be sent packing with a charitable handout. The real nightmare will come when we have to settle the Count's affairs. The guests who are expected for tea will complicate matters. I had hoped to put them off until after the police closed the case, but they are impatient.'

Penelope took charge because someone had to. When word came of the other murders in Rome on the night of Dracula's death, the elders assembled for the ball scurried out of Italy, dispersing to the corners of the world. Without their Prince, most of the Carpathian Guard felt no duty to remain at Otranto. Dead men who had stuck to their posts for centuries were gone overnight. Some exposed themselves to the sun and crumbled, out of shame at their failure to protect their master. Others less honourable simply deserted, taking with them whatever items of value they could lay their claws on. Many of the servants also hightailed it out of the palace. The retainers who stayed did so perhaps because they couldn't think of anywhere else to go.

There was all manner of mess. Penelope had rolled up her sleeves and set to clearing up.

Klove opened the door and let five people into the room.

'Good afternoon,' said Penelope, a perfect hostess.

The distinguished newcomers were Clare Boothe Luce, the American Ambassador; John Profumo, the British Minister of War; General Giovanni Di Lorenzo, head of the Italian Secret Police; Andrey Gromyko, the Soviet Foreign Minister; and General Charles de Gaulle, President of the Republic of France. De Gaulle might have come in person to make sure Dracula was truly dead.

Double doors opened and servants wheeled in a convoy of tea trolleys.

'Might I offer you hospitality?' asked Penelope. 'It is a tradition of this house.'

She was acting like the widow. As she picked up a hefty teapot and bent forward to pour, Profumo sneakily eyed the top of her summer dress.

De Gaulle snorted through his prominent beak at this British affectation. Penelope drew his attention to a decanter of brandy that evidently met with his approval. Mrs Luce, who reminded Tom nastily of his aunt, didn't take kindly to the display of indulgence; she was as ill at ease both with taking tea from a dead woman as with the presence of a known Communist. Gromyko sipped his weak, milky tea and stuck out his little finger like a charm school graduate.

'Thank you, gracious lady,' said the Russian.

'You are welcome.'

'If we could get down to brass tacks, Andrey,' said Mrs Luce. She used the Russian's Christian name like an insult.

'Very well, *Clare*,' he retorted, shrugging an apology to Penelope.

'Who is this person?' Di Lorenzo demanded, meaning Tom.

'My good right hand,' said Penelope. 'A countryman of yours, Ambassador. Perhaps you know his people.'

As it happened, she didn't. Which was a mercy.

'Miss Churchward,' ventured Profumo, 'do you have the authority to speak for the House of Dracula?'

'So it seems,' Penelope admitted. 'I've no formal position, but have been with the household long enough to be familiar with its affairs. In the absence of any official executrix, I've taken matters in hand. Thus far, I have not been opposed.'

Profumo nodded.

'You are aware of the terms of *il principe*'s residency in the Palazzo Otranto?' asked the Italian.

'Not entirely,' said Penelope. 'I understand a treaty was struck during the last war, between Dracula and the Allies. I assume that is why this party has such an interesting international flavour?'

'Dracula lived here at the sufferance of the Allied powers,' Mrs Luce stated. 'A condition of the Croglin Grange Treaty was that he make no attempt to leave.'

Penelope nodded. Tom had wondered whether Dracula might not have been some sort of prisoner.

'We were concerned, dear lady, about his engagement,' said Gromyko. 'It was never clear where the bride and groom would reside. The possibility that they might choose to leave this palace, and thus violate Croglin Grange, gave us much to worry over.'

Mrs Luce shot the Russian a nasty look. A die-hard anti-

Communist, and prominent supporter of the late Senator Joseph McCarthy, she was also known to loathe vampires. She had coined the slogan 'Never Dead Nor Red', popularised by her husband Henry's blatantly-titled magazine, *Life*.

'Sadly, that concern is at an end,' said Penelope.

'Indeed, indeed,' said Profumo, trying to smooth things over. The minister attacked the bourbon biscuits as if he'd skipped lunch.

'There is no Dracula,' said Di Lorenzo. 'There is no Croglin Grange.'

Tom didn't understand.

'Very well,' said Penelope. 'If I might be permitted to stay on long enough to settle things.'

'Of course, of course,' said Profumo. 'Does anyone have any objections?'

De Gaulle looked up from his brandy and said, '*Non*'.

Tom realised they were being evicted. The Italians wanted their palace back. It hadn't occurred to him, but of course Otranto had never really been Dracula's property.

This party couldn't just be to award the Order of the Boot to the last of Dracula's household. There must be other matters to settle, of international importance.

'Gracious lady,' said the Russian, 'we are anxious that the papers of the late Prince be disposed of tactfully.'

'There is a great deal of documentation,' Penelope admitted. 'In a variety of languages, with few of which I am familiar. Much must be of historical importance. I should hope a permanent home could be found for this Dracula archive.'

The distinguished visitors exchanged looks. Tom understood these people. They all wanted to be left alone with the papers, to search for documents embarrassing to themselves or their enemies. None trusted the others not to exploit the material for their own ends, quite correctly. They were all out for what they could get.

'The British Museum Library would be willing to take the burden,' Profumo suggested, accepting another pouring of tea.

'*Non*,' said de Gaulle.

No one else was blatant enough to put their own case. That would come later.

There was a commotion outside.

'I believe the Princess Asa is joining us,' said Penelope.

Klove, deferentially unhappy about it, opened the door again, and the princess trailed in. Asa still wore her wedding gown. Flowers were wound into her hair and spots of rouge inexpertly applied to her cheeks. She all but wailed as she dragged herself into the Crystal Room.

'Princess, dear, can I offer you refreshment?'

Penelope held a white mouse by its tail. She had taken the animal from a writhing fishbowl full of the rodents. Leftovers from the party.

Asa took the mouse and savaged it in two bites. Blood squirted down her lacework bosom.

Penelope looked at her with triumphant sympathy. She shared the expression with her guests, allowing herself the hint of a 'what can you do?' shrug.

Asa swallowed what she'd chewed and clung to Penelope like a child. The Englishwoman picked through the Moldavian's hair, smoothing tangles and extracting dead flowers.

'She's had a shock, poor thing,' Penelope explained, needlessly. 'But she'll be her own self in a few years. Won't you, dearest Asa?'

She nodded and Asa mimicked her.

26

MR WEST AND DR PRETORIUS

The remains were kept on the lowest level of the central morgue. From preserved scraps of mural, Geneviève guessed the building was built upon the foundations of an ancient Roman institution. Maybe this was where they'd brought gutted gladiators for primitive experiments in anatomy. More likely the place, like everywhere else important, had once been a brothel.

She passed down through rooms with pull-out drawers for the dead to rooms where corpses were strewn haphazardly on gurneys. Victims of age, disease, violence, and accident lay untroubled, bumped to the back of the queue by the vampire murders. Though she had only the slightest acquaintance with any of the victims, the destruction of seven elders – eight, if Dracula were included – made her think about her own mortality. If she'd left the party earlier, she might have had her own encounter with the Crimson Executioner. All the victims were of an age to have outlasted generations of fearless vampire slayers, to have survived many assassination attempts. She had no reason to think she'd have had any better luck if the man in red had come for her with a silver-bladed axe.

A trick of acoustics meant there was a constant background whispering. The voices of doctors and coroners, policemen and grieving relatives, were picked up on the building's internal wind and circulated in a sinister susurrus that sounded dreadfully like the massed complaining of the dead.

Born in an age where squeamishness was unheard of – her human father was a surgeon who had worked on battlefields, and she'd been his apprentice – and having lived through centuries too often marked by grue, Geneviève was not easily affected by empty flesh vessels or bothered by thoughts of angry spirits.

This place, however, made her skin crawl.

Through curiosity as much as duty she had consented to the request relayed from the police via the French consul. With the sudden exodus of elders from Rome, she was apparently the only person within reach who could legitimately identify the body. That she'd already done so at the scene of the crime made the whole business redundant, but forms had to be filled in and the identification made in the presence of an official witness.

Sergeant Ginko guided her through the labyrinth of the morgue. He grumbled sourly that if pressure had not been brought from above to have so many policemen at the Palazzo Otranto, then the Crimson Executioner wouldn't have had such an easy time of it in the city. She doubted that any number of men would have prevented the killings.

From his white-belted blue uniform and white beret, she knew the Sergeant was with the *polizia*, the state police. They had responsibility for violent crime, but a rivalry existed with the *carabinieri*, the red-trousered military police, who tended to boast that if it were down to them, none of this would ever have happened. Both the *polizia* and the *carabinieri* sneered at the *vigili urbani*, the municipal police, who wore blue in winter and white in summer and chiefly made a hash of directing traffic.

They came into a room the size of a swimming pool, lit like an American pool hall. Banks of shrouded lights hung over long tables. Two men worked among the dead. Geneviève understood specialists had been called on to do the forensic work.

Ginko introduced her to Mr Herbert West, of the Miskatonic University, and Dr Septimus Pretorius, who was attached to no institution. Neither gentleman gave her more than a nod. They were absorbed in examining a strew of ashes topped by a wig of long black hair and dotted here and there with teeth or tiny bones.

West was a whiny little American, with a boyish face and a fragile demeanour. A splatter of blood smeared one lens of his glasses and streaked through his tidy hair.

'Were enough blood spilled on these ashes,' West argued, 'I believe Luna Mora would coalesce and walk again. Nodes remain even on a microscopic level which could link up and recreate her body. Of course, consciousness has flown forever. We could merely reconstitute and reanimate something with the shape of Luna Mora, not the person herself. For that, we should need the physical brain, the seat of reason.'

Dr Pretorius snorted like a dowager who notices a niece using the wrong fork. He had the face of a disapproving gnome, and a bird's nest of fine cottony hair. His white smock was immaculate.

'You are a buffoon, West,' he said.

West spluttered, but made no reply. His face reddened.

'This is dirt, nothing more,' Pretorius decided, flicking some off his fingers. 'Much of it is street grime swept up with the remains. Would our lady elder care to be revived with layer after layer of dog faeces or petrol smuts shot through her body? I think not.'

'You misrepresent my views,' West said.

'We have an elder here,' Pretorius said, acknowledging Geneviève with a yellow smile. 'Shall we call upon her expertise, West? Shall we ask her whether she would be happy to be summoned from eternal night to find shards of cobblestone incorporated into her body like malignant tumours? Or shall we merely settle the matter by admitting that you are an incompetent blockhead?'

West turned away. Pretorius allowed himself a tiny twitch of triumph.

Sergeant Ginko began: 'Mademoiselle Dieudonné is here to…'

'Identify the corpse of Count Dracula,' said Pretorius. 'I know. Welcome, lady. Would you like some gin?'

He shook an unlabelled bottle of clear liquid.

'It's my only weakness,' he said, taking a swallow.

Geneviève shook her head.

'Pity. Very good for you, gin. You vampires don't drink enough, you know. Rely too much on the meagre sustenance of blood. You should all have at least a pint of gin a month. And weak tea. Or else you dry up inside. Like frogs away from water. Very nasty.'

West pushed his glasses up over his forehead. His watery eyes passed over her and he came close to look. His fingers prodded her face.

'Remarkable, remarkable,' he mused. 'The lividity, the pliability, the evident…'

'Put her down, West,' snapped Pretorius. 'Stop playing with the guests.'

'I maintain that…'

'Nobody needs to know what you maintain, fool. Excuse me, Mademoiselle. Mr West has been pursuing his own crackpot notions for a good many years. He often forgets his theories were discredited before the War and acts as if sense could be made of all this.'

Pretorius indicated the room with a flourish.

'As if making sense were anything but a convenient fiction.'

Geneviève didn't know what to make of Dr Pretorius. Like most scientists who specialised in the theory and practice of vampirism, he was not a vampire himself. He was, however, unnaturally old. She remembered his name from articles she had read at least a century ago and had the idea he had been old then. Whereas Charles had retained the outward appearance of youth for a great many years, Pretorius looked ancient. His hands were arthritic claws and his clear blue eyes nested in wrinkles, but inner steel and fire suggested a vitality that was nowhere near exhausted. Turning vampire was only the most common way of achieving unnatural longevity. A Chinese criminal Charles had encountered a time or two was believed to rely on an elixir tailored to his peculiar physiology. And there were stories of other ancients who still walked the Earth.

West was apoplectic. 'Everything is mechanical,' he shouted, prompting Pretorius to a comical, conspiratorial cringe. 'If we do not as yet understand a process, it is because we have not perceived the rules which govern its working. The dead may walk. This is a fact. There is no magic in it at all. A long-lived, as-yet unidentified virus – perhaps mutated by radium deposits in the Carpathians – will doubtless prove to be at the bottom of it. If this can be harnessed, then it will be possible for all to survive death at no cost.'

Pretorius smiled. 'How many years, West? How long have you been searching for your virus? The idea is not even original with him, Mademoiselle. He was catamite to a certain Dr Moreau, who laid down much of the groundwork for this fruitless detour. And Moreau was a collaborator with Henry Jekyll.'

'I know,' she said, interrupting the tirade.

She had met Dr Jekyll and Dr Moreau.

'Well, yes, of course you do. Before Jekyll, there was Van Helsing. And there've been others: Alexander Fleming, Peter Blood, Edmund Cordery. All squinting into their microscopes, watching the little red cells go round and round, looking for an answer.'

'Miss Dieudonné,' began West, 'do you think yourself a natural being?'

Pretorius raised a feathery eyebrow and bid her answer.

'No more nor less than I did when I was warm.'

'You see, West, you're on the wrong path. It's not that we don't understand how vampires live. We don't understand how *humans* live. We can approximate the formulae. We can create life in glass jars. We can reanimate dead tissue. We can try to sell our souls to Satan, for all the good it will do. We can have everything, except an answer that makes sense.'

'I refuse to accept that.'

'Refuse all you may, West. I have been at this a great deal longer than you. I learned many years ago that it was futile to try to explain. The deeper you get, the *less* sense there is, the more contradictions emerge.'

'You're r-r-regressing to alchemy,' stuttered West. 'What is next, s-s-sorcery?'

Pretorius grinned like a gargoyle. 'If that is the route we must take. But even sorcery is a way of systematising the unknowable. Perhaps we must accept that things do not make sense. The universe is wildly inconsistent, shifting from moment to moment, plunging from catastrophe to creation.'

'Everything can be understood, Einstein maintained…'

'Not at the end he didn't. At the end, nobody claims to understand. Talk all you will of viruses and radium deposits, or of demons and goblins, but the fact is that there are creatures who cast no reflection in a looking glass. That cannot be explained. In the eighty years the world has been forced to accept that there are indeed such things as vampires, that has defeated many a greater mind than yours, Herbert West. Remember Max Planck's Black Blood Refractive Postulate? What would you give for the laws of optics and refraction? Or any other scientific law? Not a farthing. Things that can't be, are. If there are gods, they are mad or idiot. This girl here defies all your attempts to measure, calculate, categorise, define, confine, or constrain. And what are you going to do about it, bleat?'

'You are wrong,' West said quietly.

'I think not,' said Pretorius.

Geneviève's mind was spinning. Something in Pretorius's fervour frightened her. Could be she was really afraid that he was right? She'd outgrown a youthful terror that she might be a damned soul. But if she was not a creature of science, then what was she? What was left?

'To the void,' toasted Pretorius, lifting his gin. 'To the chaos we must learn to love.'

'Mademoiselle Dieudonné is to make an identification,' prompted Ginko, who'd sat through the debate without complaining.

Pretorius reached under a black blanket and produced an object. It was Dracula's head, still unrotted, eyes angry.

'Is this him?'

Geneviève nodded.

'You have to say it,' Pretorius said. 'Officially.'

'That's Dracula,' she said.

'*Quelle surprise*,' Pretorius said, tossing the head aside like a turnip. 'I don't like to speculate without fully consulting my estimable colleague West, but I think it's safe to say the old bastard's truly dead. Is there anything else?'

Geneviève looked at the Sergeant. He shrugged.

'I think you can leave me to it then,' Pretorius said. 'You'll get my forensic report in the next week. I doubt it will be of any use to you, or indeed anyone. Good day.'

They were required to leave.

27

PROFONDO ROSSO

For a while, it was a nightmare. Having learned of the chase among the pack didn't make her a happier quarry. She did all the stupid things she'd seen people do when barracked by reporters. She flung her hands over her face, looked down at her shoes, and tried to walk on an invisible straight line through the crowd. She didn't so much as snap 'no comment' in answer to increasingly blunt and impolite questions tossed at her like grapples. She must have looked guilty as Judas.

Kate got back to the *pensione* just in time to be thrown out. The press had been there too and got a lot of interview material from the landlady's family about what a suspicious foreign slut she was. She hadn't slept in Trastevere more than twice since arriving in Rome. She'd spent most of her time at Marcello's apartment, with Charles and Geneviève, out on the street, or in prison. Nevertheless, she was required to settle an inflated bill to get her suitcase back.

She tried to telephone Marcello at his apartment but got no answer. She trudged up and down Via Veneto, but couldn't find him in any of his usual haunts.

Of course, she realised Marcello had told the other reporters about her. It was how they had been able to lay in wait outside the police station. It was also presumably why he hadn't been there. Apart from anything that might have been between them, she was a story and he ought to have been there to get it. At least he had enough gumption to be ashamed of putting her on the spot.

She still planned on taking it out on him.

While she had been in prison, the mood of the city had changed. The Via Veneto wasn't as abandoned as before, except in the sense that a great many had abandoned it for somewhere else. The Café Strega was almost deserted. The elder vampires were gone, and quite a few new-borns were making themselves scarce. If the Crimson Executioner wanted the undead out of the city, he'd scored a triumph.

She sat in the café, sipping blood. To her relief, no one bothered her. The feeding frenzy over her story had passed, and someone else would be haring around with the press at their heels. The police had announced that she was not a suspect in the death of Prince Dracula. That left the press free to speculate on increasingly bizarre conspiracies. She liked the one about the Carpathian guardsman brainwashed by the Red Chinese and transformed into a vampire slayer, though she was a lot more likely to believe it was all down to the Jesuits.

Charles was gone, and now Dracula too. Her past was being dismantled. One man she had loved, the other hated, but they had defined a world she understood. A world in which she had a place, a cause, duties, ties. The cords that fixed her in the universe were being snipped one at a time.

Was this how elders came to feel? In time, everything they remembered from life passed. They alone remained, locked into their skulls, lost in a world of pop-up toasters and television advertisements.

She felt very small and not a little afraid.

'The answers to such mysteries are very often found under the soles of our shoes.'

Father Merrin's comment stuck in her mind. He had placed a subtle emphasis on the sentence. It was something he'd intended she should remember, should think about.

What was under the soles of her shoes?

Tiles. None too clean.

And beneath that?

Eventually, earth and rock and magma.

There were catacombs, ruins, caves, lairs, cells, basements. Even nightclubs. She kept being taken underground. Rome was like an iceberg. Only a fraction was on the surface.

What lived under Rome?

Or who?

'There are tears everywhere,' Santona had said. 'The stones of the city pour forth tears.'

She remembered Santona too, her talk of *Mater Lachrymarum*, the Mother of Tears. The fortune-teller implied a link between this mysterious person and the girl who'd led Kate into Dracula's tomb. The child's pretty, evil face appeared to her still. Everything else might die here in Rome but the little girl would live on. Kate had a sense she was an ancient creature: not a vampire, but an elemental, something eternal and dreadful.

A mother must have a daughter. She kept coming back to that. Santona had said *Mater Lachrymarum* was not the girl's mother, but the city's.

How could Rome have a mother? According to Kate's old classics teacher, the city had two fathers, Romulus and Remus. No mother was mentioned, unless it was the wolf bitch who suckled the twins.

Something stirred in her heart. Not just terror, but curiosity, a need to know, to understand. It was a song she'd heard since her warm days, perhaps the overriding melody of her life.

Charles's death had knocked her out of herself. But perhaps Dracula's passing had slapped her back on course. There was something new mixed in, a tune she'd never heard before. In a sense she didn't want to contemplate yet, she was free. Without Dracula, the world was free to make of itself what it wished. And without Charles, so was she.

She wept hot tears.

She was not yet ready to be this free, this alone. It was like leaving school, leaving home, leaving society. To have no rules or measures, to have nothing but herself.

Her tears dried.

'Kate,' someone said, laying hands on hers, sitting down at the table.

She thought it might be Marcello. Despite her annoyance at him, her heart leaped.

It was Geneviève. She tried not to be disappointed.

'Kate, how are you? I hadn't heard they'd let you out.'

'I'm fine,' she said, pulling in her hands.

'You wouldn't believe the day I've had,' Geneviève said. She signalled a waiter with one hand. 'They had me identify Dracula's head.'

Kate cringed in sympathy.

'It's not rotted,' Geneviève said. 'That's baffling everyone. Age is supposed to catch up with elders when they die. Most of the Crimson Executioner's victims are heaps of funny-coloured dust. But Dracula looks fresh.'

'Next thing, they'll be saying he's a saint. Some are supposed to resist corruption.'

'Everything that could be said about Dracula has been said, trust me. You should have seen the newspapers.'

'I've been catching up. It's amazing how violent death ennobles some folk. All those people seething with hatred last week can turn around sincerely and pay tribute to a great statesman and significant figure in twentieth century history. Surely someone else must have reacted to the news by singing "Ding-Dong, the Witch is Dead" and wearing a lampshade.'

Geneviève's drink arrived and she ordered one for Kate.

They looked at each other, not sure what to say.

'I miss him,' Geneviève admitted finally.

Kate nodded. 'Me too.'

They did not mean Dracula.

'I don't know what I thought it'd be like,' Geneviève said. 'It's not as if I'm not used to people dying off around me. It's just that Charles was so *there*, if you know what I mean.'

'I do.'

It was a good thing Kate was cried out.

'There's too much mystery left, Kate. Charles would have hated that. The Crimson Executioner and your little girl. And Dracula. Who killed Dracula?'

'It wasn't me.'

'I know.'

'It should have been. In a way, I wish I had killed him. I wish I could have cut through all the compromises and decided this man did not deserve to live any longer, then stabbed him through the heart and cut off his head. I can see myself doing it, but I know I didn't. I don't know whether to feel guilty about not saving him or not killing him. I still feel his blood on me, under my skin.'

'If I can help, Kate, I will.'

She took Geneviève's hand.

'There's someone I want to visit, to talk with. Will you come with me?'

'Of course.'

'It means going somewhere our kind aren't welcome.'

Geneviève was puzzled for a moment, then understood.

28

L'ESORCISTA

It was the rankest superstition to suppose a vampire could not tread on consecrated ground. Every scrap of earth had been consecrated to some faith at some time. Being unable to step on holy turf would mean living on the high seas, outside territorial waters. In her centuries, Geneviève had been in numberless graveyards, shrines, churches, cathedrals, mosques, and temples. Always, she felt a certain frisson, the thrill of harmless trespass. However, this was a different prospect. She and Kate stood on Viale Vaticano, outside a church that was also a city.

Swiss guards were stationed at the tall gates. It was the evening and the Vatican Museums were closed to the public. The tourists had gone away, but the area swarmed with priests and nuns. Though she knew it was silly, Geneviève was uncomfortable. She'd lived through enough history to know the Vatican as a temporal institution. They only admitted the infamy of the Spanish Inquisition to play down the memory of the even more atrocious Roman Inquisition. As many murderers, villains, and degenerates had occupied the throne of St Peter as had held any other high office.

But this was the Church.

She predated the Reformation. In her time, there'd been one Church. All else was dangerous heresy. Just after her turning, she'd been excommunicated, though it remained a moot point whether she even counted as a human being with a soul.

'Come on, Gené,' nagged Kate. She was a Protestant, of course. And claimed to be an agnostic on top of that.

Kate took her arm and they crossed the road.

As someone born in the faith and fallen away (a long way) from it, was she more or less likely than a heathen like Kate Reed to combust when she set foot on Vatican territory? When did the holiness start? There ought to be a line in the road. At some point, she must cross it.

She did not explode.

Somewhere, bells were ringing. She did not put that down to an angelic miracle.

The Swiss Guards angled their pikes threateningly. Kate explained that they had an appointment with a Father Merrin.

Geneviève noticed one of the guards was a vampire. Without Dracula, a lot of Carpathians were unemployed. Mercenary forces like the Swiss Guard and the French *Légion d'Étranger* would get some unexpected recruits.

They were admitted into Momo's famous spiral ramp, which wound up from street level to the museum and library floors. A chittering of footsteps from above sounded and a small blonde woman came to greet them. She was not a nun, but a lay worker with modestly covered hair and downcast eyes. Something about her gave Geneviève the creeps. She said her name was Viridiana and offered to lead them to Father Merrin.

They were escorted through the corridors of the Belvedere Palace, deeper into the Vatican itself. They hurried across the Cortile Ottagonale, and off the tourist track, proceeding from marble floors to stone. Geneviève clung close to Kate. Long-faced priests and scarlet-robed cardinals drifted past like ghosts, all turning piercing eyes at the interloping female nosferatu.

Historically, the Church had been dead set against her kind. The communion of blood-drinking was thought a blasphemous parody of the rite of mass. It struck her that the real reason for the enmity was that the Church and the vampire were competitors. If Dr Pretorius was right and vampirism was resistant to rational explanation, then she was possessed of more demonstrably miraculous powers than the parish priest, who merely turned wine to blood. And an institution which traded in an immortality to come must be embarrassed by the prospect of easily-obtained immortality here on Earth.

Viridiana brought them into the basement that was a maze of locked bookcases. This was not the Vatican Library, but one of the Church's many private archives. Geneviève felt like asking if this was where they kept the pornography. A few lights shone in the murky distance, but darkness was the prevailing condition. The lay worker led them confidently into the labyrinth, flicking a switch every thirty paces. Weak bulbs strung overhead lit the book-lined corridor only up to the next switch and automatically shut off after five seconds. They had to hurry to keep up with the light.

They came to a clearing. Viridiana indicated a row.

'Father Merrin is along here,' she said, strangely reluctant to go further. 'He is waiting for you.'

Kate thanked the girl.

They walked between tall cases. Kate took over the switch-flicking. Books as old as she was caught Geneviève's eye, thick brassbound spines, pages the colour of tanned skin.

Kate had explained that Father Lankester Merrin was a priest and scholar, an anthropologist. He was an associate of the controversial Catholic evolutionist Pierre Teilhard de Chardin, and also – it was rumoured – one of the Church's last vampire hunters. Apparently, he'd performed rites of exorcism in Africa and banished some local predator to the outer darkness. He'd been there when Dracula died.

The priest was indeed in a pool of light at the intersection of several shelf-lined passageways. He sat at a desk, making notes. He was a thin, vigorous man.

'Miss Reed,' he greeted Kate, standing politely.

'Father Merrin, this is Geneviève Dieudonné.'

'I am pleased to meet you,' the priest said, extending a hand.

Geneviève hesitated.

'I don't think my touch will burn,' he said.

They shook hands.

'I am unsinged,' she said, showing him her palm.

He did not smile with his mouth, but his startling blue eyes were full of humour. Whatever her opinion of his Church, she had to concede this was a real priest.

'Thank you for agreeing to see us,' said Kate.

Merrin accepted the thanks without trivialising the favour asked of him. This archive wasn't open to scholars outside the Church, even by special appointment. It was a signifier of the priest's status within the Vatican that he was empowered to invite them here.

'What do you know about the Mother of Tears?' Kate asked.

Merrin nodded, as if he had been expecting the question. It was Geneviève who was shocked. When Brastov had mentioned the Three Mothers, she'd known he was trying to set a train of thought in motion, but all that had happened since had kept the train stubbornly derailed. Now she remembered her insight in Brastov's lair, that the spymaster had gone to a lot of trouble to drop a name.

'You are interested in the Mother of Rome?' asked Merrin. 'The eternal feminine of the eternal city. *Mater Lachrymarum*.'

'The name keeps coming up.'

Merrin smiled, icily. 'It would.'

Geneviève felt a slight draught. Pages lifted and settled. A building this large must have its own internal weather.

'She has many aspects,' said the priest. 'Some heretics call her the Black Virgin, mother of the Antichrist. Classical argument identifies her with Circe, Medea, or Medusa. She is the secret empress of Rome. Officially, the Church says she was a witch, like her two sisters, long dead and forgotten.'

'What do you believe?' Kate asked.

'Belief is infinitely complex. I have made no special study of *Mater Lachrymarum*. A few scholars in recent years have proposed such a venture but found no support. It's my feeling that the Vatican and the Mother of Tears are wary of each other, and choose not to go head to head. Our centres of power are on opposite banks of the Tiber.

The few volumes that make mention of this creature are not currently available to me.'

Merrin indicated the darkness of one stack.

'What does the Mother of Tears look like?'

'Traditionally, she has four aspects. A child, a young woman, a mature woman, and a crone. Of these, the child is the most terrible, for she is an innocent and has the ruthlessness of innocence. She is also, under certain circumstances, the Devil. The young woman is a saint, the mature woman a harlot, and the crone a prophetess. The child is half-blind, but the crone sees all. The saint tells the truth, but the mature woman lies.'

Kate nodded, accepting what she was told.

Geneviève was catching up. This little girl, whom Kate had seen in Piazza di Trevi and again at the Palazzo Otranto, was some sort of inhuman creature, but not a vampire. There were other monsters in the world.

'She is stronger than a vampire elder, than all the vampire elders,' Merrin continued. 'She is eternal but not ageless. In her four aspects, she is a complete cycle, a full life. Vampires are apart from the world, its changes and turmoils, but the Mother of Tears embraces them, embodies them. You are cool, she is warm. Your hearts are stilled, hers beats with the life of the city.'

'What is her purpose?' Kate asked.

Merrin shrugged, expressively. 'To continue?'

A spiral-bound notebook fluttered, pages riffling. There was a definite wind. The holy breeze of the Vatican whipped against Geneviève's face, trailing invisible fingers through her hair. She felt an icy hand reaching into her chest.

In the dark beyond their circle of light, wings flapped. Kate looked alarmed. A sharp beak struck out, swooping over the tops of the bookcases, angling down toward the priest, at the point of a long, black-winged body.

Geneviève lashed out, but missed the bird.

The beak-point sliced into Merrin's forehead, just above his glasses. Geneviève lunged for the bird. It was the size of an eagle and the colour of a crow. Yellow eyes rimmed with red. She caught its beak and held it shut.

The wings beat, hammering her chest with blows that would have broken the bones of a warm woman. The ugly bird struggled free and rose above them, hovering. Kate lay over Merrin, protecting him.

Geneviève knew better than to wonder how the thing had got in here. It flapped twice and rose out of her grasp. Talons angled down, pointed with barbs of bone.

She prayed it would leave.

And it was gone.

The effect was like a blow to the heart. She could not help but think she was the victim of a magic trick, an ancient device to reaffirm faith through the sudden imposition and removal of violent adversity.

Kate helped Merrin up and looked at his forehead. She wet a hankie on her cat-like tongue and cleaned the gash, wiping away the trickle of blood.

Merrin didn't flinch.

Geneviève knew Kate must have the smell of his blood in her nostrils, and be fighting a primal urge to fasten her mouth over his wound and suck.

'You must be careful,' the priest said. 'Both of you.'

'What was that?' Geneviève asked.

'A warning, to the Church, to me. We are to stay out of this. It is between you, by which I mean vampires, and her, the Mother of Tears.'

'Was that another aspect of her?' Kate asked.

'Only a conjuring. A little display of power. She likes her puppets, her toys. This Crimson Executioner is probably a man who has fallen under her spell, and does her bidding.'

Kate nodded. 'I thought so. In the Piazza di Trevi, it was her. The little girl. She killed Kernassy and Malenka, using the Executioner as a weapon.'

And in Otranto, Geneviève thought, what there? The Crimson Executioner was at the other end of the strings, in Rome, cutting a swath. At Otranto, when Dracula was killed, there must have been another toy, another weapon.

Geneviève felt a surge of dread for Kate.

Had her friend realised the possibility? She must have, to

have become so fixed on her course.

'Can they be freed?' Geneviève asked. 'Her puppets?'

Merrin shook his head. 'Only by death.'

Kate's face was a blank.

It didn't seem right to leave Father Merrin alone, but he insisted he'd be all right. The attack had been a demonstration not an assassination attempt, directed as much at Geneviève and Kate as him.

'Will Viridiana show us out?' Kate asked.

'Viridiana?' Merrin asked, puzzled.

'The lay worker? The young woman?'

Kate's words died as she spoke them. Geneviève tried to remember the bland, pretty face of the warm girl who had guided them here, but could not.

'Even here,' Merrin mused, smiling sadly. 'She is bold. I hope fervently you will be able to come to an accommodation with her, for no one has ever beaten her.'

They left him and retraced their path, not bothering with the lights. They needed to remind themselves they were vampires, that they were mistresses of the dark.

'If it's me, Gené,' Kate said, 'you're to kill me. Cut off my head and stuff it full of garlic. You're the only one I can trust to do it. Please, promise.'

Geneviève looked at her friend. 'I promise, *chère* Kate.'

'Thank you,' Kate said, and kissed her.

29

WHAT'S NEW, PUSSYCAT?

It was all over. Dracula was dead, properly. He wouldn't marry Asa Vajda, therefore wouldn't become a force again in the politics of the Balkans. Bond felt the knot he'd almost unpicked had been severed by an Alexandrine blow.

'Princess Asa is not very good with visitors yet, I'm afraid,' Miss Churchward told him. 'She's had a shock, as I'm sure you appreciate.'

He looked around the empty ballroom. Hangings were still left over from the party, banners with coats of arms. The buffet mice – largely untouched by vampire guests who preferred human blood – had escaped from their cages, swarming over the abandoned salads, thriving on canapés. Generations would probably breed in Palazzo Otranto.

A few liveried minions made a futile effort to tidy up.

'We have been given notice to quit, Commander Bond,' said Miss Churchward. 'I expect you knew that, being a spy and so forth.'

He didn't deny it. Everybody in Rome knew what he was. He was a bit on the high-profile side. The Diogenes Club was cultivating his colourless replacements, Grammar School civil servants with National Health glasses and Marks & Spencer's raincoats.

Miss Churchward's severe suit and diamanté sunglasses didn't entirely disguise her fine figure. At the ball, her hair had been more attractively arranged than it was now. She might be a tigress.

That American chap he had run into outside the Kit Kat Klub, the one who'd been drained white and tossed aside, was part of the household. He thought more about Miss Churchward, imagined her lips red and her teeth sinking into skin.

He gave her his card.

'When you return to London, perhaps we could meet?'

Miss Churchward looked at it, and over her glasses at him.

He allowed her a smile. She accepted it. There was a promise and a challenge in this vampire vixen. Under her tight Victorian skin was a lush, passionate, hungry heart.

Then she gave back his card.

'I think not,' she said.

He couldn't have been more surprised if she had slapped him.

'Commander Bond, you're undoubtedly a very attractive fellow and I would assume something of a success with the ladies. But you are a new-born. You don't yet have powers of fascination.'

He showed nothing in his face.

'You don't understand, do you?' she said. 'Here.'

She took off her glasses, and fixed him with a red look like a vice. He couldn't move. His knees were locked. Miss Churchward owned him. He would die for a word from her. He would throw himself into flames.

Miss Churchward touched her lips with a forefinger, and brushed his mouth with it. An electricity coursed through him, making every nerve burn. The moment lasted an eternity. He staggered.

'And that's just a touch,' she said, with a tiny smile.

Bond composed himself. The sunbursts in his head fizzled. He looked across the hall and saw how carefully Tom was moving, like an old man. He was white as a ghost and thin to the point of insubstantiality. Miss Churchward had nearly used him up.

'If you would show yourself out,' she said. 'I've a lot to see to.'

He couldn't speak.

* * *

Outside, Bond dawdled by his Aston Martin, watching the sunset behind the palazzo, smoking a cigarette. His limbs still tingled. It was as if he'd been seduced by Catherine the Great, then tortured for a week in her dungeons.

He knew very little about Miss Churchward, but Winthrop said that as a warm girl – back in the '80s – she'd been briefly engaged to the Old Man. From the demonstration he'd just had, Bond thought it worth adding a footnote to his report. Penelope Churchward would become one of the most powerful elders in Europe. And she was British.

With Dracula gone, there was a vacancy. Someone had to be Vampire King.

Bond thought the day of King-Emperors was over. The next ruler of the night could well be a Queen-Empress.

He tossed the cigarette to the gravel and slid into the sports car. He didn't have to be in London for a few days, and thought he could scare up some entertainment in Rome.

Halfway back to the city, he realised he was being followed. A familiar sensation. A black Mercedes matched the speed of the Aston Martin. Bond realised the Merc was coordinated with a pair of black-jacketed motorcyclists up ahead. He was trapped between the outriders and the control car.

He shook the last of Miss Churchward's fog out of his mind, and shifted gears.

This was more his style.

He let the Aston Martin surge forward, drawing level with the bikers, to show he was on to them. He looked from side to side, clocking them. They were twins, tiny vampire girls. Long blonde streams fanned out under their crash helmets. They wore black leather jackets over frilly pink leotards.

The girls blew him kisses and, as one, gunned their cycles, nipping ahead of his speeding car. The road narrowed, winding along the rocky coast. He thought of nudging the girls' motorcycles, but didn't want to damage the car.

The Merc caught up with them. In the rear mirror, Bond saw the driver's face. It was the thug Geneviève had called Flattop, black lips in a cruel line, heavy eyes fixed on the car ahead.

So this was Brastov tidying up.

It was possible that Smert Spionem had killed Dracula, but unlikely. The Russians rarely favoured ostentatious displays of assassination. A quiet disappearance was more their style.

No, this was personal business.

Beside Flattop, raised on a cushion, was the Cat Man himself. He was in slightly more human form, though his face was still covered with white fur. His whiskers quivered.

The Aston Martin held the road superbly. The bike girls had to lean this way and that on the curves, knees scraping asphalt, but the car cornered with ease. The heavier, armour-plated Merc screeched, tail scraping the guardrail or the rock wall.

Brastov rolled down his side window and leaned half his body out. He wore a dinner jacket and a studded leather collar. His forelegs lengthened and bulked into human arms. In claw-fingered paws he held a submachine gun.

The gun chattered. Bullets pranged against Bond's car. It was a good job the Aston Martin was armoured with lightweight alloy twice the density of steel. The glass of the rear window cracked but didn't break.

The coast road fed into the main highway. Ahead was Rome. He could lose these gnats in the city.

He appreciated the tight bottoms of the vampire twins as they leaned over their motorcycles, weaving in front of him. They must be Brastov's new bodyguards. His old crew were *hors de combat.*

Other traffic got in the way. A moon-faced priest on a bicycle wobbled and fell over as the chase passed him. Bond looked back, and saw the Merc run over the bike but not the priest, who shook a fist and cursed like a docker. Oncoming cars sensed it would be a good idea to get out of the way.

A herd of sheep were crossing the road. The girls ploughed through the animals first, knocking over some unfortunate beasts. The Merc was too hard on his rear for him to slow down, so he sped up. Animals bounced from the bonnet, leaving bloody smears that'd be hell to clean. A rain of flying sheep fell on Brastov's car, forcing Flattop to skid from side to side, sheep-guts tangled in his wheels.

Bond laughed.

A shepherd ran up to Brastov's car, shouting. The kitty-cat shot him in the face.

That wasn't sporting. It was bad form to kill civilians.

For that, he wouldn't just escape. He would teach the Smert Spionem chief a lesson. Death to Spies, indeed.

The girls were herding him as if he were a bull, skilfully nudging the Aston Martin's bonnet, dancing out of the way if he tried to knock them over. Every so often, they threw him kisses or smiles. They had pink lipstick and pale blue eyeshadow. He wondered how old they were.

They were driving through a slum area. There was still rubble from the war. Mindless zombies shambled past in pathetic gaggles. Fires were starting, spreading red light around. Whores in ratty wool jumpers and short skirts shivered by braziers, showing their breasts at passing cars.

This must be I Cessati Spiriti.

There was room on the wasteland to open up the motor and do a few spectacular circles. It was time to show the twins what the Aston Martin could do. Bond no longer wished to play bull to their toreadors. Here, where there was no property worth damaging and bystanders were hardy enough to survive or too dead to matter, he could be a shark and the girls minnows.

A wall of flame divided one section of rubble from the next. He drove through it.

The girls plunged through after him. When they came out of the fire, their pretty faces were smudged with soot. Their jackets smoked.

The Merc exploded through the flames and ground to a halt in a thick mudpatch.

The Aston Martin wheeled round, leading the bike girls in a figure eight. Bond's fangs popped from his gums, razor tips dimpling his lips. He was working up an appetite.

He eased on the brakes and came to a perfect stop.

The bikes still followed.

With his Walther in his hand, he stepped out of the car.

The bikes skidded and overturned. The girls let their machines skitter away and stood. They took off their helmets and shook out their hair. They still smiled at him, though there was more than a little pout in their full lips.

He had an idea shooting them would have no effect. But it seemed only courteous. He put bullets in one girl's shoulder and the other's knee. They giggled and danced towards him like acrobats.

There was an explosion. The Merc's petrol tank had gone up. The flameburst outlined the tall figure of Flattop and the smaller one of Brastov. They were safe.

'Good evening, Mr Bond,' purred Brastov.

'If you say so,' he replied.

'What do you think of Cathy and Pony? My kittens?'

Brastov stood between the twins, arms around their waists. His head barely came up to their shoulders and they were small. The spymaster wore leather jackboots like Dick Whittington's cat, and walked upright, more like a primate than a feline. He smoked a cigarette in a long holder and wore a red monocle over his left eye.

'Lovely,' Bond said.

'They have claws,' Brastov purred.

'So I see.'

'I shall enjoy watching my kittens play with you.'

Bond remembered what Miss Churchward's touch had done to him. If these girl-shaped creatures had a fraction of her power, he would die. Admittedly, in an interesting way, but that was no consolation.

People had come out to watch. The whores and the zombies and the others of I Cessati Spiriti. This was the modern arena, fire and rubble. Dull eyes gleamed in the dark.

It was time to put on a good show.

Pony struck first, tumbling through the air like a Chinese ghost. She had claws on her hands and feet, and they hooked into his Erik Conrad car coat, scratching through to his skin. She hissed as her chattering mouth neared his neck.

He put a hand against her face and pushed her away.

She hurtled off but landed on her feet. Her sister was already on him, wrapping her legs around his waist, tearing at his face with talons.

Cathy had a better grip, but he broke it.

Bond knew now these were comparative new-borns. They'd not be easy, but he was on an equal footing with them. He kicked Cathy in the face, and punched Pony in the stomach.

Pony tried to latch her needle-ringed mouth on his crotch. He fought panic and stepped back. Her teeth closed on nothing and he felt a wash of relief. Angry, he thumped the vampire girl on the side of her head, then picked her up and tossed her screeching at her sister.

The twins fell in a ball, foaming and spitting.

Flattop stood over Brastov, holding his master's cloak. After the girls, Bond would have to face this dead-alive thing.

Then someone new bowled into the arena.

A masked man in red tights leaped through the flame and ran across to the fight. He pushed through the spectators and embraced Flattop from behind. He gripped like a wrestler and Flattop gurgled, back bent out of shape, desperation written on his green-grey face.

It was the Crimson Executioner, the man who had killed Anibas and all the others.

'Cathy, Pony,' shouted Brastov. 'To me.'

The girls untangled themselves. The Executioner hefted the broken-backed Flattop above his head in a perfect weightlifter's stance. The muscles of his arms and legs swelled with exertion. His mouth was fixed in a manic teeth-baring grin and mad eyes shone through his domino mask.

Flattop was thrown away. He landed, groaning.

The twins crept forward, summoned by Brastov. The Executioner looked at them and laughed. Given pause, they stopped in their tracks, hissing.

Brastov's whiskers bristled. He was angry and terrified.

Bond had cause to be thankful that he was a new-born

vampire. This man killed only elders.

The Crimson Executioner, still laughing, picked the Cat Man up by the scruff of his neck and held him off the ground. His boots kicked in the air. His strangled protests sounded more like miaows than complaints.

Bond looked at the faces of the crowd. *Morti viventi*, lips rotted away to display permanent grins, watched with rapt attention, the last of their intelligence fixed on the spectacle.

Among the whores was a large warm woman, not obese or a giant, but big of frame and gesture. Something was strange about her eyes. She gave the classical thumbs-down sign.

'So decides Mamma Roma,' she declared.

'Mamma Roma, Mamma Roma,' chanted the whores.

The Crimson Executioner nodded.

He demonstrated one of the proverbial ways of skinning a cat. First, he took off Brastov's face as if it were a mask, then he pulled a red tear down through his chest, as if unbuttoning a shirt. He reached inside and extracted Brastov's red-clad skeleton from the furry skin. He tossed the fur away, and two female zombies tore it apart in an argument over its possession. Each salvaged scraps, which they rubbed against their noseless faces.

Without his catskin, Brastov was more human. He seemed to grow, assuming the shape of a full-sized man. Blood and bones and organs leaked out of him, falling with a splash around the Executioner's boots.

Bond saw mad fear in Brastov's slit pupils.

The Executioner tore the elder vampire apart and let the remains tumble. The zombies fell on the splatter of meat and bone, and began chewing. The Executioner held Brastov's beating heart and squeezed it like a sponge until it was still.

'You,' said Mamma Roma, pointing at Bond.

'Madam,' he acknowledged.

'Come here.'

He looked at the *morti viventi*, brawling and biting over the remains of Gregor Brastov. He saw Cathy and Pony helping the mewling Flattop up onto his feet.

Mamma Roma's face was implacable. She was past her

youth. Her wide hips had birthed many babies. Her full breasts had suckled children and full-grown men.

Her name was apt. She was Rome.

Her arms were out. Her mouth was open.

He went to Mamma.

30

CINEMA INFERNO

Kate expected to go through all manner of mendacity in order to get into Cinecittà, and had worked up her press credentials to suggest a reason for being in the film studio. But, mingling with a chattering crowd of girls who were massacre extras or makeup assistants, they just walked onto the lot. A relic of the fascist era not repudiated in modern Italy, Mussolini's purpose-built Hollywood-on-the-Tiber was a chaos of people.

'How do we find the Argonauts?' Geneviève asked.

Kate looked at the streams of people heading for the various stages. A troop of French cavalrymen, circa 1812, trotted double-time towards one set of thirty-foot doors, packs and rifles jingling. A circus elephant was led past by a man on stripy-trousered stilts and a woman in spangled tights.

'I imagine we should follow that, Gené.'

A shining sheepskin the size of a sail was being carefully carried past by four stagehands. Its gold paint was still wet. The Golden Fleece was carried on to Teatro 6. A blackboard by the door was scrawled with the legend '*gli argonauti*'. A ragged group of weather-beaten, false-bearded ancient Greeks loitered by the stage, smoking cigarettes and bragging in Italian about their sex lives.

They walked to the warehouse-like building. The Argonauts managed the obligatory whistles, gestures and comments, calling Geneviève 'eh, blondie' and Kate '*arance rosse*'. Red orange juice. Very flattering.

They made it onto the stage.

The vast stage was as crowded and purposeful as a riot. Her experience of film studios was confined to press calls at Ealing or Merton Park, pleasant strolls around the lot accompanied by deferential publicists, always timed to coincide with the tea break. She was overwhelmed by the *noise* of Teatro 6. Films were shot here as in the silent era: several different musical combos playing in disharmony, a building site symphony of hammering and sawing and swearing, the booming cannons of *Napoleon's Retreat* on the next stage, everyone shouting at once.

Geneviève spotted Orson Welles, raised up from the studio floor, clinging to the plaster prow of the *Argo* – which could only be shot from one side because only half the ship had been constructed – and looking up to the painted Heavens.

This Argo was a blind navigator, eyes covered by cataract lenses the colour of spoiled milk. Tears of pain ran through Welles's makeup, blobbing around the lower slopes of a monumental false nose. His real schnoz reputedly looked absurd on film, a tiny thing lost in a CinemaScope face, so he retreated behind enormous blobs of putty.

A torrent began. Rainfall from sprinklers above was whipped by vast wind machines. Water was dashed into the shipbuilder's face, drenching his robes. He clung desperately to the *Argo* and cursed the Gods.

Welles cursed in English. The Gods replied in Italian, German and French.

Actors from many countries, each a star in his or her own territory, had been carefully cast to give *Gli argonauti* 'international appeal'. In dialogue scenes, they all counted slowly up to a hundred in native tongues, a different emotion conveyed by each number. Lines were dubbed in later, often by other actors. Even Welles might lose his unmistakable canyon-deep voice and come out like Mickey Mouse.

A horde of technicians held the big sparkly blue canopy that lapped against the side of the ship, pumping their arms up and down like a synchronised weightlifting team to make waves. Water formed pools in the dips of the canopy and spilled through rips, soaking the poor souls underneath.

Argo was joined at the prow by Jason. Kirk Douglas thrust his dimple into the artificial wind, and clapped the shipbuilder on the shoulder.

'If we don't get that rug, fat boy,' he said, with feeling, 'it's your ass.'

'I'd back my ass against your chin any day of the week, play-actor,' Argo replied.

Eddy Poe was supposed to be the writer of this script, and that didn't sound like his style. More heroic lines would be provided later.

Argonauts hauled away on the oars, which battered the sea-canopy, swatting a few technicians to their knees. Curses and cries of pain rose from the depths. A divine voice from on high commanded the crew to keep rowing. In heavily-accented Austrian-English, God ordered extras to put their backs into it. Lesser gods translated the instructions into several European languages.

The torrent was a real downpour now. Some of the sprinkler-heads fell from the studio-skies, and ropes of hosewater lashed the set, twisting in the blast of the wind machines. Douglas supported Welles and water poured off them. That Argo's nose stayed stuck on was a miracle.

A carnival head broke the surface of the canopy by the boat and reared up on high-tension wires, squirting yet more water from its mouth and nostrils. Kate supposed this was supposed to be Poseidon, or one of his fishface cronies. It looked like a Gargantua-sized glove puppet, with finned ears and lobster-antennae bristling over its big rolling eyes.

The mechanical monster's fishy lower jaw hooked on the sea, and tore a section of it. A reservoir of prop water spilled through and dozens of feet slipped on the wet floor. The sea collapsed all around the *Argo*, falling away from the oars, exposing the scaffold that held up the half-ship.

Toby Dammit, the English matinée idol cast as Theseus, was discovered sneaking a crafty fag in the cutaway diagram bilges. He looked like something from the bottom of the sea, colourlessly unhealthy, pupils shrinking in the light, cheeks bulging with the internal pressure of his body. Kate had an idea there was more than tobacco in his roll-up.

'Cut,' boomed the voice of God.

Suddenly, all noise shut off. Even the quiet trickle of water wound down.

Geneviève tapped Kate's shoulder and pointed upwards. A chair on a crane descended from a platform where a motion picture camera was mounted like a siege gun. In the chair was an old man in jackboots and an open-necked shirt. One lens of his glasses was blacked-out. He carried a megaphone the size of a dustbin.

'Who let the sea get wet?' God – Fritz Lang – demanded. 'They are fired.'

Geneviève laughed, more in surprise than humour. Her chuckle echoed in the enormous space.

'She who laughs is also fired,' decreed God.

Geneviève shrugged and stifled further giggles. Kate looked reproach at her.

An Italian master technician sauntered over to Lang, hands in pockets. He spieled at length, gesturing with expressive shoulders. The director bobbed around twenty feet above, considering.

Finally, he raised his megaphone.

'We break for fifteen minutes,' he said, like a supreme court justice declaring a recess. 'While the sea is fixed. No one is allowed to leave. That is all.'

The chair ascended again, to the studio roof. Everyone started shouting at once, an explosion of babble. Some people even began working. A crew of seamstresses appeared and began to sew the sea back together. They wielded the kind of thick needles and strong twine oldtime mariners would have used to fix rent-apart mainsails. When she saw *The Argonauts* in the cinema, Kate would look out for stitches in the sea.

With an enormous sigh, Welles settled in a straining seat and popped the white rinds from his eyes. They'd found a café adjacent to the Argonauts set, and Welles – remembering them from the Palazzo Otranto – had consented to talk with them. This must have been a disused stage, converted into a cafeteria. The building was the size of a dirigible hangar, with a street winding through it and smaller buildings contained by it, like ships in the stomach of a giant whale. A row of sidewalk cafés was apparently doing great business, most tables crowded with busy young people. A tinny transistor radio played 'Dracula *Cha Cha Cha*', not a song Kate had good memories of. One table over, a bull-headed shape-shifter was boasting to a couple of party girls. She could imagine the role he was playing.

Welles's costume was still damp, but he was one of those men who seem comfortable in any situation. He dripped on the concrete floor.

Kate was less sure now than when the idea had been proposed that this would be at all useful. After all, Welles was an actor, not a real seer. But he'd been there when Dracula died, and was enough of a magician to see through most tricks.

What she was worried about, she admitted, was that he'd explain how she had done it. Everything between her descent of the cliff and Geneviève finding her covered with *il principe*'s blood was red fog. Someone – this *Mater Lachrymarum* – might have taken her mind and made use of her body. The only thing that really argued against it was the evidence. The silver scalpel, with its traces of burned vampire skin. The unmarked palms of her hands. If Welles could understand the plot of *Mr Arkadin*, could he not also come up with a story that made her a murderess and a mind-puppet?

The café was busy but no one came to take their orders.

'Two charming vampire ladies come a-calling,' Welles summed them up, fixing each with an eye. Underneath the face makeup and doughy flesh, currently further encrusted by a ginger-dyed beard, was a mischievous little-boy smile. 'This is an honour rare in the life of Old Prospero.'

'Mr Welles, we want to ask you about the ball at Palazzo Otranto,' said Kate. 'About the murder.'

Welles rubbed his magician's hands together.

'You seek me out in my capacity as a detective. I was

Sherlock Holmes once, and the Shadow.'

He wasn't very wraith-like now.

Kate had met the real Sherlock Holmes, during the Terror. She'd even run into a flier in the First World War who might well have gone on to be the vigilante they called the Shadow. If there was any role in the tangle of crime and detection fit for Welles it was Sherlock's brother, the much-missed Mycroft. Welles might well be able to fill the broad seat set aside in the smoking room of the Diogenes Club for that worthy gentleman.

'Actually, we seek you out more in your capacity as a witness,' Geneviève said.

'I'm here in my capacity as a suspect,' Kate put in. Making a joke of it did not prevent her heart cooling.

Welles's brows knit. A thin line appeared between his eyes as the top of his nose came loose.

'Oh,' he said, disappointed. 'In that case, I'm afraid I've little to add to what I told the police.'

Geneviève had played him wrongly. Kate realised her friend's directness and honesty were pre-Renaissance. Welles was a genius, a prince, a magician. He needed to be courted, flattered and cajoled. For him, a thing must be complicated or it was not worth bothering with.

'As a master of Holmesian method, Mr Welles, what impression did you form of the author of the atrocity at the Palazzo Otranto?'

The pettish genius raised an eyebrow at Kate and decided he liked her. She caught this at once and threw in a little simper that would have made Penelope proud.

Welles puffed up as he drew in a breath, cogitating visibly. A spectator in the rear circle would have seen the lines thought drew on his face. His nose was alarmingly loose, flaking away from the grooves in his cheeks.

'My first deduction was that the murderer must be a fellow of mine.'

'An American?' Geneviève queried.

'No, my dear,' Welles flapped a huge paw. 'A *showman*. You must concede it was a stroke of genius to arrange Dracula's head just so, with the cloak propped up around him, the lighting effects. It was a moment of revelation. In which you played a fine part, by the way. It seemed designed less as a crime than as a *coup de théâtre*.'

'It is the sort of spectacle you are famous for,' Kate said.

'Indeed, indeed. I had expected the police to make more of that, to think me a suspect. It is my belief that the murderer or murderess intended that. I was supposed to be the fall guy. I have already directed *Dracula* in my head. I might have staged his death similarly. I intended to film Stoker's book once, in 1940. Before *Kane*. The studio became nervous. I wanted the camera to be Jonathan Harker. I did it on the radio, with the Mercury Theatre, playing Harker and the Count.'

'Others at the palazzo that night might be called theatrical,' Geneviève said. 'John Huston, Cagliostro, Elvis Presley, Samuel Beckett.'

Welles waved away all the names. 'In that crowd, it'd be hard to find someone who wasn't addicted to the big gesture. Dracula himself was first of all a master showman. Consider his predilection for public mass executions. His sudden, cloaked entrances from nowhere, popping up through the vampire trap. His many marriages, all for publicity or political gain. No wonder he and Hitler couldn't stand to share a continent. They were too much alike.'

'You said this was your first deduction,' Kate said. 'That suggests you have had a second, or a third?'

Welles laughed, enormously. 'You're a fine one, Miss Reed. A rare thing indeed. Have you ever acted? You'd do for Mistress Quickly...'

Thank you very much, she thought.

'...no, I'm wrong. You should be Prince Hal. I'm serious. My Falstaff has never found a partner. You have it in you to play the boy, and become the man. A reversal of the traditions of Shakespeare's day. Women can play men. Bernhardt was a one-legged Hamlet. I hope to start filming next year or the year after, when the money comes together. All my great co-stars are Irish.'

'Your second thought?' Geneviève prompted.

Welles was dragged back to the moment. 'As I said, the greatest showman present, myself excluded, was the victim not the murderer. Dracula staged it all himself.'

'It was suicide?' Kate asked, wondering.

'I doubt that. No, it was fortuitous. Our murderer intervened in a spectacle already set in motion, and changed the script. Only the star's head was allowed to make an entrance. It was a calculated act of despoilment. In its own way, a moment of comedy. The intent was to ruin Dracula's entrance, to kill his reputation as much as his person, to break the spell he has held over the world for a century. I think our killer is not a showman, but rather a *critic*.'

He sat back, chair creaking, and expected applause.

A critic was a kind of journalist. Kate had written theatre and book reviews. And she'd certainly worked hard to ring down the curtain on Prince Dracula.

'Any names spring to mind?' Geneviève asked.

'Details bore me,' Welles declared. 'It should be a simple matter to fill them in, to ink over the sketch. I'm afraid I've passed on to other concerns. You may do what you wish with my insights.'

An assistant director hovered.

'Dear ladies,' said Welles, taking note of the man, 'if you will excuse me? I should be in sight of Colchis.'

He kissed both their hands and left them. Most fat men waddled, but he strode. The assistant director had to trot to keep up with him. He pestered Welles about his detaching nose.

Geneviève looked at Kate. She plainly thought this a waste of time. Kate wasn't so sure. Welles had made her think, and not about playing Henry V. In that buzz, ideas lodged. Some from him, and some he had stirred in her.

'We're not following a thread,' she said, 'we're being hauled in, like fish. People keep telling us things, as if they've been given messages to pass on. And we have these warnings, like the bird-thing in the library, to keep away from some areas and concentrate on others. He's right. It's as if we're being *directed*.'

'Service in this café is terrible,' Geneviève said.

The table was strewn with half-empty cups and glasses. No one had come to clean away or ask them if they wanted anything.

Kate picked up a glass of blood. She sniffed it.

'You aren't going to drink that?' Geneviève said, aghast.

'It's cold tea, dyed red.'

They looked around. None of the people at the nearby tables were actually eating or drinking, just raising glasses and sloshing liquid against their lips. They were laughing and talking, but the chatter was literally meaningless. The minotaur was real, but his head was plastered with swatches of painted newspaper to make him look fake.

The frontage of the café, which seemed to be contained within the studio, was actually just a front, propped up by poles. A few miles away from the real thing, the Via Veneto was recreated to the last detail. Kate wondered why anyone would go to the bother.

A camera on a rail advanced slowly through the tables and extras. A camera operator and an intent Italian director rode the mechanism, creeping up on a couple at one of the tables. The couple were brighter than everyone else, perhaps because there was a subtle spotlight on them.

The man wore dark glasses and shrugged as he smoked. The woman, redheaded and with an unflattering hairstyle, leaned over and complained at him, jabbing with an accusing finger. Kate's mind turned over. She could have been watching herself and Marcello. The man looked a lot like Marcello, and the woman might be an unfair caricature of her.

The camera glided past their table, ever closer.

'Don't look now,' Geneviève said. 'I think we're in the movies.'

31

PENELOPE PULLS IT OFF

It was time to depart in prosperity. The household was packing up, for disposal. The host was truly dead and the other guests had fled. Tom considered the Van Goghs, but they were too large and well-known to be practical souvenirs of his happy summer at the Palazzo Otranto.

Over the months, he'd built up a collection. The dead strewed their treasures any which way. Working by day, when elders were in their caskets and new-borns lulled with last night's blood, he'd harvested select, portable items. A bird of prey statuette, ugly but valuable; an Egyptian ruby scarab, with seven pinpoint flaws in the pattern of the big dipper; a tiny, withered brown hand which might be a child's or a chimp's; a model of the Eiffel Tower in pure gold; a dear little Corot no bigger than an icon. An enormous fellow Tom knew in Amsterdam might be able to do something with the loot; he was a collector and a dealer in rare, unprovenanced artifacts.

He did not, of course, hide his haul in his room where it might count as evidence. He'd found a loose floorboard in a forgotten attic and made himself a hidey-hole. If the cache were discovered, servants would be blamed. In his time, a butler and two maids had been dismissed for pilferage. Princess Asa insisted they be branded on their foreheads. Did a facial scar that read 'thief' in Moldavian hamper chances of future employment in Europe?

Presently, Asa was mad. She'd always been mad, he supposed, but the quality of her madness had changed. She was no longer the imperious monster. Penelope called her 'Princess Havisham' behind her back. She wore her ragged wedding dress and aged years every day she refrained from drinking blood. At the end of the month, she'd have to find a new house to haunt.

It was about midday. He was on a last look around. Some of the recently flown dead had carelessly left behind items of value. In General Iorga's crypt-like cell, he found a silver dagger. An old weapon, not like the bland scalpel they'd found in Dracula's heart. The workmanship was fine, the edge keen. This was an assassin's knife.

It struck him again how odd it was that so many of the dead owned silver knick-knacks. The metal was poison to them. It was either an ostentatious defiance of mortality or a need to have weapons for use against their own kind. With Dracula gone, there'd be secret wars of succession. Penelope had lectured him about it, suggesting with not a little relish that half the surviving elders would perish in the internecine squabbles. And a good job too, she said; it was time the mediaeval barbarians made way for rising generations. He pocketed the dagger, wondering if he should keep the thing. More and more dead were about. And Penelope Churchward might have long arms.

He made his way to the attic, carrying an empty suitcase he had found in one of the guest rooms. It was just the right size. He carefully packed his souvenirs, wrapping them in scarves. It was vulgar to set a price on such things, but he estimated he had enough to set him up for a good few years. He thought about France. It was time to make a home.

Whistling, he hauled the case – heavy, but not impossible – downstairs. He'd take the Ferrari, but only as far as the Stazione Centrale. It was too flashy, too easy to trace.

The case became heavier on the second staircase. He switched to his left hand and dropped it. Tom realised how weak he'd become. His neck-wounds, ragged and swollen, throbbed like mosquito bites. He made fists and flexed his arms, fighting the tingling in his depleted veins. His elbows and knees didn't quite work.

The suitcase slithered down to the next landing. Tom

stumbled after it. There was only the main staircase to the hallway, then the front door. He took hold of the case's handle, but couldn't lift it. He considered jettisoning one of the heavier items – the falcon, perhaps? – but rejected the idea as absurd. This was his nest egg.

He hugged the suitcase to his chest like a sack of potatoes and stood. It was like lifting an anchor. The weight pulled him to the lip of the stairs. His vision blurred. A dizzy spell struck. He wanted to pitch himself down the stairs and break his own silly neck.

His hip struck the balustrade and the case balanced on the long marble sweep. Tom smiled. It could slide the case down this last staircase, letting the bannisters take the weight.

He deserved this loot. He deserved the life it'd buy him.

Concentrating to make his feet and ankles do their work without interfering with each other, he went down step by step, case sliding easily beside him.

When he was through the front door, he'd never look back. And he'd never let a dead woman near him again.

'Where do you think you're going, Mr American?'

Penelope's voice wasn't raised, but it rang in his head.

He turned, mind not catching up. The case got free and slithered down the bannisters like a prankish small child, then ski-jumped across the hallway and made a bad landing, bursting open. Treasures glittered.

Tom sank to his knees, gripping the balustrade himself.

He couldn't raise his eyes to Penelope's face. He felt her looking down at him.

'You were not given permission,' she said.

His chin hit the stairs and he lost his grip. He rolled over, breathing heavily, and looked up at a fuzzy, distant ceiling. He exposed his throat to the dead woman.

Her face appeared, upside-down.

He had only one chance to escape. One treasure he had not packed in the case.

Penelope knelt by him and stroked his hair, as affectionately as she might pet a dog. She leaned forward to kiss – to bite – his neck.

Tom stuck the dagger he'd pocketed into Penelope's ribs. But her side wasn't where he thought it would be.

She twisted easily away from the silver blade. Her thumb and forefinger pinched his wrist, digging enough to jolt pain through his whole arm, numbing it from fingertips to shoulder.

The dagger fell out of his hand.

'So, our vampire killer is exposed.'

Doors opened and people came into the hall, boots thumping on marble.

'Inspector Silvestri,' Penelope said. 'Good afternoon.'

Tom's mind was fuzz and fudge.

'There's such a thing as being too clever, Tom dear,' Penelope whispered. She kissed him on the cheek, fondly. Her rough tongue licked him from chin to eyebrow, like sandpaper scouring one side of his face.

Penelope helped him stand up and walked him down.

Silvestri stood in the doorway. Sergeant Ginko and a uniformed policeman went through the case, cooing and whistling at each discovery.

'Pick that horrid thing up, would you?' Penelope asked the always-lurking Klove, indicating the dropped dagger. 'It's another one of those silver knives.'

The swirl of incomprehension began to resolve itself into a picture Tom didn't care for.

Klove fetched the dagger.

'Signor,' began Silvestri, 'this does not look well for you.'

Was this about Dickie?

Penelope handed him over to a couple of cops. They took his arms, practically holding him up. He tried to think it over, to see how he had reached to this predicament.

'You've quite come to my rescue, Inspector,' said Penelope, voice trembling to conceal her steel core. 'I fear I've had a very close escape. I never suspected we were harbouring one of those fanatics. A vampire slayer.'

Silvestri took the silver dagger from Klove.

Others were up on the landing, above Penelope. Servants. And a white spectre.

'Could it be this was the hand that struck the blow?' Penelope wondered.

Why couldn't anyone else see she was acting? Were they all blinded by her power of fascination?

His bites stung. He wanted her mouth on his neck, her tongue in the wounds.

'That question will be answered, Signorina Churchward,' said the policeman. 'For now, we shall arrest him for assault upon your person and the attempted thefts. Our investigations have turned up other questionable affairs, in New York City and Greece. Scotland Yard are involved. The other matter requires further investigation.'

The other matter? Tom couldn't stretch his mind around the phrase. What did they mean by it?

The white spectre flew at him, all teeth and nails and frayed lace. She screeched and went for his eyes and throat.

'Murderer!' Asa screamed. 'Regicide!'

Penelope gently took hold of Asa, and forced her to withdraw her hands. The Princess's face was close to Tom's, eyes enormous and insane.

'You killed Dracula! You will die!'

Only Asa showed emotion. Penelope and the cops carried the scene off as if it were a conventional conversation on a trivial matter.

Penelope gentled Asa, whispering in her ear, sorting out her matted hair.

'She has suffered a great deal,' Penelope explained.

'We understand,' said Silvestri.

Tom was tugged toward the doors. Outside, under the glare of the sun, a police car waited. He'd never drive the Ferrari again.

'May I have a moment?' Penelope asked. She passed Asa on to a servant.

Silvestri thought it over, and nodded.

The policemen let Tom's arms go. He was so weak he could hardly stand, let alone make a break for daylight. Penelope stood in front of him. She spoke quietly.

'Tom, Tom, I can't say how sorry I am it has come to this.

You're not as bad as they'll say, and you're certainly no worse than anyone here. For what it's worth, I don't believe you killed Dracula. There was no gain in it for you, and you don't murder unless by your lights you really truly have to. But you'll seem so perfect when the story of your Greek adventure comes out, so right for the role, that I fear nothing you can say or do will dissuade them. This has been a public affair, and *someone* must take the role of villain. Take comfort in the fact that the world will remember your name, and that I shall always think fondly of you. Not the Tom who'll be the famous vampire slayer, nor the Tom you'd have liked us to think you were – the affable, shallow, sincere American – but the cold, sharp man inside. I know you won't appreciate it much, but I am very fond of your true self. In other circumstances, I should have been honoured to make you my get.'

She kissed him on the lips. No teeth, no tongue. When she broke the kiss, a jewel glinted in her eye. She wiped it away.

His heart was ice. The trap was sprung.

'You may take him away now,' Penelope decreed.

The cops marched him out of the palazzo. Summer sun fell on his face. His eyes shrank and his skin tingled. He realised how badly he had been bled.

32

THE LIVING DAYLIGHTS

Geneviève supposed her luck was running true to form. For five hundred years, she'd reckoned Count Dracula the worst person in the world. He incarnated everything bad, everything despicable, everything that was not her. Now, with Vlad Tepes – or whoever he was – finally dead, it turned out there was someone in Europe older, more dangerous and worse than the King Vampire.

Mater Lachrymarum, the Mother of Tears. Boxed up among Charles's books was a volume by a modern alchemist – Fulcanelli? Varelli? – that had a section on the Three Mothers. She considered searching through the boxes but decided against it.

This time, there was no real need to find out who was behind the curtain. Charles was dead. Dracula was dead. Geneviève wasn't a detective or an avenger. Kate wasn't going to take the blame. She didn't care who'd killed the Prince. No one actually cared.

She wasn't going to be in the city much longer. Apart from anything else, there was the Crimson Executioner to worry about.

She sat in the dark in the apartment, among trunks and packing cases. It had been disturbingly easy to put away all of Charles's life. He'd only left things behind. He himself was gone.

Truly dead. She wondered what that would be like?

Suicide wasn't in her. But each year was a weight added

to her heart. How many more centuries would there be for her? She'd read *On the Beach*. It was frighteningly possible that there would be no more centuries for anyone. At ground zero, warm and nosferatu alike would be vaporised. Even Dracula had never conceived of the Hydrogen Bomb. She dreaded what such weapons would have meant in the arsenals of the chieftains of her warm days.

Kate was off, chasing her Italian lover. She was still wrapped up in her odd search for answers, but would learn. Geneviève had been the same at her age. It took a warm lifetime to accept the miraculous. Then you started questioning it, wondering what it was all for, what it was about. Who had the answers for Kate? A fortune-teller, a priest, a little girl, a warm man, a bloated genius?

For Kate's sake, she'd stay awhile. Until the smaller mysteries were cleared up. It was the least she could do.

The taste of Charles was fading in her mouth. That thinning trace was the last of him. His voice had whispered in her mind these last years. Its absence was silence.

She drifted to the balcony. Charles's chair wasn't there. She glided to the spot where it'd often been and looked down at the street, at the view Charles had favoured.

A tall, thin man in black stood on the other side of the road, under a streetlamp. He looked up at her with clear blue eyes. It was Father Merrin.

The priest crossed the road and Geneviève went back into the apartment to let him in. A makeshift lock on the door replaced the one Brastov's goons had broken.

'Thank you for coming, Father,' she said. 'I know you've been warned away from me. I appreciate your courage.'

Merrin took off his broad black hat. The wound on his forehead was neatly plastered.

'Not away from you,' he said. 'From your friend, Miss Reed.'

Geneviève offered the priest tea. There was a package of Lipton's in the kitchen. Edwin Winthrop had sent Charles monthly food parcels: Fortnum & Mason's marmalade, Cadbury's chocolate, a secretary's homemade jam.

She busied herself with making tea while the priest silently took in the packed-up belongings and the damage done by Brastov's assassins.

'This isn't about the Mother of Tears,' Merrin said.

'No. Well, I don't suppose so.'

'You have had a loss. Please accept my condolences.'

He said nothing about God or Heaven, for which she was grateful. She wanted to tell this man about Charles.

In her experience, in warm life and all the years since, priests like Merrin were rare as hen's teeth. She had no quarrel with Jesus of Galilee, but a great villain – Saint Peter the Denier, or the Emperor Constantine – had twisted His ministry. A faith for children and slaves had become a worldly nation, as rich and rotten as any other.

God might have a message for man, but churches seemed the worst possible places to receive it. Twice, she'd been put to the Question by the Inquisition. The faces of holy men were taut with lust as they worked pincers over her body. Worse still were those who truly believed they killed and stole in the name of love divine. She'd also been pursued by Puritan witchfinders in New England and stoned by the mullahs of Mecca. In the last century, she'd sought refuge in a Tibetan lamasery and found it a hive of petty intrigue and spiritual canker.

Father Merrin was better than that. She'd known few truly good men. The priest was not weak, not biddable; in the days when she was fleeing the Church, she'd not have chosen to fight with him. That he could remain in the Vatican proved all the good had not flown from the world with Charles Beauregard.

For the first time in centuries, Geneviève Sandrine de l'Isle Dieudonné felt a need schooled into her as a child.

She imagined God was in the room, with Merrin's face.

'Father, will you hear my confession?'

The priest consented and set down his cup. They were both awkward. Should they kneel? She sank to her knees on the bare floorboards. Merrin found a cushion and knelt by her.

'*Père, pardonnez moi,*' she began, in her first tongue. Her accent would be unrecognisable in modern France.

She hesitated.

'It's all right,' Merrin said. 'I understand.'

'Father, forgive me, for I have sinned...'

With the words, her heart opened and everything flooded out.

After Merrin left, she felt different. She'd told him much of her life that no one living knew, but had talked mostly about Charles. And Dracula. She'd told their story, honestly. She'd told him the true identity of Jack the Ripper. She'd admitted her love, and her failure. She had cried. And in talking to a priest, she had prayed.

She was not reconciled with the Church, not yet convinced that there was a supernatural. She was influenced by the cold insights of Dr Pretorius and the warm wisdom of Father Merrin, but was not about to change the habit of many lifetimes.

It was just that now, this very moment, it helped.

Her heart beat faster. The organ was stilled in many vampires, a ripe-to-rotten plum waiting to be pierced. In her, the pump worked. And feelings came with it.

Charles was with her still, inside. His voice whispered. His taste tingled. She had not lost the sense of him forever, just misplaced it.

She wasn't crying any more.

She looked up, reverie broken. She had another visitor. He stood in the doorway in a black tuxedo with matching tie, posing with his Walther, kiss-curl beckoning like a finger, smile calculatedly ironic, fangs bared.

Bond slipped his gun into its holster.

'Come with me, Gené,' he said. 'There's a last monster to be faced.'

His confidence was irresistible. For him, this agony was frivolous. He had a job to do and it was do or die. He could never really be hurt. It was dangerous to be close to someone like that.

But she had nothing better to do.
'I can find him,' he said. 'The Crimson Executioner.'
She stood up and went with him.

33

LACHRYMAE

The ancient villa at the heart of the city had sunk. Ground-floor windows peeped slivers of glass above street-level. Kate thought they might be stained glass: inner light made blocks of vivid red, turquoise, and amber of them.

She checked the address again. Marcello's editor had given her a vivid description: the House with the Crying Windows. She looked up. Just under the roof, a row of eye-shaped gables were angled to suggest desolation. Water trickled from gutter-spouts positioned like tearducts. The brickwork was stained green by years of sorrow.

It was striking. She wondered why it wasn't in the guide-books.

Light behind the eyes changed from red to green.

She walked across the deserted piazza.

She had almost given up on getting in touch with Marcello, but dutifully made regular telephone calls to his apartment, his haunts, and the various papers she knew he worked for. Finally, an editor told her Marcello had left instructions for her with him. He was staying at a certain address in the city, and would receive her there.

Though she still knew little about Marcello, she didn't think this was a family home. She had the idea he wasn't originally from Rome. Under his sophisticated veneer, he was a country bumpkin. And he was not from money.

This was an impressive property.

Kate ascended the steps to what must once have been a balcony and paused at the front door. It was bright blue, with gold crescents, silver stars and odd angel-faces. She had a shiver of recognition but knocked anyway. A hole opened in the centre of a painted eye.

For a moment, she was looked at. She turned round completely, hands in the air.

The door opened. The hallway was empty. A cheap trick.

She stepped inside. Portraits and mirrors and doors were symmetrically spaced along the corridor. The mirrors reflected the portraits opposite. Dried leaves drifted on the rich red carpet. The doors were locked.

The front door closed behind her. It also locked.

It occurred to her that Marcello might not have left the message. She'd seen a door like the portal of the House with the Crying Windows before, at Santona's apartment in I Cessati Spiriti. What was the connection?

Having no alternative, she walked down the corridor. In the first mirrors, she cast no reflection. But as she neared the end of the corridor, a black shadow coalesced, then resolved into a looking glass image of herself, the sharpest she had seen since her death.

She looked at her own face.

She'd been reckoned plain in life. Red hair, spectacles, and freckles weren't conventional attributes of beauty for late Victorians. Over a century, fashions in prettiness changed, and she'd been told enough times recently that she wasn't so terrible in the looks department that she'd come to wonder.

To her mind, she was still plain. Maybe she'd always be a late Victorian. Her hair looked nice cut short, though. And perhaps a different style of spectacles might help.

Behind her, in the mirror, was the face of the little girl, white with a wave of hair over one eye. Her expression re-formed from a look of desolation to a grin of malign triumph.

She spun round and found herself looking at a portrait.

It was old. Sixteenth century, by the clothes and style of painting. The face was unmistakable, though. Kate wondered at the trick of making the expression change. Was this one of those ingenious puzzle paintings so prized by cleverclogs Renaissance patrons?

She'd been too taken with the mirrors and her own silly self, to pay much attention to the pictures. Now she looked at them. The same face appeared over and over, in different styles and modes of dress. One woman was seen at four ages. Father Merrin had said *Mater Lachrymarum* had four aspects. 'A child, a young woman, a mature woman, and a crone... she is a complete cycle.'

The young woman was Viridiana, the lay worker Kate had seen at the Vatican, and the crone was Santona, the fortune-teller. The child – 'the most terrible, for she is an innocent, and has the ruthlessness of innocence' – she would never forget. Only the mature woman, somewhat blowsy and overripe, was unfamiliar, though she saw in the harlot the last traces of Viridiana and the beginnings of Santona.

A door opened. Kate was getting tired of this *Cat and the Canary* business. If this were supernatural trickery, it was nothing Orson Welles couldn't contrive with levers and distracting flourishes.

Laughter bubbled from the top of a staircase. A woman's laughter, rich and lewd. Music also sounded, very loud. A choral work, played too fast, a mass for something unholy. She couldn't help but think of this as sound effects. The walls shook with the racket.

She shrugged and climbed the stairs.

The landing was dark, but lamps came on with a lightning flicker as she set foot on the carpet. There was probably a tilting panel under it.

The music and laughter came from a room on the other side of a gallery. She went around the landing, which was a balcony in a huge ballroom. The floor below was a pool of darkness. Along with music, she heard whispers, as if every word ever said in this house were still trapped here.

This door hung open. Lights moved within the room.

Kate crossed another threshold and entered a whore's palace. The room was dominated by a four-poster bed, curtained with many tassels. Pornographic pictures covered the walls. A stench of rotten perfume hung in the air. The light was redder than blood, a solid scarlet.

The curtains opened, and she saw Marcello in the arms of a giantess, face buried in her bosom. The woman laughed, enormous mouth stuffed with food, lipstick smeared over her chin. This was the last aspect of *Mater Lachrymarum*, the harlot, the liar.

'Welcome to Mamma Roma's boudoir, missy,' she said.

Kate's heart was a stone.

She didn't care about the Crimson Executioner, about the vampire slayings. She was flattened to have been abandoned for this gross creature.

Mamma Roma shrieked with laughter and clasped Marcello so close to her mountain of flesh that he might have suffocated. Kate wished he would stifle himself on those gargantuan teats. Like all men, the only woman he could really surrender to was Mamma. He cared only for the breast, not the heart.

Was she crying? Again?

She turned and tried to flee, but tripped on thick carpet and sprawled on the landing. Something held her down.

She had to listen to their intercourse, the great gurgling, farting, squelching of it, the barks of laughter and joy, the grunts of pleasure and pain. Her own sobbing didn't drown out the din. She was shrinking inside herself. Contracted to a point, she vowed this was all she would be in the future, an appetite with teeth. Penelope had learned within days of her turning the lesson which had eluded Kate until now.

For the first time in seventy years, Katharine Reed felt like a proper vampire.

Soon, she would rise and prey.

Slim, naked ankles caught her attention. She looked up. Viridiana stood over her, robed simply, face shining. The young woman was almost sorrowful.

She helped Kate stand and straightened her spectacles.

Kate was taller than this girl. She could tear open her throat and drink her blood.

No. Viridiana was only a quarter of a creature. If she attacked, Kate would face the whole woman, the Mother of Tears, the Monster of Rome.

'Why?' Kate asked. 'Why everything?'

'I can only tell the truth,' Viridiana replied. 'I cannot explain it. Come.'

She led Kate to another room.

In the swinging of a door, Viridiana was gone. Inside, in her bower, Santona awaited.

'Why?' she asked again.

'Cities can die, Katharine Reed from Ireland. And this city is my home, my empire. Roma rises and falls like the tide, but it is always alive, in turmoil. Those who are old, though not as old as I, are a danger to the heart and soul of Roma. Creatures like you slow down the processes of life, still blood in the veins, turn a city brittle. In time, too many elder vampires will exhaust a place, make it like the things which stumble and chew in I Cessati Spiriti. I am old, older than you can imagine, but I have a reflection, a heart, a life. All I have done I have done for Roma.'

'The Crimson Executioner is your creature?'

'An actor, at my direction? Yes.'

Kate understood this woman. She felt in herself the beginnings of an elder.

'You're like us,' Kate accused. 'You don't let men's minds alone, you make them puppets. You demand blood, as we do. You demand love and worship.'

Santona nodded. 'But I can also *give*, Katharine. Can you say as much?'

She had loved Charles. She did love Marcello.

No.

She had loved Marcello. She did love Charles.

Life or death didn't matter.

'Yes,' she said, 'I can love.'

Santona considered the statement.

'I see you speak the truth. But you are changing. In the end, you all change. You have died. For you, feelings are a habit you outgrow.'

'That makes it all right to kill us? If we can't love, you can destroy us?'

'If you couldn't love, would you want to endure?'

'To endure? That's all there is for you, Mother of Tears. You live only to live on.'

'Perhaps.'

'Is it over yet? Are the elders all dead or gone? Are you now unchallenged in your reign over this bloodied ground?'

'One remains. She will be dead by dawn. Truly dead.'

Kate turned to leave the room, the house, the city.

Marcello stood in the doorway.

'Kate,' he said, 'I am sorry.'

He took off his sunglasses. Tears poured from his eyes.

'I was a fool,' he admitted. 'You are the first woman on the first day of creation. You are mother, sister, lover, friend, angel, Devil, earth, home. I love you entirely. I was misled by this creature. You are all things.'

It was overwhelming.

She slipped into his arms and received kisses. A burst of relief flooded her. The witch had been wrong. Kate Reed could love and be loved. That made her more than a zombie, gave her a right to live.

Marcello's arms were all the world to her. She nestled against his chest. Her tears were hot and happy.

One remains. She will be dead by dawn. Truly dead.

Damn. Why couldn't she forget?

'Stay with me, my love, my love,' Marcello whispered. 'Stay forever, my love.'

Now, her heart really did die.

'I can't,' she said, pushing him away.

PART FIVE

SPQR

FROM *THE TIMES* OF LONDON, AUGUST 15TH, 1959

Rome. An arrest has been made in connection with the murder of Prince Dracula. Inspector Silvestri, the detective in charge of the case, has indicated that an American citizen will be charged with attempted theft and murder. The suspect is also sought for questioning by Interpol with regards to the disappearance of Richard Fountain, an English vampire.
Prince Dracula's remains will be released into the care of his executrix, Miss Penelope Churchward. Funeral arrangements have not been announced.

Hollywood. Jeremy Prokosch, a film producer active in Europe, announces that work will begin on a three-part film biography of Count Dracula, to be scripted by Gore Vidal, Clare Quilty and Christopher Fry and shot in Spain and Yugoslavia. It is his intention that three different directors will tackle the three crucial periods of the Dracula story, with Riccardo Freda handling Vlad's warm life and rebirth as a vampire, Terence Fisher Dracula's rise and fall in Victorian Britain, and Michael Powell his exile and death. Among actors mooted for the role are Jack Palance, Francis Lederer, Alexander D'Arcy and David Niven.

London. In an interview with BBC TV's *Panorama*, Lord Ruthven, the Prime Minister, has condemned as 'utterly tasteless' the flood of Dracula-related items now entering the marketplace. He goes on to say that he does not deem the late Count's likeness or coat of arms a fit adornment for 'tea trays, toby jugs, join-the-dots puzzles, tie-clasps, watch-fobs or beach-blankets'. The Post Office will, however, issue a set of commemorative Dracula stamps in time for the Christmas rush.

Borgo Pass, Transylvania. Baron Meinster, an elder who claims to be the first get personally turned by Dracula, delivered an impromptu speech to a mostly vampire crowd, declaring himself the new King Vampire and that Transylvania should be an independent homeland for the undead. The meeting was broken up by members of the Romanian Securitate, and President Nicolae Ceauşescu has branded Meinster 'a verminous outlaw' and ordered his arrest, though he remains at large. Meinster is only the latest of several who have styled themselves 'Alucard' and claimed to be Dracula's heir.

34

THE JUDGEMENT OF TEARS

This was what Geneviève needed. To face a monster rather than herself.

Bond told her Gregor Brastov was dead, skinned and gutted by the Crimson Executioner. He had known about the Mother of Tears, had wanted them to confront her for him, so he should have known better than to tangle with her creature. The Cat Man had been trying to set her, and the spy, against the enemy he most feared, but other matters had distracted them. Charles and Dracula. A quiet war had been taking place, beyond her ken. In the end, she would have to be involved. It was inescapable.

Another elder gone, after hundreds of years. They were mostly vile, but Geneviève was used to sharing the world with them. Before Dracula's great entrance, elders had passed the centuries in travel, occasionally crossing each other's paths with wary courtesy, sometimes even gathering as a community.

Since Carmilla Karnstein, Geneviève had never counted another vampire elder her friend. They were for the most part bloodthirsty bastards. Even Carmilla was cracked.

Outside the apartment, they paused by Bond's Aston Martin. It had a few new bullet scars.

'We needn't drive,' he said. 'It's within sight of here.'

It was obvious, when she came to think of it. There was only one place in Rome for a last stand. Charles had noticed the Executioner's habit of staging his atrocities in famous public places.

Bond led her along the road.

The Colosseum stood against the Roman night, cut across like a wedding cake sliced with a scythe.

The Flavian Amphitheatre – Charles pedantically preferred the proper name – had been built in AD 72 by Vespasian in place of an artificial lake dedicated to Nero, part of an urban rebuilding scheme designed to blot out memory of the murderous Emperor. Vespasian hadn't lived to see the sand of the arena bloodied by the first gladiatorial casualties, which lasted until Honorius forbade the killing of man by man in AD 405. Wild animals, always a popular supporting act, were set against each other for a further century and a half. Geneviève knew various conscience-struck Emperors had tried to introduce Greek-style athletics contests, without fatalities, in place of the Roman games, but that the public hadn't stood for them. Only blood would satisfy the people of Rome. She supposed she wasn't in a position to be too fastidiously critical on that point.

For centuries, Romans had stolen Colosseum stone for new buildings. Blood-soaked blocks now made up portions of the Palazzo Venezia, the Cancelleria, St Peter's and many humbler structures. The plundering had only ceased in the middle of the eighteenth century when Pope Benedict XIV proclaimed it a sacred site, relying on the pious fiction that it was the site of many martyrdoms. It was a canard that Christians were fed to lions. That wouldn't have been entertainment. Instead, the followers of the fisherman were stuck on poles and set alight as a primitive form of street lighting, or simply crucified as trouble-makers. The arena was reserved for those skilled enough to make a show out of fights to the death. A thousand years and more before Dracula or Gilles de Rais or Elisabeth Bathory, the public taste for blood was already keen.

In the nineteenth century, when Geneviève had been briefly in Rome, the Colosseum was a jungle, stones buried in all manner of thriving flora. She had considered the swallowing of marble death by irrepressible life a sign of hope, but the weeds were all tidied away now and the bleached bones of the building exposed again. The two storeys of arches that made up the original outer shell stood, along with half of the jerry-built addition – replacing a wooden level struck by credibly divine lightning in AD 217 – piled on top. The terraces were still there in tiers, awaiting the return of the crowds, but the floor of the arena – the killing stage – was gone, exposing a maze of tunnels and chambers that had been below.

'I followed him here,' said Bond. 'He led me past your flat. I took that as a sign.'

'The Colosseum is a tourist attraction,' she said. 'It will be closed at this hour.'

'I doubt that our quarry cares much about that.'

'I suppose you're right.'

The Venerable Bede had written 'as long as the Colosseum stands, Rome will stand, and when the Colosseum falls, Rome will fall; but when Rome falls the world will come to an end.' She wasn't sure whether that was a comforting or threatening prophecy. A city, indeed a world, symbolised by this horrid edifice probably didn't deserve to stand.

They crossed the Piazza di Colosseo. Geneviève wondered if this was the route the gladiators had taken. No, they would have been chained under the arena, released only when the crowds had taken their seats.

Had any vampires died in the arena? There were nosferatu in ancient Rome. They would have been a novelty. She imagined Caligula – dead before this place was planned – pitting a werewolf against a shape-shifting vampire, sheathing their claws with silver knives, giving the thumbs down for the loser.

She supposed things were changing. Slowly.

Then again, Caligula hadn't thought of the Bomb either.

They strolled through the main entrance. It was too huge a space to fence off.

She smelled the stones. There were still traces of old blood.

'Look,' said Bond.

She was wrong. The blood was fresh, a vampire's. It was absurd to think the gore of the gladiators would still be in the ground.

The trail led through the great arch, into the arena.

'When we find the Crimson Executioner, Commander Bond? What then?'

He didn't answer. He wasn't there.

She knew something was wrong. Bond wasn't old enough to creep away while she wasn't looking. She should have felt the draught of his leaving, heard the tiny sounds he couldn't help but make.

Had it been him? Or someone wearing his face?

She couldn't have been mistaken. The man who had brought her here was the man she'd met before. But there was something different about him. He was the sort who always seemed to be play-acting, taking a part. But the quality of his acting had changed, become broader, less convincing. He'd been expressing himself too much with his eyebrows. The Scots in his accent had faded.

She was in a broad thoroughfare, lined by pillars. The ground was rough stone. Blood led through the labyrinth. Too obvious a trail.

Her hackles rose and the fine hair on her arms prickled. She spun around and glimpsed a red shape dart behind a pillar. Her claws popped.

She was no longer stalking a quarry. She was herself being stalked.

It had to happen, she supposed.

She must have been the last elder in Rome. She'd be the Crimson Executioner's final victim.

But not without a fight.

Kate was still reeling. Leaving Marcello, for the last time, was like pulling a thorn from her heart and throwing it away. She couldn't yet name the things she had chosen over him, but she burned with a certainty that she had picked salvation over sham, love above self. Still, it was not easy or simple. What if she were wrong, and was dedicating herself to possibilities that had died with Charles and Dracula rather than the as-yet unborn world she might have with the warm man?

She didn't know how she'd got from the House with the

Crying Windows to Parco de Traiano. But this was where she should be, where Charles had lived, where there were answers and endings.

There was vampire blood on the street. A sports car was parked across the street from the house, rear end dotted with bullet holes. Few people were about, which was odd. She was used to Rome's crowds. Whenever the extras faded away, bad things happened.

A woman came out of Charles's apartment house. Geneviève? No, this woman was dark-haired. Penelope. She wore a mid-length Gherardi overcoat, with matching stockings and court shoes in mourning black. Her hair was done up under a neat black hat.

'Katie,' Penelope acknowledged. 'I have news.'

'Me too, Penny,' Kate said.

Penelope daintily sniffed the air, and looked at the ground.

'That's blood,' Penelope observed.

Kate swam through panic.

'Penny,' she said, 'we were friends once. You must help me. The Crimson Executioner is after Geneviève.'

Penelope was exasperated. 'What are you talking about?'

'The vampire slayer.'

'You don't understand,' Penny cooed, as if everything was all fine and dandy and settled and done. 'The murderer of Dracula is under arrest. You're free to leave the city.'

Kate had to get through to her.

'There's another murderer. Maybe an army of murderers. Under the orders of someone older even than an elder vampire. Someone truly monstrous, truly ghastly. Believe me, I've met her. You wouldn't like her.'

Penelope looked at the blood trail. Her eyes reddened slightly.

'Isn't this a bit… convenient?'

Kate didn't understand.

'It's as if arrows were drawn on the road. We're being pulled by the nose, toward the Colosseum.'

'Geneviève's in danger.'

'The French person?'

Kate remembered Penelope had not liked Geneviève, though she thought the enmity washed away in shared grief at Charles's death. While Kate was off being mad with Marcello, Geneviève and Penelope had made up, hadn't they?

Penelope made a decision. 'Very well, Katie, I'll come with you. But there's something decidedly off about this. Do you see? Someone's been shooting at this Aston Martin. Can you smell that? Not the blood, the cordite.'

Charles would have looked at the road and been able to tell from smeared footprints whether Geneviève had been alone, whether she was pursuing or being pursued, and at what speed. It was a trick he had learned from masters.

Penelope was right. The trail was too obvious. But they had no choice.

'Come on, slowcoach,' Penelope said, setting off.

The ancient stands of the Colosseum weren't empty. Though Geneviève concentrated on keeping stone pillars between her and the muscleman in red, she was aware shadow-figures were filtering along the rows, settling down for the spectacle. She wondered how much the management was charging, then remembered the games were generally held at the expense of the Emperor, a pacifying gift to the people of Rome. Give them bread and circuses.

Bond was down here in the labyrinth, but she couldn't count on him. He had gone over to the Enemy. Not Brastov's side, but someone else old and powerful, the Mother of Tears.

She took off her shoes and walked on the points of her feet, darting swiftly between pillars as if they were trees in a forest. Her fangs and claws were out, though she feared they'd be outclassed by silver swords and hardwood spears.

It was disturbing that she had only glimpsed the Crimson Executioner twice, as flashes of red. He was a warm man. She should be able to scent him, know at all times where he was and how close he was getting. She was the huntress of the night, the elder vampire, the survivor of centuries. She should be the favourite.

Yet the Executioner had killed elders.

Anton Voytek and Anibas Vajda had been more dangerous than her, and it hadn't helped them. Some of the elders the Crimson Executioner had slain were shape-shifters who could become monstrous bats or living white mists. Beside those abilities, her poor talons and teeth were feeble.

The stands were thinly crowded. Were they people, or merely shades? She smelled warm blood out there, but other presences too. Old things.

There was a crack. A silver bullet struck stone inches from her face. Chips flew at her eyes. She mustn't forget Hamish Bond. He was in this game too.

A mighty switch was thrown and light burned down.

Blinking away tears of shock, Geneviève looked up. Banks of arc lights – like those she'd seen on the stages at Cinecittà – had been erected along the third tier. They came on, one bank at a time, and floodlit the stadium, turning the arena into a maze of hard black shadows and blinding white spaces.

She slipped into a shadow. A spotlight trapped her.

Blobs of dazzle floated on her eyeballs. She was used to daylight, fancied herself immune to it, but this hurt. The beams were hazy with dust and smoke. Flies spiralled in the tunnels of light.

The arena was lit up but the stands were in darkness. There were eyes out there but she saw no faces. Wheeling about, hissing, she looked to the imperial seats. Between columns of flame stood the mistress of these games, a blonde child, one eye obscured by hair. It was Kate's apparition, the girl only she – and Bond, Geneviève remembered – claimed to have seen.

Geneviève made a fist and raised it in salute.

How had gladiators felt about their Emperor?

She stood in the light and waited for her killers. There was no sense in running.

The spotlight expanded. At its edge stood a pair of red boots. As the light grew, it revealed the red tights, trunks and belt, the broad torso naked of all but paint, the balaclava hood and domino mask, the exposed teeth and mad eyes.

The Crimson Executioner loped lazily toward her, hands

opening and closing. A stench assailed her nose and she realised the red stuff on his exposed chest and face was not paint. The spoiled blood sickened her.

She danced close to him and spun around, bent over entirely at the waist, doing the splits in the air, one foot-point on the ground, the other stuck up above her head. She aimed her foot at the Executioner's Adam's apple. Her bunched, taloned toes were a dagger of skin and bone.

The kick should have fetched off his head.

Instead, he whipped to one side. Her toe-claws carved a runnel across his shoulder. His hands closed on her ankle and she was whipped off balance, up into the air. The Crimson Executioner swung her like a cat.

Her unbound hair brushed a stone pillar. On the next pass, her head would be battered against something that had stood for twenty centuries. It wouldn't kill her, but it would shatter her skull into a dozen pieces. She'd live through the next hundred years with a head like a lopsided jack o'lantern. Provided she lived through the next hundred seconds.

The crowd roared and whistled.

She let her arms fly out, above her head, and extended them at an angle from her face, heels of her hands out to take the force of the blow.

The pillar was in the way.

She felt the impact in her wrists and elbows. Her arms crumpled and her face slapped the stone, hard enough to bloody her nose.

The Executioner dropped her.

She hugged the pillar and slid down it. The blood taste in her mouth was her own.

Her red rage was rising again. She fought it. This was not an opponent who could be beaten by surrender to the animal, who'd be so terrorised by the sight of an enraged bitch vampire that his knees would turn to water.

She huddled against the pillar.

The Crimson Executioner bent and took hold of her hair, hauling her upright. His shining, empty eyes were beacons, close to her face.

Out there in the stands, a thousand thumbs turned down. This had not been much of a show.

The Executioner pressed a thumb against her neck, pinching on her jugular vein. Stolen blood pumped against the pressure but was trapped. Her heart grew swollen, her brain was starved. He could pop off her head like the top of a beer bottle. Bastard.

She tore at his sides, blunting her nails on blood-greased hide and taut slabs of muscle.

He was laughing and so was the audience.

Her fang-teeth elongated, forcing her mouth open, cutting her lower lip. But she couldn't move her head. She could only bite the night air.

She took his wrist, which was the thickness of a normal man's thigh, and dug in with hooked thumb-barbs and all eight nail-blades. She worried holes and scratched, hoping to snag a vein or a nerve.

The Executioner felt no pain.

He wasn't even her real murderer. Just the puppet of the little girl up on the imperial platform. Ghastly, hollow laughter poured out of his grin.

Red lights exploded in her skull.

'Who are all these *people*?' Penelope demanded.

'An audience,' Kate guessed. 'The senate and populace of Rome?'

'Oh, *them*!' Penny spat.

Kate saw that the crowd in the stands was mixed. Zombies at the back, faces half off the bone. The bourgeois, isolated and prim in the good seats. The rabble, thronging close to the arena, craning for a smell of blood. There must have been people here she knew but she recognised none.

Except the little girl in Nero's seat.

Kate recognised the combatants who struggled in the spotlight. This was what she had feared. Penny was appalled and fascinated by the spectacle.

'Is this some pagan revival?'

'I think it's more than that,' said Kate. 'That creature is the secret ruler of Rome. She's taken upon herself the duties of the Emperors. Maybe they were always her duties, and she let the Emperors usurp them for a few centuries. These are her games, at once a gift and a demonstration of power.'

Penelope was catching up but Kate couldn't hope to explain everything in the time they had. The fight they had come upon was nearly over. The Crimson Executioner held up Geneviève, as a tribute for *Mater Lachrymarum*, awaiting the imperial verdict.

Kate pushed through, making her way down an aisle, toward the arena itself. Penelope followed, pacifying the irritated spectators Kate had pushed aside with a flash of her fangs and a witheringly British glare.

'Bloody foreigners, eh?' Penny muttered. 'With their barbaric bullfights.'

Kate was not about to bring up fox-hunting and pig-sticking.

The cheering and calling subsided. Even the Executioner's hollow laugh shut off. The monster child pondered the verdict.

Kate vaulted a rail and landed in the arena. Broken pillars were all around. Penelope let herself down gently and brushed dust off her good coat.

'You,' Penny commanded. 'Put that woman down.'

The Crimson Executioner's head swivelled like a mechanism.

He laughed, a sound hideously familiar to Kate.

She felt cords tug at her mind. If the Mother of Tears had made a puppet of her to destroy Dracula, then she might take hold of her mind now. Having rushed here to help Geneviève, she might be forced to hold Penelope down while the Crimson Executioner finished off her friend.

No. She was not a puppet.

The British vampire Kate knew to be a spy stepped out from behind a pillar and pointed a gun at Kate and Penny.

'Commander Bond?' Penelope said.

He was the puppet here. He'd always been a thin character, too easily slotted into a stereotype. That was what made him vulnerable. He was the sort of man who always needed a mother, to cling to and to tidy up after him.

For the first time, Kate wondered who the Executioner really was. A circus strongman? An actor in peplum movies?

Bond levelled his aim between Kate and Penelope.

Penny moved incredibly fast, swifter than Kate could have imagined, and took the gun away from the new-born. She squeezed the weapon in her hand, and it popped into clunky metal components.

Without his gun, Bond was a boy whose favourite toy has been taken away. A command passed from the little girl's brain to his and he tried to put his fingers in Penny's neck. She took him by the wrists and threw him away, tossing his flapping form fifty feet or more into the air. He executed an ungainly arc and fell badly. Though broken, he scrambled around. If left alone, he would put himself back together but as a puppet he wasn't allowed to bother with his snapped bones.

A section of the crowd cheered.

Penelope gave a cheerful wave, like a member of the Royal Family arriving at a Commonwealth airport.

Kate faced the Executioner.

Geneviève's eyes were bloodied. She looked at Kate, silently imploring her not to sacrifice herself.

The Mother of Tears could not be bested. She was as eternal as the city. She was True Death, who overtakes all living things in time. She was mistress of a million puppets. She was, Kate could admit it now, *a supernatural being*.

The Crimson Executioner held out his arm and let Geneviève dangle. He squeezed and Geneviève let go of his wrist. Her bloodied hands flapped by her sides. He managed a full circle spin like a ballet dancer, slow enough to let the audience in all corners of the Colosseum see the defeated elder. He looked up to the child empress.

The little girl stuck out her arm, hand flat, thumb out.

The crowd called for death.

The hand wavered. The thumb turned down.

The crowd cheered like a hurricane.

Kate saw the muscles bunching in the Crimson

Executioner's upper arm, as the message slowly sparked along his nerves, the order to wrench off Geneviève's head.

Mater Lachrymarum was undefeatable, above and beyond all human understanding. But the Crimson Executioner was a man in her thrall.

Under her spell, Bond hadn't been free to look out for himself, even though he'd have been more use to his mistress without the shattered limbs.

There was a weakness there.

When fighting a puppet, the trick was to cut the strings.

Penelope pounced, sinking teeth into the Executioner's forearm, tearing out strands of muscle, chewing them apart. He didn't stop grinning, but his grip didn't tighten on Geneviève's throat. Penny stuck her thumb in his eye, fishing out a scarlet gout.

The crowd groaned as one, in sympathy. They could take any amount of disembowelment and decapitation, but show them one little gouged eyeball and they wanted to spew.

Kate tackled low, hugging the big man's legs and throwing a shoulder into his stomach. With three vampire women hanging off him, he overbalanced and fell like a collapsing colossus. The ground shook with the impact. A nearby column fell over.

Penelope was still tearing at his arm and neck and face. The Executioner wouldn't let go of Geneviève's neck.

Kate crawled over the fallen man, easing Penelope out of the way. She looked deep into his remaining eye, penetrating his red madness, trying to reach the man he must once have been.

There was only one way.

Penelope was working on his hand, shredding the skin and flesh from his fingers, but still not freeing Geneviève. Her hands and lower face were messy with blood.

Kate scooted around, scraping her knees on rubble, until she was kneeling at the Crimson Executioner's head, looking down at his upside-down face – *upside-down, like the reflection in the Fontana di Trevi* – and the ruin Penelope had made of his neck. Blood seeped from the wound, slower than it ought to. He was probably dying, but his mistress wouldn't let him go until the last elder in Rome was dead.

She loosened her collar and stuck a thumbnail into her own neck, opening a rent that dripped blood onto the Executioner's face. She dislocated her spinal column and pressed her wound to the Executioner's mouth while fastening her own fangs into his torn-apart neck.

She sucked his blood into her mouth and let her blood trickle into him.

There was an electric connection.

She had a sense of who he had been. An actor. She might have guessed.

His mind was still there, and her blood reached it. If he turned, he'd be her get, a responsibility for centuries. She was taking him away from his mistress. She felt his lips close on her throat. He suckled from her.

The strings were cut. New strings were forming, strings of blood between Kate and the man.

'He's let go, Kate,' Penelope said.

She heard Geneviève coughing.

The sweet strong blood was in her throat. She swallowed some and wanted more. She felt herself pouring out, into her conquest.

She had come to Rome for love. And found it.

'He'll turn,' Penny warned.

That didn't matter. With get like the Crimson Executioner, she could stand up to the Mother of Tears, could set herself up as Queen-Empress of the Night.

She thought of Charles.

And broke the connection.

She stood up and squeezed her neck-wound shut. Her blouse was stiff with blood. Ruined.

Penelope helped Geneviève, holding her upright as her crushed neck filled out and healed.

'Hail to *la vampira*,' someone shouted. The cry was taken up. Flowers rained from the sky.

The Crimson Executioner – whoever he had been – was shaking in his death throes. Kate's blood was in his mouth, but he didn't swallow. He choked and vampire blood poured out of him. The Mother of Tears had lost her toy but wasn't going to let anyone else claim him.

A man died. He'd had a name once. A life.

As he died, the crowds left. Kate, exhausted, slumped by him, holding his cooling hand. Geneviève couldn't speak yet, but was gasping gratitude. Penelope, elegant despite the gore smeared on her face, was still puzzled by the drama into which Kate had impressed on her.

The people of Rome went back to their dreams. Kate saw Inspector Silvestri and Diabolik, Cabiria and Marcello, Pier Paolo Pasolini and Palmiro Togliatti, the waiter from the Hassler and Elsa Martinelli. And hundreds of others, from all walks of life and death. Everyone she had met since coming to the city, and those who had been there but unnoticed. A circus parade and a funeral party, a riot and an orgy, a communion and a community.

Were they even here physically, or had the witch girl summoned their phantasms, roping them in on her private games? This spectacle was shut off from the everyday life of the city, but could not be taken out of it. The city was a great, beating heart, and all hearts need blood as much as any vampire. *Mater Lachrymarum* gave the night-selves of the populace the games, and the memory would not outlast the dawn. But the spilled blood kept Rome alive.

How often did this happen?

Kate felt death as the blood in her mouth went rancid. She spat, and wiped her mouth on her hand. The Crimson Executioner was gone.

Penelope gave Geneviève to Kate. They hugged, fiercely.

Again, all three vampire women were crying.

'Thank you,' Geneviève croaked.

'That's all right, m'darling,' said Kate. 'Least we could do.'

They broke the hug.

The Mother of Tears was with them. Now, she was Viridiana, the saintly adolescent with the glowing face. Her purity was hard, unsympathetic. According to Father Merrin, she told only the truth. Under some circumstances, Kate would have preferred to deal with Mamma Roma, who told only lies.

'Elder vampire,' she said, addressing Geneviève. 'You must still die.'

This thin stick of a girl could pour forth fire.

For the first time, Kate was truly terrified.

Viridiana's eyes grew, pupils whirling spirals. Geneviève was struck, gripped by an invisible force. Kate tensed, feeling an impulse to throw herself between the two. Was that brave or stupid? She couldn't decide.

Suddenly, Penelope demanded 'And who are you to judge, missy?'

Penny didn't understand who she was dealing with. That made her brave and stupid. She walked towards Viridiana, ready to give this impertinent chit of a monster a good slapping as if she were some careless shopgirl not the secret mistress of an eternal city. Penny would be *destroyed*. Kate couldn't let her step into the line of fire without understanding.

Kate didn't think about it. She stood in front of Penelope and Geneviève. It made her calm.

'You'll have to get to my friends through me,' she said.

Viridiana thought about it.

'Miss Reed,' she said, 'the love of your life chose this elder over you, and yet you're willing to die for her. Miss Churchward, you don't even like this elder, and yet you're willing to kill for her.'

The saint was genuinely puzzled, but still cunning. Her shot went straight to Kate's heart.

'We've been through a lot together,' Kate said. It sounded feeble, put like that.

Viridiana stepped back into the darkness and stepped forward as Santona. Her *'ndrangheta* servants lurched out of the shadows of the columns.

'Such feelings will pass, Katharine Reed,' the fortune-teller foresaw. 'Vampire elders cannot feel. They are heartless as these walking remnants are mindless. Their souls have flown. As have yours, missies. You only feel out of habit. It will pass.'

The *'ndrangheta* raised silver-tipped spears.

The Mother of Tears evidently had a killing pack to spare in case her chief puppet failed.

Geneviève laid her hands on Kate and Penelope's shoulders. She gently pushed them aside like doors, and stepped forward.

'I'll stay,' she said, croaking. 'But my friends will go. Unharmed.'

Santona's gnarled face wrestled with a puzzle.

If Geneviève was willing to die for her friends, then she could love and hate and feel. And *Mater Lachrymarum* was wrong about elder vampires.

Santona considered Geneviève.

Kate realised they were saved. Not just for tonight, but for all time. If Geneviève was genuine, then it was possible to become an elder and remain a real live girl. Kate did not have to yield to that gradual withdrawal from the world she'd begun to think the inevitable lot of her kind.

Dawn was breaking. Pink light rose in the sky.

Geneviève, though torn, was not broken. Her hair caught the dawnlight and shone. Her face reformed, perfectly. Her fangs receded. Her hands lay on Kate and Penny's shoulders, like a real mother's, a firm grip that said you were protected, that no harm could come.

Mamma Roma was with them now, bedraggled and weary after a night servicing the lusty men of the city. She was disgusted by what she was learning.

'You are gambling, elder,' she said. 'You are faking emotion you do not feel. You cannot love.'

There was contempt in the whore's accusation, but it made Kate's heart burst with joy.

'You're lying,' Kate said, exultant. 'You always lie.'

At the last, there was only the little girl, nameless, silent, cruel, lost. For the first time in millennia, the Mother of Tears had been forced to change her mind. She wasn't happy about it but that didn't stop them from leaving the Colosseum. This was only a temporary thing. The little girl was as half-blind as a one-eyed jack, as capable of taking one side of an argument as the other. Another night, *Mater Lachrymarum* might decide the other way and they'd all be cut to pieces by silver blades.

Kate and Penelope supported Geneviève between them. They left the arena.

35

LYING IN STATE

Bells tolled and crows circled in the night. The funeral party clung to the cliffs of Fregene, negotiating a narrow path that led from the Palazzo Otranto down to the beach. The coffin went first, carried by the faithful Klove and the top-hatted, long-nailed Zé do Caixão, undertaker to the wealthy and notorious.

Geneviève fell in with the procession. Kate and Penelope were a little in front. This would be her last appearance in Italy, she decided. The warning issued at the Colosseum had taken and she would quit Rome, never to return. She still didn't entirely understand the personage who'd nearly killed but finally spared her. Her throat wasn't quite healed and she spoke with a froggy rasp.

Attendants held flaming torches to light the path.

If it hadn't been for the Crimson Executioner, all vampire society would have been here. As far as the world knew, he was still active, set on exterminating any elders who trespassed in his city. An actor named Travis Anderson, who had mysteriously disappeared a few years ago, had been found dead in the Colosseum but no official connection was made with the Executioner.

On the beach was a bier of driftwood. The coffin was laid on it and Klove lifted off the lid. Geneviève looked at the corpse. It was indeed Dracula, head resting on a pillow placed above his body. He still resisted corruption.

Princess Asa wailed her grief. Penelope comforted the elder.

They would wait till dawn, then fire the bier. Cremation had the advantage of demonstrating that Dracula was indeed definitively dead.

The vigil shouldn't last more than two hours.

Geneviève looked at the faces of the few mourners. Most were members of the soon-to-be-dispersed household. Kate's Italian reporter was here; she was pointedly not speaking with him.

'It must have been Commander Bond's hand,' Geneviève said. 'Guided by the Mother of Tears. He killed Dracula.'

Kate nodded. 'I don't care, as long as it wasn't me.'

Bond had survived the night of the games, but Geneviève thought he'd never be the same man again. He was on his way back to the Diogenes Club.

The Princess knelt at the foot of the bier and shrieked at the dying night. She was quite unhinged.

'Princess Asa is an elder,' Kate said.

Geneviève didn't follow.

'The Mother of Tears said only one elder remained in Rome,' Kate continued. 'You, Gené. Why didn't the Princess count?'

Geneviève looked out at the sea. 'Fregene is outside the city proper,' she said. 'Beyond the Realm of Tears?'

'In that case, why kill Dracula? He never left the palazzo, never went into the city.'

Geneviève had no answer.

'She was here, though. I saw her.'

Kate was thinking something through. She was like Charles, sparking swiftly from one thing to another, piling up evidence, filling in gaps with deductions.

Suddenly, she climbed up on the bier, exciting another wail from Asa, and pulled Dracula's right hand out of the coffin. She showed Geneviève the thickly-haired palm. A weal was scorched across it.

'Remember the silver scalpel with vampire skin burned on it?' said Kate. 'The proof that a vampire struck the killing blow with a bare hand? What happened was that Dracula was stabbed and took hold of the knife-handle himself, trying to pull it out. He couldn't keep the grip and let go, his hand falling by his side. Nobody looked at his hairy palms.'

'Kate, what do you think you're doing?' Penelope demanded.

Kate hopped down onto the sand.

'I'm catching you out, Penelope.'

Geneviève saw at once that Kate had guessed right.

Kate took Penelope's hand.

'You wore gloves, Penny,' she said. 'You're careful.'

Penelope did not deny the accusation.

'You arrange things,' Kate said. 'Receptions, parties, funerals. Other people's lives. And you arranged a murder, just as you do everything, with a touch of style, but without wanting to take too much credit.'

Geneviève stood by Kate. If Penelope attacked her friend, she was ready – no matter what she owed the Englishwoman – to save her.

Long moments passed.

'Very well,' said Penelope, coolly. 'I'll tell you what happened. I can't claim to explain anything, but…'

36

PENELOPE'S SHROUD

I sought to be what I have become. You both know that. I made a bargain with Arthur, Lord Godalming. He turned me, in exchange for… well, I expect you can imagine. I'm not like you, Katie, or you either, Geneviève. I was taught that life is trade, that favours must be bartered, not given. It's a very Victorian attitude, one that served to make whores of all girls, panders of all men. We spoke of 'the marriage market' and of a girl's 'value'.

Can you remember what it was like to turn? From an early age, I knew I had power. Over my parents, over my friends, over men. It wasn't just being pretty. Katie, you were cleverer than I. And more honest. That's why Charles preferred you. But you could never have hemmed him in to proposing to you. This, you must remember, was when I was alive and just a girl. Imagine how much stronger I became as a vampire, when I could exert a spell of fascination. At first, I was drunk with the possibilities.

Then, as you know, I became unwell.

Other new-borns drank tainted blood and shrivelled to death. That wouldn't happen to Penny. But it did. You, Geneviève, saved my life when you stopped that quack Dr Ravna from sticking more of his leeches to me. I still have the scars. I can only wear high-necked blouses.

I may have grown, may have changed, but at bottom I am still Penelope Churchward. Pretty Penny. Bad Penny. It may not be an entirely happy position. I admit that I envy you both. You have freedoms I have never known. Charles favoured you both over me and I do not blame him. Once, in the first throes of life as a vampire, I thought I hated you all. I tried to avenge myself upon you by taking Charles. I could have drained him and turned him and, I thought then, made him my slave.

I did not. I came close, but his blood *changed* me.

That's something no one told me before I turned. I was given to understand vampirism was just a physical thing, the drinking of blood. From the first, I was shocked by all the other things that came with that hot copper gush. The feelings, the contradictions, the *information*. I didn't know that turning vampire made Penny Churchward a vessel, and that taking blood could fill me up with other persons. A weak vampire, such as I was, can drink too much of a strong warm person and lose her own self, become a reincarnation of her victim. I didn't bleed Charles enough for that. If I had, he would have been drained dead. But I took enough to see myself through his eyes, to see Pamela's face over my vanished reflection, to see the monster I was even before I sought the Dark Kiss.

I fought the blood in me. I struggled to purge myself of Charles. Since then, I have only drunk from the weak, the hollow and the professional. Weak tea, with lots of milk.

I was putting the blame in the wrong quarter. Charles Beauregard did not make me what I was, did not colour my world with blood. Nor, really, did Art. Behind it all, behind the Changes, was Dracula.

He was Prince Consort then. Later, he called himself everything from Graf to Prince, Emperor of the Night to King of the Cats. I always think of him as he first presented himself to Jonathan and Mina Harker, to my poor friend Lucy Westenra, as the Count.

We thought too much of titles then. No, I am being unfair. *I* was the one who thought too much of titles. When Lucy said she was to become Lady Godalming, I was green with envy. I would only be Mrs Charles Beauregard, though I had hopes he would earn and accept a knighthood, perhaps a peerage. Nevertheless, Charles could only be a new-born in society, while Art was an elder.

Dracula. Yes, I shall get to him.

I recovered slowly from my unwise predations, over a decade. I made myself a coven of new-born get. Most of my brood perished in the First World War and the years afterwards. I had chosen only those who wouldn't put up a fight and would accept me as their mistress. I couldn't fit them for survival. That was a great sadness. There are remnants of my bloodline, the Godalming line. I boasted of them to you, Katie. That was the old Penny, I'm afraid. They are degraded beyond redemption. Sometimes they turn up, after a handout of money or blood. Most are wraiths, consumed by an appetite larger than their personalities.

England became difficult for me. Women got the vote, you remember. Secretly, I had always thought we should have it though I couldn't imagine why any woman should waste herself in politics. I knew that voicing suffragist opinions – as you did, Katie, heroine of the age – devalued one's worth in the arena that really counted. My mother died, my warm friends grew old. Fashions changed, hemlines rose. Everyone talked on the telephone all the time. I was a butterfly with a pin through it, kept under glass, admired sometimes, not really cared for. You, Katie, were always in the thick of things. You didn't turn into a wax flower. That proved it was not an inevitable part of becoming a vampire. It was something in me, in Penelope. Bad Penny's Blues. It became of paramount importance that I find some use for myself.

After the Second World War, I sought out the Count.

I secured an introduction through Mina, of all people. She was his get, after all, and had kept in touch with his household. When Dracula was established here, at Palazzo Otranto, I visited, and placed myself at his disposal.

It would be an exaggeration to say he accepted my offer. He did not resist.

Picture the scene. I arrive at the palazzo above this beach. My head is full of the stories. Of Jonathan Harker ascending that mountain in Transylvania, arriving at Castle Dracula to be greeted by the King Vampire and his bloodthirsty harem. And of Charles and you, Geneviève, venturing into Buckingham Palace when the Count held court there, to put an end to his red reign.

I thought I knew what to expect. If Dracula chose to kill or enslave me, I would accept that. I owed him that much.

There were soldiers on guard, then. It was 1946, and the fires of Europe still smouldered. After delays with the guards – I was shocked to find I was required to bribe them – I was admitted into the Royal Presence. I was prepared to be crushed by the sheer weight of his person. I knew second- and third-hand that the Count was like a whirlpool. Those who went near him risked being caught up by the currents and swirled under.

Dracula sat in a chair, not on a throne. I was not crushed, not whirled. I was not killed, not enslaved.

I thought, at first, that he was dead. Truly dead.

Then an eye opened. Bright scarlet in that mask of withered grey.

I had one of those blood flashbacks, a scrambled memory from an old lover. I was Charles, in Buckingham Palace in '88, silver scalpel in hand. All around was spilled blood and threat, roused monsters moving swiftly.

Then, nothing.

The red eye regarded me with no apparent interest. All my apprehensions washed away. It was most disappointing. I had half expected to throw myself into this maelstrom, to lose the last of the old Penny. If I had become one of Dracula's brides, it would all have been over.

Instead, I found myself mistress of the monster's house.

It was a position someone had to take. I was there.

It was something of a surprise to me, a shock even, that the Count was so biddable. I do not mean that he was weak-willed. Rather, that he no longer had an interest in the world.

It had all become too much for even him.

This is the secret I have kept. Dracula was not what he had been. He slept much of the time. In his waking hours, he would feed and wander in his thoughts. History had caught up with him, and passed him by.

Once, he had been passionate, obsessed with novelty and energy, with new inventions and new slang. I found evidence of his bygone enthusiasms everywhere, from half-built war machines to reports from scientists and scholars, commissioned long ago and now cast aside unread. The papers are under that coffin, waiting to be burned. I give myself the credit for that. I have been under pressure to turn the material over to various factions. Mr Profumo of the War Office appealed to my patriotism, Mrs Luce of the United States to my paranoia, and Mr Gromyko of the Soviet Union to my pacifism. I have resisted them all and Dracula's secrets shall die with him.

That Dracula, the plotter and schemer, the waiter in the wings of history, was dead. I became governess to his ghost, the walking shell of the King Vampire. I don't know what it was that changed him. Hiroshima and Nagasaki. All his get who perished in the Nazi Death Camps. A Labour Government in England. The ringing down of the Iron Curtain. Some infection from the *morti viventi* of Italy. That damned song, the 'Dracula *Cha Cha Cha*'.

The man who had mastered *Bradshaw's Guide* and could whistle airs from Gilbert and Sullivan could not cope with broken sound barriers and rock 'n' roll. You can take so much on board, Katie. I've read your articles on Kerouac and Eddie Cochran, on the Mau Mau and Brigitte Bardot, and my head spins. I've tried to keep up, honestly I have. I've read *Peyton Place* and *The Catcher in the Rye* and *From the Terrace*. But sometimes, I just want it all to stop, to be frozen as it was. That's the sliver of ice that first pricks the heart of a vampire who is on the way to becoming the wrong sort of elder, the type the Crimson Executioner was stalking. I understand why the Count wanted to climb into his coffin and pull down the lid.

As you said, Katie, I am an arranger. I was trained to be a Victorian wife, which involved a combination of self-effacing tact, ruthless bookkeeping and stage management. Any of my class could run a country, an army, or a listed company with far more efficiency and imagination than the overgrown schoolboys who hold positions of power. If mankind is to survive the century, I advocate dedicating society not to the principles of Karl Marx or Henry Ford but those of Mrs Beeton.

When I became the effective head of the House of Dracula, I finally found a position. These last few years, I have been Dracula. I have maintained his correspondence, played off the world leaders who've flirted with him. I have procured for him, found him warm bodies to bleed. And when he lost interest even in willing sacrifices, I have fed him, bloating myself on young blood and squeezing it from my veins into his mouth.

The House of Dracula is one of the great fortunes of the world, and will now be dispersed as I see fit, to deserving causes throughout the globe. The House of Vajda, as represented by poor Princess Havisham, wished an alliance so they could return in triumph to their homeland. I am not sure what I thought would happen after the wedding. This was one of my attempts to stir the Count from his lassitude. It was plain he would never consider me a fitting consort, but Asa had bloodline, breeding, and pre-Renaissance savagery. It was my hope that the marriage would wake him up, make him Dracula again.

I suppose I loved him. I suppose I loved Charles.

I came close to killing Charles. While I was delirious and dotted with leeches, I dreamed of simply tearing out the heart you had taken from me, Geneviève, and squeezing it dry in your face.

I did kill Dracula.

I have told myself Charles freed me finally to do the deed. By dying. He was the last of my warm life. I'm sorry, Katie, but you're not alive. Like me. With Charles's death, I passed from living memory and became a ghost.

It was my position to destroy the monster who had changed the world, who had spread the rot of the twentieth century. I know I was living a contradiction. For years, I'd thought I was bringing Dracula to the point where he might enter again on the international stage, but I was always aware that in the end I would kill to prevent that great return. I am a woman. I am entitled to change my mind, to hold two opposite things in my mind at once. I know you understand me, my sisters.

I laid the groundwork long in advance. I had the weapon brought to the palace by the warm tool I then schooled to take the blame. I used Dracula's own gold to purchase the silver scalpel of Jack the Ripper, the weapon that killed Art and the old Queen, that was the symbol of the revolution against Dracula in which you, Katie, distinguished yourself. It was stolen for me by a vampire cracksman of our vintage, a fine Victorian scoundrel, and smuggled here by the American who will soon be charged with the murder of Count Dracula. Don't feel too sorry for him. He is a genuine and unprincipled vampire slayer, and a thoroughly bad lot, if amusing at times.

I had the scalpel for months. I had in my mind Charles's memory of holding the knife, and now I held it myself. I would put on gloves and play with it, enjoying the tingle of silver through cotton. I touched its point to my tongue once, and shocked myself unconscious. I am sorry not to have it still. It has so many associations. I am glad that I could give it yet one more layer of meaning.

Maybe I was waiting for Charles to die.

Maybe I was waiting for an audience.

Maybe I was waiting to be convinced against my plan.

This story is not all to my credit. I admit Princess Asa proved to be a great personal trial. I saw I had miscalculated and that she intended to force me out of this household after the marriage. She was furious that Dracula would not come out of his crypt and meet with her and even began to suspect an imposture was being practised. She remembered the Count's habit of employing doubles to take his place on the field of battle – do you recall that Hungarian actor who perished in the First World War, Katie? – and wondered if I was not trying to palm a survival of that practice off on her.

If I were a passionate murderess rather than a scientific one, I should have cut her throat and left her to drain. As it turns out, that might have been a mercy. Whatever happens, I shall see she is taken care of. In her current state, she's no harm to anyone. The passing of Dracula was like the sinking of a continent, and Princess Asa's mind has been sucked into the maelstrom by the whirlwaves.

Dracula meant so much to us all. When the elders gathered for the ball, you saw how many were imitations of him. They dressed in fashions he once set and then abandoned, all those red-lined black capes and starched evening shirts. They styled themselves Counts and Princes and Barons as he did. They relived excerpts of his biography, like the leading men of provincial touring companies, echoing his deeds always.

Why was it I who killed him?

Do you remember Van Helsing, Katie? And you know how Mr Stoker in his strange book imagined the professor and his stalwart band pursuing the Count and cutting him down? In Mr Stoker's world as it should have been, they were all strong – Mina, Jack Seward, Jonathan, even Art – and in the ordinary course of the world as it was, they would have been strong enough. But Dracula was more than a man, more than a vampire elder. He was an idea, a philosophy, a big simple answer for an age that was tiring of complicated questions. We cannot blame him. We chose him.

It was time someone ended all that.

I was best placed for it. I was not, so far as I am aware, a puppet of that creature we encountered in the Colosseum. She was there, though. You were right about that, Katie. I think her ideas about vampire elders were shaped by his presence, just beyond the boundaries of her territory. Everything she assumed about him and read in the hearts of those who were imitations of him, was untrue of you, Geneviève, as it will be untrue of you, Katie. But it will be true of me.

My heart is dead. My loves are gone. There will be no more.

When I entered his tomb, the Count made no attempt to resist. It was not a scene like the one Mr Stoker describes: the timid vampire slayers approaching the overwhelming monster and standing up to him, invoking forces of great good to overcome titanic evil. I believe he was expecting me. He waited in silence. He did not want to go to his own party.

I killed him because I hated him, and everything he had done to my world. I killed him because I loved him, and wished to save him from the humiliation that would come if his condition were public knowledge. I killed him because I could.

I stuck the scalpel into his heart. He took hold of it – very perceptive, Katie – not to pluck it free but to hold it in place, as if he didn't trust his heart not to spit it out of his chest.

You see, in my crime, I had an accomplice. Count Dracula himself.

At the end, as his heart burst, I saw the old life in his eyes. He had triumphed over death for so many years, but his final victory was over life. His own. It took all his great strength, and he could not have done it without me.

I think I was his creature, as the Crimson Executioner was that witch's creature. He took me in and, through subtle influence, shaped me into the sword he would fall upon. Maybe I am reading too much into a few glances, trying to heave the guilt from my shoulders. That would be quite in character, as I'm sure you can attest, Katie.

I left him to die alone.

It was the child, I am convinced, who took off his head and made a plaything of it. As we know, she is inclined to the theatrical. I think we were supposed to see that flourish, the head on the pike, as a warning. She didn't make me do what I did, but she knew what I was doing. I can't explain that, but I think we have learned not to ask for explanations with regard to her. You got caught up in all that, Katie. You were the one there when the girl fetched off his head and all the blood poured out. I am sorry. I did not mean for you to be hurt. This was a private matter, between myself and the Count. But it could not remain private, for you must always blunder or force your way into everything. That used to annoy me a lot. Now, I am thankful for it.

There. Now you have it. My story.

37

ON THE BEACH

Kate realised she had cried a little. Only she and Geneviève had heard Penelope's confession.

'We're free now,' she said.

As the sun rose, Dracula dissolved. Torches were hurriedly touched to the bier. Flames rose and licked around the coffin. The corpse writhed as if galvanised. Decay, staved off for so many years, thrived in the Prince's body.

Princess Asa was restrained from throwing herself into the pyre like an Indian widow. Penelope took a broad black hat out of her bag and set it on the Princess's head, shielding her from the dawnlight.

Kate watched Dracula's coffin burn and felt no triumph.

There was a burst from the heart of the fire and a column of ashes and sparks rose from the pyre. The body caught light and burned up entirely. There was now only wood to burn.

Kate felt the heat of the fire and the chill of the morning.

Penelope passed Asa to Klove and turned away from the fire. Geneviève had walked down to the water's edge. Kate linked arms with Penny and walked with her, treading carefully on the wet sand.

An Orthodox priest – representing Vlad's original faith – droned a prayer.

Marcello, hidden behind his dark glasses, walked back toward the cliffs. Her desperate love was burned away, but she had no ill-will for him. He was as lost as everyone else. She understood he'd given up journalism and become a publicity agent for all the new Malenkas.

Charles, Dracula, Marcello. All gone.

Kate was dizzyingly free of all but the ghosts.

The three women stood by the sea.

'I'm on a flight back to London this afternoon,' Kate said. 'I'm not sorry to go. Things will have piled up. And I need to earn some money. The *Guardian* wants to pack me off to Cuba, to cast an eye over this Castro fellow and see what I make of him.'

'I'm going to Greece,' Geneviève said. 'Then, maybe Australia. I thought I'd look into this rocketry business. I've been staying put these last few years. It's time to travel again.'

Unspoken between them was that they all thought it best to stay away from Rome. If they met any vampires, elders or not, they'd advise them gently to give the eternal city a wide berth. There was someone there quite old enough, and jealous of her position.

Penelope paddled, letting the water into her shoes.

'I'd like to visit Pamela's grave,' Penelope said. 'It's in the hill country, in India. My cousin was important to me. I realise now how I have deliberately veered between trying to be exactly like her and trying to be nothing like her.'

Penelope explained as if asking permission.

Kate didn't know what to do. She ought to break the story. Penelope would be a heroine to many. Funds were already being raised for the defence of her fall guy.

She had only just forgiven Penelope for everything else that was between them. This latest addition to the load would take some coping with.

'I'll never tell,' Geneviève said. She still croaked a little.

Penelope thanked Geneviève and shook her hand.

Dracula's smoke poured out over the sea.

'Me neither,' Kate said. 'Probably.'

Penelope smiled coldly and kissed her.

'I only said "probably".'

'I know what you mean. I've always known what you

meant. And remember that, despite everything I have told you and everything we have been through together, I am still Penny and you are still Katie.'

Kate saw the frost in Penny's eyes. She was changing again, emerging from another cast-off snakeskin.

'Tag,' Penny said, 'you're it.'

Penelope tapped her shoulder solemnly and ran off toward some rocks.

Geneviève didn't understand at all.

'It's a game, Gené,' Kate explained. 'We were children together, remember?'

The elder vampire looked solemn and seemed younger than ever.

'Tag, You're It?'

'That's right,' Kate said, tapping Geneviève's chest. 'And now you're it.'

She ran away, not very fast.

Geneviève caught on, and by the time Kate reached the rocks, her friend was waiting for her, to tag her back. Laughing, Kate feinted towards Geneviève – who eluded her with the fleetness of a vampire elder and the cunning of a sixteen-year-old French girl – and leaped across a pool to tag Penny, who fell over, splashing, and reached out to find Kate had darted away.

'Tag, you're it,' Kate said.

She ran past the still-burning pyre, skipping through the ashy sand, dodging between the undertaker and the attendants, furiously pursued by Penelope.

'I'll get you yet, Katie Reed,' Penny shouted, without malice. 'Just you wait…'

Kate ran along the beach, away from the fire.

ANNO DRACULA 1968

AQUARIUS

1

Sunday morning, before nine. A godly hour, the smug might say. Church bells were pealing in Greenwich and Blackheath. Merciless June. A cloudless sky. Blazing sun. Shade hard to find.

Like most vampires, Kate Reed was no fan of early summer. Nights passed in seconds, days crawled for a week. Her cheeks and the backs of her hands tingled with the beginnings of burns. She ought to be senseless in her tightly curtained flat, cocooned under her continental quilt. Ideally, she'd be in the Southern Hemisphere.

Grass shone golden-green, as if coated with reflective paint. She had a choice: oversize el cheapo sunglasses and calming turquoise blur or clear National Health specs and headache-making focus. Prescription shades, her idea of decadent luxury, cost what she made in a month. A *good* month. For a while, she'd got through daylight with the home-made option: granny glasses, tinted with felt-tip pen. Those got trampled by a police horse outside the American Embassy. *The Guardian* spiked her copy on the Grosvenor Square demo. Too partisan. And where was the vampire angle? Editors looked to her for that.

This morning, there was a vampire angle. So she could sell it…

…if the papers had room for a little murder. Monday: Andy Warhol shot in New York… Wednesday: Robert Kennedy killed in California… Yesterday: James Earl Ray, assassin of Martin Luther King, arrested at Heathrow Airport... Ongoing death tolls: Vietnam, Biafra, Kôr. Soviet tanks massing on the Transylvania border. American riot cops loaded for bear in Watts, Selma and Jerusalem's Lot. France preparing an above-ground Gamma Bomb test on Bali Ha'i. The Troubles kicking off again in Belfast.

That was the week, that was...

Twelve months ago, 1967 – the year of The Monkees. The Summer of Love. Kate had certainly been *in* love last summer. Twice. Not concurrently. She wasn't *that kind of girl*, or hadn't been so far. Now, 1968 – the Year of the Monkey. The Summer of Something Else. The Burning Season? She'd lost the taste of last year's loves: a warm Hells' Angel, Frank Mills, and a vampire vicar, Algernon Ford. Neither trustworthy, both 'trips'... as the young were saying. The young also said 'never trust anyone over a hundred and thirty'. She wasn't that old. Yet.

It was coming down. The Age of Aquarius. The Permissive Society. The Kali-Yuga. The Revolution. Flower Power. Helter Skelter. The Hallucination Generation. Fear and Loathing. The White Heat of Technology. The Green Green Grass of Home.

No more water... the fire next time.

Jesus Saves... with the Woolwich.

Go to work on an egg! Burn, baby, burn!

Commercialisation. Radicalisation. Decimalisation.

People who'd been excited or apprehensive were now elated or terrified. It was no longer enough to report news. Journalists had to *anticipate*, comment on breaking waves, name and package trends for general consumption.

She was writing more for *New Worlds* than *The Grauniad*. Michael Moorcock, the editor, encouraged her to chronicle the New Terror. He reminded her of Frank Harris, her father-in-darkness, but was a much better writer. Mike coaxed something half-decent out of her. Along with the porny purple passages of Horatio Stubbs's serial *Harelipped in the Bed*, her supposedly inflammatory piece lost *NW* its Arts Council grant. She was still waiting to be paid. Mike was rattling out *Seaton Begg* paperbacks for rhino to plough back into the magazine. She needed fashion commissions from *Woman* or *Compact* to pay the rent. Unless they came through, she'd have to ghost 'confessions' to go between pin-ups in *Bikini Girl* or *Wow Magazine*. 'I Was a "Groupie Girl" for a Gore-Crazed Groover!' 'House of Thwacks!' 'Soho After Sunset!'

Squinting through Tizer-bottle specs, she acclimatised to the glare. She was in Greenwich, just outside Maryon Park. Some students wanted to use the tennis courts. They were kept back by blue-uniformed, tit-helmeted policemen.

As soon as she saw fuzz, Kate realised she was dressed like a burglar: black pocketless fly-on-the-thigh trousers, horizontally striped black and orange t-shirt with a cartoon bee on the front, black plimsolls, slightly ratty grey cardigan with sleeves long enough to cover her hands, oversized black peaked cap with a pom-pom. Her shoulder-bag wasn't labelled 'SWAG', but was cavernous enough to stash loot.

She showed her press-card. Fred Regent, a young plod she knew, let her pass. Kate was expected. A posh athlete complained and was ignored.

This was once Hanging Woods, a haunt of highwaymen. Then, Charlton Sandpits. Now, the place was tamed. One of those leafy public spaces the English loved to keep tidy but would prefer people not use. No litter, no dogs, no children, no vampires. A familiar, alien place, like the abandoned suburbs, cracked launch-pads and drained swimming pools J.B. Graham wrote about in *New Worlds*. So quiet you wouldn't know you were in a city.

Keeping to the path, she passed the tennis courts and walked over a gentle hill. The park was mostly grassy slopes, trees straining against dark green slat fences. She saw people near the treeline. A copper got in her way, gauntlet out in sign language for 'stop in the name of the law'. His helmet's blue visor was down, blanking his face.

Being a woman, mouthy, Irish, a leftie and a blood-drinker, she'd had her differences with the police. Even before the Terror, peelers shoved her about. Kate had been arrested as a suffragette and insurgent, as a rebel and rabble-rouser.

She'd marched to Aldermaston and against Vietnam. She'd been force-fed, hosed down, truncheoned and garlic-sprayed. She'd been interned without trial, locked up for her own protection and bound over to keep the peace.

Helmet-head wasn't a riot cop. The visor meant something else. He wore B Division sleeve flashes. He was a vampire.

'Let her through, Herrick,' said a plainclothes officer. 'You know who she is.'

The pig stepped aside like a robo-man. Without seeing Herrick's face, she could picture his expression. Lips a straight line. Eyes red flints. No love lost.

Press credentials wouldn't get her into Maryon Park this morning if she were only on a crime beat. The early morning call made that clear. She was invited in her capacity as Associate Member of the Diogenes Club. Her *shadowy* capacity. Funny how you could be an enemy of the state and a secret civil servant at the same time.

She knew the OiC, Detective Superintendent Bellaver. He had a doleful, surprisingly groovy moustache. Most officers under him were vampires, but the Yard liked a living super at B Division. Old coppers' tales about the undead being not 'creative' enough for high-level police work were still trotted out. Your basic biter made a decent enough plod, all right. Nothing puts the wind up a scrote like a fang-flash and a speed-burst. But when it comes to a whodunit, you want a live mind on the job. The thinking was shite, but Kate was happy to leave that argument to vampire cops. Bloodsuckers in blue did her few favours. If anything, *nosferatu* filth tended to be bigger bastards than warm police just to prove they weren't soft on their own kind.

Detective Sergeant Griffin, a vampire, handed Bellaver a polystyrene cup of tea. The swirly violet pattern of Griffin's trendy Nehru jacket hurt her eyes. Bellaver took a swig of brown liquid and made a face as if a tramp had pissed in it. He looked like that most of the time, and no wonder.

B Division was Scotland Yard's unit for crimes involving 'the vampire community'. Kate thought being called a 'community' was one step from mandatory bat symbol armbands. After that came internment camps, then scythes and stakes.

Anticipating a Soviet crackdown on the limited reforms of Transylvania's Premier Torgu, Central European undead had been arriving in Britain since spring. Six weeks ago, the Tory MP Enoch Powell delivered an alarmist speech about Carpathian immigrants. He invoked 'rivers of blood' and not in any metaphorical sense. Lord Ruthven threw him out of the Shadow Cabinet, which only made him more popular with an aggrieved, resentful section of the warm population. Powell's followers were as keen on marching as any radical student and more prone to bursts of the old ultra-violence. Enoch was too patrician and parliamentarian to endorse street-fighting. Others were happy to carry flaming torches. Extremists like Lorrimer Van Helsing – supposedly descended from Dracula's arch-enemy, though Kate knew Abraham Van Helsing and couldn't remember him having children – came close to advocating extermination. The boot-boys had a craze for what they charmingly called 'Drakky Bashing'. Early morning assaults on lone vampires by gangs of short-haired thugs seldom prompted thorough police investigations.

'Enock is Rite' was scratched on her front door, above a crude cartoon of a bat with a stake through it. The building's other tenants were also vampires: Morgan Delt, an artist semi-permanently shifted into long-armed apeshape 'to make a statement', and a quiet Japanese girl whose nameplate was a *kanji* which meant 'Mouse'. Delt had Kate sign a petition against some Van Helsing rally and asked her out to a counter-demo, but she'd had enough of police horses. Even she thought it best to keep her head down rather than risk deportation. In *Éire*, vampires had by law to be referred to as *Dearg-Dul* to keep the *Ghaeilge* word in use. Silver-toting priests strode about Dublin in a righteous fury which made Enoch seem vamp-symp.

'Hello Katie,' said Bellaver. 'Sorry to keep you up after bed-time.'

'What's it all about, Alfie?'

'Nasty business. Potentially political. We've already seen off

Peculiar Crimes. Bryant and May want to bolt it onto their Leicester Square case. It's no surprise your lot want it too. The Diogenes Bloody Club.'

'My lot aren't exactly mine.'

As ever, the situation between her and the British Secret State was delicate.

'I heard something about that. They'll never cut you loose.'

'They might not be them any more. Not in any sense I recognise. It's the Diogenes Happening now. Next it'll be the Diogenes Experience. Mycroft Holmes would not have approved.'

She'd eventually have to go to Pall Mall and report to Richard Jeperson, Chair of the Ruling Cabal. He got a lie-in and the Sunday supplements in his big circular bed. She risked spontaneous combustion. It was ever thus.

'Why was this place called Hanging Woods?' Bellaver asked, out of the blue.

'Why d'you think?' she responded. 'They hanged people here.'

'In a minute, you'll be sorry they stopped.'

'I've never been in favour of capital punishment.'

'Good for you, Katie,' said Bellaver. 'Twenty years on the job and I'm in favour of capital punishment *in schools*.'

The Super led her towards the trees. More uniformed police stood about, all vampires, one a woman. WPC Rogers' regulation hat came with a practical black veil. She darted birdlike looks about the park, quickened senses attracted to tiny sounds, scents and sights. It was overwhelming at first. Donna Rogers had the beginnings of a focus which would be handy in police work and offputting in her personal life. She could spot a new pin in a lawn and a peroxide hair on a lapel.

Geoff Brent, the warm police surgeon, was grave and useless. He wore a 1961 cream mac to spite the fabber world of this end of the decade. A sheet lay over someone on the ground. They weren't taking a nap.

'What makes this one of yours?' she asked Bellaver.

'It's a vampire murder, ducks.'

Flashbacks. Whitechapel, 1888. Jack the Ripper. France,

1918. The Bloody Red Baron. Rome, 1959. The Crimson Executioner. If there was a string of vampire murders, she tended to trip over it. She had to admit it looked suspicious.

'Not *that* kind of vampire murder,' Bellaver said, knowing what she was thinking. 'The other kind. Meet Carol Thatcher…'

He nodded. Griffin lifted the sheet.

A young woman. Formerly warm, now dead. Blonde, open-eyed. Make-up caked. Orange-and-pink Mary Quant dress torn off the shoulder, purple-and-taupe Balenciaga tights shredded, one white Courrèges go-go boot missing. On her neck, two ragged punctures. The classic 'Seal of Dracula'.

Kate looked at Bellaver.

'How long since… ?'

'I knew you'd ask, so I checked out Edgar Lustgarten's *Big Book of British Murderers*. In London, this is the first one of these since the Blitz. 1944. The Blackout Bloodsucker. John George Haigh. Remember him? Disposed of the drained *delicti* with sulphuric acid. Guillotined 1949. Peculiar Crimes' Leicester Square case is a meat-skewer stabbing made to *look like* a vampire murder. Otherwise, there are rumours. But we scotch rumours. B Division is particular about closing those cases.'

Kate knelt by the dead girl, Carol.

'Vampires kill, all right,' said the Super. 'We don't need Edgar Bloodlustgarten to tell us that. Vampires kill like every other sod. You know the songs. "Couldn't stand the wife's nagging any longer so I shut her up." "He called my pint a poof so I went for him." On top of that, vampires get carried away and suck some poor popsy dry. A very specific type of manslaughter, Katie. I've seen too many bloated, befuddled mugs when sun comes up and the girlfriend's cold.'

She hadn't been there herself, but dreaded the possibility. The warm didn't understand what a mouthful – even a *taste* – of blood was to a vampire. Some vamps had contingency plans for how to get rid of the body, cope with the guilt and carry on. Kate cared more about not being a monster than about getting away with it when the red thirst became the red *mania*. Too many otherwise decent vampires lost self-control while battening on innocents. She wasn't immune. She was only a hundred and five, seventy-nine years a vampire. Her elder friend Geneviève confided that over the centuries she'd killed three people without meaning to.

'There are vampire villains out there too,' Bellaver went on, warming to the subject. 'Proper impalers like Waldo Zhernikov, smug leeches like Big Bloodsucker Hog and motorcycle maniacs like the Living Dead. They certainly kill people. And use teeth and claws to do it. But they kill because they want to or to prove a point, not because they need the blood. Blood's everywhere, Katie. You can buy it in a Wimpy Bar. Since they're at each other's throats all the time, vampire villains mostly kill other vampire villains. They'd do their own mum if she got between them and a payroll blag. Tears are not shed in B Division, truth be told, when the likes of Jack "the Bat" McVitie fetch up with tent-pegs through their ribs.'

Griffin gathered up the sheet and made a mess of it. WPC Rogers took it away and folded it properly into a square.

Kate had an impulse to touch the dead girl's wounds.

'This is what vampires used to do,' she said. 'B.D. Before Dracula.'

'On the nose, Katie. It's new and old at the same time. What you mob were like when folk scarcely believed you existed. Drag a bird off the street, bite her neck, suck her like an orange, chuck the peel in the bushes.'

'He'll do it again,' she said.

'Or *she*,' said the WPC.

'Good point, Rogers,' admitted Bellaver. 'Female of the species and all. But, returning to the nub – yes, he or she will most likely re-offend. Kill again. Haigh did six before Inspector Hornleigh nabbed him.'

Kate was sick to her stomach, disgusted with the way her fangs sharpened and the *need* pricked in the back of her throat. She knew this would be bad. There were *implications*.

'So here we are again,' Bellaver said. 'In the vampire-hunting business, God help us. Any tips?'

'Take early retirement?'

'No such luck.'

'Then, get a shit-proof sou'wester. When Carol gets her picture in the papers, it's going to start pouring.'

From his face, Kate saw Bellaver had already worked that out.

2

The Super left Griffin in the park, overseeing vital work. Bins and bushes had to be gone through. Few killers were considerate enough to discard engraved calling cards or one-of-a-kind signet rings at the scene of the crime, but there was a chance something incriminating might turn up among the used Durexes and Sky Ray wrappers.

Carol Thatcher's body was collected by an ambulance and sent for autopsy. Bellaver found Kate space in one of B Division's battered blue Austins. She left her four-year-old red Mini Cooper in the Charlton car park.

'We've invaded the local nick,' the Super told her. 'Dixon has set up an incident room. The Shooter's Hill woodentops aren't happy about us getting comfy on their manor, but such is life. Regan's bringing in Carol's gentleman protector, one Timothy Lea. From the state of Timmy's bird, I'd say he hasn't done a bang-up job of protecting her lately. We can hold "living off immoral earnings" over the ponce until he coughs up anything he knows. Strewth, what's this…'

The car stopped.

'Bloody students,' said Peter Steiger, the driver.

'Not another demo!' Bellaver said. 'What is it this time? Ban the bomb? Stop the War? Free the pit-ponies?'

A solemn, fancy-dress funeral procession blocked the road. White-faced youths in black robes and cowls carted a twelve-foot cardboard coffin with 'Old Britannia' scrawled in its side in red paint. A mime brass band waved silent instruments.

Some wore distinctive black-and-white striped scarves.

'It's Rag Week,' said Steiger.

'Stone the crows and plough on through. You have a horn, man. Honk!'

'It's Sunday morning, sir,' the driver protested.

Bellaver leant over and punched the horn. Students turned and leered, snarling through kabuki make-up. Some wore fake fangs over real ones. Most were vampires, of a more recent vintage than their dress-up costumes. New-borns playing at being elders. There'd been masses of those when Kate turned. The murgatroyds of the '80s. What happened to them? The same thing that would happen to these sharp kids. They'd die off or grow up.

As a last resort, the Super turned on the *nee-naw-nee-naw*. When a passing police siren made her stick fingers in her ears, she hadn't thought how much more irritating the two-tone was if you were *inside* the cop car. She felt the noise in her teeth. At least the siren startled the students into making way.

Bellaver wound down the window and shouted, 'Turn out your pockets, get your hair cut…'

The coffin fell, disclosing a giant white papier maché skeleton. Packets of pills hit the street.

The crowd made oinking and grunting noises.

'My daughter's at the University of Watermouth,' Bellaver said. 'She tells her mates her dad's a lavatory cleaner. Anything's better than being a copper.'

The students were from St Bartolph's, a college well away from the city centre. It didn't have the firebrand rep of the L.S.E. but was a minor hub of suburban student unrest. Vice-Chancellor Walter Goodrich was one of those Establishment worthies constitutionally unable to open his mouth without prompting a sit-in or freak-out. Banning the sale of *Socialist Vampire* outside lecture halls had led to scuffles between staff and bussed-in radicals. Among the first institutions to boast a School of Vampirism, St Bartolph's had made controversial appointments. Kate was appalled that Caleb Croft, her least-favourite vampire elder, held the Chair of Sociology. Croft, Dracula's Chief of Secret Police during the Terror, had lodged in the security services for the best part of sixty years before retiring to teach.

The *Mail* indicted St Bartolph's as a hotbed of Maoist revolution. The *News of the Screws* alleged kinky nude blood frolics in the Halls of Residence. *Bikini Girl* ran a lay-out of topless student vampire girls in dramatic poses.

Lately, St Bartolph's biggest stories came out of the formerly obscure School of Botany. After years of tedious, unfruitful research into fungus parasites on wheat, Professor Bowles-Ottery happened on a powerful, naturally-occurring hallucinogen. His ergot derivative was a hit with astral voyagers and hippies who dreaded missing the magic bus. The American SF legend E.B. Fern chewed Bowles-Ottery Pellets, known as BOP, like winegums. Fern came to London to take personal receipt of an unprecedented *New Worlds* advance, but got distracted by BOP. Moorcock had yet to see a word of Fern's serial *Dr Shambleau, or: The Whores of Axos*, though Fern had sent in seven rice paper Rorschach blots and said that was the first instalment.

Bellaver shut off the siren.

A young vampire doffed a tall hat and bowed, magnanimously letting them pass. He was dressed as an undertaker, ringmaster or conjurer, head-to-foot in black but for crimson cravat and scarlet sunglasses. The new-born looked like a cock: livid and healthy, sculpted raven hair, Kirk Douglas chin. All his teeth were fangs. Such a handsome lad would have no trouble glutting himself on the willing warm. He must miss mirrors, though.

'Want a suspect?' she asked Bellaver.

The policeman considered the mockingly gracious vampire. He wasn't impressed.

'What does that flash git think he's playing at?'

'He doesn't think he's playing,' she said.

Steiger drove them through the gap in the rag procession. The new-born buck swivelled, eyes on her. He all but licked his lips.

'Bring back National Service, I say,' muttered Bellaver.

That face – red, red mouth, as if stained – would stick in

her mind. Who was the student leader? Greenwich's answer to Dany le Rouge?

The cop shop on the corner of Well Hall Road was a redbrick castle, built on the site of yet another London gallows. At least the condemned had a good view before taking the drop. Shooter's Hill was one of the highest points in London. You could see for miles and miles and miles. The late Count Dracula bought property here, following a fourteenth century instinct to put fortresses on top of mountains.

Steiger pulled up outside the police station in time for Kate to observe a textbook Good Cop/Bad Cop procedure. A growling, red-faced detective in a stained, wide-collared suit dragged a long-haired, complaining youth along the pavement. At the front doors, a grandfatherly uniformed sergeant offered the lad a cup of tea and his choice of biscuits.

'Get inside, you horrible hairy,' shouted the detective, Jack Regan. 'Or we'll have your lungs out for carrier bags.'

'Mind how you go on the steps, son,' said the uniformed man, George Dixon. 'You don't want to have a nasty accident.'

Kate guessed the youth was the aforementioned Timothy Lea. His muslin shirt was bunched up under his arms and around his neck because Regan had a big-handed grip on most of it. Lea's unbelted, bell-bottomed jeans flew at half-mast, exposing milk-chocolate-with-white-trim y-fronts. Barefoot, he bled from his soles, smearing the pavement. Regan and Dixon showed fangs.

'Get sticking plasters for his footsies and shove him in an interview room,' said Bellaver.

'I never done nuffing,' whined Lea.

'That's a double negative, son,' said Bellaver. 'You'd better sharpen up now you're assisting the police with our enquiries. If you never done nuffing, you must have done somefing. Stands to reason.'

Regan roughly yanked an arm. Dixon politely helped with the other. They could easily tear the poor kid in two. Regan's scowl and Dixon's smile were both hungry. The terrified Lea went whiter than a sheet fresh-washed in Omo. Bellaver and Kate followed them into the station. The local fuzz – all warm – kept out of B Division's way, not wanting to appear ticked off by an undead invasion. She spotted empty patches on a noticeboard and scrunched-up pro-Enoch posters in a wastepaper basket. Even before running into Desk Sergeant Tom Choley, Kate knew Shooter's Hill plods were not generally well-disposed towards 'the vampire community'. She'd lay odds that, around here, Drakky Bashing was considered high spirits rather than criminal assault.

Choley had to let vampire coppers pass unimpeded, but took against her. The desk sergeant's non-regulation hair crept over his collar. His smirk was highlighted by a beauty mark on his cheek. He had no crucifix to hand so he barred her way with a lengthy form. Bellaver was a smart cynic, Regan a canny thug and Dixon a born beat-walker; different methods, all good coppers. Choley was a proper pig – the sort of police who'd done well when Caleb Croft was in charge. A self-satisfied sadist, his position gave him enough power to be exactly as much of a monster as he dared. Without the guts to wade into a demo or kick in a villain's door, he could do his damage, and get sick jollies, from behind a desk. He behaved as if stripes made him untouchable. For all she knew, they did.

'What's the hold-up, Skip?' Bellaver asked.

Kate handed over her filled-in form. Choley picked up the paper by a corner, as if it were contaminated. He pinned a visitor's badge to her shirt, effecting an accidental nipple-knuckling in the process. He smiled. She thought about his soft neck and strong pulse.

Being a vampire was like having a loaded gun on your hip. Every irritation was a reminder you were lethal. It'd be so easy to let the teeth slide out…

She kept her mouth shut.

The palaver with Choley took up enough time for Timothy Lea to get settled in an interview room.

Bellaver and Kate examined him through a one-way mirror. Left alone by the vampire sergeants, Lea had reverted to a sullen composure. He wasn't under arrest, so his pockets hadn't been emptied. With a pencil-stub, he drew a naked, headless, limbless woman on the table top. Not the first art on this classic theme scratched into the surface.

The Super had Lea's thick folder.

'Student?' she asked.

Bellaver snorted. 'Not our Timmy. Chucked out of school for being a useless herbert. String of mickey mouse jobs, off the books. No PAYE for Timmy. Window cleaner, driving instructor, holiday camp… pop performer, it says here. Not in any hit parade I know. If they needed a picture of a long-haired layabout for an encyclopedia, Timmy Lea would pose for it. Fall asleep halfway through the sitting.'

'Anything violent?'

'Not him. Too much like hard work. He's soft as cottage cheese. Strictly rubbish crime. Hopes to get away with it with his cheeky grin. Tried being a drug dealer, but hasn't the head for sums. That's modern crookery for you. Got to be good at arithmetic or you get docked more than a gold star when it comes to settle-up time. He's not even much of a ponce. Only had the one girl. Lord knows how he'll get by without Carol to bring in the readies.'

Timothy Lea seemed very young to her. She wasn't fooled by his pose. The lad was scared to his bones.

'Let's have a chat with the specimen, shall we?' Bellaver proposed.

Bellaver held the door open for her.

At the sight of Kate, Timmy shrank like a salted slug. She glanced over her shoulder, into the mirror where she didn't reflect. No doubting what she was now.

'Relax, Timothy,' said Bellaver. 'You're not here to be bitten. This is Miss Katharine Reed. She is a civilian observer. Not a policewoman.'

Kate tried to seem even less threatening than usual.

Sergeant Dixon came in with a mug of tea and a plate of custard creams. Bellaver confiscated them at once and sat opposite Lea.

'If it's about those pills I sold that geezer in the Winchester,' the youth blurted, 'they were Trebor mints coloured with purple pencil, not BOP. Just a giggle.'

'A hilarious prank, I'm sure,' said the Super, dunking a

biscuit. 'But of no present interest. You are well acquainted, as they say in the papers, with a Miss Carol Thatcher.'

'What about Carol?'

No one had told him. Kate had a conscience pang. Timmy Lea wasn't a vampire, so he wasn't a suspect.

And he didn't even know the girl was dead.

'You and Carol came to the Smoke eighteen months ago,' said Bellaver, reading from the file. 'From somewhere called Oakham. Her dad's a mortician, which will be handy. She'll get a cut rate. Since then, she's been a busy little tart. Made many friends. Paying friends. Businessmen, actors, politicians, oil sheiks. Wad of fivers in an envelope, shoved into your hot little hand while she earns it on her back? She's "modelled" for the Neville Hetherington and Sybil Waite Agencies. Names well known to the Vice Squad. Still, what's a few mucky pictures between friends, eh? You put her in blue films. *Sixth Form Girls in Chains*. *The Science of Sex*. *Bathtime with Brenda*. Can't say I've seen those at the Essoldo, but my tastes run more to musicals. Me and the Mrs thought *Half a Sixpence* was smashing. For a complete nit, you were doing nicely with your pet scrubber, weren't you?'

Lea said nothing, but fairly eloquently. Bellaver shut the file.

'That's in the dim and distant, Timmy. Not at all what concerns us, though I suppose we could bung the file over to Obscene Publications for a larf. No, we're interested in the last few hours. Would you be aware of Miss Thatcher's movements over the weekend?'

Now, Timmy had more than an inkling. He looked at Bellaver, at her, at the mirror.

'Where's Carol? What's happened?'

Now, he *knew*.

'Do you recall who Miss Thatcher was – ahem – *with* between the hours of two o'clock this morning and sun-up? Come on, lad, you must keep a diary. Little black book of names and times and places? Standard business practice in your line.'

Timmy was bled-white pale.

'Carol went on from the party last night,' he said. 'It was a scene, man. Not a thing. You dig?'

'I don't speak Raver. Do I need to get a translator in? Katie, have you the foggiest what Mr Lea means?'

'Who was Carol with when you saw her last?' she asked.

Damn. Bellaver had made her Nice Cop.

She didn't like being included in this. It might yield results, but she was uncomfortable with cruelty.

'A crowd, you know,' Timmy said, relieved to talk with someone – anyone – who wasn't a policeman and might conceivably take his side. 'People, you know. That photographer bloke? Some of his birds.'

'This photographer?' said Bellaver. 'Presumably, he has a name.'

Timmy was distracted. He would soon ask questions himself, but now he had to concentrate. He can't have had much sleep. And he'd been on the piss last night. Dope, too. If it was a scene, not a thing.

'Nolan,' he said. 'Thomas Nolan.'

3

Carol Thatcher still sewed her name in dresses. When she went to big girls' school, her mum probably bought a supply of tags which had lasted a lifetime. Griffin – less of a musicals fan than his Super – said he recognised Carol from his spell on the Ob Pub Squad, but official identification was necessary. Models – that was the deceased's profession on the tax books – habitually shared and stole fab gear, so there was a slim chance another bird was kitted up in her clobber. Timmy Lea was packed off to the morgue with WPC Rogers to view the body. Bellaver said he could go home after that, provided he didn't stray too far.

Before leaving, Timmy asked Kate something she'd heard before.

'Will she come back? Like you did? As a…'

He made fang-teeth with curled forefingers.

'It doesn't work like that, Mr Lea. She'd have to have drunk vampire blood before, ah, death.'

His face fell, hope squashed. He got in the Austin with Rogers, who lifted her veil to drive. B Division cars had slightly tinted windows.

'Did anyone tell him how Carol died?' she asked Bellaver.

Bellaver looked at Regan, who shook his head.

'Then how does he know?'

'Pimps' intuition?' Bellaver suggested.

Regan made fists.

'Another thing,' said Kate.

Bellaver looked at her, glumly.

'How do we know Carol's attacker *didn't* make her drink his blood before draining her?'

It was a longstanding irritation to the police that, by law, autopsy couldn't be carried out until three days post mortem on the off-chance the deceased might turn. That had happened, but rarely. The three-day delay meant coppers twiddling their thumbs before they knew whether or not they were on a murder enquiry.

'We couldn't be that lucky,' Bellaver said, 'but someone will sit shiva just in case. She was white-lips.'

White-lips. She knew the expression. A victim drained to death without the benefit of the Dark Kiss. No tell-tale vampire blood about the mouth. There were other callous terms: throwaways, non-returnable bottles, dolly mixtures.

'I suppose the bastard could have wiped her off with a hankie just for jollies,' mused Bellaver.

Most, if not all, new-borns passed through a transitional state indistinguishable from death. Kate's lasted only six hours. Three days seemed to be a cut-off point. The few who turned after then were brain-damaged ghouls, bereft of personality or intellect. Different clergymen cited the fact that Christ rose on the third day to characterise vampires as blessed or blasphemous. Legal precedents had been hashed over for eighty years. Turning someone against their will was a crime, but not murder. It sometimes led to lengthy, expensive lawsuits, referred to in chambers as Tepes v Westenra cases. The boon of *potential* immortality was weighed against the social opprobrium and medical inconvenience which came with turning vampire. Even with the National Health, a frighteningly high proportion of new-borns didn't survive their first year. Among the fatal perils: allergy to sunlight, rapid ageing, out-of-control shapeshifting, self-destructive mania and a wasting condition whereby a new-born's body literally ate itself from the inside. Oh, and being murdered by Drakky Bashers. Kate argued that vampires who were profligate with bestowing the Dark Kiss on short-lived get should be subject to the penalty of law, which added to her already considerable unpopularity among the more traditionally arrogant, high-handed and thick-headed undead.

The dead girl might resurrect and identify her assailant. Kate couldn't see it happening.

From Timmy, they had a rough itinerary of Carol Thatcher's last hours.

Yesterday afternoon, she had been with the plastic surgeon Sir John Rowan. Timmy tried half-heartedly to pretend she had a consultation about mole removal, then admitted it was sex for cash. Sir John was one of Carol's regulars. Bellaver blanched at the list of ministers, big shots, famous entertainers, diplomats and crooks Timmy came up with. He envisioned another Keeler Affair – the kind of scandal-festooned investigation which gets vast press coverage, but also leads to officers on the case being quietly demoted to traffic duty in Welwyn Garden City. Carol generally shied away from vampires. Timmy thought she'd never been bitten (before), but she was a sometime professional arm-ornament for Baron Meinster, a disciple of Dracula who proclaimed himself the late Count's successor. The Baron took the trouble to appear in public with a succession of glamour gals, especially since his 1953 conviction for 'importuning for immoral purposes' in gents' conveniences around Chelsea. Meinster was in Rome just now, reputedly prostrate at the feet of Helmut Berger – so he was off the list of suspects.

After leaving Sir John's space age penthouse, Carol went shopping at Biba in Kensington, buying more clothes to sew tags in and never wear, toting them back to her Chelsea flat in an 'I'm Bleeding Britain' bag. She met Timmy at the Prospect of Whitby in Wapping, where they tallied up her week's take over fish and chips and a pint. Timmy didn't mind talking – bragging – about sex, but blushed like a convent girl when the subject of the money was raised. At the riverside pub, they met Clive Landseer, a young man with no visible source of income, and his latest discoveries, white-blonde male and female twins who 'came together'. Timmy was in awe of Clive, who'd been tossed out of several posh schools and talked like a toff. He'd also recently turned. The five of them went to a 'scene', which is to say a party, thrown (but not attended) by the Persian-American millionairess Syrie Van Epp on the *Fevre Dream*, a Mississippi riverboat reassembled on the Thames as a floating pleasure palace. Timmy dropped more names from pop music, fashion, industry and films. There were vampires among this in-crowd. Sebastian Newcastle, now a tycoon, bloated and replete after his hostile take-over of the Cyril Lord carpet empire. Herbert von Krolock, Baron Meinster's amusing ex. Mrs Michaela Cazaret, collector of art and artists. Paul Durward, the pop singer. Canon Copely-Syle, Black Cardinal in the Church of Satan, a frequent, combative guest on *Late Night Line-Up*. And Professor Caleb Croft, with a retinue of favoured students.

Kate would love to pin Carol on Croft. Again, they couldn't be that lucky.

The professor was most likely the biggest monster on the guest list. But she didn't see him being tripped up by a clumsy lust-murder. He'd been getting away with far worse for centuries. As a prime specimen of vampire behaviour B.D., he was the poster boy for rapine. Born Lord Charles Croydon, he'd been an eighteenth-century Hellfire Club rake. Even before turning, he used up and threw away wenches, relying on title and connections to evade the gallows.

Yes, there were drugs at the party. Half the guests were on Bowles-Ottery Pellets, which Bellaver guessed one of Croft's bright young things had likely brought along to spread the goodwill. Of course, there was sex. Kate felt sorry for Timmy, who spent more time totting up Carol's fees than having anything like a good time. Even he couldn't keep track of who went with who, though he reckoned Clive tried to get Carol together with the twins to put on a show for a newspaper columnist who 'liked to watch'. He knew Carol nipped into a private berth with one or more members of the band Forever More, just for kicks. More seriously, she balled the Emir Abdulla Akaba with Plainview Oil picking up the tab. A busy night's work. Timmy got seasick, though the boat was solidly moored. He didn't say so, but Kate supposed Clive Landseer put something amusing in Timmy's gin fizz. He was lucky not to wake up tattooed and ring-sore.

Bellaver wasn't happy with the jet set *dramatis personae*. The sort of people it was hell to have as witnesses, let alone suspects. Being famous, beautiful, wicked and rich in various combinations meant they all felt the rules – not to mention the law – didn't apply to them. Just getting them to answer questions would be a colossal chore. Most would be too spacey to provide evidence which would stand up in court.

Eventually, Timmy came round to where he'd come in.

When he last saw Carol, she was talking with Nolan, the photographer. He had a couple of tall, scary birds with him. Girls with hungry eyes. Not tarts, but your actual fashion models, too skeletony to get by in Carol's trade. Probably not vampires, since they'd need to show up on film to make a living. Timmy said Nolan expressed an interest in shooting Carol.

'I'll tell you who wants shooting,' Bellaver muttered. 'The lot of them.'

Then, Timmy lost track of Carol. There was nothing to say she didn't give Nolan the brush-off, latch on to Newcastle or Croft or Durward or Vampires Unknown, and stagger off down whatever tragic life-path led to Maryon Park. But Bellaver had to start somewhere and Thomas Nolan was elected. There was even a smidgen of evidence: Griffin came back from litter duty with a flattened cardboard package found near the body. It had contained a roll of photographic film, and not the cheap stuff they developed at Boot's.

The Super told Griffin to hop off and track down Nolan's gaff.

WPC Rogers came back with the official word. Timothy Lea had verified the identification and gone off, pale and shaking. Carol Thatcher's pencilled name could be rubbed off the forms and replaced with biro ink.

'If she'd got stabbed or overdosed, nobody'd give five new pence,' Bellaver said. 'But she had to get fanged.'

Rogers – a thin-faced, weirdly attractive woman – had colour in her cheeks. Kate wondered if she'd nipped Timmy in the car. He was the type who'd do whatever a woman in uniform told him.

Griffin came back. He'd found the address of Nolan's studio. Pottery Lane, Notting Hill. Evidently, the photographer lived there too, over the shop.

But Griffin had other news. He brought in a Super 7 transistor radio.

'What's the matter, lad? Can't bear to miss *Two-Way Family Favourites*?'

The lunchtime news was on. Kate recognised the voice.

'…if this is indeed the first case of its kind since the War, and not merely the first case to have been *publicly owned as such*, we can take little comfort in that, for it was an *inevitable consequence* of government after government turning a blind eye to the escalation of the situation. A girl – *a young girl* – is dead, has been sacrificed… Let her not die in vain, let us draw a line and say "*this far, and no further*".'

'Enoch,' said Bellaver. 'Flaming Enoch.'

The snippet ended. In accordance with the BBC's policy of balance, a vampire clergyman – Kate's old boyfriend Algernon Ford – came on next. Algy uttered sympathetic platitudes about the friends and family of the victim and insisted the fiendish, probably foreign culprit was unrepresentative of the long-established, patriotic British vampire community.

'Griffin, did I or did I not make it plain that certain details of this case should not reach the press?'

'You did, Super.'

'And yet those details are now on the wireless?'

'Yes they are, Super. None of our lads is responsible.'

Kate knew it was unlikely that the information had come from inside B Division. It could have been Brent, the police surgeon, or whoever – she hadn't thought to ask – found the body in the first place. Most likely, it was a local copper. Every nick had some friendly officer willing to swap a pint for tit-bits. Kate had sources like that. Griffin was one of them when in the mood. This was more likely a malicious leak.

'It'll be Choley,' she said.

'Who?' asked Bellaver.

'The desk sergeant with the black spot and the greasy fingers.'

'If so, he will rue the ruddy day. Griffin, you're too wet for what I have in mind. Rogers, go and dragoon someone terrifying, like Herrick or lawd-help-us Berkeley-Willoughby, then set them loose on these premises, fangs full out. I want this shop locked tighter than a fraidy cat's arsehole. Intimate that throats will be ripped if I hear any more of this on the news before we have the murderer clapped in silver in the dock at the Old Bailey.'

Griffin nodded and took his radio away. Rogers went out in search of an attack dog.

'Too late,' Kate said. 'The fraidy cat's out of the bag.'

Bellaver looked sour but did not disagree.

4

Even on a Sunday afternoon, the high-ceilinged waiting room of Thomas Nolan's studio was crowded with aspirant models of all sexes. Kate had never seen so many long legs, knobbly vertebrae and knife-blade cheekbones. Pulses throbbed in throats, wrists and ankles. She wouldn't know where to bite, for fear of scraping bone. Pretty creatures perched on low, backless couches like uncomfortable grasshoppers. They wore in fancy dress: astronaut, flamingo, cowgirl, Boy Scout. Glass-top tables had still-life arrangements of foreign-language magazines the waifs couldn't read and exotic fruits they wouldn't eat.

Big black-and-white movie star posters hung on whitewashed walls. Bogart in a white tux, Rita Hayworth as Gilda, Jack Andrus as Ulysses, Bardot on a motorbike, Byron Orlok as Clayface, Theda Bara as Countess Addhema, Toby Dammit gaunt and drugged. Someone had reddened their eyes with magic marker and added fangs to black-lipped mouths. She didn't get the point. A chrome-and-crystal American jukebox played Procul Harem. She glanced at the selection panel: 'A Whiter Shade of Pale', over and over.

...her face, at first just ghostleeeee, turned...

Nolan's Chinese personal assistant was present, issuing orders to minions. Kate was surprised – the PA was the woman she knew as the Daughter of the Dragon. She'd used more elaborate names, but now called herself Lin Tang. Kate hadn't kept track of the woman, but heard the Lord of

Strange Deaths, her father, had joined his ancestors. Before the ceiling fell in on his Limehouse lair, he had issued his customary statement, 'the world shall hear from me again'. So far, it hadn't.

'Kate,' Lin Tang acknowledged, stone-faced. 'And some official gentlemen.'

Shorter and slighter even than her, Lin Tang wore a black miniskirt, vinyl kinky boots and a sleeveless top consisting of gold rings sewn together. Her hair once fell unbound to her knees. Now, she had sharp-cut fringes and showed the nape of her neck. Kate remembered the Daughter as a *hapkido* whirlwind in 1896, dicing Carpathian Guardsmen with twin scimitars in the Battle of Lamb's Conduit Street. Did anyone else here realise the tiny woman was more dangerous than the bald, pockmarked wrestler who barred the inner doors? He was for show: arms crossed like the genie in *Aladdin*, single earring, flower painted on his forehead. Lin Tang might have inherited him from her father.

In the '90s, a time of odd alliances, Kate and the Daughter had served in different branches of the Underground dedicated to the overthrow of Prince Dracula. Then, Lin Tang dutifully carried out her dreadful father's bidding. Later, she turned against him – for love, Kate understood – and made her own way in the world. Good for her. Not a vampire, she seemed about the same age as she had eighty years ago. Her family had access to potions and elixirs. Like vampirism, they carried a high, invisible price. The Lord came to resemble a Chinese mummy. Lin Tang's painted face might crack yet.

Bellaver searched through his pockets for his warrant card, and found it only after Griffin had flashed police I.D. at Lin Tang.

'We'd like a word with Mr Nolan, miss… ?'

Lin Tang gave nothing away.

'It *is* a serious matter,' Bellaver insisted.

The wrestler shifted a little.

In this bubbleworld, B Division's authority was scarcely recognised. No wonder the Super was wary of the case.

When Kate started as a crime reporter, policemen found it almost impossible to interview anyone of superior social standing. Well-born ruffians of the 1880s, like Caleb Croft and his chums generations earlier, could more or less get away with anything. In this egalitarian age, being famous – no matter what for – earned the privileges which once came with title and estates.

'Thomas is not to be disturbed,' said Lin Tang.

The doors opened behind the wrestler, bumping him out of the way. Thomas Nolan, more wasted than Toby Dammit in the poster, stalked out, blond hair wild, brick-dust streaks on his blinding white jeans. Not a tall man, he displaced a lot of air. Behind him somewhere, a woman sobbed.

Lin Tang noticed the Presence.

'Thomas looks disturbed to me,' said Bellaver.

The photographer began inspecting the crop of models, pinching chins and staring into eyes. None spoke.

'Hopeless, useless, spotty, malnourished, too tall… *t'chah*! The lot of you, out out out!'

The astronaut misted up the inside of her plastic bubble helmet and passed out. Her spacesuit had a vent which exposed her miraculously flat midriff in a manner not advised for extra-vehicular activity.

Lin Tang clapped her hands, like her father signalling that more Western barbarians be tossed into the river. The models were banished, though Kate guessed they'd be replaced by interchangeables within the half-hour. The cowgirl took the spacegirl with her.

'You must be joking,' he said to Bellaver.

Then he came to Kate…

'…but you… interest me.'

He made a square with thumbs and forefingers and looked through it at her.

'Snappy snappy,' he said. 'Teeth please.'

'He means smile,' said Lin Tang.

'I means teeth,' said Thomas.

Kate opened her mouth, as if for the dentist. Her fangs slid out of gumsheaths.

Often, her teeth noticed she fancied someone before her brain did. Thomas Nolan. She felt a sting of interest. Meanwhile, he saw her as an object. Damn. She'd been here before.

'Lovely gnashers,' he said. 'Come in and we'll expose some film.'

'But I'm… I don't… no reflection. No pictures.'

He smiled, tightly. 'Let's see if we can do something about that, luv. You're definitely what I want.'

If this was the only way in, then…

Thomas led her into the inner studio. The wrestler thought better of stopping Bellaver from following.

The building was a former carriage-works. The studio still smelled of wood and horses. Large sheets of white or pastel paper were tacked to the walls. Cameras and lamps perched on stands.

The sobbing woman was a vampire, another tall blonde bone-bag in a silvery evening dress. Barefoot, her soles were grubby from the uncarpeted floor. Kate recognised Barbara von Weidenborn, a professional artists' model under the name Barbarushka. A twig of the Dracula family tree, she was now in abject distress, like a harem bed-warmer who has failed to please the sultan and is doomed to the *oubliette*.

Lin Tang snapped long-nailed fingers. The wrestler escorted the Dracutwig off the premises. Kate trusted there were no trapdoors hereabouts for such poor things. The Daughter must have moderated her methods of disposing of people, though brief acquaintance suggested Thomas Nolan could be as cold-blooded as the Lord of Strange Deaths.

Kate saw what Barbarushka's problem was.

Scattered on the floor were developing Polaroid photographs, all of strange shadows on white paper.

'I won't photograph either,' she insisted.

Nolan summoned an attractive, auburn-haired woman. She wore a black sweater and britches and had a cinema usherette's tray slung around her neck, full of cosmetics rather than ice cream tubs.

'Edwina,' he ordered, 'do your magic.'

The woman started puffing powder at Kate's face.

It tingled, oddly. Her eyes watered.

'That's got silver in it,' she said, gripping Edwina's wrists.

'It's so you'll show up,' Nolan said.

'I don't necessarily want to,' said Kate.

Edwina was strong, Kate realised. She might well be up to a tussle.

Bellaver stood back, amused. Kate had not signed up for whatever this was, especially if it involved disfigurement.

'Mr Nolan is working on processes to photograph vampires,' Lin Tang explained.

'You have such a *look*,' the photographer said. 'But if it's not on film, it's wasted.'

'That argument only works on girls who get older,' she said.

'Wouldn't you like to see your own face?'

'Not really. People weren't kind about it.'

Nolan was puzzled.

'She means she has red hair,' Lin Tang said. 'When she was warm, Western women with red hair were considered hideous…'

Kate must remember to thank the Daughter of the Dragon for her concision.

'And glasses,' Kate said. 'And freckles.'

Nolan peered at her and didn't see a problem. Which ought to be cheering. The snapper spent his days peering through viewfinders at Jean Shrimpton and Penelope Tree. If he saw nothing wrong with specs, frecks and ginger, it was one in the eye for all those lads in cricket caps who made droll remarks about pillar-boxes and owls when not asking her to dance in 1886. They were mostly dead, of course.

He picked up a camera and started snapping at her.

'Lovely,' he said. 'More fang, please. And the eyes. Flash 'em, luv. Teeth and smiles. That's the business, darling. Oh yes.'

Flashbulbs popped.

She was backed against a sheet of butchers' paper, which fell down. The photographer advanced on her. Click click click.

Edwina also had a camera – the Polaroid, which spat out instant images.

She showed one to Nolan, who took a photograph of her holding it out to him.

Kate saw Edwina's photograph. There she was, in it. A pale, round face. The blank circles of her specs. Prominent eyeteeth, a defensive snarl. Even her hair. The magic had worked.

Despite herself, she was interested.

Annoyingly, she looked startled in the picture. Like every long exposure taken when she was alive and had to sit in a chair with head-pincers to be photographed.

Bellaver failed to stifle laughter. Griffin was smirking too.

She'd make them pay later.

'Now, stop all this,' she said. 'We're here about something serious.'

To Thomas Nolan, this *was* serious. He shot more pictures, with various cameras, fixed on tripods and hand-held.

She tried to exert her will on his. It wasn't one of her talents, but she'd been a vampire long enough to pick up some of the tricks.

Nothing.

Each snap was something taken from her. A layer of skin? It was like being bitten, being drained – which she'd only gone through *once*, albeit profoundly – being turned. She was worried she would fade.

Like ice in the sun, I melt away…

Edwina and Lin Tang stood to one side, attendant harpies. Why didn't he photograph them instead? They were pretty.

A big lens was close to her face, like the probe of the Martian War Machine in the film of *War of the Worlds*. She had no reflection in it. The shutter irised inside the camera.

Click click click.

She shrank, cringing, almost in terror. Nolan went down on his knees, over her, aiming down, still shooting. She put a hand behind her, and felt the floor.

She was strong. She could throw him off.

She was thirsty. She could bite him.

Click click damnable click.

She didn't resist. The clicks were kisses now. Her teeth cut her own lips. Her mouth would be reddened.

'Stop,' she said, firmly.

Nolan gripped her thighs with his knees. He bore down on

her, a cyclops. The upper half of his face, above his cherub lips, was all camera, a big eye on an extending stalk.

There was an automatic quality to his clicking. He took a shot and rolled the film on, again and again.

She was wrung out, limp.

She saw what was wrong.

'Bellaver,' she said. 'Get him off me. It's about the case.'

As the Super stepped forward, Kate reached up and took away Nolan's camera. He still made click-and-roll motions. He cooed at her, trying to capture the *look*.

He was in a daze, imagining himself taking photographs.

'Luv,' he said, 'come on, luv…'

Griffin and Bellaver helped him stand up. His hands still made motions. He wasn't seeing anything.

His studio girls showed little concern. They were used to not questioning bizarre behaviour.

'Lin Tang,' she said. 'He's been fascinated. Barbarushka?'

The Daughter snorted contempt. 'Not that one.'

'Another vampire, then. Recently. How long has he been like this? Manic, not all here…'

The question didn't mean anything to Lin Tang.

'Good news and bad news, Super,' she told Bellaver. 'Nolan must know – must have known – something. But a vampire has got into his head and locked it up.'

The photographer was quieter now, suggestible. Edwina sat him in an egg-shaped chair that hung from the ceiling on a chain. His feet dangled, scraping the floor. He muttered, and his hands worked an invisible camera.

'Were either of you with Nolan last night?' Bellaver asked. 'On a boat, and then somewhere else?'

Lin Tang nodded. Edwina shrugged.

'Did he take any photographs last night?' Kate asked.

'Of course,' said Lin Tang. 'He always takes photographs.'

'Have they been developed?'

'No. He does that himself.'

'We'll need the film,' said Bellaver.

'That won't be possible,' said Lin Tang.

'Make it possible, Lotus Blossom. Or we'll find something

to charge you with. Obstruction, most likely. If Insidious Fiendishness isn't an actual offence, we'll make it up specially.'

'My name isn't Lotus Blossom, Inspector Plodder. Or Suzie Wong.'

'I did make it clear this is a *murder* enquiry.'

Lin Tang was unimpressed. Given who the woman was, Kate understood why. A murder? Only one?

'Nolan will need help,' Kate said. 'To fix his head. You'd best cooperate.'

'Very well,' said Lin Tang. 'But I will develop the film myself. One of you may join me in the darkroom.'

'An offer you don't hear every day,' said Bellaver. 'Katie, I'm assuming you can see in the dark.'

'Like a cat,' she said.

'Miaow away, then. I'll find someone to unscramble Tommy Sunshine's brains.'

5

Access to the darkroom, a former stable, was via an airlock set-up. Two black blankets pegged on clotheslines. When Kate came out with the wet contact sheets, Bellaver's pet hypnotist was shining lights into Thomas Nolan's unseeing eyes.

Marcus Monserrat was a venerable, bowed gent with leg-braces and crutches, deeply suntanned or part-Asian, sporting a neatly trimmed white beard. A brain specialist, he'd returned from a sojourn in Tibet with a supposed mastery of ancient mesmeric techniques.

She remembered the '20s and '30s craze for going to Tibet and acquiring the power to cloud men's minds. *The Disappearing Diplomat*, James Hilton's biography of Hugh Conway, inspired a lost generation of fatheads to freeze their extremities off trudging up snowy Himalayas in search of Shangri-La, Shambhala or K'un-L'un. Kent Allard, a flier she'd known during the First World War, was one of the few who came back. With Tibet occupied by Red China, would-be mystics favoured the Maharishis of India. She understood *serious* dark postulants had moved on to a new continent. They hung about Ayers Rock soliciting Aboriginal shamen for the secret of killing via shouting or bone-pointing, as if there were a crying need for cleverer ways of murdering people.

For Monserrat, supernatural powers hadn't meant material wealth. He didn't seem to have set out to be an ascetic. Once a prosperous Harley Street neurologist, he now had cards up in newsagents' in Marylebone High Street. His clientele ran to cash customers who wanted to give up smoking or biting their nails. Kate didn't know how Monserrat came to be on B Division's books. He must have helped on previous cases. This wasn't the first time a witness to vampire crime had been *fascinated* into keeping schtumm. Clearing the fog would be a useful trick. If it wasn't arrant quackery. Which, in Kate's opinion, it was.

Nolan sat limply in his egg-chair, hands in his lap. Monserrat had at least got him to stop taking imaginary snaps. The subject was awake, but unresponsive.

Hypnotism had progressed from 'watch the watch'. An array of multi-coloured lights mounted on one of Nolan's own tripods flashed in arcane sequence. With 'A Whiter Shade of Pale' leaking in from the waiting room, the studio was like a duff discotheque. Kate wished they'd change the record. After hours of Procul Harem, she'd have taken 'Any Old Iron' or 'I Was in Kaiser Bill's Bat-Staffel'. Or, for preference, 'The Sound of Silence'.

Bellaver stood to one side, with Griffin and WPC Rogers – who'd brought Monserrat to Pottery Lane – and a slim, white-haired, elderly woman. Monserrat's wife was a vampire, which meant she *chose* to seem the age she looked – probably to match her husband. Kate had come across that before and was not one to criticise whatever people did to make relationships work. But… Mrs Monserrat was bright-eyed and a little creepy. She stared hungrily, fangs out, at the young man under her husband's 'fluence. Kate didn't need a package holiday in India to know what she was thinking. It was a good job Enoch Powell wasn't here: the expression on Mrs Monserrat's face was exactly what vampire-haters were afraid of.

Monserrat was getting no response from Nolan.

Bellaver, bored, came over to look at the pictures.

'Any joy?' he asked.

'Fifteen rolls of it,' Kate said. 'Lin Tang is making prints of every exposure, but here are the contact sheets. The *Fevre Dream* stuff could go to the *News of the Screws*. It's what you'd expect. Rich, beautiful, famous, horrible people having a knees-up.'

'So you don't get invited to Syrie Van Epp's parties?'

'Please – if I ever fall in with that mob, stake me. They're the worst sort of useless.'

'Any pictures of Carol?'

'Lots. At the party, and… afterwards.'

'How afterwards?'

'In a cab, I think. And in Maryon Park.'

Bellaver was reminded of another avenue of inquiry. 'Griffin, have we rousted out last night's taxi drivers?'

'Yes, Super. No luck yet, but if Carol Thatcher went from the boat to the park in the small hours the cabbie should be traceable.'

'If it's easy, it should have been done by now, lad.'

'Yes, Super,' said Griffin, looking at his pointy shoes.

'She must have got to the park just before dawn,' said Kate. 'There are twilight photos. Sun-up is – what? – four, four-thirty, this time of year?'

Kate laid out the contact sheets on an artist's table. An overhead light brought out the sheen of the photographic paper. Columns of glistening images, in black and white and colour. She gave Bellaver a magnifying glass.

'What's that pong?' the policeman asked.

'Chemicals,' she said. 'No need to call the Drug Squad.'

The spell in the darkroom with Lin Tang had made her slightly light-headed. Lack of blood, exposure to sunlight and general irritability were working on her too. She wasn't seeing something.

She arranged the photographs in chronological order, trying to find a story in them. She had to go against instincts and read down columns rather than across. Even that might be a mistake. The sheets read deceptively like a Japanese-Italian photo-comic, but Nolan didn't always catch relevant moments. He hadn't known he was compiling a record of the last hours of Carol Thatcher's life. More false leads than true clues.

'Let's play Spot the Ball,' said Bellaver, peering through the glass. 'Professor, can you haul Golden Boy over here?'

Monserrat commanded Nolan to get up and go to the table. The hypnotist had more difficulty crossing the studio than his subject. His wife had to help. Annoyed, he tried to shrug off her firm arm-grip.

Blankly, Nolan stood at the table.

'Does this ring any bells?' the Super asked.

'He only hears my voice,' said Monserrat, lisping softly. 'Look at the pictures, Thomas. At *your* pictures.'

Nolan hung his head and ran his fingers over the wet sheets, as if they were secret messages in Braille.

The photographer mumbled. Snatches of lyrics. Songs from the party?

The most interesting thing about Nolan's pictures was that vampires showed up in them. Edwina can't have sprinkled silver talcum on everyone. Lin Tang said Nolan was conducting experiments with chemical processes and new makes of fast film. It was an obsession: finding a way of taking good likenesses of vampires. Kodak had marketed a film for the undead in the 1950s, Kate remembered. Results were iffy. Nolan wasn't fully there yet, and maybe it couldn't be done, but vampires at the party weren't invisible. Some were negative images, some see-through and some sketchy or featureless – but they were captured on film. Bellaver was interested, too. Taking mug-shots of vampires was a challenge, let alone using photographs in evidence. Some were incautious about public behaviour, since revealing pictures would *not* show up in the scandal sheets. If Nolan's work continued, contingent upon him getting his wits back, habits would have to change. Was Carol's death incidental? Could the real purpose of the crime committed in Maryon Park be to stop Nolan developing the art of vampire photography?

'Recognise any of these spooks?' Bellaver asked her.

'Surprisingly, yes,' Kate admitted. 'That's Herbert von Krolock in the lime-green shorts and t-shirt, snogging that actor from *A Kind of Bleeding*. What's his name, Alan Bates? The pretty boy is Paul Durward, an elder who sings a bit. I don't know the warm blonde with the cleavage who's all over him. This one is unmistakable, though I can't name any of his coterie…'

She tapped a picture of a grey man. His hair was more bouffant than when she'd last seen him. He kept 'with it' in a wide-collared dayglo suit and frilly-fronted, floppy-cuffed orange shirt. But his face was congealed death. Nolan's process showed up patches of rot on his cheeks and forehead which might not be visible to the naked eye.

'Caleb Croft,' said Bellaver.

Kate shuddered at the name. If ever a vampire were a monster…

Professor Croft was flanked by vampires in matching monk-hoods. Their faces were indistinct, hollows in the cowls. One wore a black-and-white St Bartolph's scarf. This year, everyone was seeking a guru. The thought of Croft getting his teeth or – worse – mind-hooks into young people, warm or vampire, was appalling. That scarf caught her attention. Having noticed it once, she saw it over and over. Not always on the same person.

'These pictures,' Monserrat said to Nolan. 'They are not last night, they are now. Tell us what's happening.'

'I'm on a boat,' said Nolan. 'It's a trip. A far-out trip.'

'Is there a girl?' asked the hypnotist.

Even deep under the fluence, Nolan smiled. 'Girl. Girls.'

Nolan photographed any woman who crossed his viewfinder. He even took a few exposures of Lin Tang, who had – somehow – changed her outfit two or three times during the party. Kate recognised fabulous birds from films, telly and the rotogravure. Julie Christie, Catherine Cornelius, Sandie Shaw, Moira Kent, Anita Pallenberg, Fontaine Khaled, Julie Ege, Ayesha Brough. One shot caught actress-model-singers Gillian Hills and Jane Birkin, giggling conspiratorially, regarding the camera with a gleam at once promising and predatory. Penelope Churchward, who moved in these circles, wasn't at this do; Kate thought Penny was in New York just now, keeping secrets.

'One girl,' said Monserrat. 'Carol.'

In the party photographs, Carol went from extra – cut

off at the sides of pictures – to leading role. She had caught Nolan's attention: a whole sheet consisted of shots of her at the party, sometimes chatting or dancing with others, but mostly on her own, smiling or puzzled. Why her, of all the girls there? Did Nolan have an instinct for spotting the soon-to-die? If so, Kate should be wary since he'd snapped off a reel on her too. Was Carol flattered that the cyclops singled her out? Or spooked? For a model, but Kate thought Carol seemed uncomfortable at being photographed. That could have been pathetic fallacy, an awareness of the tragic ending shadowing innocent looks with spurious meaning. Timothy Lea was in a few early shots, stuffing his gob with canapés, then got lost in the crowd. Had he been got rid of? Lin Tang, Edwina and the wrestler – Milton – were in the pictures. Might they have hustled Timmy out of the way to give Nolan a clear run at the girl?

Now, Nolan saw the ghostface girl and mumbled.

'Carol,' he said.

'Is he remembering?' asked Bellaver.

'She's a white flame,' said Nolan.

Beyond the party photos, they came to shots taken inside the taxi Carol had been in sometime between the boat and the park. The Daughter of the Dragon said Nolan took off without her. Kate intuited that Lin Tang was still irritated by that escape, and would have been even if it hadn't ended in murder.

In the cab, Carol wore the St Bartolph's scarf. Nolan used high-contrast black-and-white film. Other people were in the back of the taxi, but Nolan was working close, shooting Carol's face whenever light came through the windows. Shadows chopped across the pictures. These exposures would be blown up. Perhaps a hand – with one of those fabled, distinctive rings – might be resting on her knee in one shot? Or an array of blobs would coalesce into a recognisable culprit? Kate thought they couldn't be that lucky.

Nolan was interested in *Carol's* face. Not some vampire licking his lips in the shadows.

Even hypnotised, he was drawn to her. He put fingerprints on the sticky pictures.

Having seen Carol dead, Kate was struck by how alive she'd been. She understood why so many wanted to get close. Timmy Lea was lost without her. Not that he'd have been able to hang on in her life if she were taken up by Nolan's circle. She was, or seemed in stills, luminous. Or perhaps Kate was projecting on a blank, dead slate.

The last contact sheet was a roll of colour, taken in Maryon Park in the blue light of pre-dawn. Magic hour. Carol, trailing that scarf, walked a path towards the trees, looking over her shoulder, smiling. At Nolan, of course, but also at others. Shadows clustered on the ground.

Kate couldn't help but hope Croft was there. She'd waited decades for him to be caught red-mouthed. It was as likely Carol had snatched the scarf from a student and run off with it as a trophy. Why should she latch onto a mouldy professor and his inky followers? So many more exciting, dazzling, dangerous persons were on hand.

'That scarf,' she whispered to Bellaver. 'Was it found near the body?'

The Super checked his notebook. 'Nope. Unless Griffin missed it.'

'There was no scarf,' confirmed Rogers, defending the sergeant.

Nolan was shaking now, quite alarmingly.

'What are you seeing, Thomas?' Monserrat asked.

'Red,' he said. 'Sunlight, like blood. No. Blood, like sunlight.'

Ideally, the final photograph would have shown Carol in a clinch with a gore-smeared monster – his (or her) face captured perfectly in the light of dawn, fanged maw open wide and guilty. Instead, it was an empty frame, or a *seemingly* empty frame: a blur of bushes and grass and jagged shadow, and Carol's torn-open neck and shoulder.

'Who's here?' Kate asked, pointing at the photograph. Monserrat passed on her question. 'Who's with Carol?'

'Eyes,' he said. 'Sunrise eyes. Burning blind.'

'He doesn't know any more,' Kate told Bellaver. 'If you push too far, he'll break.'

'Who is in this picture?' Monserrat insisted.

'Can't say. Eyes, ice, aieee!'

Nolan's mouth was full of white froth. Some leaked onto the photos.

'Bring him out of it,' said Kate to Monserrat. 'Or he'll shrink inside his head. You'll never get him back.'

Monserrat wasn't taking instructions from her, but Bellaver gave him the nod.

'Wake up, Thomas,' he said, 'in three-two-one…'

Monserrat snapped his fingers and Nolan collapsed. A *Thunderbirds* puppet, suddenly unstrung. Despite the hypnotist's order, the photographer hadn't woken up. He'd gone to sleep, which couldn't be good. WPC Rogers caught Nolan easily and heaved his deadweight upright. He came round, then found himself in the grips of a uniformed vampire and took fright.

'What?'

Rogers patted him down as if he were a Saturday night drunk and handed him to Edwina. The make-up girl led Nolan away, promising a nice cup of tea and a suggestive biscuit. Thomas Nolan was insulated like a child. He had people to nanny him after his tantrums and coddle him when he was showing off.

Bellaver looked at the disarrayed photographs and shrugged. 'I'd say "every little helps", but it doesn't, does it?'

Kate had to admit he was right. She took the magnifying glass and twiddled with it.

She kept going over the contact sheets. There was something she wasn't seeing. Or something she was seeing she shouldn't. A notion fluttered, demanding attention – but when she looked again, through the glass, at particular pictures, she couldn't see what it was.

It was mid-evening, still light out but cool. The sun that had risen on Carol Thatcher's death was going down. Kate, bone-tired and headache-hammered in daytime, felt senses sharpening with the coming of night. With dark-adapted eyes, she might see more.

Edwina came back then. She had corralled someone else to make the tea.

'Phone call,' she said. 'For the Superintendent.'

'Probably the Chief Constable, dishing out a bollocking,' Bellaver said to Kate. 'He doesn't like being bothered by your lot – journalists – on Sundays, or any other time. And he likes to spread the joy.'

Bellaver went to the waiting room.

Kate was intrigued by Edwina's healthy throat. She was a very English girl – almost prim – with an attractive little croak in her voice.

'If you're thinking of biting me, luvvy, you can shove off,' she said.

Kate shut her mouth and – she was sure – went red. She'd be looking like a pillar-box again. She didn't drink from other women, except in the most antiseptic, unromantic of circumstances. The possibility, even, only occurred to her during dry spells. She supposed she was still a Victorian. Not that the Victorian times she remembered were any less omnisexually adventurous than the swinging '60s; people were just better about keeping quiet.

Bellaver came back, obviously bearing bad news.

'The Chief Constable?'

'Worse. George Dixon. There's been another one. A dead girl. Another white-lips. He's not going to stop at that, is he? The bastard. It's a flaming spree.'

6

Arc-lights rigged inside the police perimeter made the building site seem like a film location. The harsh, fizzing glare hurt less than the sun. At midnight, Kate felt sharper, less muddy-headed than at dawn.

Griffin lifted the smeared polythene as if it were a see-through shroud. Laura Jane Bellows was folded up inside a wheelbarrow. She had long dark hair and white, white skin.

'Gawd,' said Bellaver.

Rogers looked critically, as if judging the murderer's aesthetic sense in posing the corpse. Dried blood was smeared around the girl's throat. Whoever had bitten her made a mess of it. On her last night out, Laura had worn a black bikini, black thigh-boots and a black crochet poncho. Witnesses would remember the outfit.

The dead girl had been identified quickly. Her dabs were on file from a pot bust. She hadn't paid her fine. So far as anyone could tell from a quick ring-round, Laura was an ordinary flower child. From Hatfield, originally – where was that? – she'd shared a flat off the King's Road with two other girls. After dropping out of college, she'd worked in a coffee bar and a travel agents but hadn't stuck to either long. She'd been scrounging rent money from her parents and going to parties she wasn't really invited to. Kate recognised her as one of the incidental pretty faces in Nolan's photos of the *Fevre Dream* bacchanal. Girls like Laura Bellows were welcome anywhere. Heavies who might resolutely guard a door against speccy reporters would step aside at the flash of a smile and the twirl of a poncho-fringe. There was a downside. Girls like Laura Bellows and Carol Thatcher weren't in short supply. Their murderer wasn't alone in seeing them as disposable, to be used once or twice and thrown away.

Laura's friends admitted she'd been knocking about with Clive Landseer, who'd soon be quizzed about his unfortunate habit of knowing murder victims. As a paid-off parasite, Landseer's duties included trawling for biddable popsies to dress any social occasion. On Saturday, he'd roped Laura in to decorate Syrie Van Epp's boat bash. She told her sceptical flatmates she was only expected to dance on the *Fevre Dream*. Kate knew how the game worked. *Have a drink, have a pill, have some more, they're just like Smarties... This is an MP, be nice to him, chicken... yes, he likes you, who wouldn't?... Go into a cabin and have some fun... you've seen him in the papers and on the telly, and he likes you loads... We're all fancy-free, chicken... have another drink, another pill... three's not a crowd, you know, it's an* experience... *Try this, it's called a purple passion... you've no hang-ups, love, you're not square, you're an angel, a princess... nothing you don't want to do, and I'll make it up to you, but I'd appreciate it... another drink, another pill, another man... hang loose, babe.*

Some time last night, Laura Bellows had been bitten and bled out. Some time today, she had been dumped in a wheelbarrow.

'We were supposed to find her tomorrow morning when work started,' said Bellaver. 'But kids "playing" turned her up. Probably on the scrounge for stuff to nick, bless 'em.'

They were in Deptford, not far from Maryon Park.

Five streets of back-to-back houses had been flattened, wrecking balls from Langly Construction accomplishing what the Luftwaffe couldn't. Three tower blocks were due up here. Currently, it was a ghost community: the shells of homes, a bulldozered playground, street-signs thrown in a pile, rubble and rubbish. She'd been at the press launch where Sir Billy Langly proudly showed off the plans for his high-rises. Critics likened them to vertical rabbit hutches or battery farms in the sky. To Kate, they looked like coffins.

She'd spent decades trying to stay out of coffins.

The dead girl had been left in place until B Division took a gander at her *in situ*. The discovery of a body on the site wouldn't hold up work. The police – and Laura – should be gone before the builders brewed up their first Monday morning round of tea.

The body was supposed to be found. Whoever the killer was, he didn't care about secrecy. He might *want* a high profile. These maniacs were often frustrated showmen. He'd copyright a 'trade-name' next, like Jack the Ripper or the Steel Claw or the Peeping Tom.

The Super told Griffin to take away the polythene.

A St Bartolph's scarf was knotted round Laura Bellows' white arm.

'There it is, Katie,' Bellaver said. 'You were asking.'

'Funny place to wear a scarf, Super,' said Griffin.

'The murderer must have tied it there,' said Rogers.

'I hate the ones who play parlour games,' said Bellaver. 'The silly buggers imagine they're matching wits with you, sending their darling little messages, planting clues all over the place. It means they think you can't touch them.'

'Sometimes they're right,' said Rogers.

Bellaver shook his head. '*Anybody* can be nicked. Maybe not for what they've done, but for something.'

That chilled rather than cheered Kate. She remembered other policemen with that attitude.

'Caleb Croft teaches at St Bartolph's,' she said, neutrally. 'That's a St Bartolph's scarf.'

'You think Croftie's a drinka pinta nighta man?' asked Bellaver. 'Two pintas, one nighta?'

'He'd drain London dry if he could get away with it.'

'Leaving the empties tied up with a bow?'

She shrugged. That didn't seem like the grey eminence she knew. But the scarf meant something.

Was she acting like a Black and Tan? Trying to fit up someone she didn't like even if it meant the real culprit went free? She worried about such niceties. That told her she was still herself, still Katie Reed. She wasn't (yet?) only the

Vampire Katharine. She held herself to a higher standard than she expected of the monsters. Which didn't mean Croft wasn't guilty, just that a case against him had to be based on more than prejudice. She wouldn't frame him, even if he was the worst vampire unimpaled in Britain.

Laura Bellows might have been killed *before* Carol Thatcher. The girls had certainly been exsanguinated within an hour of each other. Kate's first thought was *feeding frenzy*. A pack of leeches, battening on the victims. Your basic blood orgy. The Living Dead, the vampire bike club, supposedly enjoyed regular Gang Fangs, to initiate new members or get rid of wasted groupies. In that scenario, the girls would have suffered multiple bites. Carol and Laura had only the classic neck punctures. Autopsies would have to confirm it, but that suggested a single biter. So: one killer, wolfing two victims at a time. That indicated an overpowering *red thirst*. Nolan's photos suggested Carol died where she was found. Laura was killed somewhere other than the building site where she was dumped. Maryon Park? Leaving the bodies in different places didn't fit the profile of a vamp gone blood simple. Spree-killers weren't hard to catch: they kept tearing into people until they were brought down with silver or the stake. This monster wasn't going to make it easy. They were dealing with a cunning, ruthless, *experienced* murderer. Bellaver was right: that scarf was a message… an invitation.

In the daytime, St Bartolph's College was within sight of this place.

The Super chewed the trailing ends of his moustache, thinking it over.

'Tell you what, Katie – you go, with the blessings of B Division, and beard the beast in his den. If you can make a case against Croftie, bully for you.'

'If not, you haven't pissed off a member of the Establishment for no good reason? It'll have been radical muckraker Katie Reed barking up the wrong tree?'

Bellaver gave a 'take it or leave it' shrug.

'I daresay the Diogenes Club could shoulder some of the blame,' he said.

'While I go back to school, where will enquiries take you?'

'Chummy Clive Landseer is an obvious first port of call. He smells like as right a tree to bark up as any. Fact: he knew both women. Fact: he's a new-born vampire. Fact: he's an excessive little shit.'

Kate couldn't disagree. Past the dome of artificial light, she saw the silhouette of a spire. St Bartolph's chapel. She was being reeled in. It was as if that scarf were knotted around her neck.

7

The next morning, she reported to the Diogenes Club. Richard Jeperson was still in bed, though he was a warm man and everyone else in the building was a vampire. Their doorstep order was fifteen pints of blood and two of milk. Vanessa, one of Jeperson's Lovely Ladies, came to reception to see her. The tall girl's enviable hair was as red as Kate's but long, straight and untangled. Vanessa explained that the Chairman of the Ruling Cabal was sleeping off a psychedelic dream-quest. That sounded like taking a nap after a nice long rest but Kate admitted she wasn't attuned to the switched-on generation.

What would Mycroft Holmes or Charles Beauregard have made of Diogenes in the Age of Aquarius? Danny Dravot was a rare survivor of their era still in service. The thoroughly unlovely sergeant was off in Welsh wilds, supervising brutal training courses, which left Pall Mall to the Lovelies. As a reporter, Kate just about kept straight the international roster of cat-suited, karate-chopping vampire women: Whitney (American), Maureen (Irish), Louise-Ésperance (Barbadian), Lady Celia (English), Quelou (French), Zarana (Egyptian), Nezumi (Japanese) and Lorelei (German). Nezumi was her upstairs neighbour, the quiet Miss Mouse. Kate assumed that, when not undercover as fashion models or go-go dancers (this lot couldn't go undercover as school dinner ladies to save their lives), the Lovelies were abseiling out of helicopters to assault the mountaintop lairs of megalomaniac gazillionaires.

This Monday, they were draped elegantly over the stuffed leather couches and armchairs where once were parked the substantial bottoms of unsociable Victorian clubmen. The fanged pussycats wore what looked like swimming costumes and didn't even pretend to read *Go Girl* or paint their nails; the Lovelies just awaited their master's bidding. Kate's Associate Member status meant she didn't qualify for Jeperson's entourage-cum-harem-cum-strikeforce. She didn't lose any sleep over that.

Vanessa passed her to Corri, another Lovely. The Club's archivist – a *Playboy* cartoon librarian in slit skirt and too-tight blouse – had a beehive hairdo fixed by crossed pencils, was drenched in *ylang-ylang* and fiddled with diamante eyeglasses worn on a long chain like an ornamental fan. Corri unsealed the file on Caleb Croft aka Charles Croydon aka Adrian Lockwood aka the Worst Vampire Who Ever Lived. A century or two into his potentially long life, Croft had a spotty record of cruelties B.D. and a considerably nastier sheet A.D. Kate knew all too well how he'd served the Crown while Dracula was wearing it. Kept on by Lord Ruthven after the Terror, he'd burrowed deep into the British Secret State, moving from one acronym to the next: MI5, MI6, CI5, GCHQ, WOOC(P). It was all the Circus: civil servants playing Cowboys and Indians at taxpayers' expense. With reorganisation of the intelligence services following the Second World War, Croft had even been up for membership of the Diogenes Club. A single black ball – Charles Beauregard, Kate would have bet anything – denied him. In the 1950s, he was designated 'C' at Universal Exports, then 'Mr Hunter' at the Section. The game stayed the same: handing down kill orders to laddish thugs who code-named themselves Sandbaggers or Scalphunters. Forced out of the Circus in the purge of the old guard prompted by Kim Philby's defection in 1963, Croft took up teaching. He grew his hair over his collar and wore foulards. At St Bartolph's, he was a popular lecturer.

Corri found a 1923 report by Edwin Winthrop, an old attachment of Kate's, on the subject of a conference held at Mildew Manor (what a name!) where Croft tried to play kingmaker and foist a new arch-vampire on the world. Winthrop wrote that Croft was at least self-aware enough to realise his countenance was not suited to public rule. He was by nature a behind-the-throne, corridors-of-power *eminence grise*, an enforcer of ruthless dictats. 'C' for Control. Not a King of the Cats, but a master of cat's paws. Was he also a rash murderer? Had he killed two girls over the weekend? In his new-born days, he *had* been that sort of monster, but he must have grown more restrained to last this long. Still, over the years, one weakened. If his inner beast was off the leash, he needed to be taken out and shot. The stake wasn't enough. He was a silver-bullet-to-the-brain case. That had been his favoured means of executing vampire dissidents. Sometimes, Kate forgot she was opposed to capital punishment.

Before leaving, Kate gave Vanessa a run-down of everything she knew about the victims and an update on B Division's progress. The Club kept abreast of the way the murders were reported. Ripples were tracked across the city. While Enoch Powell gave polite interviews on the wireless and television, Lorrimer Van Helsing held angry meetings in pub cellars. There was talk of demos and direct action. The Midnight Mess, a vampire restaurant in Richmond-Upon-Thames, suffered an after hours/mid-morning arson attack. Plainview Oil denied they employed Carol Thatcher or, indeed, anyone who serviced clients the way Carol did. Laura Bellows' parents sold her life story to the *Mirror*. Kate pitied the poor hack who'd have to write that, and reckoned the series would break down ten per cent life to ninety per cent death. Screaming murder headlines forced Harold Wilson, after weeks of holding out, to make a concession to a faction in his own party who were as prejudiced as Powell but less patrician about it. The Prime Minister announced a Royal Commission of Enquiry into 'the vampire problem' and plucked James Manfred, O.B.E. – a time-server at the Department of Administrative Affairs – to serve as Chairman. Depending on the fall-out, Manfred could expect a knighthood or early retirement after he turned in his findings.

Not unkindly, Vanessa asked Kate if she'd like anything

from the Box of Tricks. A vinyl shoulder-bag with hidden compartments full of knock-out gas, grappling wire and skeleton keys pricked her fancy, but it was a shocking pink which didn't match her outfit and wasn't kind to her complexion.

8

Back when this settlement was called something like Grenewyche, the monastery of St Bartolph's commanded a river view which meant the abbot could exact tithes from cargo ships. The monks' taxing reputation was inflated by tales of missing maids and subterranean oblations at obscene altars. With the Dissolution of the monasteries, Henry VIII used St Bartolph's as a prison for a while. The mediaeval building crumbled under the Tudors and Stuarts. Sir Christopher Wren and his assistant Nicholas Dyer rebuilt it in 1710 as an afterthought to the Royal Naval College, semi-officially known as the School for Discipline. In 1869, the cadets lashed Admiral-Headmaster Ashleigh to death with his own cat o' nine tails during a dry-land mutiny. After that, the Navy got shot of St Bartolph's. It became an outpost of the University of London.

Between the wars, Professor Elwyn Clayton and the 'St Bartolph's Set', a clique of Victorian new-borns and Carpathian left-behinds, made a noise about a project to uncover (or whitewash) the vampire heritage. Kate had owned a copy of Clayton's *The Whole History of the Undead* since its 1938 publication, and still not finished reading it. During the War, St Bartolph's was requisitioned back into naval use as a facility for training saboteurs. Needing extra classroom space to perfect infernal devices, the Navy threw up huts in Wren's spacious quadrangle. Typically, the prefabs remained in use. Kate dreaded to think what state they were in. One wing of the college was destroyed by a V-weapon in 1945. Clayton, who stayed in his chambers against direct orders from Winston Churchill, was killed by the rocket. Disciples talked of his eventual return. The School of Vampirism he founded remained the foremost in England, if not the world. Lately, however, its status was challenged: St Bartolph's was often outbid for important documents by Faber, an American cow college with alumni endowments to spend and a policy of not admitting vampires to study their own history. The blown-apart wing was replaced by a controversial plate glass-and-concrete hothouse designed by Santonix, the award-winning but certifiable architect. Jim Graham said the St Bartolph's annexe was a masterpiece – but he lived in Shepperton and never had to look at it.

This was the last week of the academic year at St Bartolph's. Many Third Year students must have beetled off after taking finals, and would be back – or not – for graduation, or at least the posting of their results. Kate arrived mid-afternoon, after the shadows started lengthening to offer refuge. Like all educational institutions with a mixed warm-vampire student body, St Bartolph's offered a staggered day: one set of lectures and tutorials starting at nine in the morning; another, overlapping set starting at four in the afternoon, the out-of-the-coffin hour. Young bloods could get their studies done and be ready to go out on the town at midnight. Tutorial groups weren't strictly segregated, but the split schedule nudged the living and the living dead to stick with their own kind.

A group of tanned, long-haired kids came out of the old wing – their lecture just finished. Among paisley blouses, denim bell-bottoms, appliqué sunflowers and Donovan hats, Kate saw a tall girl enveloped in a violet djellaba, half-masked by blue aviator goggles. A token vampire? She hung adoringly on the arm of a warm boy. He wore a *Shane* fringed jacket and had a guitar slung over his shoulder. Was the girl called a 'scab hag' by other vampires? Did live birds who fancied her boyfriend call her 'viper' behind her back? Hey, maybe everyone liked the pale kid? A morning spent contemplating the works of Caleb Croft had poisonous after-effects.

'Hello,' she said to the students.

'Fuzz,' a youth sneered. 'Vampire fuzz.'

'No,' she said, omitting to mention she *was* working with the police. 'I'm a reporter.'

'Worse,' said a girl with Indian braids and a headband. Did she pack a scalping knife under her embroidered waistcoat?

Kate had a fold-out map of the campus, but all the names had been changed, seemingly in the last five minutes. As a ploy to avert Revolution, Vice-Chancellor Goodrich let the student body vote on what their lecture halls were called. British heroes were out, radical chic was in. The Harry Paget Flashman Refectory became Che Guevara Hall, the Horatio Hornblower Library was now the Jean-Luc Godard Collective. Professor Bowles-Ottery's George Edward Challenger Biology Laboratory transformed into the Unlimited Dream Factory. A dayglo psychedelic mural exhorted passersby to 'Pop a BOP'.

'If it's about Bowles-Ottery, man,' said the vampire's boyfriend, 'he's on sabbatical. Floated away on a multi-coloured cloud. Awaa' wi' the fairies.'

Many journalists had filed stories about Bowles-Ottery.

'I'm trying to find the Sir Francis Varney Theatre,' she said.

If her immediate reception was lightly chilly, dropping that name inspired a big freeze. If they'd known anything about Sir Francis, it'd have been worse. But they stopped ragging her.

'Varney – that's Mamuwalde, isn't it?' said one of the warm guys. 'Dru?'

The warm youths looked to the vampire girl. She shrugged in her djellaba.

'Oh yeah,' she said, reluctantly. 'The Tent. You can't miss it. Go past the main building and it's in the meadow. The Prince Mamuwalde Theatre.'

'And watch out for the Black Monks,' said Dru's boyfriend.

The vampire shuddered and her friends laughed.

Kate was surprised these kids had that much sense of history, then perceived they didn't mean ghosts of the pirate monks of the Middle Ages. These Black Monks were some new shower. A pop group, a motorcycle gang or a political faction, perhaps? A variety of hallucinogenic mushroom? The students moved on before she could ask for an explanation.

'Ricky Strange is appearing at Groover's tonight,' Dru told her boyfriend, 'and I'm not missing the freak-out of the month because of bloody Enoch!'

The vampire girl had been reminded she wasn't like her friends. There'd be a lot of that about, if things kept up. Kate remembered the Notting Hill blood riots of '58. Then: Teds with razor-edge crucifixes; now: skinheads with silver-toed Doc Martens. The haters of '68 had adopted a bubblegum hit as an anthem of what they called 'human pride', mockingly chanting 'Hey, ninety-eight point six, it's good to have you back again'. Body temperature lower than the norm was a trait of all vampire bloodlines.

Beyond the main building, she found the Prince Mamuwalde Theatre.

The outdoor stage was shadowed by a vast, bat-shaped canvas roof stretched over a frame, like a circus tent lifting off in a high wind. White chairs were arranged for an audience. This graduation ceremony would be here, but it was a music venue too. Reparata and the Delrons played here last month, according to posters. Jethro Tull were booked in a week. The College Dramatic Society would stage a reading of *MacBird!* next Friday if Goodrich didn't ban it.

Professor Croft was using the shade for his seminar group.

He was in front of the stage, perched on an umbrella shooting stick. He wore a dark-purple corduroy blazer, a mod hip-length cape, a straw hat which didn't suit him and a long St Bartolph's scarf. He gestured and talked, hands more expressive than his face.

Now Kate understood who the Black Monks were.

They sat in a semi-circle at Croft's feet, cowls down. His students wore black habits. A small group, eight or nine: mostly men, all vampires. The robes were academic as much as monkish, and marked them out as a group, a tribe. She'd seen the Black Monks before, she realised: at the demo yesterday and in Nolan's party pics. They mostly wore their hair like Croft: long, but styled – a Regency dandy look, not let-it-all-hang-out hippiedom.

Janey Mack, of all the vampire elders in the world, Corpseface Croft gets to be a style icon!

Kate swallowed her spit and drew in her fangs. She sat in the back row, and eavesdropped.

Croft was talking about the Dracula Declaration. Everyone alive in 1885 remembered where they were when they heard the news – vampires were *real*, they were here, they were taking over! People her age competed to see their first vampire, to talk with one… and, though few said it out loud, to be bitten, *turned*. If her family hadn't been in Dublin that year, Kate would've had bragging rights. She was friends with Lucy Westenra and Mina Harker, Dracula's first English get. Considering what happened to poor Lucy, Kate might not have had the courage to turn if she'd seen her chum as a vampire. Which was getting ahead of her memory. Kate's *first vampire* was a Carpathian Guardsman named Kostaki, who visited the Reeds' Chelsea home when her father, a Classics Professor at Trinity and London, brought his family back to London. Kostaki quizzed Father about his circle of suspect friends, which included enemies of the state like Bram Stoker and Abraham Van Helsing. The vampire wore the sort of uniform she associated with comic opera, but it wasn't funny on him. He had a handlebar moustache and pointed ears, and turned out to be more honourable than most elders. Kate's *second* vampire, she realised years later, was the Englishman who sat in the unmarked carriage outside the house while Kostaki paid his call. Caleb Croft, already a secret policeman.

The Dracula Declaration meant something different to Croft.

For him, already a vampire, it was the moment when he could come out of hiding.

'Until the Declaration, we hadn't even known how many other vampires there were, how spread across the world,' the Professor said. 'A few vampires imagined themselves unique, the only creatures of their kind ever made. Those cats were in for a shock, you better believe it! Many shunned humans except as prey, living like mad hermits in castles, caves or tombs. I passed for warm, hiding among crowds. My fortune was gone, dribbled away over decades. My connections, once of the highest, came to mean nothing, zip, nada, zilch. My title and estate passed to heirs when I could no longer explain why I was still alive…'

…and why all those chambermaids were sickly or dead.

'I got good at changing my name, home and profession every dozen years. When Dracula came, I was in London, one of the few vampires already in the city he would make his capital. I was a thief-taker. Not an official Scotland Yard pig with a badge and rules to follow, but what they called in the Wild West a bounty hunter. Back then, "dead or alive" mostly meant dead and there were no complaints if the beef was paler than on the wanted poster.

'I'd tracked and killed Styles, the Haymarket Strangler. I bled him white. I turned the corpse in at Islington Police Station. While I waited for my five sovereigns blood money, a constable named Thackeray showed me the *Dailygraph*. Queen Victoria was to remarry. Thackeray was more fussed that Prince Dracula was a foreigner than that he was four hundred years old. It didn't sink in when the warm were only told. They had to *see*. But for me – for vampires all over – being *told* was enough. We were reborn, baby, reborn! Most of us knew who Dracula was, what kick he was on. King of the Cats, yeah? Some even put him down for it, like who did he think he was, you know? At that moment, I was pretending to drink tea. Whenever Thackeray was distracted, I poured a slosh into a plant pot. I'd mastered the skill of pretending to eat and drink, a trick none of you have any use for.

'When Thackeray said "What does it mean, *vampire*?" it was like a blood-rush… a sudden clarity, a profound change. I openly poured away my tea and showed my fangs. Thackeray didn't understand. A woman saw my face and screamed. Some vampires went on a tear. Too early. They were caught and killed. Dracula had them impaled himself. That was my first job for him…'

It struck Kate that Croft might never have actually *met* Dracula. Even at the height of his power, he was a jumped-up thief-taker. He only betrayed the Count when his patron did. Lord Ruthven had carried off living among the warm better than Croft, periodically returning as a bogus son and inheriting his own title. It was a forgotten division in the community. For centuries, vampire elders from 'civilised' nations like Great Britain and France looked down on Central European brutes of the Dracula stripe. None of them stirred from elegant lassitude to bring off anything on the scale of Dracula's coup, so most bent the knee, accepting Vlad Tepes as King of the Cats.

Croft had stuck with the name he happened to be using at the time of the Declaration. He didn't reclaim the title of Lord Charles Croydon.

'Vampires who turned after lived a different world,' Croft continued. 'Your world, my friends. Many – most! – didn't last. They changed too fast, had a false sense of invulnerability, couldn't see how things really were. Dracula was their God and their downfall. That must shock you. But, remember, Dracula didn't survive, didn't hold power long. Now he's truly dead. Dead and gone and done with and put away and finished. Endsville, man. As vampires, we must get past him, get around him. Tomorrow, I want to talk about his long fall, and what we can learn from it. Do you dig?'

Kate expected applause.

Instead, a young man nodded sagely and said, 'Yeah, we dig.'

Kate recognised the hat-doffing undertaker/ringmaster from the Sunday morning procession. The chin and the grin. The sexy sadist.

'I expected no less, Mr DeBoys,' said Croft.

Two vampires appeared, sat either side of Kate, leaning in to grip her arms. Tiny, blonde French dollies with identical faces. One with bunches, the other with a pony-tail; one with heart-shaped sunglasses, the other sucking on a lollipop. They wore halter tops, short-shorts and flip-flops. They looked under fifteen, but were older than sin. Kate remembered the sisters from Rome, where they'd freelanced for the Soviets. Cathy Castel and Pony Tricot, the yé-yé vampire twins. They weren't students: there was nothing they needed to be taught. So, Professor Croft hired bodyguards? Not commonplace in the groves of academe. Had he fed Carol and Laura to the twins? They shared a vicious, nasty streak.

Croft deigned to notice her now.

'Katharine Reed,' he said, introducing her. 'You'll remember I assigned you her journalism from the Reign…'

That was what Dracula cronies called the Terror! She always forgot.

'You can learn a great deal from Miss Reed.'

…not that he'd learnt anything from her when he was out to have her head on a pole and smash the hidden presses which printed her newssheets.

DeBoys eyed her, grinning ferally. She felt that stab of attraction. She guessed he was just playing at being dangerous. He was Head Boy: the sort who might leave a plump, bleeding baby on Teacher's desk. The other Black Monks had followed his lead at the demo.

The twins eased her out of her seat and walked her towards the seminar group.

They were shorter than her by inches and she was reckoned titchy. Kate knew that since quitting Rome and Smert Spionem, Cathy and Pony had worked for Mossad – kidnapping the American Nazi propagandist Howard W. Campbell Jr to stand trial in Israel – and the *Unione Corse*, the Corsican mafia. The Diogenes Club had a report that the twins had fallen out and taken opposite sides of the barricades in the recent Paris street-fighting. If that were true, they'd patched things up since May.

'What might we do for you, Miss Reed?' asked Croft.

She shrugged out of the twins' grip. More accurately, they let her go.

'An interview, for the eightieth anniversary…'

'Of what?'

'The downfall. You were just talking about it.'

'Ah, yes, I suppose so… the Old Queen's passing.'

'I'm sure you've more reminiscences you'd like to share, or are they just for this select circle of… students?'

'I am happy to rap for your article, but there must be *quid pro quo*. If I consent to an interview, you must share your perspective with the group. My young friends will have many questions for you.'

'Yes Miss, we'd be ever so interested,' said DeBoys, silky smooth.

'Of course,' she said, hoping she hadn't made a mistake.

9

The seminar moved indoors to Croft's rooms in the Santonix wing. He had a suite to himself. That must infuriate the lesser lights of the School of Vampirism.

The outer office was the domain of Miss Brabazon, a middle-aged secretary. One lens of her Lennon specs was black. She gave Croft a sheaf of messages he handed back dismissively. The twins settled on low, amorphous orange chairs. Bored with blowing bubblegum balloons through fangs, they lit Gitanes. Pony shoved a tiny button in her ear and tuned a transistor radio to whatever the Light Programme changed its name to last year (Kate knew it was BBC Radio 1 but wouldn't admit it). She nodded mindlessly to The Move, The Flower People or The Small Faces. Cathy flipped through *Cue* and found pictures of Toby Dammit in open-necked shirts. Kate had written for 'Britain's first teenage newspaper' until her interview with Jimi Hendrix – mostly about Vietnam and Malcolm X, until the subs got to it – came out headlined 'that's the man who plays guitar with his teeth and says each frizzy strand of his hair is a vindication'.

Kate followed Croft into an inner sanctum.

Remembering her father's cluttered study, she was surprised Croft could teach without a single book in sight. No pictures hung on the black walls, though a neon-faced twenty-four-hour clock might count as art. Executive toys were stranded on his concrete slab desk: a Newton's Cradle and a Drinking Bird. Students sat in chrome-tube-and-leather slings. The

Professor had a diabolical mastermind swivel chair with a control panel in one arm. He pressed a button. Tinted window-blinds rolled down, minimising painful sunlight. Conceivably, other buttons opened a trapdoor to a piranha tank or fired laser beams at the School of Humanities.

She considered the Black Monks.

Eric DeBoys, star pupil and leading light, stuck close to her all the way into the building and up to this room, showing off his teeth and – she could swear – trying to exercise a power of fascination on her. She'd developed immunity to vampire mesmerism before detachable shirt collars went out. Was DeBoys smitten? More likely, he tried it on with any woman who crossed his path. She slapped herself mentally for her instinctive prickle of interest. The last thing she needed in her life (or her knickers) was another vampire knob.

If he wanted trouble, he could always apply to the twins. Cathy and Pony would leave Eric DeBoys lying in a pool of blood and laugh about it all the way home.

She had gathered names and noted significant traits of the rest of the seminar group.

The blokes were a mixed bag. Most were negligible knock-offs of DeBoys. Scrawdyke, a scruffy git with a strident, Northernish voice, projected lethargic aggression. Hair sprouted from every part of his face except his chin. Withnail, a slender glutton, possessed thirsty eyes and an actorish gait. Moïse King, a brutal toff, had scars around his little boy mouth and, she suspected, exercise books full of poetry he'd never let anyone read. Simon Armstrong was a bespectacled, over-eager swot; the others picked on him because he let his infatuation with Croft show.

Two of the men were more interesting. James Eastman, a long-armed, sceptical American, was hollow-eyed and black-stubbled, and spoke in a whispery, dry rasp. In this group, the symptoms were unusual. He was fasting, defying his vampire hunger by abstaining from human blood. A spiritual trip? Self-punishment? Plain masochism? He didn't wear the black robes, and looked like an outlaw biker in stained denim jacket and scuffed leather britches. Keith Kenneth, a vulpine predator, was Eastman's mirror: a decadent rather than an ascetic, pallor pinked with recent indulgence. He wore a loose purple silk shirt and matching velvet trews under his robe. A choker of love beads didn't quite cover a maroon bruise on his throat. How did he get that? If anyone here was Bellaver's killer, Keith was the most likely prospect. She could see him prowling noisy disco darks for biteable pick-ups. Had he sighted Carol or Laura and just pounced?

There were two girls. Anna Franklyn approximated monk's habit with a shimmering green-black sari and headscarf. A dark, exotic woman with a pixie haircut, she showed a stretch of tight olive-tan midriff. No longer a new-born, Anna might be about Kate's age, a Victorian holdover. She was of an odd bloodline, Indian *rakasha* or Malay *naga*. Her sinuous, serpentine manner betokened a reptile totem, not the bat or rat of a European *strigoi* or *nosferatu*. She was notionally Simon's girlfriend, if only because DeBoys didn't choose to take her away yet. Fran, a full-bodied vamp, was no one's but her own. She wore a black velvet dress with a plunging front that showed off ginormous bazooms; the only monklike aspect of her ensemble was a rope-belt resting on generous hips. On a whim, she might pass an afternoon in bed with one or more of the unattached (or attached) lads, but she was a free agent. Fran had newly healed bites which matched Keith's. Had they torn into each other? In Kate's day, new-borns were advised not to attempt mutual vampirism, which tended to lead lovers to bleeding each other out. This new generation were up for any kink. She wondered if Fran had laid Caleb Croft, then realised that of course she had. Ice grinding on ice. Ugh.

Most of the Black Monks followed DeBoys' lead, as if he were the apostle who passed on the Professor's dictates. None of them loved or liked him, or each other, much. That was a problem with small, mostly-male, exclusively vampire groups: so much competition for attention or favour, they never got anything done. Who'd split the order and strike out on his own? Who'd stick around and wither away? Eastman was a prime candidate to hit the road, with Sartre, Camus and

Roquentin packed in his Harley's saddlebags and mirrored sunglasses over red eyes. Armstrong would be here until he was a used-up shell. In two hundred years, he'd be parroting Croft's lectures to new generations of soul-dead students.

The Professor sat behind his desk. He set the Newton's Cradle clacking. The perpetual motion bird dipped to drink. The eye and ear were drawn to the desk and the man behind it. Like Marcus Monserrat's disco lights. Hah, Croft needed *tools*! His eyes weren't enough. His powers of fascination were weak. It was unlikely he'd mindwiped Thomas Nolan. Unless this was a feint. He wouldn't be the first vampire to adopt a pose of feebleness to gull prey, only showing steel, sinew and fang at the last moment. She was not a good detective: she could talk herself out of any insight, consider a knot from so many angles she never got her fingers into it.

'Would you care to sit here, by me?' Croft asked her.

Of course, she would not care to. But she did, in a plain wooden guest chair.

'Point of order,' said Scrawdyke. 'Does the group recognise the visiting speaker's status as a vampire elder?'

Kate showed her teeth, satisfying everyone except Scrawdyke.

'I don't shapeshift,' she said. 'And it's still rude to ask a lady's age.'

Scrawdyke was going to say something, but DeBoys slapped the back of his head, stirring up an unwashed bird's nest of hair. Reluctantly, Scrawdyke didn't press his point. Technically, she wasn't an elder, but she let it ride.

Croft leaned back like a guest on *Dee Time*, waiting for a question to prompt an anecdote. She'd asked for an interview after all. Croft set it up as a performance piece.

'"A profound change", you said,' she began. 'I believe you meant the Dracula Declaration changed us all.'

Croft nodded. 'Obviously,' he said.

'I'm interested in what you changed *from*, Professor Croft. The vampire you were when the world didn't believe in vampires.'

He was wary. 'As I said, I was an itinerant... a ghost of myself.'

'Why didn't you take back your name? Most did.'

'Charles Croydon was dead. His life gone. Part of the past.'

'Forgive me if this seems indelicate, but how did he feed? Charles Croydon?'

'As a predator feeds,' he said. 'By fascination or force. You must dig this. We are all vampires here.'

Anna Franklyn's head oscillated like a cobra's. James Eastman ground his fangs.

'The practicalities were different,' she said. 'When you couldn't admit what you were, when there were no socially acceptable ways of drinking blood.'

'Social acceptability is an artificial construct. We are far beyond those. By our nature.'

'Our nature as vampires?'

'Our nature as predators.'

The living – she couldn't even think of the expression 'the warm' – Lord Charles Croydon had been exactly like the vampire Caleb Croft. Only money and influence saved him from being strung up in Hanging Woods. 'By fascination or force.' She knew what he meant. He was a murderer and a rapist. Frilly shirts and bright shoe-buckles didn't make him any less a thug. Turning enabled him to *predate* on a larger scale. Centuries on, he was an *old* murderer and a rapist. He survived by growing *cautious* and adapting to the times. But how easy was it to stop being an unrestrained monster? If Croft thought he'd get away with it, he'd use and dispose of Carol Thatcher and Laura Bellows in a trice. But *could* he think he'd get away with it?

'You were born with a title. Do you still feel *entitled*?'

Croft wasn't rising to that. 'That's just wordplay,' he said. 'Sophistry, man. We're beyond that here. I expected better of you. Reed, as I get your vibe, you've always wanted to be equal… *equal with whom*?'

'I remember when women didn't have the vote.'

Scrawdyke put his hand up, was ignored, and put it down again, yawning to pretend he just wanted a stretch.

'So, you want to be equal with men? Cool. And, since you're Irish, equal with the English, right? Under the law…'

'In Ulster, right now, the rights of the Catholic minority are…'

'But you're not Catholic. You're the daughter of Dr Pierce Plunkett Reed, of Trinity College and King's, London. A Dublin Protestant… an Ascendancy Prod, right?'

She admitted it.

'And, darling girl, you're a vampire. You are not equal, you can't be equal. You have *risen above*.'

Croft swivelled in his chair, and addressed his circle.

'Friends, get this: Katharine Reed is still here, *eighty years* A.D. Consider the Galapagos turtle. They can live for centuries. Like us. But they hatch in the sea and new-borns have to crawl across the beach to safety. Sea birds, *predators*, haunt the beach, and snatch – how many hatchlings? Five in ten, nine in ten? It's a feeding frenzy. Carnage. The slaughter of a generation. Of the weak, or the unlucky, or the unwary. It was like that for new-borns in the wake of the Dracula Declaration. Most didn't make it across the beach. Kate Reed did. Study her, learn her secret. It may save your life.'

She was uncomfortable. DeBoys eyed her wolfishly.

Anna – who was Kate's age or older – looked at the floor. Croft had never made a turtle speech about her, evidently.

Of course, in this story, the Professor *was* the butcher bird. Some new-borns of the 1880s succumbed to disease or carelessness. Not a few were killed in the Terror. The regime's chief shrike was Caleb Croft.

'What is your secret?' asked Armstrong, notebook ready.

'"Diet and lots of sleep",' she said.

'That's from Elisabeth Bathory's paperback,' said Moïse.

'And she took it from Herbert von Krolock,' Kate responded. 'Almost all the witty things ascribed to vampire socialites are Herbert *bon mots* passed around and polished up. Most of us lose the ability to be funny after a century or so. If an elder makes a joke, he usually has to say "ho ho ho" afterwards to be sure you know to laugh.'

'Point of etiquette,' said Scrawdyke. 'Generalisations are unhelpful. Give specific instances.'

She smiled and shrugged.

'You've ducked the question, luv,' said Keith Kenneth. Or was he Kenneth Keith? 'Keeping your secret?'

'It wouldn't be a secret if I blabbed everywhere, would it?'

If Kate had a secret, she didn't know what it was. Not of the Dracula bloodline, she escaped the rot which cut down many of her generation, but it wasn't as if she was particularly careful. She'd put herself in harm's way often. Too often. How many times can you be sole survivor of some catastrophe and shrug it off? On the principle that a tightrope walker shouldn't look down, she didn't like to consider the occasions when she'd nearly tumbled.

Even now, she was in a lions' den, taking questions from cubs.

'I wouldn't take me as an example,' she said.

Armstrong wrote that down.

'What are your thoughts on the Before?' asked DeBoys.

'Point of explanation,' said Scrawdyke. 'DeBoys means...'

'I know what he means,' she said, hastily. 'B.D. Before Dracula. I had little experience of it. We didn't know what was coming. It wasn't like decimal coinage. We weren't told the thing would happen, given a date to expect it by and charts in the papers to learn so you're ready for it. When I was a girl, when I was *warm*, we'd barely heard of vampires. They weren't even worth not believing in. Angels or ghosts or the soul or a truly good man... we talked often about whether those existed. My father wrote *A Counterblast to Agnosticism*. He was one Protestant who took the "protest" part seriously. He had decided opinions on *Irish* beliefs. At a meeting of the Home Rule League, he told Parnell that Ireland would never be a nation until we stopped wittering on about the wee folk. He had no patience with the Celtic folklore with which some Nationalists dressed up the Cause. Before the Dracula Declaration, vampires seemed like fairies. Children's stories. The scholars who credited them, Calmet or Hesselius or Abronsius, were marginal crackpots. One thing which happened A.D. was a revival of all manner of nonsensical beliefs on the principle of "if there are vampires, then why could there not be..." boggarts or gorgons or the Easter

Rabbit or two-headed llamas? That took a while to die out. There are modern equivalents of such foolishness, like flying saucers or the vanishing police box.'

If more people knew about the Mother of Tears, the epidemic of credulousness might take fire again. That was the least of the reasons why Kate hadn't written about the creature who secretly ruled Rome.

Scrawdyke tried to put up his hand, but several of the others stopped him.

'So you admit you can't understand what it was like for Caleb B.D.?'

DeBoys used Croft's Christian name. The name he had *taken*. Why Caleb? Was the former Charles Croydon sticking with his initials? Vampires often did that, so their names matched the initials on their luggage. Or else they went in for anagrams like 'Carmilla' or 'Alucard'. Croft might be working his way through Bible names. Caleb of the Tribe of Judah was one of the spies Moses sent into Canaan, who came back and said the land could be taken.

'Oh, I can *understand*,' she said. 'I can understand what it was like – what it *is* like – for a lot of people in a lot of situations. It's called empathy. A trait not often associated with vampires and virtually absent in elders...'

DeBoys grinned.

'...but it has its uses.'

'There were glories in the old days,' said DeBoys. 'When there was more of a nightly challenge... when we – vampires – weren't so *common*...'

The Black Monks would defend their Black Abbot, of course.

'I didn't expect to hear that at a university. Aren't children today into throwing off the dead weight of history? It's the time of the season, the age of Aquarius, the Now Generation, the Happening Thing. Aren't you *with-it*?'

'Mr DeBoys follows his own course,' said Croft. With pride, or resignation, or... something else?

'And we follow it with him,' said Withnail, smirking to show he saw the joke in that. 'Black Monks all, and hellfire to quaff...'

All the students snapped their fingers. A private joke. A pre-arranged response to a trigger phrase.

Scrawdyke snapped so hard he broke bones. He winced, gripping the finger while it healed.

Eastman, a hold-out against the joke, scowled. Kate decided she liked him.

Croft allowed himself an indulgent smile. She'd forgotten how disgusting that was.

'What are the Black Monks?' she asked.

DeBoys' fangs glinted. 'We are vampires among vampires,' he said.

10

Outside, the seminar done, it was still annoyingly light. These long summer evenings were a bore.

Kate didn't know if she'd learned anything.

The Black Monks were a scary concept – the disciples of Caleb Croft, yearning for the good old days of unfettered slaughter and *hellfire to quaff* (snap!) – but mostly ridiculous individuals. Weary Withnail or Apologetic Armstrong couldn't get it together to hurt anyone, though she supposed they might hold the others' coats in any group atrocity. Moïse King would swallow any evil impulse and redirect it into a sonnet sequence. Anna Conda and Full-Bosomed Fran were just passing through. Neither were so into the Black Monk scene they wore the habit, though they cared enough not to clash. James Eastman was not of this party – to squelch a pang of embarrassing desire, she decided she fancied the brooding biker *much* more than DeBoys.

Which left Evil Eric, Carnal Keith and Scruffy Scrawdyke on her active suspects list. DeBoys was the obvious Top Cat in this alley ('He's the boss, he's the pip, he's the championship… he's the most tip-top…') while Keith was a fashion-plate sensualist with brawlers' knuckles. Point of information: Scrawdyke was a vicious misogynist. He'd glared at her throughout the seminar, waves of loathing spilling over onto Anna and Fran. When Croft dismissed the group, Scrawdyke wheedled, trying to get Anna to lend him notes on a lecture he'd missed. A painful performance. When generally powerless people thought they could hurt someone without consequence, they were terrifying. Still, he'd have to stir from his coffin and show some initiative to hurt anyone.

The open, mostly concrete space between the college and the river was busy. More Rag Week shenanigans. Mummified medical students trailing bandages were chased around yellowing grass and by Groucho-loping whitecoats with big butterfly nets. 'They're Coming to Take Me Away, Ha-Haaa!' roared from speakers. The routine – and the song – ended and hats were passed for small change. A white-faced mime shook a shako at her. She got rid of some threepenny bits from her purse. What charity were they supporting?

Sat around a fountain was the negative image of the student gang she'd run into earlier: six or seven vampires, mostly not dressed in black, and one warm girl in a grey shroud. Croft wasn't the only lecturer with a seminar group in the School of Vampirism – this must be another clique. Now the lunatics' act was over, a vampire boy in a kaftan, eyes bright with recent feeding, took up an acoustic guitar. Fingers strumming faster than humanly possible, he combined Robert Johnson's 'Cross Road Blues' with Tony Hatch's 'Theme From *Crossroads*' in one too-clever-by-half racket.

The scarf knotted around Laura Bellows' leg could lead to any vampire at St Bartolph's. Student or faculty. Or the murderer might want to direct attention here, away from themselves. Clive Landseer or Syrie Van Epp or Sebastian Newcastle or U.N. Owen-Vampire?

'Kate,' barked someone.

She scanned the area. First, she clocked her bodyguard. Nezumi, her mousy neighbour, must have been marking her since she left the Club. Dressed in claret blazer, skirt and straw boater, she solemnly joined a warm schoolgirls' skipping game. She was, as might be expected, expert. Though they lived in the same building, Kate hadn't talked much with the young-old Japanese girl. Thanks to an insufficiently soundproofed ceiling, she knew Nezumi was a devoted listener to *Junior Choice* on Saturday mornings. She often played children's or novelty singles on her Dansette. 'Nellie the Elephant', 'I Am a Bat and I Live in a Hat', the Goons' 'Ying-Tong Song'. As a Lovely, she was presumably lethal. To match her uniform, she carried a battered, bandaged hockey stick – a formidable weapon in a street-fight. However, it was hard to see Nezumi as a samurai sex kitten when she looked thirteen and sang along in a thick accent to 'A Mouse Lived in a Windmill in Old Amsterdam'.

Nezumi hadn't called out to her, though.

Sergeant Griffin sat alone on a bench, pretending to read the *Mirror* (ENOCH SAYS 'NO MORE VIPERS'). Every student who passed grunted or snorted like a pig, so being in plainclothes – if an electric blue suit and crimson shirt could be counted as plain – wasn't working. He might as well wear a tit-helmet with a blue lamp on top. A wag in a *Magic Roundabout* t-shirt set fire to an enormous roll-up and exhaled a marijuana cloud. Griffin told the kid to push off and take a dip in the Thames.

Kate had no choice but to go over and sit next to the vampire copper.

'It takes all of ten minutes to read the *Mirror*,' he said. 'Including the flippin' horoscopes and Andy Capp. I've been here an hour... it's been a pain.'

'You should have brought a book. I always have one on the go.'

She was in the middle of J.P. Donleavy's *Meet My Maker the Mad Molecule*.

'I'm stuck on the first chapter of *Valley of the Dolls* and don't want to carry the thing around in public.'

A warm student kindly put a hand-drawn 'BEWARE OF THE PIG' sign on the bench next to Griffin. The policeman flicked out fangs. The student flashed the peace sign and scarpered.

'Is Bellaver calling me off? Did Landseer confess?'

'Far from it. Bastard's got an alibi. Edward Langdon, MP, no less. While the girls were being drained and dumped, the Honourable Member was getting sucked off by our Clivey. After arm-twisting, Langdon gave up a statement. Checks out, too. Wouldn't you know it, Langdon is on the Manfred

Commission. At least he can't be prejudiced...'

'Don't you believe it, Sergeant. Some of the loudest Enochites cover love-bites with make-up. You know the type. Spend the week screaming we should be impaled and burned and buried at the crossroads in graves sprinkled with salt and sown with garlic, then crawl round the viper bars on Saturday night begging for a little nip. Remember that shrink in the 1950s who said he could "cure" vampirism? Dr Holstrom. Held the Hyde Park rallies which kicked off the Blood Riots. He turned out to be one of Lis Bathory's cast-offs. He turned. After all the trouble, I doubt he's been embraced by "the community".'

Griffin folded his paper and chucked it in a bin. He threw the funny sign after it.

'If you're hoping for a culprit here, I can't give you one,' she said. 'Every vampire I've seen today looks guilty. Including you.'

'I have an alibi too. I was on duty Saturday night. Until the call came in, it was a boring shift. We played Monopoly in the B Division squad-room in Holborn. Bellaver cheats. Keeps a "Get Out of Jail Free" card up his sleeve. What about you?'

'If either of my neighbours were home, they'd have heard typing from my flat. One thousand words for *Woman* on bright red or royal blue Bri-Nylon long-johns for the younger – or younger-seeming – girl.'

She didn't mention that she could produce a neighbour with a loud whistle. The Diogenes Club liked to keep some separation from the authorities – the *other* authorities.

'Thin. You could have a fascinated minion hitting random keys for hours while you were off haunting the night in search of your prey.'

'If I had a fascinated minion, all sorts of things would be much, much easier. Still, if I'd drained two girls an hour or so before I saw you in Maryon Park, I'd have been practically purple.'

Two tall warm girls in mini dresses walked by. Griffin's eyes nearly popped. They sat on the lawn, arranging their legs into lotus positions. The dope-smoker offered his huge reefer and they took substantial hits. Grass did nothing for Kate but give her a headache. The drug revolution turned up all sorts of hallucinogens and narcotics which didn't work on vampires, and one or two which did. Griffin ogled the pretty girls. They were swan-necked as well as long-legged.

'Volunteer for this?'

'The Super sent me with a heads-up for you. B Division will be all over this patch tomorrow. Those flower children had better not be passing around that Camberwell Carrot. The Drug Squad has invited itself into the investigation. Sergeant Pilcher is itching for an excuse to get his size-elevens up the fundaments of the chemical hippies of this parish...'

'Is this one of those pacify-the-papers shows? To prove you're doing *something*?'

'Ah-hah, we'd like you in the press to think so... because you'd still have to pat us on the back. But there are wheels within wheels. There's a real reason...'

'Are you going to make me try to *fascinate* you into coughing it up?'

Griffin enjoyed playing I've Got A Secret, but let it go. 'The autopsies, love. *Trés* interesting. They called in Hardy...'

The pathologist Dr John Hardy worked with the Home Office on high-profile cases. He ruled Stephen Ward's death a suicide and Joe Orton's a murder.

'...and he found something which would have been easy to miss. When the blood's gone, it's difficult to test for, say, alcohol...'

'But the blood's never *all* gone, is it? Even in white-lips cases.'

'No, there's always something. The brain, they say, is a retentive sponge. All those little capillaries. If you suck them dry, would you pick up the dying thoughts of your victim, do you suppose?'

Kate looked at Griffin. He can't have been a vampire more than a year.

'Try not to use emotive terms like "victim",' she said. 'Irks the Enochites.'

Griffin shrugged and carried on. 'Hardy found enough blood in the cerebella to test. Both girls were high when they popped off... tripping on quality BOP, manufactured close to the source. Which would mean in that building over there. The one with the mural which looks like the Dulux dog spewed up fifteen shades of non-gloss on the wall.'

'The dead girls were on Bowles-Ottery Pellets?'

'Handfuls. Not that it should make a difference. One'll do the trick. Serious bopheads drip liquid Bowles-Ottery onto a sugar-cube. You could have it in your breakfast cuppa and take a trip to work. Semolina Pilchard gave a speech about ways and means of turning on. He's like your secret vampire lovers. Rabbits on and on about filthy drugs. The thought of duffing up a long-haired pop singer and copping a stash gives him a week-long stiffy. He times his raids when the dim herberts are with groupies so he can get an eyeful.'

Sergeant Pilcher collected famous hippie scalps. He'd busted Mick Jagger, John Lennon and Jerry Cornelius, and had American singer Lionel St Dubois turned back at Heathrow. A policeman with a press agent, Pilcher sailed close to the wind in staging his headline-grabbers. In court, Horace Rumpole, Cornelius's brief, proved Crown Exhibits A through C were herbal cough medicines. Pilcher knew a lot about drugs but couldn't spot the good ones. He should have led with Exhibit D: Chew-Z cut with vraxoin, bug powder and dreamshit. So dangerous a cocktail Jerry didn't nerve up enough to drop it until the seven-day party thrown in Derry & Tom's Roof Garden to celebrate his acquittal. He was still in a happy coma and seemed to have changed colour.

'I assume everyone at Syrie Van Epp's bash was on something?' she said.

'Uh-huh, and we can guess how the BOP got from here to there. With one of your Prof's pals.'

'He's not *my* Prof.'

'Bellaver's not happy.'

'Front page news?'

Griffin shrugged. 'He doesn't like the way everything in this case leads to St Bartolph's.'

'He's right. It's too neat and tidy. Little arrow-signs. Pointing here. Makes you think we should be looking somewhere else.'

The sun was down now. Blessed shade.

Griffin took a small pack out of his pocket. 'Opal Fruit?'

'Ta,' she said. 'Lime, please.'

'Connoisseur, eh?'

He shucked sweets from the tube like bullets from an automatic, till he found a lime. He took a strawberry one.

They sucked and chewed. Her taste buds still worked. She got no thrill from cocaine, opium or vintage champagne (yes, she had tried), but Opal Fruits – 'Fresh with the tang of citrus! Four refreshing fruit flavours!' – made her mouth water. And saliva brought out her fangs.

'At least these never let you down,' said Griffin, looking at the individually wrapped sweets in his hand. 'Not like…'

'Drugs?'

'Blood.'

Kate knew how Griffin felt. She'd got past the disappointment a long time ago. None of Croft's Black Monks had shown the signs, and most must have turned about when Griffin did.

'Know why I became a vampire, Kate?'

She didn't.

'Donna…'

'WPC Rogers?'

She had known they were going out but keeping it quiet.

'Know why *she* turned? B Division. As a viper, she was a cert for promotion… Otherwise, she'd stay a glorified traffic warden. Warm WPOs have a hard time in the Met. Best she could hope for is Vice Squad. Dressing like a tart and entrapping kerb-crawlers. But in B Division… well, there are opportunities for advancement. So, she was all fired-up for the turn. Good Old Cheery Old Jolly Old Julian went for it too…'

Kate hadn't known Griffin's first name.

'No one told us about vampire couples. It's not in that little leaflet you get at the doctor's.'

Kate understood. Turning quickened every sense, but realigned them too. No more booze or sunny days on the beach… but Opal Fruits triggered your pleasure centres.

'Some stay together,' Kate said, well aware she'd never stayed with another vampire for more than a few weeks. 'Some marry.'

'And become those two-in-one monsters. Mind-melded forever. Can't tell where one leaves off and the other begins.'

'Isn't that love?'

'Maybe, but it's terrifying. Most of the ones you're talking about are elders, right? They got together when there weren't so many vampires walking about.'

Croft had been married, Kate remembered. Lady Croydon was burned at the stake in Massachusetts in the eighteenth century. Perhaps that explained him – he was only half a person. Not that it was any excuse.

'If one partner's strong in the head, the other dwindles,' said Griffin. 'I've read about Dracula's "wives"...'

The ghost of Lucy Westenra walked over the grave Kate wasn't resting in.

'I doubt WPC Rogers is a psychic quagmire like Dracula.'

'It's not that, though. It's the bedroom, isn't it? You can do all the things you did before and they're... well, nice. Strawberry Opal Fruit nice. But it's not blood. And for blood, you have to find... other people.'

Kate understood. Frank Harris, the vampire who turned her, lost interest the moment she ceased to be biteable and became a rival. She had sought him out in the first place because he could give her an experience but wouldn't fill in her dance card. She'd – scandalously – slept with him, becoming 'a woman who did'. It seemed a waste not to. She knew turning vampire would enrage her father so much he wouldn't trouble to be bothered about additional harlotry.

'When we were warm, we'd lie there... afterwards. Smoking, dozing, sticky. Together. Now, after we have it off, I know what Donna's feeling because I feel it too. Red thirst, screaming in the brain. I want to get out of bed, get away on my own, and find someone to...'

She held his hand.

'I know. It's part of turning. I've been a vampire for eighty years. Sometimes I don't know why I did it. Except I'm still alive and I get to see how the story turned out...'

'What story?'

'All of them. Do you want me to talk with Donna?'

A new vocation – Agony Auntie. Katie Reed's Advice to the Lovelorn. Many of the men in her life would laugh at that.

'Too late for that, love,' he said, letting her hand go. 'We're on different courses, now. We're not the same kind of viper.'

Few vampires used that word. Griffin retained the prejudices of his former life. Scratch him and he probably agreed with Enoch Powell. He hadn't yet accepted that he was one of the monsters.

'You're a catch, Julian,' she said, trying to mean it.

He was a new-born, not one she responded to. It wasn't a matter of fancying or not fancying him. She had extra senses. This was like glancing at a field of horses and knowing the winners from the also-rans before the race. She didn't see the spark, the hint of sharp ivory in a smile, in Sergeant Griffin. In DeBoys and Eastman and even Donna Rogers, she did – they would be *great* vampires. Griffin was fated to be Good Old Cheery Old Jolly Old Julian. Just like she was always going to be Carrot-Top Katie, Four-Eyes Reed, the Freckled Freak. Not that she wanted to be great, just *good*.

There was a commotion on campus.

'Talk about careless driving,' said Griffin.

A blue-and-white Volkswagen van swerved off the approach road to the car park. It ploughed across the lawn, making ruts. Students scattered out of its way. The dope-smokers were befuddled by the sudden excitement. One of the girls was together enough to shift her friends. Their blanket was ground under the wheels of the juggernaut. The VW's unusually bright headlights hurt her eyes. Heraeus metal-halide incandescents. Sun-lamps, developed in Germany for military use. Extra beams were mounted on the roofrack.

Kate was fully alert.

Griffin stood. His fangs were sharp and his eyes reflected red.

'Oi, you,' he shouted, hand up to shield his face from the dazzle.

The van wrenched to a halt. Its side-doors opened. Several men jumped out. They wore white boiler-suits with crusader crosses on their fronts – vertical bar from crotch to neck, horizontal from armpit to armpit – and heavy Doc Martens, plus cheap plastic masks of *Beano* and *Dandy* characters. Dennis the Menace, Plug from the Bash Street Kids, Desperate Dan, Biffo the Bear, Korky the Cat. Students laughed but this wasn't another Rag Week stunt.

Plug and Korky had crossbows, Biffo a blowtorch. Dennis and Dan touched rag-wrapped sticks to the flame, and they caught. The firebrands advanced across the lawn, waving flames at any creatures of the night.

One of the vampire kids – the lad with the guitar – got in the way, and his kaftan was set on fire. He screeched and rolled on the grass, extinguishing the flames. The comic characters stepped over him. Korky stuck the boot in, landing a vicious kick to the kid's ribs. His Docs had metal toe-caps. Steel or silver.

Kate had her claws and teeth out.

'Knock it off, you lot,' said Griffin, producing his warrant card. 'Police officer.'

Plug raised his crossbow and fired.

The bolt pierced Griffin's eye, its silvered tip punching out the back of his head.

The policeman dropped his ID and buckled at the knees.

Kate caught Griffin and tried to let him down gently. His good eye stared, angrily. Blood gouted from his wound. His whole body spasmed. She didn't know what to do. How to start to help. His mouth opened and closed. Word-chains leaked out.

Most of the students legged it.

Kate saw Nezumi running towards her, hockey stick raised, boater blown off. Plug fitted another quarrel, turned and fired. Nezumi leaned out of the way of the dart but didn't break step.

Biffo made 'quick quick' hand-gestures.

Dennis and Korky grabbed Kate and dragged her towards the van. She lost hold of Griffin, who was left behind on the grass. She twisted and got an elbow in her face. Her glasses flew off in pieces. A gloved hand closed over her mouth. She tried to bite, but shock flew through her fangs. Silver plates under canvas. The Bash Street Gang had come prepared for vampires.

Fire was held close to her and she went slack. Biffo nodded approval. He was in charge.

She was nearly in the back of the van.

Griffin wasn't moving. Plug put a bovver boot on the policeman's chest and pulled out his bolt. Silver tips were costly. Dan stuck his firebrand against Griffin's side. That polyester suit caught light, sheathing Griffin in flame. He didn't writhe or screech.

Sergeant Griffin was truly dead.

She couldn't let herself be taken into the van.

Nezumi charged through, bringing her hockey stick down against Plug's knee. Biffo dropped his blowtorch and took a revolver out of his hip pocket. Could the Japanese vampire dodge bullets?

Kate grabbed Dennis's wrist, where the skin was bare, and extruded her nails into his meat. He let go of her mouth and she scratched, hoping for an artery.

Nezumi stood, demurely. Biffo aimed his pistol at her.

Dennis got his arm free of Kate's claws. He dropped his flaming torch and pulled a lathe-sharpened length of wood from his tool-belt. She bobbed and ducked like a boxer, shifting her torso so a heart-stab wouldn't be easy. Especially through the eyeholes of a plastic mask. Dennis ripped off his face – she didn't recognise him, but he had the close-cropped haircut she associated with Enoch's nastier followers – and concentrated on her. Blood flowed freely over his gauntlet. She felt inconvenient red thirst.

Korky, Dan and Plug joined Dennis. They made a ring around her. Dan jabbed with his torch. Korky and the limping Plug held crossbow bolts like stakes. She wheeled about, hissing. She resented being reduced to this defensive cartoon. She saw in a bloody blur.

They were herding her towards the van.

Then, Dan's torch was ripped from his grip and tossed away. It arced high over the lawn like a distress flare. Dan's mask came off, disclosing a plump, bland, scared white face. An instant later, his face came off. Wild eyes stared out of a red ruin.

Black shapes mixed in with the comic characters, moving swiftly, tearing and biting and breaking. Plug screamed when his bolt was taken from him and stuck into his back before he could see what had attacked. Korky's arms kinked the wrong way and he was dragged yards away from the light. Dennis, undeterred, knocked Kate down and got his knee on her stomach. She crossed wrists over her heart as he raised his stake high. For a moment, she saw clearly – the clean wooden point. This would kill her.

And she'd never know how this story turned out.

Then Dennis was wrenched upwards and off her. She heard the squelch of the stake ramming into something with bones and flesh.

Dennis was struggling with a Black Monk.

It was Eric DeBoys, grinning though he had a stake stuck in his shoulder. He took Dennis – a much bigger man – by the throat and lifted him off the ground. His thumb-barb dug into Dennis's neck, rooting for the pulse, nail edging near the purple worm of the jugular vein.

All vampires knew their human anatomy.

Dennis spat at DeBoys and tried to call him a viper. DeBoys dropped him and he clutched at his own throat, stanching the seepage. DeBoys licked his thumb like a cake-spoon.

The other Black Monks, cowls up, stood over the fallen thugs. Biffo lowered his gun in surrender. Nezumi darted back into shadow, leaving credit to the student vampires. Eastman found the dope-smokers' blanket and used it to put out the fire that had sprung up around Griffin.

Dan touched his wet face in horror and screamed. Anna Franklyn slipped close – green scales on her forehead, forked tongue darting across her lips – and sank needle-fangs into his neck. Her venom paralysed his vocal cords and shocked him into immobility. He might even live. From now on, he'd have more use for a mask.

Four of the Bash Street Gang were down. Only Biffo stood. Now the ring was closing around him.

'Let's have a sight of you, Mr Bear,' said DeBoys, removing the mask.

Biffo was a thin-faced, bright-eyed, middle-aged man. His thin lips twitched over nicotine-discoloured teeth. His thin hair stuck up in odd directions. He looked utterly mad.

'I'm not afraid of you,' he lied.

Kate recognised Lorrimer Van Helsing.

11

The Bash Street Gang called itself the Circle of Light. Lorrimer Van Helsing's Knights Templar were Joseph Hawkins, Adam Cochran, Reginald Bird and Peter Craven. The names meant nothing to her. Most were known to the police, with violent previous. It wouldn't surprise her if this shoddy little lot ended up famous. Martyrs to their cause.

They all went back to Shooter's Hill in black mariahs.

The press had been told to wait for an official statement, but weren't having any of it. The crowd of reporters outside the police station was agitated. Long after the warm pubs had shut, they gave off a beery, inky funk. Kate tried to shrink and hide among big policemen. Surely, the Fourth Estate would be more interested in who'd been arrested than which journo was getting privileged access. Fullalove of the *Gazette*, a Fleet Street veteran, recognised her and called out, 'What's the story, Katie?'

She pretended not to hear him.

'Come on,' he insisted. 'You've the ears of a bat. Cough up.'

'I'm a witness, Jamie,' she said, making a hands tied gesture.

'Witness to what?' asked Stenning of the *Express*.

She was hassled by hacks she owed drinks, favours and money to and hacks who owed drinks, favours and money to her and hacks she wouldn't trade drinks, favours and money with if the earth caught fire. They tried to invoke a solidarity none of them would have felt with an exclusive at stake.

'Enough of that,' said Bellaver. He pulled her away from the wolfpack and escorted her up the stairs into the nick. 'Do I have to lock you up too?'

She assured him she wouldn't talk. He let her go. The nick was crowded. Anger in the air.

Bellaver was sick to his stomach and his men were on the dangerous side of irritable. Even placid George Dixon flashed fangs at the holding cells, while Regan and Herrick showed wolf faces and growled through peepholes at the Bash Street Gang. If the Circle of Light had thought vampires were out to get them before, they should be happy now.

Bellaver gave a 'hands off' speech to his men and summarily told WPC Rogers to end her shift. With one of the Squad on the way to the morgue, he knew there was a risk of unfortunate accidents. The Super wasn't like DCI Charlie Barlow, whose New Town Task Force was famous for never bringing a felon to arraignment without something broken. On Bellaver's watch, suspects in custody did not 'fall down stairs'. Persons helping the police with their enquiries were not to fetch up drained dry and packed under a cell-bed.

Donna Rogers was partially out of uniform, herringbone civilian coat and chiffon headscarf over blue serge skirt and white blouse. She arranged with the night desk sergeant – not the odious Choley, but a trustworthy Northern Irishman named Lynch – for her duties to be covered. She dealt with the practicalities as if she were off home to cope with a burst pipe rather than a dead boyfriend.

Kate couldn't read Rogers. Was the vampire woman so far gone she didn't feel anything? Some new-borns got hard fast. Griffin had said they were cooling. Leaving the WPC in the wind right now was a bad idea – though her Super, and everyone else, had so much to deal with it was unlikely she'd get special treatment.

It wasn't as if there was any big mystery. B Division already knew what the attack on campus was about.

The Circle of Light had set out to even the score for Carol and Laura. Two vampires for two warm girls. They hadn't reckoned on their first viper kill being a police officer. Van

Helsing, at least, must realise how big a mistake that was. His merry band of thugs were too stupid or sullen to see it. Yet.

Dr Hardy wouldn't be required to suss cause of death. The hole in Griffin's head, made by wood and silver, would have killed anyone. Due to the pioneering efforts of Jack the Ripper, the world knew a stake or silver through any major organ – not just the heart – brought true death to a vampire.

Kate could imagine what the Bash Street Gang would have done to her in the back of Van Helsing's VW.

Tom Lynn, the boy in the kaftan, was in hospital, healing rapidly. He wouldn't be showing off his guitar skills for a while, since his hands were burned into claws. From experience, Kate knew that being able to grow back skin and sinew was all well and good but it still hurt like a bastard. For months. After eighty years, there were no analgesics which worked on vampires. Heightened senses meant heightened pain receptors. Part of the deal. Oh, you didn't look at the small print when you turned? Tough luck, chum.

Finding time to take pity on her, Dixon brought a cardboard box from Lost Property and told her to take her pick from a selection of specs. She tried random pairs until she found something close to her prescription. Red horn-rims with flamingo-wings. They could have belonged to Danny LaRue.

She could see again.

Detective Superintendent Bellaver was fending off phone calls from interested parties. He would not be pressured into making statements until he had to. While he had the Circle of Light in custody, they'd get the proper grilling.

None of the Bash Street Gang were masterminds. Even Lorrimer Van Helsing, a Professor of Anthropology, was pretty much an imbecile. He'd been kicked off the faculty of St Bartolph's after his one-man sit-in failed to disrupt Mrs Brabazon's office routine in the School of Vampirism for even a morning. Croft had been away at a conference that day, or he'd have taken the would-be vampire hunter's head. Vice-Principal Goodrich had no alternative but to sack Van Helsing. An anti-discrimination complaint was working its way through the system. Leading a guerrilla raid on campus would presumably shift those forms to the bottom of the pile.

This personal history explained why Van Helsing chose to target the college in his 'retributative strike'. Bellaver suspected the Circle had a source on the force, and had followed B Division's lead back to St Bartolph's. After a lightning moment of deduction, Kate suggested the Super give Sergeant Choley his turn under the interrogation room lamps for further information.

The sorry crew were booked, had their dabs taken and posed for pictures. Adam Cochran, aka Desperate Dan, didn't resemble his previous mug shots. They could do wonders with plastic surgery, nowadays. Sir John Rowan could transplant Cochran's bum skin to his face, if he could be bothered.

A reporter had telephoned Enoch Powell, waking him in the small hours. The MP told the papers he didn't endorse Van Helsing's circumvention of the law and recited a paragraph which explained this was exactly the sort of violence that would become commonplace if the vampire population were allowed to grow unchecked. That was like saying it wouldn't rain so much in England if they had fewer church fêtes.

After she'd given her statement to a sour-faced Jack Regan, Kate was allowed to look through a two-way mirror at Joe Hawkins aka Dennis the Menace. He had a thick pad of bandages stuck to his neck. She identified the bovver boy as her assailant. Hawkins was comfortable in custody. It was what he expected. Wanted, even. This proved he was right to hate and fear and strike first. Against procedure, Regan showed her Hawkins's form. He was a passionate Drakky Basher, usually as part of a gang.

If Eric DeBoys, who was giving his statement elsewhere, had killed Hawkins, Kate wouldn't have cared. Even if it weren't a fair fight. If Hawkins were waylaid by an entire order of Black Monks and chewed to bits, it'd be no more than he deserved. She hated Hawkins all the more for making her think like that, think like *him*.

Hawkins scratched at his wound. Even through glass, Kate smelled blood. Her thirst quickened. She sucked air over her teeth. He looked at her as if she were in the room.

He blew a kiss and smiled. His shorn head made him seem like a big baby.

'If it wasn't vipers, it'd be something else,' said Jack Regan. 'Joey hates students and hippies and blacks and coppers as much. Going to love doing bird, he is. Toads like him thrive in prison. Should hang the lot of 'em.'

She reminded herself she didn't believe in that.

Peter Craven – Plug, Griffin's murderer – would not go to the gallows. He was sixteen, still in school. He'd have to wait two years and murder someone else if he wanted to hang.

Kate and Regan walked along the dimly lit corridor adjoining the interrogation rooms. One-way windows made each room like an aquarium tank.

Craven shifted, handcuffed to the table, trying to strike up a conversation with the mirror. He had shoulder-length hair and smiled too easily, but his eyes were already like Hawkins's. Nailheads in a board. He whined about his knee, which had taken a bash – Nezumi's handiwork. He seemed relieved it was all over. He thought he'd just get to finish his schooling in Borstal. She wondered if he even knew he'd killed a copper. At the least, Craven would be detained at Her Majesty's Pleasure. For a long time.

She tried to see the boy as a victim, cajoled and manipulated, threatened and lied to. His monstrousness had been fanned. She turned vampire overnight. It had taken years to turn Peter Craven into what he was.

His mum was outside, talking to the reporters. She'd already started asking how much her story would go for on the open market.

'Why is he so chirpy?' she asked Regan. 'He's dead to rights.'

'He's got in with his mates. It's why he was so eager to fire the first bolt. The others have crosses tattooed on their sides. Hawkins has three. Craven can get his, now. He's done one of us. A step up from Drakky Bashing. He's FVK now. A Fearless Vampire Killer.'

'So they've done this before?'

'Or say they have. Two of 'em are full of shit. Probably turned up with a coal scuttle full of ash and bone and said they'd topped a Carpathian. No doubt about Hawkins. Nasty piece of work. Herrick's digging up what we can get to stick on him. Put names on the crosses.'

'What's the answer?' she asked. 'Education?'

'I'd educate 'em all right,' said Regan. 'All the way up to an exam they wouldn't pass.'

For the next few hours, Kate looked through interview room window-mirrors as if flicking between TV channels. Bellaver took Van Helsing, who had dragged in his brief, Jasper Lakin. The lawyer's argument was to claim that the attack was only supposed to be an act of guerrilla theatre to draw attention to the vampire problem at St Bartolph's, but Van Helsing's lads got out of hand. Van Helsing said as little as possible and let Lakin do the talking for him.

Regan was given a free run at Craven, who mainly wanted his viper-killing quarrel back so he could get it framed. He freely admitted his part in the raid and was proud to be the only one to stake a vampire last night.

Bird was given to a couple of B Division newcomers, Perryman and North, who went round the houses with him and couldn't get him to remember his own name, occupation or place of residence.

Cochran was in hospital, under guard, having his face seen to. His interrogation would have to wait.

Hawkins, the most interesting face, would have been Griffin's. He'd had a knack of getting through to the harder nuts. Bellaver had to trust Pickering, a little, whiny, bald, fanged fanatic, to take a run at the unresponsive skinhead. Hawkins, bored, said nothing but kept staring at the mirror.

According to Dixon, DeBoys and the other Black Monks were helpful. They gave articulate, concise statements which agreed with each other. They'd make impressive witnesses in court, earning them gold stars in any copper's book. Observing a commotion, they'd taken steps to cool the situation until the police could respond. Kate wondered how cool Cochran was just now: he was only alive because Anna's venom had anaesthetic/narcotic properties (which she hoped someone was analysing).

The students were polite. Dixon made sure they stayed out of the incident room which was papered with pictures of Carol and Laura, alive and dead. DeBoys politely asked if they could leave before dawn. Bellaver had no reason to keep them around. The Super disapproved of the general public taking action in such cases but had to thank them for thinking fast. Kate knew they'd saved her life. Nezumi had slipped away and no one mentioned her; not even Craven of the shattered knee, who didn't want to admit he'd been nobbled by a schoolgirl.

'Besides poor Julian, the worst thing about this is the distraction,' said Dixon. 'An open and shut case which is going to get a lot of ink. The papers will be all over it. By tomorrow, the public will be against us and for them. In the meantime, whoever killed those girls is free and liable to do it again. We have to waste time on these monkeys. They're stopping us catching the vampire murderer.'

'The murderer is their wet dream, though,' she said. 'As long as he's out there, killing innocent warm women, then *all* vampires are monsters, fit only to be staked. He's the best recruiting sergeant the Circle of Light could have.'

Could there be a tie-up between the killer and Van Helsing? Croft and he had been on the same faculty, after all.

All the interrogations ended at five a.m.

Kate glanced along the windows and saw the interviewers standing, gathering their notes, and leaving. Their subjects remained seated. Uniformed constables came into the room to take breakfast orders.

Only in England… commit a murder, and have your pick of tea and jam or marmalade on your toast.

'Hello hello,' said Dixon, 'what's going on here then?'

It took a moment for Kate to register what he'd seen. In Craven's room, a WPC jammed a chair under the door-handle. Donna Rogers. She'd either not gone home when ordered or snuck back when everyone was busy.

Kate had a track-and-zoom moment.

Rogers turned. Craven gave her an insolent smirk. He quite fancied himself with the ladies.

Then he noticed the WPC was a vampire and shut off the come-on.

Donna Rogers' mouth grew to four times its usual size. Lamprey-teeth projected. She drooled bloody spittle. Her eyes were red marbles.

Craven looked to the mirror with the beginnings of panic. He rattled the chain that fixed him to the table. Uncuffed while answering questions, Regan had shackled him after the interview was wound up. Was that procedure? People were going to ask. Rogers tore Craven's chair out from under him. He fell with a bump, chin against table. That drew blood. Rogers wiped a smear off his face and licked it with a long, liver-coloured tongue.

The murderer was crying for his mummy now. So loud Kate thought the woman might hear him from outside the nick.

The door shook. Bellaver's voice sounded through it.

Kate made a fist and smashed the mirror. Blood scent caught in her nostrils.

'Donna, no,' she said.

Rogers, realising she was out of time, picked Craven up and took a bite out of his neck which exposed bone, severed arteries and scraped away meat. She chewed and swallowed and let gore gush into her maw.

Dammit, Kate's fangs sharpened.

The chair under the doorknob dislodged. Bellaver and Regan rushed into the room and restrained Rogers.

Craven fell, dead. Kate saw it as if in slow motion. Gobbets of blood went everywhere. His wrist was still fixed to the table. His head flopped back, loose. His neck was nearly bitten through.

In sudden death, the boy's eyes showed expression – pure terror. Then nothing. Until Rogers bit him, Peter Craven hadn't really bought all the vampire-hating stuff Van Helsing poured into him. He just wanted to be like his mate Hawkins, hard and feared. He wanted to earn his cross and be part of the gang.

Finally, Donna Rogers had put the fear of vampires in him.

'Well done, love,' said Bellaver, sarcastically. 'Know how

difficult it's going to be to clean up this mess?'

Rogers' face was back to its normal configuration, but everything below her eyes was painted with blood.

She spat out meat and gristle.

12

Word got out to the press. Mrs Craven's story was worth more now her precious boy was not just a vampire slayer but a vampire victim. Fullalove had a note smuggled into the station, offering Kate a column in the *Gazette* if she'd write up the killing. If she took him up on it, she'd never get access to B Division again. However, judging from Bellaver's face after a phone call from the Home Secretary, there might not be a B Division after this hash.

The story had changed and not in any useful way.

Vampires were monsters. Julian Griffin's death wouldn't get an inch under the racing results. Donna Rogers and Peter Craven would be on the front page for weeks.

'Bellaver,' Kate called, getting his attention, 'give Craven's mug shot to the papers.'

'Why on Earth should we do that?' he asked.

'The only other photos of him will come from his mum. He'll be in school uniform. He'll be the naughty, cheeky lad who sits at the back of the class. At least the picture you took last night makes him look like a murdering thug.'

'If our press officers thought like you, they'd run the Yard.'

'It'll come,' she said.

The Super took her advice. He also ordered Dixon to find 'couply' snaps of Donna Rogers and Julian Griffin from before they turned to release to the press. Though policy was to discourage relationships between officers serving in the same unit and he wasn't supposed to know they were going out. Things were escalating. Griffin for Laura and Carol. Craven for Griffin.

Someone had to put Rogers under arrest, for form's sake.

During the hub-bub, Sergeant Lynch clocked off and Kate's old playmate Tom Choley showed up bright and early. He couldn't stop smiling as he went through the formalities of booking Rogers. The WPC hadn't wiped her face. She looked like an Apache squaw after scalping the Cavalry troop who massacred her village. Handcuffs hung loose on her thin wrists. Jasper Lakin gave her his card.

Choley had scared up a Shooter's Hill plod to escort Rogers down to the holding cells. Kate caught the ice glint in her eye.

'Unless the bars are silver, you're putting her within reach of the rest of Van Helsing's mob,' she warned Bellaver. 'She'll be out of her cell and in theirs in seconds.'

The Super thumped his forehead.

'Damn, Katie... are you the only one here thinking?'

Bellaver had Dixon take Rogers away from the local woodentops.

'Give her a wash and haul her back to Holborn.'

Dixon fetched a wet towel and dabbed the blood off Rogers' face like a Bank Holiday mum cleaning a mucky lad with the spit-wet corner of a hankie. She didn't resist.

'Neither of you are to talk to the reptiles outside,' said Bellaver. 'Rogers, you are ordered not to say you've been arrested. You're just another plonk, savvy?'

Plonk. Person of limited or no knowledge. Prejudiced male officers called policewomen plonks. She'd never heard Bellaver use the word before.

Rogers nodded. She felt no guilt over murder, but her Super's disapproval stung. Bellaver had hopes for Donna Rogers. *Had* had hopes.

Dixon took out the key to take her cuffs off. She broke them before he could get to the lock and gave him the pieces.

'Enjoying yourself?' Bellaver asked, incensed.

Rogers was sobered. It was all crashing in on the woman now. She hadn't thought past the killing. Which made her just like Peter Craven.

Dixon and Rogers left through the front doors, despite Choley's protests about Rogers being a Shooter's Hill catch not B Division's. With the sun up, Rogers had to roll down her veil.

Kate looked through the open doors as Dixon and Rogers went into the harsh light. The reporters were baying.

On the steps, Rogers' sleeve was tugged by Mrs Craven.

'When can I see my lad, miss?'

Rogers laughed in Mrs Craven's face.

Mrs Craven screamed and tore away the veil. Rogers' red eyes shrank in the dazzle of sunlight and her face steamed. A monster being dragged to the stake.

Cameras went off. Rogers had better pray she didn't show up in photographs. She was not displaying the ideal front page face.

The police station was in chaos. The shift change made things worse. Everyone had heard different versions of the night's events.

Choley was putting in multiple complaints about the vampire invasion. After this shambles, he'd be listened to.

Breach of the peace, grievous bodily harm and accessory to murder charges still had to be laid against Van Helsing's Circle of Light. Now that booking Craven for the murder of a police officer would be problematic, his mates' crimes risked being viewed as high-spirited misdemeanours. As Bellaver said, 'Who *doesn't* want to set fire to a long-haired guitar player?'

Then, Norman Pilcher of the Drug Squad arrived, with his best hippie-kicking size elevens on, fired up to raid St Bartolph's. When told circumstances had intervened and that little adventure would have to be postponed, he was gutted. He threatened to make complaints. Bellaver laughed and told him to queue up behind Sergeant Choley and every other bugger in London.

'You can't let these addicts win,' said Pilcher. 'Or society falls, mark my words. Look at her…'

Pilcher meant Kate. His nostrils twitched, like a bloodhound's.

'This is a police station and she's "on" something. Out with it, "flower-child"? What's your "bag"?'

'Sunshine, man,' she said, flashing the peace sign. 'Sunshine.'

13

Raiding Shooter's Hill Lost Property again, Kate acquired a tatty floral parasol which meant she could go out in the pre-noonday sun.

Her car was parked at St Bartolph's.

She avoided conversation with any of her colleagues in the press and set off on foot.

As was embarrassingly obvious, her *red thirst* was more than rising. She'd seen so much blood – vampire and human – spilled last night that her need was as sharp as her teeth.

In a newsagents, she bought three half-pints in 9d cardboard Tetra-Paks. The shop kept vampire stock in the chill cabinet with the milk and fizzy pop, which meant a frustrating wait for breakfast to warm up enough to be drinkable. Cold blood was like an electric shock to the fangs and gave her brain-freeze. So as not to seem too obsessively bloodthirsty, she also bought an Aztec bar and tinted clip-ons for her foraged glasses.

The papers were out, but she was too depressed to want to read their coverage of the night's grief. As she fondled a Tetra-Pak to warm the contents, she lingered by the rack outside the shop and took in headlines. Early editions led with the policeman killed on campus, implying a student riot. The mid-morning papers came in with the story of Craven and Rogers. A warm teenager killed by a vampire policewoman while in custody.

She bit off the corner of the tetrahedonal carton and sucked.

The newsagent's boy, who was restocking the paper rack, looked alarmed. He also looked *delicious*.

She squeezed the Tetra-Pak and gulped down blood.

It came from cows, but Unigate did something to make it taste human. Cheap stuff had a vaguely sweet aftertaste, from the anticoagulants put in to make it keep. When in funds, she'd sometimes treat herself to Gold Top at ten bob a half-pint. It was milked from human donors ('fresh from the neck').

By the time she was back at St Bartolph's, she'd glutted herself and was almost floating.

A lone policeman, Fred Regent, guarded last night's scorched, bloody battlefield. He had his helmet on but was in shirtsleeves. Some hippy-dippy had braided together a necklace of buttercups and daisies and hung it around his neck.

She told him he could have to wait to be relieved. Bellaver might have forgotten he was stuck here.

'I'm not surprised, Katie,' he said. 'I heard what happened with Donna.'

She gave Fred her Aztec bar out of pity. He told her she had a little smear around her mouth.

She warned him not to accept funny cigarettes and found her Mini in the car park. Students favoured Mini Coopers, Mini Mokes and Mini Vans. Her plain red car stood out amid psychedelic paint jobs, artificial eyelashes for headlamps and made-up vampire coats of arms. A Volkswagen bug covered with staring x-ray eyes had 'the BOPMOBILE' written on its bonnet.

A rack of scooters would make her Hells' Angel ex-boyfriend sneer. Among the Vespas and Lambrettas, like a wolf in the flock, was a motorcycle Frank would grudgingly approve – a chopped Norton Commando, with stars and stripes on the petrol-tank.

An American flag on a British bike?

'Had to leave my Harley in California,' said the owner, stepping out of the shadows under a tree. '*Namaste*, Lady Kate.'

James Eastman. His face and arms were greased against the sun.

'Like to take a ride?'

She smiled but turned him down. She'd had enough wind in her face with Frank. She said it was a cool bike, though.

Eastman took a cigar from his top pocket, punctured the end on a fang, and lit up with a Zippo. He must go through several packets a day to cultivate his throaty growl.

'How you hangin'?' he asked, concerned. 'I heard what went down at pig plaza after we split. Heavy scene.'

'You could say that.'

'When the buzz hit the wires, I thought *you* were the sister who'd iced the FVK. Righteous.'

Kate was slightly shocked anyone would think that.

'I like to think I have more self-control, but your Professor Croft would say I'm delusional.'

'Big Daddy? He's not *my* professor, he's my… hah, nothing.'

Kate's reporter senses prickled. Though he ran with the crowd, Eastman wasn't a proper Black Monk. Was he an exchange student? Had he turned before he got to the UK or been bitten here?

There weren't many American vampires outside isolated townships in New England and ghettos in New Orleans, Las Vegas and San Francisco. Whenever the craze was about to catch fire, some national insanity came along to discourage it – from Prohibition in the 1920s to the Un-Human Activities Commission of the 1950s. Times were a-changing, but Yanks still trained cheerleaders in stake-twirling gymnastics and recited pledges before star-spangled crosses. As a nation, America remained afraid of vampires.

'Why are you *really* here, lady?' asked Eastman. 'It's the murders, isn't it?'

'What murders?'

He wasn't fooled. 'The dead girls. You're here for them, right? The trail leads to St Bartolph's, like drops of blood. I grok you're hanging with the fuzz, but you're no pig. I read up on you. Big Daddy never tells the whole story, but I know all about the Terror. Do you think the vampire killer is on campus? Wild.'

She remembered thinking the clues pointing here were contrived, like a paper chase. Eastman wore a St Bartolph's scarf like a neckerchief, tight about his throat and tucked into his sleeveless denim jacket.

The Black Monks hunted in a pack. Eastman was a solo act. Laura and Carol had been bitten, but only once. Kate could do the sums.

'You take care, Lady Kate,' said the American. 'World needs more suckers like you. And fewer like Big Daddy. Dig?'

'Ah, dug. Thank you, I think.'

Eastman walked away, shoulder muscles bunching and unbunching. She decided she liked being called Lady Kate, but not enough to rule out James Eastman as a suspect.

14

She needed to crash. Besides all the excitement, she'd spent too much time in the sun lately. With a pint and a half in her, she was drowsy. Not in the best shape to drive, though there was no breathalyser for vampires.

She switched on the car radio and caught the BBC news headlines. The well-spoken announcer quoted Bellaver as giving 'no comment' about the death in custody of Peter Craven. Donna Rogers wasn't mentioned, though a woman was said to be 'helping police with their enquiries'. As if to remind her that the rest of the world was a mess too, the other stories were about the incident at My Lai in Vietnam which the US army were not calling a massacre; the arrests of the assassins of Bobby Kennedy and Martin Luther King; and a strike by women workers at the Ford car factory in Dagenham. Kate wished she was covering that. She'd written about the match girls' strike of 1888, and conditions hadn't changed enough since then.

Kate kept the wireless on, to fight off sleep. After the news was a repeat of last night's *The Bowmans*, the long-running serial ('an everyday story of country folk') with the irritating theme music. Since Sister George rose from the grave, and Fenella Fielding took over the role, the show had become more and more focused on its token vampire, though this episode was all about brucellosis at Bowman Farm and the vicar's shoplifting habit. Television soap operas *The Northern Barstows*, *Cowley Mansions* and *Crossroads* all followed *The Bowmans* by bringing in domineering female vampire characters – always played by warm actresses with false fangs.

She got back to Holloway Road and parked her Mini in the hard-fought-for space outside her flat. Collecting a sheaf of post she could afford to ignore until later, she went upstairs and let herself in. Her flat was one large room used as study and crypt, with a small kitchen area marked off by a bar, and a separate bathroom. Many vampires would use the bath as a coffin, but she liked to soak and think sometimes. She kept a sleeping board in the main room, surrounded by book-piles. As soon as she stepped inside, the fuzziness in her head became thicker. She saw grey spots – a sign of impending lassitude. She lowered and locked the blinds, expelling light from the flat. She took off the clothes she'd been wearing too long and put on pyjamas. In the bathroom, she used the loo and cleaned her teeth. A framed Aubrey Beardsley print hung above the sink where the mirror had been.

She lay on her sleeping board. The lights went out.

Technically, vampire lassitude was deep coma, not temporary death.

No dreams, though. Vampires didn't dream. Warm critics who said vampires would never create harped on about that.

Two days later, at nightfall – well past nine o'clock – her eyes opened.

She sat up on her board and found she wasn't alone. Nezumi perched on a bar-stool. An anglepoise light was on and she was reading *Bunty*. Someone lay senseless and face-down on the carpet. A young, warm woman. Shaggy blonde hair and a long white dress. Barefoot and bleeding a little.

'What did I miss?' Kate asked.

Nezumi solemnly folded the corner of a page and shut her comic.

'The flattened filly is Jessica,' Nezumi said. 'I had to slosh her on the noggin. She was carrying this. For you.'

Nezumi picked up a sharpened stick.

Kate was alarmed. She must remember to thank Richard Jeperson for providing a bodyguard.

Refreshed, Kate sprung up. She crouched by Jessica.

'Did you kill her?'

'No. Just packed her off to Bedfordshire for a forty winks.'

Kate stood and went to the bar. A fringed leather shoulder bag she didn't recognise was plumped on the counter, contents removed and arranged neatly.

'Who is she again?' Kate asked.

'Jessica Van Helsing,' said Nezumi, holding up a student union card. 'You met her grandfather last night.'

So, the feud was passed down to another generation.

'This isn't going to end, is it? Did she come to kill me?'

'Not seriously, I suppose. She hummed and hahed and bit her lip like a clot for minutes. And she didn't prepare properly. She forgot to bring a hammer. To be on the safe side, I tapped her on the bean to make sure she couldn't give you a poke with a sharp stick.'

'Thanks.'

'Anything for a chum,' said Nezumi.

Jessica Van Helsing moaned, stirred and tried to push up. Nezumi reached idly for her hockey stick.

'Do you like her hair?' asked Nezumi. 'I mean, not now, with blood in it, but in general… ? I was thinking of going blonde. For a lark.'

Kate pulled on a dressing gown.

'We better take care of the silly goose,' she said.

Kate and Nezumi turned Jessica over. The tang of leaking blood hit both their palates at the same time and their fangs flicked out. They giggled and wrestled the warm girl onto the sleeping board.

Jessica's eyes fluttered open. She saw two vampires looming over her. Her face started to contort.

'Please don't scream, dear,' Kate said. 'Would you like a cup of tea? It'll have to be lemon. I've not got milk in.'

'I'll brew up,' said Nezumi, flitting into the kitchen area. She knew where everything was.

Kate had forgotten the Japanese girl was an elder. She was so *fast*.

Jessica put her hand to her head and said, 'I could murder a cuppa.'

'Be thankful that's the only thing you're murdering, girl,' said Kate, twiddling Jessica's stake. 'What on Earth were you thinking?'

'Sorry. It's Granddad. He's locked up… he left instructions for… well, for reprisals.'

'No offence, but your granddad is a loon.'

'A gibbering loon,' Nezumi elaborated.

Jessica was embarrassed. 'I know, I know… it didn't used to be so bad, but when he lost his job because of vampires, he went potty… and when I started seeing Paul, he went pottier…'

'Paul?'

'Paul Durward. He's a Karnstein, twice removed.'

Jessica's eyes and cheeks shone when she mentioned her beau. Kate knew who Durward was. Blond and too pretty. Knee-britches, tight weskits and ruffle-shirts had come back into fashion and let him enjoy a third or fourth stab at golden youth. He'd signed with Decca and recorded an album of folk-inflected covers ('Season of the Witch', 'House of the Rising Moon', 'Quinn the Eskimo'). He had a three-octave range but little character. Paul Durward was not only a vampire with no reflection; he was a vampire with no echo. He'd been at Syrie Van Epp's party. Kate realised she'd seen Jess in the crowd photographs, too. The blonde with the cleavage.

The girl had new and old love-bites.

Kate dug out a first-aid kit and treated Jess's head-wound. She'd have a lump and an ache but nothing permanent.

'You're not in the Circle of Light?' Kate asked the girl. 'Pledged to destroy all vampires?'

'Far from it. I think vampires are *dreamy*.'

Kate's kettle whistled a shrill comment. Nezumi brought over a stoneware teapot Kate had bought from a craft shop in Somerset and what cups she could find. Kate feared her crockery wouldn't satisfy a Japanese anglophile. Nezumi poured tea into a mug with a Mondrian design, a plastic beaker salvaged from a broken thermos flask and the last surviving china teacup from Kate's mother's Sunday set.

'So what's up with the stake?'

Jessica couldn't say. She was a sheltered twit, but not essentially malign.

'Why's it all so complicated?' Jessica asked, and burst into tears.

Kate hugged the girl, gingerly. Jess presented her neck shyly, which Kate pointedly ignored. What kind of creature did this girl take her for?

So Lorrimer Van Helsing's granddaughter was going out with a viper? He must take ribbing about that in FVK circles, what with his endless speeches about avenging the wrong done to his beheaded ancestor. Vampire haters always went on about monsters 'coming for our women'. If they spent less time fulminating, maybe 'their women' wouldn't be so inclined to seek out a fang on the side. Kate suspected the Circle of Light was at bottom a neurotic response to this affront. The Professor's grudge probably began with minor sleights, like Caleb Croft getting a nicer office and invitations to bunfests with the Vice-Chancellor, then escalated until it seemed vampires were behind all his disappointments.

15

While Kate was dead to the world, a lot happened. None of it good.

Graffiti appeared all over the city. '3-1'. Or, spelling it out, 'Vampires 3, Humans 1'. So far as anyone could gather, unconnected people were responsible… Warm supporters of the Circle of Light, crying vengeance after their failed attempt to equalise… and a certain aggrieved, gloating, nasty-minded species of vampire crowing over a petty lead.

The score wasn't likely to stay level long. Soon, it wouldn't be a football result. It'd be a rugby result. Then, it would be impossible to keep count. Again. With so many long-lived folk walking around, Kate thought they'd have learned something. Evidently not.

Van Helsing's group weren't the only defenders of humanity on the streets. Donna Rogers wasn't the only vampire ready to meet fist with fang.

Enoch Powell was *everywhere*, making speeches and giving interviews. He called for calm in a manner calculated to inflame the extremists he loftily disavowed. Marcus Obadiah, a defrocked priest, said outright what Powell hinted at, declaring Holy War against the unclean monsters who lurked among pure humans and should be exorcised with fire, silver and the stake.

Someone had cheekily vandalised the Sir Francis Varney Memorial in St James' Park, chiselling a hole in the chest of the statue of the former Viceroy of India – a reference to the Second Mutiny, when the unlikeable Varney was strapped over the barrel of a gun and had a cannonball fired through him. Two eccentrics, Seán Manchester and David Farrant, were picked up by the Kingstead Night Watch while trying to break into Lucy Westenra's long-since-vacated family tomb. They claimed they only wanted to make sure the girl remained truly dead. Having fallen out with each other, Manchester and Farrant were conducting an entertaining feud in the letter columns of the local paper. Poor Lucy – if she'd been let lie, the world might be a better place.

A Unigate delivery tanker was hijacked by men in Beatles wigs and Sgt Pepper tunics and five hundred gallons of blood poured into the sewers. That would congeal into a vile lagoon. Old rumours circulated about the things which lived under the city. The blood was said to be the staple diet of the Black Swine of Hampstead, the India-Rubber Men and the Ghost of Guy Fawkes.

Prominent vampires, including Lord Ruthven, Baron Meinster and – would you credit it? – Paul Durward, were called on to condemn Donna Rogers and all weaselled out of saying much. The vampire murderer might be sulking that his quiet killings were driven off the front pages by public bloodletting. In his absence, Rogers became the Bloodthirsty Monster of 1968.

The papers ran photos Bellaver issued of the warm WPC, graduating from Hendon with a smile, but darkened and retouched to make her a cross between Myra Hindley, Cruella de Vil and Graf von Orlok.

Kate had imagined right-wing commentators would be torn between labelling Craven a cop-killing tearaway who deserved what he got and a heroic vampire-slayer saving womankind from monstrous affronts. The fact that Craven's victim was a policeman carrying out his duty to protect the public was so seldom mentioned she suspected newspaper proprietors had issued a dictat that this was to be suppressed. The story was out in distorted forms, skewed for the prejudices of whoever was retelling it.

The Manfred Commission convened early, and was taking

depositions from whoever it could haul in, starting – of course – with Enoch Bloody Powell. The real action would be on the streets rather than in Whitehall committee rooms. *Private Eye* was already running clever-clever jokes about the 'Sangfroid Commission', whose chairman found excuses to hold meetings in Soho basements to examine testimony from exotic dancers. Kate had heard rumours that James Manfred was a private connoisseur of kink.

Jessica's granddad was stuck in jail but protesters were calling for the 'heroes of humanity' to be freed. If the Circle of Light had killed Kate instead of Griffin, they'd be out on bail. Despite the papers, the Metropolitan Police couldn't let people who murdered their officers get away with a rap on the knuckles and a 'don't do it again, son'. Peter Craven, a minor, couldn't be named by the press in connection with the murder he'd committed, but could in connection with his own death – prompting a high degree of squirming circumlocution which served to confuse the man on the Clapham Omnibus. A delegation from the *Socialist Vampire* showed up in Holborn to protest the arrest of Donna Rogers, though it must choke them to take a stand on behalf of a pig lady who was also a *nosferatu* sister. The presence of rival protestors suggested imminent street-fights which would make the Blood Riots look tame.

Jessica Van Helsing, Kate's new best friend, said she'd persuade her Paul to stage a rally for peace between the warm and the undead. She thought he could get John Lennon and John Blaylock to appear and headline a free concert in Hyde Park. Kate had to admit Jess and Paul made a pretty poster couple for human-vampire love, but reckoned peace had already had its chance. Everyone was picking sides for war. Also, she didn't need to hear Blaylock sing 'The Laughing Gnome' ever again.

The worst news was that Bellaver was out. Someone had to take the fall for letting Rogers get at Craven. He was the obvious candidate. Over half his personnel – pretty much the only vampire detectives in the Met – were suspended or reassigned. Norman Pilcher, of all people, was temporarily running B Division. He knew how to make a BOP bust but not how to run a murder investigation, so there was no progress on the Carol Thatcher/Laura Bellows killings. Among the coppers in the frame as replacements for Bellaver were Charlie Barlow of the New Town Task Force and James Anderton of the Cheshire Constabulary, warm men known for sweeping implementation of brutal policies. From now on crimes involving vampires would not be investigated by vampires. It was a short step towards the Met deploying Vampire Slayer units more efficient than a crowd of crossbow-waving yobs in Beano masks.

Assaults by the warm against vampires skyrocketed in the daylight hours and well into the evening. With the Circle of Light busted, a group calling itself The 98.6 – after that song – was active. They were careful about being caught, inducing bouts of amnesia in witnesses which Marcus Monserrat couldn't cure. The Unigate blood tanker stunt was one of theirs. There would be an equal or disproportionate response from the vampire community. New-borns who'd been painted with CND signs and searching for mystic inner peace last month formed little circles around Carpathian Guard left-behinds whose expertise in guerilla resistance was a prized commodity. The Living Dead, the vampire motorcycle gang, patrolled suburban streets, claiming they'd protect any viper hassled by The 98.6. The shady entrepreneur Hogarth – Big Bloodsucker Hog – put extra undead bouncers on his nightclubs. Imposing bodies stood on every corner of the West End Jungle.

According to Nezumi, the Diogenes Club were caught up in high-level politics. Richard Jeperson had to get out of bed, while the Lovelies took to the corridors of power in order to dissuade pin-striped dolts from courses of idiocy. Even their powers of fascination were strained. Doubtless chuckling at his luck, Harold Wilson was presently on holiday in the Scilly Isles, waving his pipe at reporters and posing in a Ganex mac which didn't suit the climate. That put the hardly inspiring Home Secretary Jim Callaghan in the hot seat as acting Head of Government. All police leave was cancelled.

The Home Office ordered teargas and garlic spray in bulk. These preparatory measures were leaked to the press. Lord Ruthven, scenting blood in the water, made noises about a snap election. He came back early from *his* holiday in Scotland to make the Prime Minister look bad.

Carol and Laura were still dead. Whoever was responsible was still at large. As of now, only Kate Reed seemed interested in bringing them to book.

16

'I was surprised when you called,' Kate told Eric DeBoys. 'I didn't think a new-made blood like you would be interested in an old stick like me.'

DeBoys grinned, showing off his chin dimple as well as his teeth. 'I'm at St Bartolph's to learn from my elders.'

'I'm not a teacher. And I'm not an elder.'

'No, but you're an example.'

The School of Vampirism had its own dusk till dawn student bar, The Deconsecrated Chapel. Pampered vermin nestled in straw-filled cages hung from the vaulted ceiling. Mice, rats, piglets. Movie posters hung in alcoves, replacing sacred images. Someone had magic-markered red eyes and fangs onto Rudolf Valentino in *The Count*, W.C. Fields in *Never Give a Sucker an Even Break* and Orlon Kronsteen in *London Screams* and lipstick-kissed heart-shaped wounds on the necks of Jean Harlow in *Red Dust*, Jane Fonda in *Cat Garou* and Mavis Weld in *Clara Croft*. She'd seen that before, at Thomas Nolan's studio – the work of the same alteration artist, or just a trend she'd not noticed till now?

Just in case this date was more than social or – perish the thought! – romantic, she had let Nezumi come along and sit in the corner. Not that Kate could have stopped her bodyguard. The underage elder drank sugared blood through a straw. The high glucose content was added artificially, not because the donors were diabetic. She shooed away a couple of warm boys who tried to chat her up.

Most of DeBoys' fellow Black Monks were in the bar. Armstrong and Anna were having a quiet argument while Keith and Withnail posed in the dark at the edge of the dance-floor.

Dru, the vampire girl she'd seen with a warm crowd a few days ago, was here, alone. She sported a black eye and a simmering, angry attitude. Grabbing one of Nezumi's cast-offs, she nuzzled his neck with alarming attack.

Things were changing on campus, as folk found out who their real friends – or real enemies – were. In the pulpit, Moïse King played records. The Zombies' 'Time of the Season', The Crazy World of Arthur Brown's 'Blood', Question Mark and the Mysterians' '96 Tears'. Cathy and Pony go-goed in perfect sync on a chessboard floor with lit-up white squares. Scruffy guys watched the twins, fascinated.

No sign of James Eastman. She supposed this wasn't his scene.

King spun The Royal Guardsmen's 'Snoopy vs the Red Baron' – *not* a favourite pop pick of Kate's. Responding to the song, Nezumi finished her drink and started dancing with the French girls. They responded aggressively, like basketball players marking a star shooter. Noticing Nezumi, King gave her a Japanese theme, playing Biff Bailey and His Jazzmen's 'Sukiyaki'. She sang to the instrumental, in a clear soprano. '*Ue o muite arukō*.' 'I hold my head up high.' If King had known Nezumi's tastes, he'd have dug out 'Three Wheels on My Wagon' or 'Nellie the Elephant'.

Kate and DeBoys drank Gold Top. The Boy Eric wasn't on a student grant budget. She guessed he was from money. Everything about him was expensive. He had a Norman name. DeBoys. DeBois. Of the woods. That made sense: he had a big bad wolfish aspect, like someone who rode to hounds but longed for game more dangerous than the fox.

She hadn't drunk Gold Top in a while. She tried not to think who it had come from. This was good stuff. If she stood, she'd be a little giddy.

'What do you want to be when you grow up?' Kate asked.

'*Do* we grow up?'

'I wonder sometimes,' she admitted.

'My degree is in Law… but I might go into politics.'

'Which party?'

'That's the problem. None of them appeal.'

'Traditionally, thanks to Lord Ruthven, the Tories are the Vampire Party. Enoch Powell has probably undone that. A well-spoken lad like you'd be welcome on the editorial board of the *Socialist Vampire*.'

'A bunch of Scrawdykes,' DeBoys sneered. 'So many Points of Order, never a Point of Action.'

'Do you want Action?'

His eyes gleamed. 'Indeed I do. Elders go still, you know…'

'As I said, I'm not…'

'I never said you were… I mean Professor Croft. He's like a lizard. He never moves. He hasn't moved. He's found his crack – his coffin – and he's comfortable in it…'

So, Croft's disciple might have outgrown his master? Or wanted her to believe that.

'Don't underestimate him,' she said.

'I don't. He's survived centuries. But he's stuck. When I turned, things sped up. It's the same for the rest of us.'

'The Black Monks?'

'You could call us that.'

This evening, he wasn't wearing robes, but a black velvet Carnabetian suit. His cream ruffle shirt was unbuttoned. Medallions – inverted crosses, a boar's head, a *Blue Peter* badge, a ruby-eyed Aztec skull – clustered on his hairy chest.

It was a good thing she'd dolled up. Kate wore a Jean Varon outfit, a purple minidress with a mesh midriff and matching lace-up boots. Not something she'd buy for herself, she'd demanded the gear as a gift from Richard Jeperson. The Diogenes Club were obliged to pacify her after a simple job went south on a cross-channel ferry.

'We move fast, Kate. *Think* fast. We should call ourselves the Quick.'

'Do you have a motorbike?'

DeBoys laughed. 'Like Jimmy the Yank? No, Lord no. I drive a Jag.'

'*I* drive a Mini.'

'But you're Quick. I can see it.'

'Maybe I used to be. Then I... well, I did grow up. I was always the Sensible One. They called me that when I was alive, as a polite kind of insult. "Sensible" meant "unmarriageable".'

Why was she telling this lupine toff her life story? Was she fascinated? Or was it the Gold Top? Her brain was fizzing.

'Where are "they" now?'

'My friend Penelope – who is mostly who I mean when I say "they" – is still knocking about. Though she *didn't* get married, as it happens. Bit of a failure, there. Goes to show you shouldn't gloat too much.'

'You've a cutting edge, Miss Reed.'

'I shouldn't be mean about Penny. She's not had an easy time of it. Nothing turned out the way she expected, either.'

The man who hadn't married Penny hadn't married her, either. Or Geneviève, even. He was gone now. Sometimes, when the wind blew a certain way, she saw the faintest trace of Charles Beauregard in Richard Jeperson, who now sat in Charles's chair on the Ruling Cabal. More often, sadly, Richard reminded her of Edwin Winthrop, another Most Valued Member of the Diogenes Club. She didn't much care to be reminded of Edwin, still alive with some of her blood in him, sustaining his sharpness. Eric DeBoys had an Edwinian streak: a glint of *wanting* something and being willing to rip it out of you with a smile and some flowers. A walk in the woods with DeBoys would end up with rough and tumble in the chase. She wondered if she should put him up for club membership – give the Lovelies someone to squabble over.

A fuss broke out at the other side of the bar. Simon Armstrong, red-faced, shouted something which didn't carry over 'The Legend of Xanadu'. Anna Franklyn crossed her arms and stood back from him. Armstrong flinched at the whip-cracks in the song and made a show of storming out in a huff, snarling at the warm lads in an attempt to put a vampire face on things. He completed his exit, then needed to come back for his duffel coat – ruining the dramatic effect. Armstrong slunk off for good this time and the warm lads jeered.

'Uh oh,' said Kate, 'Anna's in the wind.'

The snake-woman walked across the dance-floor. Her tiny, sari-inhibited steps showed off her hips. Her head cobra-wobbled. Cathy and Pony stood aside as she glided past. They were still in a dance duel with Nezumi, who matched them step for step. Kate realised much of the stomping on her ceiling was Nezumi practising the frug, the monkey, the batusi and yosaki naruko.

Without invitation, Anna sat at their table. A lit candle was stuck in an empty, wax-encrusted wine bottle. Her face was olive-green in the flickering light. She blinked sideways.

'Simon's in a tizzy,' she said.

'Simon's *always* in a tizzy,' said DeBoys. 'He's a wet and a weed.'

''Tis true,' Anna sighed. 'Marshes and mires are not wetter and weedier than he.'

Anna ignored Kate and started fiddling with DeBoys's sleeve, stroking the velvet nap like cat's fur, then rubbing it the wrong way, then smoothing it again.

DeBoys smiled at Kate, unashamed.

Anna started stroking his arm with her cheek. Now, she was looking at Kate too, with unreadable serpent eyes.

Kate wondered if she should find a reason to leave, but didn't think DeBoys wanted her to go. Far from it. He was hatching ideas, enjoying himself. He was even close to opening up, she thought. If he could tell her anything, then he'd cough it up when he felt he was in power.

That might be what Eric DeBoys most wanted – from the Law, from politics, from life – power over others. And control. So: sexy fascist vampire dandy. This was Machiavelli's Prince '68-style.

'This scene is a drag tonight, Eric,' said Anna. 'Let's go out.'

'Ladies?' asked DeBoys.

'Sure,' said Kate. 'I'm game.'

'I'll just bet you are,' he said.

The crack wasn't worthy of him. A chink in the armour of cool.

They stood. Anna pulled a saffron shawl over her sari. DeBoys settled a scarlet-lined opera cloak over his shoulders, fastening it with interlocking snake-heads. A platinum clasp; not silver, of course. Kate's ensemble came with a midi-cape, but she never wore it. A cloak screamed 'I am a vampire', playing up to stereotype. Obviously, DeBoys disagreed – or, rather, was comfortable with stereotype. Kate kept asking herself who this young blade was *really*, but wondered if the surface – the grin and the chin and the cape and the elaborate hair and the *quickness* – was just what there was of him.

Glancing backwards as she was guided out of the Chapel, Kate saw Nezumi make a move to leave the dance-floor and follow. Her path was barred by Cathy and Pony, who adopted hostile dance stances. Nezumi held her hockey stick like a samurai sword. The rest of the patrons got off the chessboard.

'Looks like we picked the right time to seek new meat,' said DeBoys, arm firmly around Kate's shoulders.

'Could be entertaining,' Kate ventured.

'You've seen one cat-fight…'

He nodded at the French twins, who demonstrated their *swiftness*. Nezumi blocked their first blows with her stick and leg. Kate would have taken bets on her bodyguard, though she realised this fight was about keeping the elder busy, not putting her down.

Cathy and Pony were mercenaries. Was DeBoys paying them over what they got from Croft? Or did the Professor have them guard his disciples when they weren't protecting him?

King put on the Amen Corner's 'Scream and Scream Again' and packed all his other precious records in a sturdy cardboard box. Yes, things were going to get broken. If 'Hey, Ninety-Eight Point Six' was the anthem of the militant warm, then 'Scream and Scream Again' was the violent vampire signature tune. It was loud enough to cover the racket of a scrap.

Nezumi whacked Pony about the head and dodged a *savate* kick from Cathy.

Kate was gently but firmly steered out of the bar.

Keith Kenneth was with them, now. He ditched Withnail and fell in behind DeBoys.

Beyond Keith, Kate saw Nezumi put Cathy on the floor by sweeping her feet out from under her but take a scratch to the cheek from Pony.

Then, she was out of the Deconsecrated Chapel.

The din continued, muted by the old building's thick walls. The Amen Corner thumped along. After midnight, the campus was otherwise peaceful – though, thanks to the School of Vampirism, far from deserted.

PC Regent had finally gone home, but tape was still up around the burned grass.

'If Van Helsing's comic cuts come back, we're ready for them,' said DeBoys. 'Louts and oiks and rabble.'

'They're not my favourite people, either,' she said.

'The vampire who was killed…'

'Griffin.'

'…you knew him?'

'I'd *met* him,' she said, hoping the dark would hide her blush of shame. She didn't want to deny Griffin, but wanted to keep her police connections quiet-ish. As if they weren't general knowledge. If the Black Monks had marked Nezumi, they must know about her official capacity.

'We've always expected attacks,' said DeBoys.

'Eventually,' said Keith.

'You responded quickly,' she said. 'I'm grateful.'

Expected? Or *known about in advance?*

'It's in the open, now,' said DeBoys. 'That's better. In a stand-up fight, we'll win. And everyone will see us win.'

They were walking across the campus. Kate didn't know where to.

'If it comes to an all-out fight, we'll lose,' Kate said. 'Trust me. We will all lose. I've seen it too many times.'

DeBoys turned to her, smiling. His cloak whirled with him.

'Maybe you're an elder after all, Miss Reed.'

'I just don't think you should be so eager for a scrap,' she said.

She knew she sounded weak.

Anna was attached to DeBoys now, slipped under his cloak, lacquered nails tapping his medallions.

'We're thinking a great deal bigger than a scrap, my darling,' DeBoys said.

'Black Monks all, and hellfire to quaff,' said Keith.

DeBoys, Anna and Keith snapped their fingers. At her.

Anna separated from DeBoys. Keith moved away. They had her surrounded.

They were in a quadrangle between the biology lab and the School of Vampirism. In the centre of the grass was a Marcel DeLange bust of Elwyn Clayton on the scale of an Easter Island head. An alarming thing. Its eyes spiralled like pinwheels. Its jowls dribbled.

Kate knew her nails were growing. She felt threatened. Or flirted with. Or both.

The three students walked around her, taking mockingly slow steps followed by vampire-swift flits. She turned, trying to keep her eyes on DeBoys, who led this game of ring-a-rosy. As they moved, their faces shifted. Anna's was scalier, forked tongue darting from a lipless mouth. Keith's was harder, rougher, stiff and distorted by big, chunky fangs. DeBoys' was a leonine mask, sculpted hair now flowing from his cheeks and neck, magnificent yet pantomimish.

She knew something they didn't. Something about herself.

She was *quicker* than them. If she concentrated, they seemed to slow even when they thought they were at their fastest. If she chose, she could step out of their circle easy. She could scale the walls of the Unlimited Dream Factory. She could be gone into shadows their eyes couldn't penetrate.

Why did she feel so confident?

Had DeBoys put something in her drink? She shouldn't have fallen for that.

She stopped turning and stood still, serene. They weren't ringing her in. They were dancing tribute.

Lord, she *was* becoming an elder!

She clapped her hands, once, loud as a rifle-shot. And the dancers stopped.

It took seconds for DeBoys'cloak to settle, but he was rigid in an instant. He was in front of her, eyes fixed on hers.

'Very nice,' she said. 'Is this an initiation?'

DeBoys laughed, charmingly. He might even be a little self-conscious about the game. Anna and Keith were too serious.

'Or is this foreplay?'

'Or a play for four?' said Keith, touching her face.

That made her skin creep. Keith was DeBoys with all the pleasing qualities scraped away. DeBoys would use flowers before force, and apply the spurs lightly; Keith would bend her over a dustbin and rut like a stag.

She jammed the flat of her hand against Keith's chest. He was lifted off his feet and barrelled backwards across the quad. Anna was there to catch him, but he was furious and shocked.

'Didn't expect that, did you?' she said.

She had an urge to punch him until his face was a mess. She knew she could do it.

Her teeth were extended. Her mouth was a little miracle. Fangs like razors sliding from gumsheaths like velvet. She never bit her tongue.

'Come upstairs, Kate,' said DeBoys. 'We've a present for you.'

17

Somebody – who could only be The Boy Eric – had definitely put something in her drink. It was now in her brain.

Not BOP, because that did blow-all to vampires. Not aspirin, because she had the beginnings of a headache. She wished she'd paid more attention to all the drugs experts – E.B. Fern, Jerry Cornelius, Semolina Pilchard – she'd run into lately. But they were all so *boring*, like people who tell you their amazing dreams or enthusiasts for new systems of physical jerks. Lord, she remembered Frank and Oscar cracking on about absinthe making the art grow fondlier in the '90s… the haunted puffers who patronised the Lord of Strange Deaths' chain of opium dens… and the discovery, upon turning vampire, that all it took to get high as a bat was human blood. *Mmmm, ninety-eight point six!*

The lair of the Black Monks was a student common room with crepe hangings and a portrait of Dracula propped up in front of the unused fireplace. Joss-sticks burned in pots. The Count was angry, as if he smelled the incense and didn't like it. Dracula's snarl was in slow motion. His cloak riffled in Carpathian winds. The folds of crepe moved too.

She shut her eyes and saw busy red squiggles. Rats.

Someone chortled in the room and it frightened her.

She looked again. Things crawled in the periphery of her vision, as if the world were melting just beyond her eyeline.

DeBoys manoeuvred her around the furniture. Transparent inflatable chairs, a low plastic coffee table, a couch shaped like giant lips. Four lava lamps were placed around the room at the poles of the compass. Competing multi-coloured liquid swirls slid across the ceiling, the walls, the faces…

On a large round soft thing like an upended paddling pool, one woman held another down, restraining, comforting and/or groping her. The woman on top was Fran, the Black Monkess. Black Nun? Her robe rode up on her thighs – her flanks were reptile-scaled by the lava light – and her hood was down, unloosing her cascade of hair. The woman underneath was Jess Van Helsing, stoned out of her tiny little mind. She was the chortler. Her white shift was cut low in the front. Boob spill was inevitable. Did every sweet young thing these days have a 'sacrificial victim' dress in their wardrobe? Kate saw the pulse in Jess's throat. Red-and-blue traceries of veins flowed under her skin.

Another vampire sat in a blow-up chair, watching with soulful eyes. A beautiful boy in a white fur coat and turquoise trews. Paul Durward, of course. He had pageboy blond hair and girly lips, though his mouth was forced open by his full fangs. That always gave vampires an imbecile look. Durward drooled a little. On the point of feeding, *everyone* was an imbecile, she supposed. Instinct took over. She was no different. Especially not now. Her mouth was wet too. She could *taste* blood.

Fran held an open razor in front of Jess's face, drawing her gaze, catching the shifting light. Pearl handle, steel blade. Fran slow-waved the cutthroat with a limber wrist, hand turning a circle like an owl's head.

Even if she weren't tripping, Jess would have been *fascinated*. Kate couldn't take her eyes off the sharp edge, either. A drop of blood trickled along the blade as it turned, forever almost falling free but turning back.

'We're not all students in our little group,' DeBoys explained. 'Paul is as much a Black Monk as any of us. He's been very generous to the Cause…'

'Hellfire to quaff,' said Durward, deadpan.

Dutifully, fingers snapped. Even Fran joined in, with her free hand.

Kate couldn't snap her fingers. She'd never got the trick. She couldn't wiggle her ears, either. Though she could touch the tip of her retroussé nose with the point of her vampire tongue, so there!

She actually did that now. To prove to herself that she was in control. Her body would do what she told it to. Except she wasn't demonstrating anything of the kind. She was being silly. Double rats. Though steady on her feet, she was losing her moorings.

The Black Monks had seen this before.

She was tripping.

Fresh cuts on Jess's arms and breasts were sealed by Elastoplasts. Kate could smell the blood.

Gold Top.

She knew what DeBoys had done. To Jess, to her. Also, to Carol and Laura.

She'd been only partially right in thinking herself immune to the effects of Bowles-Ottery's hallucinogenic ergot. Just swallowed, it did nothing to vampires. Morgan Delt, for one, had tried it and been disappointed. But… if a warm person took BOP, it entered their bloodstream. If a vampire drank that blood, then…

SNAP. CRACKLE. BOP.

She hadn't drunk much in the Chapel. Just ounces. Very fresh. DeBoys must have decanted it into her glass when he went to the bar supposedly to buy her a drink.

What a gent. What a git.

Maybe the druggies were right. Thinking clearly, along neural paths she didn't usually tread, she put it all together. The BOP in Carol's and Laura's blood. The bitemarks on Fran and Keith's necks.

She understood Eric DeBoys' kink. The girls took the drug, the designated murderers drank their BOP-laced blood, then DeBoys bit them. The high passed up the chain to the Grand Master of the Black Monks. Like Renfield, Dracula's first British disciple, DeBoys saw himself at the top of a pyramid of predation, absorbing lower forms of life. But that wasn't how the Siphonaptera Syndrome worked…

Bigger fleas have little fleas, upon their backs to bite 'em,
And little fleas have littler fleas, and so, ad infinitum…

Eric DeBoys wasn't Grand Master. He was the Littlest Flea. If he needed a murdering trade name, it shouldn't exalt his status. He wasn't Jack the Ripper, the Gorilla of Soho or the Boston Exsanguinator. He was the Mite. The tiniest tick, the pinprick pinhead. There were no lower forms of life.

He hadn't touched the girls, directly. But he was the killer. The absence in Thomas Nolan's photographs… the vampire who scrambled the photographer's brains… the culprit B Division was after. Case closed. Now, all she had to do was live through the night and bring in her man.

Determined and angry, she darted close to DeBoys. She was older and stronger than him. Her talons traced his face. She wound a nail into his chin dimple. Her tongue slid over his finely stubbled throat. She could taste the smell of Brut. She thought about ripping his face off his skull. She thought about kissing him till he passed out in orgasm.

He pushed her away firmly and took hold of the back of her neck, as if she were a cat who might scratch. He guided her across the room. Towards Fran and Jess. She stiffened, but Anna and Keith gripped her arms. She was not stronger than all of them together.

She was being led to water. She was to be made to drink.

Anna hissed in her ear, not in any language she knew.

'Once we were hunters, Kate,' said DeBoys, lecturing again. 'Now, we're pets. That's against nature. Croft has lost his way, stood back, left us free. We respect the example he set, B.D. – when we could live by our wits and teeth. Before we were coddled, registered, stamped, folded, numbered, briefed, debriefed and shut in coffins. We are vipers, my darling. We should be proud. It's not war; it's the wild. The natural state of things. This pretty bird is for our pleasure, our sustenance. Jessica is our gift to you, Kate. She's nothing. A circulatory system with a national insurance number. Her grandfather would understand. We respect Van Helsing. This murder is a tribute to the name.'

This murder?

Was Kate the weapon or the culprit?

She tried not to be forced further. That bloody St Bartolph's scarf had been a snare. It had pulled her to this.

'You must see we're not doing something wicked to you, Sister Kate,' said DeBoys. Anna murmured agreement and Keith smirked nastily. 'We're helping you find out who you are. We admire you, sincerely. More than Croft. More than *Dracula*. We want to help you unlock your potential, as your example has shown us. You can be a Black Monk. A Black Abbess, even. Just drink, pretty creature. It's such a small thing. Killing one of them. But it's a liberation. This bird's pals know about it. They ink crucifixes on their bodies for each of us they cross off. We don't need to keep tallies to impress each other or scare our enemies. That's not our bag, baby. Our trophies and markers are under the skin, in the blood, in the head. Once you're free, you'll see…'

Her red thirst *raged*. Her teeth tore the inside of her mouth. She tasted blood and wanted more. She was angry with the Black Monks, *furious* at DeBoys… but that compounded her *need* for blood. She couldn't resist or attack or hurt the people who were doing this to her – and, no mistake, even zooming through the ionosphere on BOP, she knew *something wicked* was being *done to her* – but Jess Van Helsing lay there, available, unresisting, ripe, delicious, *bleeding*…

Fran played the razor over Jess's wounds. She teased an Elastoplast off the girl's bosom, scraping away the just-formed scab… but didn't slice off any more skin.

Blood welled from the cut.

She saw, in microscope vision, every pore. She flew on leather wings across a vast human landscape – the breast a hillside, the veins underground rivers, the wound a crevice, the blood a geyser.

'Go on, woman,' said Keith, 'get some in!'

She froze. The flesh map under her was a person. Kate was expected to bite, to suck more blood and BOP. To surrender humanity, to unleash her inner vampire. To take a trip.

To trip was to embark on a voyage of discovery. But to trip was also to stumble and fall.

Life was a trip. Love was a trip. Murder was a trip.

Jess's eyes were open but empty. With even a small amount of Jess's blood in Kate, they had a connection. The girl's trip – different from Kate's wooziness and wavering realities – washed over her. The barriers between their minds thinned. Jess heard Paul singing *la la la* in the middle of a plain of long grasses, crowned by a circlet of fluttering cartoon butterflies. Kate was overwhelmed by the girl's feelings. Her own heart caught on tragedy.

DeBoys wanted her to see Jess as a thing, a token, a convenience, a snack. A centrefold filled to bursting with strawberry milkshake. That was what blood-drinking was for him. That was what *murder* was for him. A moment of struggle and inevitable dominance, then supping from an empty vessel. He didn't get *communion*…

…Kate was nauseated by how much she felt for Jess, a girl she barely knew. This *connection* was easy to mistake for love. She'd done that before. Too often.

In Jess's mind, something impossible happened… Paul, *her* Paul, was singing '*Hey, ninety-eight point six, it's good to have you back again…*' Not '*Scream and Scream Again, oh baby, scream and scream again…*'

Impatient, DeBoys pressed Kate's face to Jess's breast. As always, intimate contact with a warm person was a pleasant shock. *Warm* meant 98.6° Fahrenheit… warmer than Kate, warmer than any vampire. One thing vampires rarely told their warm friends – kissing them was like kissing a hot-water bottle.

Kate rolled her face against Jess's bosom. Was she remembering her mother… or a long-gone wet-nurse? Red wetness seeped between the girl's skin and her cheek.

Kate's mouth found the open wound. Blood stung her tongue.

The Black Monks repeated 'hellfire to quaff' as if on a tape recording played at the wrong speed, elongating the words to meaninglessness.

She was in a *quick* moment.

Fran whispered 'Bite her'. So did the others. *Bite her, bite her, bite her…*

Bite. Bitter. Bat. Her. Herr. Hair.

Jessica's blood was sweet as the filling of Cook's cherry pie.

BOP and Gold Top took her back to childhood. Was hers a trip to the nursery? The womb?

Kate's fangs ached. And all her bones were fangs. Fangs around her eyes, at the ends of her fingers, in her belly, in her vulva, budding from the insides of her elbows. She had more mouths than skin.

'She's holding out,' Keith said to Fran. 'Longer than you did…'

'She's a stubborn sister,' said DeBoys.

Kate's lips were stuck to Jess's chest, as if by black frost. She couldn't pull away without leaving skin. The vacuum in her mouth drew blood from the superficial cut.

Rainbow pathways. Faces in clouds. Kaleidoscope eyes. Lemonade pies.

Even Jessica Van Helsing's hallucinations were shallow. It was a wonder she didn't hear sitar music and see a hookah-smoking caterpillar.

She just heard and saw her Paul, ululating her own love back at her. He didn't need a reflection while he had Jessica.

Kate's eyes were bloody with tears.

This poor idiot was going to die under her fangs and she couldn't stop. Jessica Van Helsing would be the next victim. Kate Reed would be the next murderer.

Some detective. She had caught herself.

'Bite her,' said DeBoys, issuing an order, not making a suggestion.

He was getting impatient. That came with privilege. Being the man on the horse looking down at the peasant in the field. And being a junky. That was the other thing, the thing he'd covered up. He needed his fix. BOP, human blood, vampire blood. His drug cocktail. Eric DeBoys was sweating blood. Great bullets of it stood out on his forehead. Trickled in his chest hair. Made sticky patches on his shirt. He was starting on the shakes.

Take away the black robes, the hellfire salutes and the pseudo-philosophy and this was all about shooting up. She was almost disappointed.

But that was a tiny quibble.

Jess's heartbeat sounded like a galley drum. Standing speed. Racing speed. Ramming speed. Biting speed.

Kate's *red thirst* could be restrained no longer…

Her jaws gripped like a bear trap and her fangs sank into meat. Sundered blood vessels emptied into her mouth. She nuzzled against ribs, probing for a vein and a steady pulse… Jess's heart thumped her skull.

If unrestrained, she'd break Jess's sternum and pry away the bones. She'd chew towards her heart and tear into the aorta, the body's mother lode, the great river surging through the trunk…

She would swim and tear through flesh and bone and exult in killing with no shame.

Only…

She stopped.

'What's wrong?' asked someone. 'Why's she not…?'

Only *she wasn't that kind of girl.*

She was the Sensible One. She knew – had always known, despite the stings of Penelope's put-downs – that she could be as *sensual* as *sensible*. She wasn't prim. She wasn't an old maid. She wasn't what they'd expected her to be.

But she had her limits. This was one.

Dammit.

She was cold sober now. Jess was tripping enough for the both of them.

DeBoys grunted in frustration and anger.

She took her mouth out of her victim's chest. She'd bitten a sizeable hole. The girl was bucking and bleeding. At last, she was afraid – her rainbows shone black and her butterflies metamorphosed into giant wasps.

Fran bent to drink from Jess's wound, but Kate blocked sharply with the heel of her hand. She felt the vampire's nose break. Fran was pushed across the floor and knocked over a lava lamp. She yelped as the hot object stuck to her bloody face. She flailed with her razor and slashed an inflatable pouffe. The thing hissed and collapsed like a burst soufflé.

Kate pressed her fingers over Jess's bite-wound, stanching the blood.

'I told you, Eric,' said Anna. 'She's weak.'

'No,' he said. 'She's strong. That's her problem.'

Kate concentrated on the warm girl. Jess wasn't safe yet, the little fool. Her eyes flicked away, towards the impassive youth who'd watched all this happen.

'Paul,' she said, imploring, '*Paul...*'

'Look at me, Jess,' said Kate. 'Me. It's Kate Reed. Remember.'

Of course, her face must be red with Jess's blood. Scarcely reassuring.

She hadn't bitten anything vital. Jess would dribble blood for a while, needed to to be careful about infection and would have an unsightly scar that might make her buy some high-necked blouses, but she would live – or, at least, not die from anything Kate had done to her. A pint of Bovril and a mustard plaster and she'd be right as rain. Providing she was let alone now.

A cold metal ring pressed into Kate's temple.

Eric DeBoys held a gun to her head.

'Her. You. Choose.'

18

Click. The hammer was drawn back.

Kate didn't move.

She held Jess in her arms. The girl was in a swoon. She was an awkward weight. In the moment, Kate heard Jess's beating heart.

Keith helped Fran stand up, get her robe straight and stem the blood pouring from her nose with paper tissues. Kate had another insight. Keith, the callous predator, was more into Fran than she was him.

DeBoys took the gun away from her head and showed it to her. A revolver. The cylinder was full. Matt silver bulletheads. That ammo would settle her hash, all right. He took aim again. His floppy cuffs were damp, stained with his own bloodsweat.

She couldn't expect help from the others.

Saying anything was likely to annoy DeBoys enough to finish her quickly. He could have Anna bite Jess, then glut himself on the snake woman, so he wouldn't miss his fix.

The door opened. A figure was outlined.

James Eastman. Not a Black Monk. She was saved.

The newcomer stepped into the room. Lava light rolled over his face. Not James Eastman.

Caleb Croft.

The last person in the world who'd want to save her. Indeed, someone who'd be only too happy to watch her execution. He'd been cheated of it during the Terror.

If DeBoys shattered her skull with silver in front of Croft, it would be like putting a ripe red apple on the Professor's desk. He'd get a first class degree without sitting any exams.

Kate relaxed and let Jess roll out of her arms. The unconscious girl rucked up the carpet and ended up face-down. Her sacrificial dress was backless. She had fluff and grit stuck to her bare skin and white silk-covered rump.

That might be the last thing Kate ever saw. A Van Helsing's bum. She would have words with God – if He existed – about this turn of events. Perhaps she'd get a better answer from the Other Fellow.

'Sir, she's not worthy,' DeBoys said. 'She won't kill.'

Croft smiled, a matter of a twitch of his dead mouth over jagged fangs. Blue and green blobs of light fought over his face, an eternal yin-yang struggle.

'Won't she indeed?'

'She's not a real vampire, sir.'

Croft chuckled, a sound like a shower of razor-blades.

Between the beats of Jessica's heart, between the ticks of Croft's expensive wristwatch, Kate stood up, shoulder-slammed DeBoys against the wall, took his gun away, rammed its barrel under his ribs, and shot him, firing upwards, bursting his heart with silver.

She let him go.

He took a step away from the wall and turned – red speckles grew in a circle a foot across on the back of his cape, as if the lining were leaking through – then fell.

Anna hissed. Kate pointed the gun at her.

'You're not a killer,' she said, forked tongue darting.

'I'm not a murderer,' Kate explained. 'I don't believe in capital punishment. I'm not a sadist. I don't enjoy killing, but…'

'Kate Reed was – is – a terrorist, space kidettes,' Croft told his remaining students. 'If Mr DeBoys had paid attention to my lectures, he'd know that.'

'I haven't had to kill anyone since…'

She didn't need to tell these people that. She had no nostalgia for the Terror or the Irish Civil War.

DeBoys looked like he didn't believe he could die.

She wanted to kick the smug, dead bastard. He'd made her

go against her principles, after all. He *had* turned her into a killer. With that annoying clarity she hoped would soon wear off, she saw she'd served Croft's purpose too. The Black Monks' antics brought on him attention he did not seek. She'd ended that. If anyone was Grand Master of the Black Monks now, he was.

Of course, she could shoot him and have done with it.

She'd come up in the dock just after Donna Rogers. With a few character witnesses and equivocal testimony from the other Black Monks – who would, she guessed, feel disillusioned with their masters and mentors about now – she might get away with it. Penny, for one, had skated off after worse. And Geneviève. Lord, what other vampires had done…

But, annoyingly, it remained. She was not that kind of girl.

The doorway behind Croft was crowded. A gunshot always drew attention. Everyone wanted to know what had happened. James Eastman was there, just behind Croft.

Another unwelcome intuition. She'd mistaken Croft for Eastman in silhouette because they looked alike. It wasn't common, but some vampires could father children on warm women. Eastman called Croft Big Daddy. And hated him. Kate could only guess what the former Lord Charles Croydon, despoiler of warm wenches, had done to some poor Californian in about 1940. She gave Eastman the gun. How he used it was his decision.

Also in the crowd was Nezumi, one sock rolled down around her ankle, scratches on her face, hockey stick on her shoulder. Neither twin was there. Nezumi blew upwards, shifting her fringe out of her eyes. She flicked a glance at the dead man on the floor and nodded approval.

Kate accepted that she had saved herself, and not waited for someone else to do the dirty work. She could live with the guilt. The five or six others she'd killed had all been trying to murder her too. She'd not drunk any of their blood. She would not let being a vampire define her like that.

Now, with an audience, she needed to make a gesture.

She knelt by DeBoys, stuck her fingers in the ruin of his back, and licked them clean.

Images and impressions sparked. A big house, riding to hounds, flogging and being flogged, a *lot* of women, black candles and goat-heads, a beer glass smashing on an old man's face, pain, pain, blood, blood, blood… and nothing.

She stood.

Anna Franklyn came at her, spitting venom. Nezumi twisted the handle of her hockey stick and drew a steel short-sword from it. She placed the edge of the blade against the snake-woman vampire's throat. Anna closed her mouth and shed scales, showing a new, as-yet-unused face. Nezumi nodded, seriously, and Anna stepped away from the sword.

Someone must have called the police by now.

19

Kate was lucky. Pilcher was in bed, dreaming of hippies jumping off a cliff. The call was taken by Sergeant Lynch at Shooter's Hill. He rounded up Dixon and Regan, suspended or not, to go to St Bartolph's.

If Sergeant Choley were on duty, Kate would be in a tumbril.

The drug was burning out of her – she didn't know how much sharper or more perceptive or monstrous she'd have become if she'd drained Jess dry – but she could still explain what she'd worked out.

Keith, Fran and Anna were in separate interview rooms. Two were murderers, one an accomplice, but it had all been Eric DeBoys' fault. He had intended that all the Black Monks take part in his blood-and-BOP ritual, binding them to him as accessories to murder if not in some mystic commingling of drugs and human sacrifice.

Obscurely, it was all about Croft, who would walk away free, as usual. DeBoys had been trying to get his loved-hated mentor's attention, but also hoped to turn Croft back into the vampire he used to be, the unashamed murderer and rapist who inspired the Black Monks. James Eastman wasn't the only member of the seminar group who saw Croft as the father who must be appeased, pleased, revered, replaced and destroyed.

DeBoys had let Nolan tag along to take photographs Croft would appear in and laid that silly trail with the scarf. It was his way of pressuring the professor. Bellaver often said some fools seemed to want to get nicked. Infusions of the blood-and-BOP mix – which had only been brewed up twice, but now had a street name: Crimson – nourished the rake's feeling of being beyond the reach of the law.

Anna, who could most easily cut a deal, kept schtumm. She resented the way Kate had been bumped in front of her – the next victim should have been hers, though her venom in Jess's wounds would have tipped off Dr John Hardy at the autopsy. Keith and Fran were in a classic prisoners' pickle – each not knowing if the other had turned Queen's Evidence. Fran would cut the deal first. Stressing DeBoys' powers of fascination, she might be able to plead manslaughter through mind-warpery.

The truth would come out, or as much of it as these cretins could give.

DeBoys had nurtured an inflated notion of his place in history. Using Carol as a lure, he'd fascinated Nolan to provide illustrations for his unwritten biography. At that, he'd be successful: someone – not Kate! – would write a paperback about this. No one knew how completely Nolan could be un-addled, though Monserrat was claiming some success with his hypnotic procedures. The snapper was on the party scene again, with a fresh interest in fast cars and renewed enthusiasm for dolly birds.

Kate and Nezumi had to make statements. Nezumi was happy to give details of which hospital – St Swithin's – she had sent Cathy and Pony to. As a follower of Shinto, she Brownie-swore to the truth of her testimony.

Jessica Van Helsing was in the same hospital. Michael Upton, a medical student who came with the ambulance, said he was more concerned by her drug intake than the cuts and bruises she'd suffered at the mercy of bloodsucking fiends. The side-effects of Bowles-Ottery pellets included acute stomach pains, which proselytisers seldom mentioned could be agonisingly fatal. Upton called vampires 'bloodsucking fiends' to her face, the cheeky sod.

Jess came round enough to ask for Paul Durward to sit in the ambulance with her. He'd done it, too. Kate didn't need a drug insight to see that the nit would stick by the boyfriend who'd been happy to see her killed. She hoped Jess would at least corner the feckless viper into marrying her and then drain *him* of his feeble life essence with her woolly-minded yet steely bounciness.

Inappropriately, before leaving the scene of the crime, Upton asked for Kate's phone number. Even more inappropriately, she gave it to him. If she wasn't arraigned for murder, she could look forward to a date in another bloody student bar. This time, she'd get her own drinks in. Medical students had access to drugs which made BOP seem like Maltesers.

At the police station, Kate told George Dixon everything except what she'd guessed about Eastman. If the biker ever assassinated his father, she hoped he'd be out of the country before B Division got on his case.

After they were done, Jack Regan popped his head into the room and said, 'Own goal, eh? That'll muck up the score.' She hadn't thought of that. It had dawned on her, as she told the story, that Jessica's granddad wouldn't be grateful to her for saving the warm girl's life... much less, bringing in the murderers of Carol and Laura. To the Circle of Light, Enoch Powell and The 98.6, she was still a monster. The vampire community wouldn't be happy with her either. As a Fearless Vampire Killer, she could get a cross tattooed under her arm.

Dixon bade her good morning and said he'd tell Bellaver how it had shaken out in the end. She promised to go and see the Super, who was pruning his roses and boning up on parking regulations and the *A to Z of Welwyn Garden City*. It was wrong he wasn't here to see the end of it. She'd report to the Diogenes Club as soon as she was able. If solving the murders served their long-term, mysterious purposes, she supposed she should be happy about that.

Just before dawn, when vampire and warm alike were at their lowest ebb, calls started to come in. The School of Vampirism was on fire. The 98.6 were claiming responsibility. A full-scale student protest, fomented by the *Socialist Vampire*, got in the way of the Fire Brigade. The firemen had been run ragged all night by lesser arsons designed to distract and exhaust them before the big burn-up of 1968. The press were out in force, too. And the members of the Manfred Commission. The Battle of St Bartolph's was just beginning.

Kate's ears still rang. If you fire a gun in an enclosed space like a student common room, that happens. She also heard sirens, fire alarms, telephone bells, police whistles, steam kettles, the wireless pips, screams.

As the sun came up, the din got louder.

ANNOTATIONS

As with the new editions of *Anno Dracula* and *The Bloody Red Baron*, this section is not exhaustive or definitive. Again, first and foremost, the key source is Bram Stoker: without *Dracula*, derivatives like this series wouldn't be conceivable. In this book, I must obviously also acknowledge primary debts to the filmmakers Federico Fellini, Maro Bava and Dario Argento, and the authors Ian Fleming and Patricia Highsmith. For more on my sources, see the original Acknowledgements.

PART I THREE CORPSES IN THE FOUNTAIN

Well before *La dolce vita*, the Trevi Fountain was made internationally famous by the film *Three Coins in the Fountain* (1954), based on John H. Secondari's novel *Coins in the Fountain* (1952). A major commercial hit in its day, Jean Negulesco's wide-eyed yet stuffy movie was one of a run of glossy 1950s productions – *Roman Holiday* (1953) was the keystone in the cycle – showcasing European locations. The premise was always that down-to-Earth Americans find romance abroad with fantasised Europeans (often Royal) in an era when international tourism, hitherto exclusive to the rich or the bohemian, was for the first time a middle-class pursuit. There's a Dracula connection: one of the romantic leads is Louis Jourdan, later notable in *Count Dracula*. Casting a Frenchman as an Italian Prince is typical of Hollywood's 'they're all foreign so what's the difference?' attitude. *Three Coins*, *Roman Holiday* and company present Europeans rather as the *Twilight* franchise does vampires: glamorous, romantic, non-threatening, wealthy, beautiful objects. I use the basic premise of *Three Coins* for *Dracula Cha Cha Cha*: three foreign women in Rome, having romantic complications. The overripe Jule Styne-Sammy Cahn title song, a number one hit for The Four Aces (US) and Frank Sinatra (UK), outlasted the memory of the movie.

Princess Asa Vajda: the vampire villainess of Mario Bava's *La Maschera del demonio* (1960), also released as *The Mask of Satan*, *Black Sunday* and *Revenge of the Vampire*. The dark-haired, striking English actress Barbara Steele earned her horror-movie immortality – tagged 'the only girl in films whose eyelids can snarl' by Raymond Durgnat – in the dual role of Princess Asa and her descendant Katja. Notionally based on Nikolai Gogol's 'Vij', the film was written by Ennio de Concini and Mario Serandrei. Steele plays Gloria Morin, the character based on Sophia Loren, in Fellini's *8 ½* (1963).

Dracula's wives are not to be confused with Dracula's brides. Ilona Szilagy, Queen Victoria and Sari Gabòr are real people, though only Ilona was married to Vlad Tepes in our history. Elisabeta is Vlad's perhaps mythical first wife: she's supposed to have committed suicide upon hearing a false report of his death, as dramatised in the prologue of *Bram Stoker's Dracula* (1992). Marguerite Chopin comes from Carl Dreyer's film *Vampyr* (1932).

Hugh Walpole's Castle of Otranto is in the province of Otranto, in the heel of Italy, well away from Rome.

CHAPTER 1: DRACULA *CHA CHA CHA*

'Dracula *Cha Cha Cha*'. Composed and performed by Bruno Martino, the Italian pop song first appeared (briefly) over the end credits of *Tempi duri per i vampiri/Uncle Was a Vampire* (1959), in which Christopher Lee (just a year after his first performance as Dracula) plays comedian Renato Rascel's inconvenient ancestor. The song, a bigger hit than the film, is also used in Vincente Minnelli's *Two Weeks in Another Town* (1962), where Barzelli (Rosanna Schiaffino), another character based on Sophia Loren, dances to it in macabre circumstances. 'Dracula *Cha Cha Cha*' has been covered in multiple languages by Henri Salvador, Rod McKuen, the Tango Saloon, Los Dandies and Bob Azzam; a selection of versions can be found on YouTube. Martino also recorded a sequel song 'Draculino'.

Count Gabor Kernassy. When populating the vampire jet set of *Dracula Cha Cha Cha*, I naturally looked to Italian vampire movies of the period. Kernassy is played by Walter Brandi in *L'ultima preda del vampiro/Playgirls and the Vampire* (1960).

Malenka: the name comes from Amando de Ossorio's *Malenka* (1969), also known as *Malenka – The Niece of the Vampire* and *Fangs of the Living Dead*. Like *La maschera del demonio* and *L'ultima preda del vampiro*, it's one of those films in which the lead plays the vampire ancestor and a lookalike descendant. The dual role of Malenka and Sylvia Morel is taken by Anita Ekberg; the Malenka of *Dracula Cha Cha Cha* also stands in for Sylvia, Ekberg's character in *La dolce vita*.

Paparazzi: the term *paparazzo* comes from the character played by Walter Santesso in *La dolce vita*. That Paparazzo was based mostly on the photographers Tazio Secchiaroli and Marcello Geppetti; screenwriter Ennio Flaiano took the name from a character in George Gissing's novel *By the Ionian Sea* (1901).

CHAPTER 3: *GIALLO POLIZIA*

Giallo (literally, 'yellow') is an Italian term for a brand of thriller originally published in yellow covers (just as the term film noir derives from the French *Série Noir* imprint). In Italian cinema, the term is associated with a cycle of gruesome, stylish, cosmopolitan murder mysteries.

Inspector Silvestri (Thomas Reiner) appears in Mario Bava's important *giallo Sei donne per l'assassino/Blood and Black Lace* (1964).

The Crimson Executioner (Mickey Hargitay) appears in Massimo Pupillo's flamboyant *giallo Il Boia Scarlatto/Bloody Pit of Horror* (1965).

CHAPTER 4: MYSTERIES OF OTRANTO

Richard Fountain and Chriseis come from Simon Raven's vampire novel *Doctors Wear Scarlet* (1960); Patrick Mower and Imogen Hassall play them in Robert Hartford-Davis's film *Incense for the Damned* (1972). Raven, incidentally, contributed to the script of *On Her Majesty's Secret Service* (1969).

CHAPTER 8: JOURNALISM

Maciste, the Hero of Rome: the eternal strongman, a recurrent figure in Italian pop culture, was created by writer Gabriele d'Annunzio for the film *Cabiria* (1914), a spectacular of the Punic Wars. Played by burly Bartolomeo Pagano, Maciste returned in adventures with varied historical (even contemporary) settings throughout the silent era. Series entries highlighted the versatile hero as Maciste the Mountaineer, Maciste the Detective, Maciste the Medium, Maciste the Athlete and Maciste in Love. His 'versus' movie fight-card includes *Maciste contro la morte/ Maciste vs Death* (1919), *Maciste contro Maciste* (1923) and *Maciste contro lo sceicco/Maciste vs the Sheik* (1925). The Dante-inspired *Maciste all'inferno/Maciste in Hell* (1926) was the first film the young Federico Fellini saw: he claimed his entire career was an attempt to recapture the impression it made on him. In the 1960s, after the success of the Steve Reeves Hercules films, a great many mythic muscleman movies were made in Italy and Maciste returned, played by Mark Forest, Gordon Mitchell, Kirk Morris and others. These movies mostly have ancient settings, though a new *Maciste all'inferno* (1962) finds the hero fighting evil in seventeenth-century Scotland and combines muscle-flexing action with the brand of gothic horror created by *La maschera del demonio* (its English title is *The Witch's Curse*). Gordon Scott starred in *Maciste contro il vampiro/Goliath and the Vampires* (1962). In dubbed versions, the 1960s Maciste films often rename the character to make him a more internationally prominent hero: Atlas, Goliath, the Son of Hercules or Hercules himself. D'Annunzio used the name Maciste because it was understood to be a surname of Hercules – after a temple in the Tryphilian town of Macistus – and intended that the character be an avatar of the classical hero.

CHAPTER 9: *LIVE AND LET DIE*

Gregor Brastov: the vampire villain of Charles L. Grant's *The Soft Whisper of the Dead* (1982). Charlie's classic monster trilogy is completed by the werewolf novel *The Dark Cry of the Moon* (1986) and the mummy book *The Long Night of the Grave* (1986). My story 'The Chill Clutch of the Unseen', about another archetypal fiend, was written in homage to the series.

CHAPTER 10: CAT O'NINE TAILS

The Three Mothers: this mythology – drawn from Thomas de Quincey's *Suspiria De Profundis* (1845) – underlies Dario Argento's trilogy of films, the classic *Suspiria* (1977) and *Inferno* (1980) and the belated footnote *La Terza Madre/Mother of Tears* (2007). A different take on de Quincey's vision appears in Fritz Leiber's novel *Our Lady of Darkness* (1977).

CHAPTER 11: THE DANCING DEAD

Anthony Aloysius St John Hancock: the character played by Tony Hancock in *The Rebel* (1961), of course. Created by Ray Galton and Alan Simpson.

Nico Otzak: later known for her association with Andy Warhol and the Velvet Underground, Nico has a small role in *La dolce vita*. She'll be back in *Johnny Alucard*.

It's unfair to say the American couple follow the fashion set by Quilty and Vivian: it's the other way round. Though Charles Addams didn't name the character until the TV show *The Addams Family* (1964), he'd been drawing his wasp-waisted, black-shrouded ghoul woman since the 1930s. The obvious model for 1950s horror hostess Vampira, Morticia might also have influenced the style of Vivian Darkbloom (a much cleverer anagram than most vampires use) in Vladimir Nabokov's *Lolita* (1955). Marianne Stone's Vivian, in Kubrick's 1962 film, and Carolyn Jones's Morticia are lookalikes.

CHAPTER 16: KATE IN LOVE

telefono bianco: during the Mussolini era, the heavily state-controlled Italian cinema industry turned out trivial, reassuring films known as white telephone movies: domestic dramas and romantic comedies with a fantasised upper- or upper-middle-class milieu and art-deco decors (the white telephone being a signature luxurious touch). Significant titles include *La dama bianco* (1938), *Inventiamo l'amore* (1938), *Centomila dollari* (1939), *Luce nelle tenebre* (1941) and *Il fidanzato di mia moglie* (1943). How these reflected the real lives of Italian audiences of the period can be judged by the fact that the cycle ran to a movie called *La vita è bella*, released in 1943. The critic Tom Milne coined the term *telefono rosso* to characterise the *gialli* of the 1960s and 1970s, which have a similar social milieu (and emphasis on set and costume design) but add black-gloved, masked murderers who slash their way through the wealthy, superficial characters.

CHAPTER 19: THE PARTY

Dorian Gray: the Italian actress Maria Luisa Mangini (1936–2011) took the name of Wilde's character (who passed briefly through the *Anno Dracula* series in 'Vampire Romance'). Her credits include Fellini's *Le notti di Cabiria/Nights of Cabiria* (1957), Michelangelo Antonioni's *Il Grido* (1957) and (as Antiope) the sword and sandal *La regina delle Amazzoni/Colossus and the Amazons* (1960).

Dr Hichcock. Dr Bernard Hichcock (Robert Flemyng) is the villain of a key title in the Italian horror movie cycle of the early '60s, Riccardo Freda's *L'orribile segreto del Dr. Hichcock* (1962), aka *Raptus, The Horrible Dr Hichcock* and *The Terror of Dr Hichcock*. 'The candle of his lust burnt brightest in the shadow of the grave,' shrieked the posters. Mrs Cynthia Hichcock is played by Barbara Steele, who also appears as Mrs Margaret Hichcock, wife of Dr John Hichcock (Elio Jotta), in a follow-up *Lo spettro* (1963).

Lex Barker, a former screen Tarzan, is in the crowd in *La dolce vita*. In 1959, Gordon Scott was the official ape-man, starring in *Tarzan's Greatest Adventure*; soon, he would play Maciste (in *Maciste contro il vampiro*, 1961), Remus, Zorro, Coriolanus, Hercules and others in Italian-made muscleman movies.

Mrs Honoria Cornelius and Colonel Maxim Pyat recur throughout the multiverse of Michael Moorcock. From Mike, I learned that every novel should have a party scene; this guest-list is a tribute to him.

CHAPTER 20: *OPERAZIONE PAURA*

The chapter title comes from the 1966 Mario Bava film, also known as *Curse of the Dead* and *Kill, Baby, Kill.*

CHAPTER 21: *CEMETERY GIRLS*

The chapter title comes from the US re-release title of Javier Aguirre's *El gran amor del conde Drácula* (1974), in which Paul Naschy plays Dracula.

CHAPTER 22: *THE MAGIC SWORD*

The chapter title comes from the 1962 Bert I. Gordon fairytale film, which features Maila Nurmi (Vampira) in the role of Hag.

CHAPTER 24: *CADAVERI ECCELLENTI*

The chapter title comes from the 1978 Francesco Rosi film, also known as *Illustrious Corpses.*

CHAPTER 26: MR WEST AND DR PRETORIUS

Dr Pretorius is played by Ernest Thesiger in James Whale's film *Bride of Frankenstein* (1935), scripted by John L. Balderston and William Hurlbut. The version who appears in the *Anno Dracula* series was created by Paul McAuley in the stories 'The Temptation of Dr Stein', 'The True History of Dr Pretorius' and 'Dr Pretorius and the Lost Temple'.

CHAPTER 27: *PROFONDO ROSSO*

The chapter title comes from the 1975 Dario Argento film, also known as *Deep Red* or *The Hatchet Murders.*

CHAPTER 29: *WHAT'S NEW, PUSSYCAT?*

The vampire twins were created by Jean Rollin as roles for actress sisters Catherine and Marie-Pierre Castel (sometimes billed as Cathy and Pony Tricot). They first appeared in *La vampire nue/The Nude Vampire* (1970) and recur throughout Rollin's filmography, notably in *Levres de sang/Lips of Blood* (1975). Alexandra Pic and Isabelle Teboul play non-identical variations on the roles in Rollin's late *Les deux orphelines vampires* (1997).

CHAPTER 30: CINEMA INFERNO

The vampire trap. Invented for London's Lyceum Theatre in 1820 – not the site associated with Bram Stoker, which took the name later in the century – the vampire trap is a stage trapdoor which allows instantaneous appearances and disappearances. It is so called because it was first used in a production of James Planché's *The Vampire, or, The Bride of the Isles*, an adaption of Dr Polidori's 'The Vampyre'.

CHAPTER 31: *PENELOPE PULLS IT OFF*

The chapter title comes from the 1975 Anglo-German sex comedy starring Linda Marlowe and Anna Bergman.

CHAPTER 33: *LACHRYMAE*

The four aspects of the Mother of Tears derive from pillars of European art cinema… the child is the Devil (Marina Yaru) from Fellini's *Toby Dammit* (a segment of *Histoires extraordinaires/ Spirits of the Dead*, 1968); incidentally, Fellini was influenced by the child ghost of Bava's *Operazione paura* (both, in turn, influence the Devil of Martin Scorsese's *The Last Temptation of Christ*, 1988); the young woman is Viridiana (Silvia Pinal), from Luis Buñuel's 1961 film; the mature woman is Mamma Roma (Anna Magnani), from Pier Paolo Pasolini's 1962 film, though I was also thinking of the fleshy fantasy whores who recur in Fellini's movies (especially in *Roma*); the crone is La Santona (Ida Bracci Dorati), from Vittorio de Sica's neorealist classic *Ladri di biciclette/Bicycle Thieves* (1948). In Argento's films, Mater Lachrymarum appears as a pouting model, played by Anna Pieroni in *Inferno* and Moran Atias in *La terza madre*.

Jack Palance, Francis Lederer, Alex D'Arcy and David Niven have all played Dracula, appearing in *Dracula* (1974), *The Return of Dracula* (1958), *Blood of Dracula's Castle* (1969) and *Vampira* (1975).

CHAPTER 34: THE JUDGEMENT OF TEARS

The original US editions of *Dracula Cha Cha Cha* were retitled *Judgment of Tears*; I've always preferred my title (as the UK spelling). Bibliographers and book collectors get frustrated by things like this: the Carroll & Graf US hardback of *Judgment of Tears* is the novel's first edition though it contains a misleading 'first published in the UK' notice (schedules were rearranged and the British edition came out a year later).

ACKNOWLEDGEMENTS

Various thanks are due to Dario Argento, Mark Ashworth, Dana and Pete Atkins, James Bacon, Nicolas Barbano, Suzanne and Richard Barbieri, Martine Bellen, Sarah Biggs, Anne Billson, Sebastian Born, Faith Brooker, Jennifer Brehl, Monique Brocklesby, Sara and Randy Broecker, John Brosnan, Molly Brown, Gian-Piero Brunetta, Eugene Byrne, Susan Byrne, Mark Burman, Pat Cadigan, Jenny and Ramsey Campbell, Kent Carroll, Daniela Catelli, Valeria Cavalli, Jackie Clare, Jeremy Clarke, Lorenzo Codelli, David Cross, Darryl Cunningham, Les Daniels, Ellen Datlow, Julie Davies, Meg Davis, Martina Drnkova, Alex Dunn, Val and Les Edwards, Kris and Dennis Etchison, the staff of Fantafestival 1990, Martin Feeney, Leslie Felperin, Jo Fletcher, Martin Fletcher, Barry Forshaw, Chris Fowler, Christopher Frayling, Neil Gaiman, Tony Gardner, Lisa Gaye, Pandora Gorey, Paula Grainger, Charlie Grant (whose cat I've borrowed), the cast of *Gypsy Angel*, Carlos and Pia Hansen, Mike Harrison, Antony Harwood, Rob Holdstock, Andre Jacquemetton, Alan Jones, Rodney Jones, Stephen Jones, Laragh Kedwell, Mike King, Karen Krizanovich, John Phillip Law, Cathy Leamy, Christopher and Gitte Lee, Pat LoBrutto, Tim Lucas, Chris Manby, Paul McAuley, Maitland McDonagh, Lisa McGuire, Maura McHugh, Marie-Helene Méliès, Cindy Moul, Julia and Bryan Newman, Jerome Newman, Sasha Newman, David Newton, Quelou Parente, Katya Pendill, Marcelle Perks, Adriano Pintaldi, Stuart Pollok, Ann and

David Pringle, Lorenzo Quinn, Alberto Ravaglioli, Andy Richards, Lisa Rogers, Kate and Nick Royle, Geoff Ryman, Jane and Russell Schechter, Dave Schow, Adam Simon, Helen Simpson, Millie Simpson, Sally and Dean Skilton, Robert Sklar, Mandy Slater, Brian Smedley, Michael Marshall Smith, Jane and Brian Stableford, Frank Stallone, Steve Thrower, Jean-Marc Toussaint, Tom Tunney, Caroline Vié, Nick Webb, Connie Williams, Doug Winter, Jack Womack, Kate Worthington, Mark V. Ziesing.

Books, films, CDs: Michael Anglo's *Nostalgia: Spotlight on the Fifties*; Michelangelo Antonioni's *L'avventura* and *L'eclisse*; Dario Argento's *Profondo rosso*, *suspiria* and *Inferno*; Mario Bava's *La maschara del demonio*, *Sei donne per l'assassino*, *operazione paura* and *diabolik*; John Baxter's *Fellini*; *Beat at Cinecittà* (Crippled Dick Hot Wax); Peter Bonadella's *The Cinema of Federico Fellini* and *Italian Cinema: From Neorealism to the Present*; Antonio Bruschini's *Bizarre Sinema!: Horror all'italiana 1957–1979*; Antonio Bruschini and Antonio Tentori's *Malizie perverse: il cinema erotico Italiano*, *Mondi incredibili: il cinema fantastico-avventuroso Italiano*, *Profonde tenebre: il cinema thrilling Italiano 1962–1982* and *Operazione paura: i registi del Gotico italiano*; Antonio Bruschini and Igor Molino's *Made in Hell: A Pictorial Voyage Through the Italian Horror*; Simon Callow's *Orson Welles: The Road to Xanadu*; Charlotte Chandler's *I, Fellini*; Costanzo Constantini's *Fellini on Fellini*; *Eyewitness Travel Guides: Rome*; Roger Corman's *A Bucket of Blood*; Donald P. Costello's *Fellini's Road*; Robert Day's *The Rebel*; Federico Fellini's *Le notti di Cabiria*, *La dolce vita*, *8½*, *Giulietta degli spiriti*, *Toby Dammit*, *Roma* and *Intervista*; the exhibition catalogue *Fellini: Costumes and Fashion*; Ian Fleming's *Casino Royale*, *You Only Live Twice* and *On Her Majesty's Secret Service*; Paul Ginsborg's *A History of Contemporary Italy*; Jean-Luc Godard's *Le Mépris*; Joan Gordon and Veronica Hollinger's *Blood Read: The Vampire as Metaphor in Contemporary Culture*; Barry Keith Grant's *The Dread of Difference: Gender and the Horror Film* (which contains Robin Wood's essay 'Burying the Undead: the Use and Obsolescence of Count Dracula'); Peter Haining and Peter

Tremayne's *The Un-Dead: The Legend of Bram Stoker and Dracula*; Patricia Highsmith's *The Talented Mr Ripley*; *Italy After Dark: Italia Nostalgica* (especially Romina Power's 'Que sera sera'); Kenneth Rayner Johnson's *The Fulcanelli Phenomenon*; S. Masi and E. Lancia's *Italian Movie Goddesses*; Clive Leatherdale's *Dracula: The Novel & the Legend*; Bob Madison's *Dracula: The First Hundred Years*; Pascal Martinet's *Mario Bava*; Maitland McDonagh's *Broken Mirrors/Broken Minds: The Dark Dreams of Dario Argento*; Vincente Minnelli's *Two Weeks in Another Town* (in which Rosanna Schiaffino dances the 'Dracula *Cha Cha Cha*'); Alberto Moravia and Sam Wagenaar's *Women of Rome* (Patrizia Nappi, the girl in the first photograph, is what I think Geneviève looks like); *Murder For Pleasure: Giallo & Thriller Original Soundtrack Themes* (Gatto Nero Records); Amando de Ossorio's *Malenka, la nipote del vampiro* (with Anita Ekberg); Luca M. Palmerini and Gaetano Mistretta's *Spaghetti Nightmares*; Pier Paolo Pasolini's *Mamma Roma*; Stewart Perowne's *The Pilgrim's Companion in Rome*; David Punter's *The Literature of Terror*; Massimo Pupillo's *Il boia scarlatto* (aka *Bloody Pit of Horror*, with Mickey Hargitay as the Crimson Executioner); Simon Raven's *Doctors Wear Scarlet*; Piero Regnoli's *L'ultima preda del vampiro* (aka *Playgirls and the Vampire*); Charles Richards's *The New Italians*; Nino Rota's *Greatest Hits*; Irwin Shaw's *Two Weeks in Another Town*; Alan Sillitoe's *Saturday Night and Sunday Morning* (Arthur Seaton really does rant about vampires), David J. Skal's *V is for Vampire*; O.F. Snelling's *James Bond: A Report*; David Thomson's *Rosebud: The Story of Orson Welles*; *Tutto Fellini* (Cam's Soundtrack Encyclopedia); Leonard Wolf's *Dracula: The Connoisseur's Guide*.

FINE

About the Author

Kim Newman is a novelist, critic and broadcaster. His fiction includes *The Night Mayor*, *Bad Dreams*, *Jago*, the *Anno Dracula* novels and stories, *The Quorum*, *The Original Dr Shade and Other Stories*, *Life's Lottery*, *Back in the USSA* (with Eugene Byrne) and *The Man From the Diogenes Club* under his own name and *The Vampire Genevieve* and *Orgy of the Blood Parasites* as Jack Yeovil. His non-fiction books include *Nightmare Movies* (reissued in 2011 by Bloomsbury in an updated edition), *Ghastly Beyond Belief* (with Neil Gaiman), *Horror: 100 Best Books* (with Stephen Jones), *Wild West Movies*, *The BFI Companion to Horror*, *Millennium Movies* and BFI Classics studies of *Cat People* and *Doctor Who*.

He is a contributing editor to *Sight & Sound* and *Empire* magazines (writing *Empire*'s popular Video Dungeon column), has written and broadcast widely on a range of topics, and scripted radio and television documentaries. His stories 'Week Woman' and 'Ubermensch' have been adapted into an episode of the TV series *The Hunger* and an Australian short film; he has directed and written a tiny film *Missing Girl*. Following his Radio 4 play 'Cry Babies', he wrote an episode ('Phish Phood') for Radio 7's series *The Man in Black*.

His official website, 'Dr Shade's Laboratory', can be found at www. johnnyalucard.com